Praise for Colleen Cambridge and the Phyllida Bright mystery series

"Two words describe this book: absolutely delicious. . . . A a near-perfect traditional mystery." —*First Clue*

"What if Agatha Christie's housekeeper was the best detective of all? In this delightful book, she is! You will love watching Phyllida spot the clues the authorities miss when a dead body shows up in Agatha's library."—Victoria Thompson, *USA Today* Bestselling Author of *Murder on Wall Street*

"Cambridge weaves in just the right amount of historical detail and references to classic Christie novels while placing Phyllida and her intelligent sleuthing skills front and center. . . . Dame Agatha would be proud." *–Publishers Weekly*

"Cambridge balances Downton Abbey–style period charm with a tight plot that twists and turns right until the end, with utter believability . . . The real-life historical players make only brief cameos, but Cambridge creates such a compelling cast of fictional characters that they are hardly missed. Reminiscent of Jessica Ellicott's 'Beryl & Edwina' series, this novel will please readers with its historical world and a plot that would satisfy Poirot." *– Library Journal*

"Agatha Christie the person plays a very peripheral part in the proceedings, but Agatha Christie the writer haunts every page of this delightful book that both pays homage to the Queen of Crime, but also embroiders on her work with a fresh character and a fresh look at a part of her life. This is a wonderful series debut." *–Mystery Scene*

"A good cozy to read with a cup of tea on the patio." —*New York Journal of Books*

"Excellent." —*Mystery & Suspense Magazine*

"Delicious fun—would a writer kill to be published?—and the locked-room mystery is a homage to the queen of crime herself." —*Historical Novel Society*

T0021415

Books by Colleen Cambridge

The Phyllida Bright mystery series

Murder at Mallowan Hall
A Trace of Poison
Murder by Invitation Only

The American in Paris mystery series

Mastering the Art of French Murder

A
TRACE
of POISON

Colleen Cambridge

A Phyllida Bright Mystery

KENSINGTON
PUBLISHING CORP.

www.kensingtonbooks.com

This book is a work of fiction. Names, characters, businesses, organizations, places, events, and incidents either are the product of the author's imagination or are used fictitiously. Any resemblance to actual persons, living or dead, events, or locales is entirely coincidental.

To the extent that the image or images on the cover of this book depict a person or persons, such person or persons are merely models, and are not intended to portray any character or characters featured in the book.

KENSINGTON BOOKS are published by

Kensington Publishing Corp.
119 West 40th Street
New York, NY 10018

Copyright © 2022 by Colleen Gleason

All rights reserved. No part of this book may be reproduced in any form or by any means without the prior written consent of the Publisher, excepting brief quotes used in reviews.

All Kensington titles, imprints and distributed lines are available at special quantity discounts for bulk purchases for sales promotion, premiums, fund-raising, educational or institutional use. Special book excerpts or cus-tomized printings can also be created to fit specific needs. For details, write or phone the office of the Kensington Special Sales Manager: Kensington Publishing Corp., 119 West 40th Street, New York, NY, 10018. Attn. Special Sales Department. Phone: 1-800-221-2647.

The K with book logo Reg. U.S. Pat. & TM Off.

ISBN: 978-1-4967-3248-4
First Kensington Hardcover Edition: November 2022
First Kensington Trade Edition: September 2023

ISBN: 978-1-4967-3249-1 (ebook)

10 9 8 7 6 5 4 3 2 1

Printed in the United States of America

"I promise that my detectives shall well and truly detect the crimes presented to them, using those wits which it may please me to bestow upon them, and not place reliance on, nor make use of, Divine Revelation, Feminine Intuition, Mumbo Jumbo, Jiggery-Pokery, Coincidence, or Act of God."

—Oath taken by members of the Detection Club

AUTHOR'S NOTE

While Agatha Christie and her husband, Max Mallowan, along with the Detection Club, actually existed, the Listleigh Murder Club, Mallowan Hall, Phyllida Bright, and her staff—as well as the deadly incidents described in this book—are purely figments of the author's imagination.

CAST OF CHARACTERS

DETECTION CLUB MEMBERS (actual historical figures)

Agatha Christie: celebrated detective story writer; creator of the Hercule Poirot, Miss Marple, and Tommy and Tuppence Beresford stories

G. K. Chesterton: popular crime writer of the Father Brown short stories; president of the Detection Club

Dorothy L. Sayers: famous writer of the Lord Peter Wimsey mystery series

Anthony Berkeley: suave, well-dressed, and upper-class writer of detective novels, including *The Poisoned Chocolates Case*

LISTLEIGH MURDER CLUB MEMBERS
(fictional characters)

Digby Billdop: local vicar for the Church of England; writer of the Father Veritas mystery stories

Alastair Whittlesby: local solicitor, president of the Listleigh Murder Club, and writer of the Inspector Belfast mystery stories

Miss Crowley: a single, drably-dressed woman who writes about the rakish and adventuresome Filberto Fiero

Vera Rollingbroke: a wealthy, well-heeled woman who is rarely without her notebook and who writes stories about an upper-class woman named Bunkle and her crime-solving cat partner, Mrs. Cuddlesworthy

Louis Genevan: antiques dealer who owns a shop in Belgravia and writes mystery stories about a spinster woman

Dr. John Bhatt: Listleigh's local physician who has begun to create his own crime-solving lab and who writes stories about a detective named Dr. Graceley

MALLOWAN HALL STAFF

Phyllida Bright: housekeeper and amateur detective extraordinaire

Mr. Dobble: Mallowan Hall's very proper and often intimidating butler

Mrs. Puffley: cook at Mallowan Hall who insists that murder is no excuse for inadequate meals

Bradford: the chauffeur, who has adopted an adorable canine named Myrtle

Molly: first kitchen maid and a favorite of Mrs. Bright's

OTHER CHARACTERS

Father Tooley: pastor of St. Wendreda's Catholic Church, at which the Murder Fête is being held to raise money for St. Wendreda's orphanage's roof

Rita: maid at St. Wendreda's rectory

Lettice Whittlesby: wife of Alastair Whittlesby

Eugene Whittlesby: estranged brother of Alastair Whittlesby, who nonetheless lives in the same house

Old Mrs. Whittlesby: mother of Alastair and Eugene; is bedridden and "dragon-like" in her personality

"Rolly" Rollingbroke: Vera Rollingbroke's doting husband

Drewson: the Whittlesbys' butler

CHAPTER 1

"*I* JUST DON'T SEE ANY WAY AROUND IT. HE'S SIMPLY *GOT* TO BE DONE away with," said a hushed voice.

"Right. The problem is . . . *how* to do it . . ." replied another voice. "Soon . . ."

While anyone else overhearing such an exchange would surely be alarmed, Phyllida Bright merely smiled to herself and went about the business of counting tablecloths for the welcome luncheon at the Listleigh Murder Fête.

Being the housekeeper at the vast and elegant Mallowan Hall, the home of the famous novelist Agatha Christie and her husband, Max Mallowan, Phyllida was quite used to overhearing—and participating in—discussions about murder and the finer points of how to permanently do away with an inconvenient person.

Whether abovestairs or belowstairs, there was always some conversation going on about which poison to use, whether a knife or a gun would be more or less bloody when employed than the other, and if a blow to the head would actually do the deed or whether a spike shoved into the back of the neck would need to be added to complete the task before stuffing the body of a maid into a downstairs cupboard.

"Poison . . ." replied the first person, whose words were becoming less audible. Perhaps they were walking away. "Coffee. Or a drink . . . ?"

"There is . . . that," replied the other. ". . . his new car, eh?"

Phyllida was fairly certain the first was a man speaking, but it was difficult to be certain as she was inside the social hall at St. Wendreda's Catholic Church and the voices were coming through an open window. Regardless, surely it was one of the detective fiction writers who were here for the Murder Fête. There were dozens of them milling about—both published and unpublished writers—many hoping to get a glimpse of some of the popular and well-known authors, such as G. K. Chesterton or Dorothy L. Sayers.

"Yes, poison . . . wouldn't it? . . . something . . . done," replied the companion, whose sex was indistinguishable due to its hushed tone. "And soon . . . cannot *bear* his boastful, overbearing nastiness any longer." These last phrases became stronger and more distinct, clearly indicating the frustration of the speaker, whose voice was low and crusty enough to be either male or female.

Phyllida tsked to herself, wondering how writers could come to dislike characters they'd created. Of course, not being a writer herself, she couldn't imagine such an occasion.

However, there was a time only recently when Agatha had become weary of and annoyed by her most popular fictional detective, Hercule Poirot. Like Sir Arthur Conan Doyle, whose Sherlock Holmes had so become the bane of his existence that he actually killed off the character—only to be required to revive him in order to silence his fans—Agatha had become fed up with Poirot and his persnickety, bombastic ways.

Fortunately, Agatha hadn't actually plotted to kill the little Belgian detective—an event that would have prompted Phyllida to have a pointed and impassioned conversation with her employer. For Phyllida had what one might term a literary tendre for the brilliant, mustachioed detective.

Of course, the discussion to which she was currently privy

might very well be about a villain rather than a meddlesome crime fiction detective, but she quite doubted it. The tone of voice implied a person very much at the end of their rope in dealing with the individual, which implied someone well-known to the speaker, such as a recurring character.

She hoped it wasn't Dorothy Sayers speaking about her detective character Peter Wimsey. Not that Lord Peter could hold a candle to Poirot, but Phyllida certainly enjoyed his detective work—and having recently solved a real-life murder herself, she highly approved of the intrepid Harriet Vane as his partner (although she was no comparison to Agatha's spunky Tuppence Beresford).

"Mrs. Bright, ma'am, the flowers for the tables are here. The vases are on their way."

Phyllida turned from her stack of tablecloths to speak to Ginny, the first parlourmaid from Mallowan Hall. Presumably, the person standing next to her was Amsi, the gardener from the manor house, but it was impossible to tell for certain as the figure was completely obliterated by the mountains of roses, Michaelmas daisies, and gladioli in the cart he was pushing.

"Excellent. When they arrive, line up the vases on the table there and you may arrange them—five roses, six daisies, and two gladioli for each. Make certain the glads are in the center, mind, and mix the colors," Phyllida told her, even as she scrutinized the fresh apron and uniform her maid was wearing.

Not one straggle of honey-gold hair escaped Ginny's cap, and her stockings were sleek and smooth—as they should be. Phyllida had extremely high expectations of her staff at all times, but she was particularly exacting when they were to be interacting with the public.

She turned to the second of the maids she'd brought with her from home. Despite being a kitchen maid and not usually seen by guests or even the family, Molly was just as clean and pressed and starched as Ginny was—and could be counted on not to gossip quite as much. Phyllida mentally nodded approval. "Molly, you can put out the tablecloths—there's a rectangular one for the head table and the rest are circular—and then help Ginny place the flowers. Directly in the center of the tables, if you please, with three spaced out across the head table."

Phyllida gestured to the tablecloths she'd just finished counting. As anticipated, there were sixteen round ones, which left two extra since there were fourteen luncheon tables. Phyllida always had an extra of everything.

Except patience, when it came to Myrtle—who'd just made her appearance.

"What is that beast doing in here?" she demanded as the dark, curly-haired mop of a puppy barreled into the hall.

Bradford, the Mallowans' chauffeur and Myrtle's master (Phyllida used the term loosely, for she wasn't quite certain who was the master of whom when it came to the two of them), came casually strolling into the room as if he had not just unleashed a hellhound in a church hall. He was carrying a large crate that presumably held the vases. "She wanted to come with me," he replied, as if it were the least bit permissible to allow a puppy to run rampant through a luncheon hall. "Where do you want these, Mrs. Bright?"

Every time he said her name in that drawling, ironic tone, Phyllida's hackles went up. She couldn't help it. The man was impossible and simply *filled* with arrogant criticisms and unwanted observations. "On the table there," she replied frostily. "Dogs are *not* allowed in the luncheon hall."

Myrtle was tearing about the space, her tail flying behind her like a banner, barking, bouncing, skittering, and generally making a nuisance of itself. Phyllida removed herself quickly from the beast's path as it streaked past her. Since Myrtle's invasion of the grounds at Mallowan Hall, Phyllida had had to retire three pairs of silk stockings due to rents from the creature's paws, as, for some reason, the beast seemed particularly enamored with her.

Needless to say, Myrtle was not welcome inside Phyllida's domain of the manor house.

"Of course not, Mrs. Bright," replied Bradford as he set down the crate. Was he chuckling at her quick footwork to avoid the beast? "But the luncheon isn't for four hours. She'll be long gone by then."

Phyllida was interrupted from a tart reply about the remnants of Myrtle's hair being everywhere by the arrival of Mrs. Agatha, Miss Sayers, Mr. Chesterton, and Mr. Berkeley.

"Good morning, Phyllida. I see you have everything well under control here," said the lady of Mallowan Hall. There was a hint of laughter in Agatha's voice, for upon her entrance, Myrtle had come charging up to her, tail wagging wildly. "Yes, you *are* quite adorable, aren't you?" As Agatha bent to scratch the wriggling four-legged bundle of curls, Phyllida smothered an acerbic comment.

She and Agatha had become friends during the Great War, when women were eagerly conscripted for all sorts of jobs. At the time, both were single women, and since they were about the same age, their rapport was natural. Agatha had worked in the dispensary at the hospital—which was how she'd learned so much about the poisons she used in her books—and Phyllida had worked as a nurse at the same hospital before going to the front lines. They were great friends and had got along tremendously for more than ten years. The fact that Phyllida had chosen to take the position as housekeeper at Mallowan Hall had not altered their relationship in the least, although they did take pains to keep from being too familiar around each other in front of the other servants or guests.

One thing housekeeper and mistress did not agree upon was an affection for dogs. Mrs. Agatha had a wire terrier named Peter, and when Bradford had brought Myrtle to live with him in the garage apartment, both of the Mallowans had taken to the beast with rapturous affection.

Phyllida had not.

"Mr. Bradford promises to remove it well before the food arrives," she told Agatha primly, knowing he was listening. "But of course we will have to sweep again due to the dog hair." She shot the chauffeur a dark look and was rewarded by him ignoring her.

"I have no doubt everything will be in strict shipshape with you at the helm, Phyllida." Agatha straightened, leaving Myrtle to find another victim.

Phyllida quickly sidestepped the slathering, drooling, panting beast once more, and so the mop transferred its attentions to Miss Sayers.

"You'll be sitting at the head table there, G. K.," said Agatha. She was speaking to Mr. Chesterton, who had agreed to be the Grand Master for the Murder Fête, as it was a charitable event being sponsored by the Detection Club.

The Detection Club was a group of detective fiction writers, including Agatha Christie, G. K. Chesterton, Dorothy L. Sayers, Anthony Berkeley, Hugh Walpole, Freeman Wills Crofts, and a dozen or so other popular authors. They met regularly in London to discuss the techniques and travails of crime fiction writing and to provide support to one another. Each had taken an oath to be fair to their readers in creating and presenting the solutions in their stories, but whether the oath was anything more than an inside joke, Phyllida wasn't certain.

The Murder Fête in Listleigh was a weekend event that had been arranged to allow aspiring writers of detective stories the opportunity to meet successful writers of such works, as well as for the public to come and listen to the authors speak and to buy their books.

The aspiring writers paid a fee for the first day, which included the private Welcome Luncheon at half past one with the Detection Club attendees who were present—Sayers, Chesterton, Berkeley, and Christie—along with short classes taught by some of the published writers. The highlight of the first day was an outdoor cocktail party in the evening, giving the hopeful writers another chance to hobnob with the author celebrities. Along with their entrance fee, each amateur author had been offered the opportunity (for an additional fee) to submit a short story for a contest to be judged by the professionals. Tomorrow, Saturday, the fair on the grounds of St. Wendreda's would be open to the public for book sales and a general festival. On Sunday at teatime would be the awarding of the Murder Fête Grand Prize.

As Grand Master, G. K. Chesterton would speak at the luncheon today, and on Sunday he would give out the prize for best short story to one of the aspiring authors. The prize was a publishing contract for the story in both England and the United States. Phyllida was privately rooting for Dr. Bhatt to win, for she'd read some of his work about a physician turned amateur detective. She thought it was exceedingly good.

Listleigh had been chosen as the site for the Murder Fête because of the local writers' club. After John Bhatt, the town's doctor and a member of the local club, heard about a fundraiser the Detection Club had participated in in London, he conceived the idea of a local fundraising event. This one was for the nearby orphanage and school for wayward children sponsored by St. Wendreda's, which needed a new roof. Dr. Bhatt had sent a very compelling proposal to Mr. Chesterton, by way of Mrs. Agatha. The publicity such an event would afford the writers, the money it would raise for children in need, and the opportunity to get out of London during the hottest part of the summer prompted the Detection Club to accept the Listleigh writers' club's proposal.

Because of Agatha's involvement, Phyllida had readily taken charge of the planning and execution of the event. Not only was this sort of activity exactly what she loved to manage—and was exceptional at doing—but also being at St. Wendreda's for several days during the setup and event meant she was *not* at Mallowan Hall, and therefore did not have to interact with Mr. Dobble, the butler.

"Very well," Mr. Chesterton replied after he looked at the table. Approaching his sixties, the writer of the popular Father Brown stories had masses of thick dark hair and habitually wore a pince-nez. He was a bulky, imposing man whose dark clothing merely added to his commanding persona. "How many aspiring writers will be here?"

"There are fifteen of them who have registered, and paid, of course," Agatha told him. "They aren't all from Listleigh. Some are coming from as far away as Wales." She had declined the local club's request to be the Grand Master, for she was quite shy and preferred not to speak in public or even in small groups unless she knew them well. It was a monumental decision for her to agree to participate at all, for Agatha disliked publicity and the press—but she could hardly decline with the event being such a local undertaking.

Being instrumental in the planning and executing of the event afforded Phyllida the opportunity to help keep her reclusive friend out of the public eye as much as possible, and the only public event was tomorrow's book fair and the announcement of the grand prize winner.

"I trust you all received your copies of their short stories— there were only ten submitted—for the judging?" Agatha asked her colleagues.

"Yes, indeed," replied Miss Sayers. "I received my packet a fortnight ago, which gave me ample opportunity to read them— although I had to finish the last on the train here." Dorothy Sayers was a large, boisterous woman who tended to wear long black frocks that ebbed and flowed around her. Her dark hair was cut short in a style called the Eton crop, giving her a mannish appearance despite her draping clothing. "Some of them were actually quite good."

"Quite. I thought so myself. Might be some competition at the publishers for us," said Mr. Chesterton with a chuckle.

As she watched Ginny make up the vases and Molly finish the tablecloths, Phyllida couldn't help but listen in hopes of overhearing any hint about who might be awarded the prize.

"Father Tooley has had all of the rankings since Monday of this week," said Agatha. "So no one can accuse us of falling to any undue influence once we begin mingling with the writers." She smiled.

"Indeed," replied Mr. Chesterton. "A holy man counting the tallies would be above suspicion."

"Have you decided on a favorite yourself?" asked Miss Sayers.

"Oh, yes," replied Agatha. "There was one tale that particularly stood out to me. I found it quite entertaining, as well as clever. But there were several others with great merit. It should be quite interesting to see where we all stand with our preferences."

Before she could get any indication of which story that was, Phyllida was required to move out of earshot when Myrtle discovered the swaying tail of a tablecloth that had just been placed.

"Leave that be, you little recalcitrant, annoying, hairy, beastly thing," Phyllida said as she marched over to stop the nonsense. "Mr. Bradford, if you would remove this nuisance at *once.*"

Looking not the least bit abashed, the chauffeur swooped up the motley beast. As Myrtle began to slather his face with what passed for affection, Phyllida couldn't help but notice that the beast's thick curls were indistinguishable from her master's unruly mop of hair. *Two of a kind,* she thought irritably. *Both lacking any sort of decorum or respect.*

"All right, then, Mrs. Bright," said Bradford. The bridge of his arrogant, blade-like nose was shiny where the dog had been licking him. Phyllida suppressed a shudder. "We'll take ourselves off, then. What time shall we return to bring you back?"

It was Phyllida's current private hope that the Mallowans would either hire a second chauffeur or that Bradford would leave—and take his dog with him—for some greener pastures or greasier garages. Having to ride in the Daimler with him whenever she wanted to go into town or anywhere else was nearly as trying as dealing with Mr. Dobble.

Nonetheless, she was the consummate professional, and she had learned over the years that she could get along with anyone, regardless of how irritating or sardonic they might be, as long as they did their job. And unfortunately, Bradford was more than equal to his job.

"I should like to be picked up at three o'clock, and then I'll need to return here by half five in order to see to final preparations for the cocktail party, if you please, Mr. Bradford."

He looked at her from over the top of the panting puppy's

head. The beast's little pink tongue was lolling from the side of its mouth like an unfurled ribbon. "Right, then. Myrtle and I will be here to collect you just before three o'clock." He gave her a cheeky grin, obviously knowing how much she loathed the idea of being trapped in a vehicle with that slathering menace.

"Thank you, Mr. Bradford."

A loud thud followed by an ominous crash had her spinning from further repartee with the driver.

One of the tables had somehow been upended. Flowers, water, and a shattered vase were all over the floor.

It was a good thing Phyllida had extras . . . of everything.

"I'm so very anxious about meeting all of them!" said Digby Billdop. "All of those famous writers!"

He was the vicar at St. Thurston's Church, C.O.E. His parish was located across the village green from St. Wendreda's, the papist church in Listleigh and the bane of his existence due to competition for flock members.

He was still annoyed that St. Wendreda's had landed the distinction of being the location for the Murder Fête instead of his own St. Thurston's, which didn't have an orphanage with a conveniently bad roof.

As if that should have made a difference.

Both churchyards were shaded by many maples and oaks and had colorful gardens, as well as residences for the vicar and priest, respectively. Digby grudgingly admitted that even though St. Thurston's yard was larger, St. Wendreda's did have the nicer lawn, for it was bordered by the small river that ran through the village. Tomorrow it would be filled with tents and festival-goers.

"I'm certain it will be far less taxing than you imagine," said Harvey Dobble, the butler at Mallowan Hall. "Meeting all of them."

They were sitting at the same table at which they played their weekly chess game at the vicarage. Dobble had risen unusually early and slipped away from his duties at Mallowan Hall this morning in order to buck up his friend before the Murder Fête luncheon—and to make certain the vicar didn't back out of going at the last minute. Digby was prone to anxiousness and he had delicate nerves, but in Dobble's opinion, the vicar was a gifted writer, as well as a worthy chess opponent.

Digby clasped his pudgy fingers together on the table in front of him as if to keep them from fluttering. "To meet Mr. Chesterton in particular is quite upsetting my insides, because he's simply . . . but you know how he's my *inspiration.* Oh dear . . . what if none of them liked my story?"

Dobble shook his head. "Not at all, Digs," he said. "I've read your stories and they're eminently publishable. Why—and don't repeat this—I find your Father Veritas to be far more compelling than Mr. Chesterton's Father Brown. He overdoes the umbrella bit, Mr. Chesterton does, and *'little'* Father Brown—as he continues to describe him—is far too doddering for my taste. Gives the clergy a bad name when he's so rumpled and vacant-eyed."

"Do you really think so?" replied the vicar, his eyes hopeful.

"I certainly do." Dobble gave him a warm smile—something that would never be seen by any of the staff at Mallowan Hall. "Don't I always insist on reading your new pages the moment I arrive, even before dinner? Father Veritas has become my favorite detective—after M. Poirot, of course."

"Oh, thank you for saying so," replied Digby, clasping his hands even tighter together. His eyes glittered with raw emotion. "That is quite a compliment, as M. Poirot is simply . . . well, *parfait*—as he would say—as is Madame Christie." He gave a little chuckle that trailed off into a sigh. "I know I must sound silly, but Alastair Whittlesby is always picking at every little detail in my stories, and sometimes I simply can't help but wish *he'd* run out of ideas, or that his words would dry up, or . . . or that his pages would get accidentally dropped into the fire and destroyed. Or . . . or that *something* would happen to him. Even though it's not very Christian of me," he added ruefully.

"Alastair Whittlesby is an unmitigated arse, and *I* have no qualms about wishing his papers would go up in flames—or worse," Dobble said stoutly, for there had been more than one occasion when Digby had been near tears after a Listleigh Murder Club meeting. Mr. Whittlesby reigned as president of the group and, in his mind, as the as-yet-undiscovered Shakespeare of Detective Fiction. "From what his butler tells me, the man is no more civil at home than he is at the writers' club meetings. Drewson claims the rows between him and his brother are something to behold."

Alastair Whittlesby was meddlesome, opinionated, and often-times rude and cruel. But he was the only solicitor in the village, and his father had had a baronetcy and a bit of money, so the man thought himself above most everyone he encountered even though he was barely considered a gentleman.

"Even Wednesday, when we were all there at his house for tea and cocktails, he was simply insufferable. He's so very certain he will win the story contest and the publishing prize—I'm certain that's why he had us all there. To gloat in advance," said Digby.

"Was everyone there?" asked Dobble. His attention slid—not for the first time—to the cake sitting on the counter, and he was feeling quite regretful that his friend hadn't yet cut into it. A piece of whatever it was—a luscious white confection—would be an excellent partner to the tea he'd been sipping. Digby's house-keeper was a formidable baker, a fact which Dobble would never even think of acknowledging in the hearing of Mrs. Puffley, who reigned in the kitchen at Mallowan Hall.

"All of the members of the Murder Club were there," replied the vicar, seemingly oblivious to Dobble's interest in an early-morning dessert. "Even Miss Crowley, who refused to touch even a glass of sherry." Digby sighed. "If Whittlesby does win the prize, I might have to quit the club. He'll be utterly intolerable! I just wish something would *happen* to him, to . . . to put him out of the way."

"Now, now, Digs, let's not put the cart before the horse. You've as good a chance of winning as anyone—save Vera Rollingbroke."

They chuckled, and Dobble was relieved that his friend seemed to relax a little. He very much hoped that Digby would win, but more than that, he desperately hoped that Alastair Whittlesby would *not*. Even if Dr. Bhatt won instead of Digby, it would be far better—though in that event, Dobble would have to contend with Mrs. Bright's subtle, but smug, satisfaction.

Dobble glanced at the clock and saw with a start that it was past time for him to return to the manor house to see that breakfast had been cleared, and tea and dinner were being prepared. For the last few days during the preparations for the Murder Fête, the residence had been unusually quiet. This was mainly due to the long absences of Mrs. Bright. She'd taken her impudently bright hair and her righteous temperament to St. Wendreda's—along with some of her staff, which had actually left Dobble in a rather trying position, keeping the meals coming and tea on time. But that inconvenience had been balanced by the fact that Mrs. Bright had been blissfully and regularly *not present* at the manor house.

"I'd best be off, then, Digs," said Dobble, once again looking sadly at the cake as he stood. "Mrs. Bright has left the household in quite the straits as of late, and there's no one to set it right but myself."

"Why, that's not very sporting of her, is it?" said Digby, rising as well.

"Not in the least," Dobble replied as he settled his hat in place. "But it does afford me the opportunity to ensure the maids are doing their work to *my* standards. There's simply so much *lace* and *chintz* everywhere, I've taken the opportunity to decrease its presence." And he'd made certain those blasted cats of Mrs. Bright's hadn't so much as poked a whisker from outside of her sitting room. Their frustrated yowling at the door had brought a smile to his face.

"I do know how indispensable Mrs. Bright is up at Mallowan Hall," Digby said earnestly. "She's quite a wonder, isn't she? So clever and well turned out, and so very civil, too, if a bit intimidating. It must be very trying with her being absent so much this weekend."

Dobble stiffened a little. "*Wonder* is hardly a word I would use to describe that woman, Digby. She's . . . well, she's slightly more than adequate at her position—which, incidentally, I cannot begin to understand how she acquired, with her surely never having been in service until Mrs. Agatha brought her on."

"Oh!" replied Digby with a conspiratorial smile. "I didn't realize you'd finally ferreted out that information! What *did* she do before she came to work for the Mallowans? I've been simply *dying* of curiosity."

Dobble's mood soured even further. "Well, I haven't actually determined for certain that Mrs. Bright hasn't been in service before. The woman is extraordinarily tight-lipped about her past! Why, I don't know much of anything about her other than she knew Mrs. Agatha during the war, and it seems she was a nurse at the front lines. And whatever happened to her husband is a mystery as well. For all I know, Mr. Bright might arrive at Mallowan Hall someday and murder us all in our sleep!"

"Oh." The vicar's eyes widened behind his round glasses. "So you did find out that she was married, then?"

"Well, not precisely," Dobble was forced to admit. Why *did* Digby have to be so interested? Couldn't he just allow Dobble to grumble without asking questions? "And quite honestly, I'm not certain *who* would marry someone like her, anyway, so perhaps she never *has* been married after all. One absolutely doesn't know a thing about her past. The problem with Phyllida Bright is that she is simply *not* suited to being a housekeeper."

"Quite. At least you'll be able to get things done properly with her out of the way," replied Digby, soothingly.

"Thank fortune for that," Dobble replied. "Although of course she has taken all of the better maids with her to St. Wendreda's and left the lesser ones for me to contend with, along with some extra ones—and you know that managing *maids* is simply not done by a butler!" Dobble frowned. Had he remembered to tell the extra maids about the damper in the sitting room?

"Perhaps one of the footmen could manage the maids for you," said Digby, patting him on the arm.

Dobble sighed and shook his head. "And that is why you are a vicar and have no servants to speak of, other than an old day maid-cook, Diggy," he said. "One does not put footmen in charge of maids if one does not want little ones running amok nine months later."

After a quick glance to be certain no one was walking past the vicarage, he bent to give Digby a quick kiss. "That's for luck today," he said, and then slipped out the door.

CHAPTER 2

Friday evening

THE WEATHER COOPERATED, AND THE MURDER FÊTE COCKTAIL party went off just as Phyllida—and the Detection Club—planned. The maids had hung Japanese lanterns in white and black (representing the printed page of the detective novels) throughout the little courtyard at St. Wendreda's rectory. They'd set up circular, waist-high tables for drinks and ashtrays, and each was covered by a white tablecloth and decorated with intricate paper roses constructed from newsprint, in keeping with the theme. Beneath each flower vase was a piece of red felt cut into an amorphous shape to suggest a pool of blood. A squat black candle on a saucer burned next to each one—safely distant from the paper roses, of course.

The small, walled-in garden was filled with clusters of white rosebushes spilling countless blossoms and filling the air with their sweet, floral scent. Throngs of boxwood edged the space, and the pathways were dirt, edged by clumps of creeping phlox. It was just seven on a July evening and still light outside, so Phyllida had not seen the need to employ extra lanterns or strings of electric lights—although she had, of course, brought some.

Although the enclosed garden normally had only two benches, both situated near a statue of St. Francis of Assisi, for this evening's event Phyllida had added three other wrought iron benches brought from Mallowan Hall, and placed small, low tables in front of them.

"You've really pulled this off swimmingly, Phyllie. The whole event, but this outdoor gathering is simply perfect. It looks so innocent and lovely," Agatha murmured to Phyllida as she touched one of the fragrant rose blossoms. They were standing just inside the main gate to the courtyard so Agatha, arguably the most popular and famous of the writers, could take a short break from socializing. "One would never know there's murder in the hearts of everyone here."

Phyllida laughed. "Quite so! If overheard, the conversations would surely give Scotland Yard a pause." She sipped from her glass of champagne—for Mr. Max had insisted she enjoy the festivities after all of her hard work—and surveyed the fruits of her labor, reminded of the conversation she'd overheard this morning.

She wondered which of the writers had been plotting to poison someone, and eyed the small crowd for suspects.

There was Mathilda Crowley, an olive-skinned woman of forty-five who was an active member of the Listleigh Murder Club. She had gray-threaded dark brown hair fashioned into a roll that settled around the back of her neck, and Phyllida knew that she wrote stories about a dashing young man named Filberto Fiero, who spent much of his time in the French Rivera. Dr. Bhatt had told her the stories were more fanciful than based in reality, but they had some entertaining parts . . . and some particularly gruesome murders.

Miss Crowley wore a severe, summer's wool skirt and jacket of dark brown more suited for secretarial tasks than a cocktail party. Most of the other women—Phyllida included—were dressed in frocks of light, flowing material with bright patterns or solid colors, belted neatly at the waist, accented by shoes with high heels. Their hats were colorful and trimmed with lace and feathers, whilst Miss Crowley's chapeau was little more than a squat brown box atop her head. In a single nod to adornment, there was a single small black bow affixed to its front.

Miss Crowley, who lived by herself in a cottage at the end of

Firth Street, held a teacup in her gloved hands instead of a coupe or flute, and surveyed the garden as if trying to determine whether she should step into the fray or remain stationary. She'd positioned herself near the table of macarons and thumbprint tarts, however, and based on the sprinkle of crumbs at the corner of Miss Crowley's mouth, Phyllida suspected the lemon, strawberry, and chocolate treats would win out over navigating through the partygoers.

Digby Billdop, the vicar from the Anglican church of St. Thurston's, wore his customary owlish expression above a deeply cleft, pudgy chin that reminded Phyllida of a plump and rosy apricot. He was standing in G. K. Chesterton's proximity—near enough to hear whatever the writer was saying, but seemingly unable to work up the courage to venture close enough to participate in the conversation. The vicar clutched a glass of champagne and nodded silently, his eyes fastened worshipfully on the creator of the most famous of parochial detectives.

Besides the hovering vicar, Mr. Chesterton was discoursing to an audience of two more, both of whom Phyllida recognized as the other members of the Listleigh Murder Club.

Vera Rollingbroke, an attractive blonde in her early thirties, was an enthusiastic and prolific writer of as-yet unpublished detective stories about an unmarried, wealthy lady nicknamed Bunkle and her cat, Mrs. Cuddlesworthy. (According to John Bhatt, there was good reason they were as-yet unpublished, for who would believe a talking cat?) Her hat was a cunning yellow disc of felt that sat atilt just above her left brow and sported a single dark blue feather tacked around its shallow crown, and Phyllida felt absolutely covetous about it.

Vera was married to the gregarious Sir Paulson Rollingbroke, familiarly known as Sir Rolly, whose family seat was just to the northeast of Listleigh. She seemed to have disdained gloves, sparkling wine, and macarons for a notebook, into which she was feverishly making notes. It appeared that she had attended tonight's gathering without her husband.

Crowding in next to her and effectively blocking the vicar from edging in closer was Louis Genevan, who was holding two glasses of champagne in one hand whilst clamping a cigarette between two fingers of his other. Presumably one of the vessels had belonged to Mrs. Rollingbroke before she forsook it in favor of note-taking.

Louis Genevan was an antiques dealer from London who divided his time between Listleigh and his little shop in Belgravia. He was an elegant, well-groomed man with brown skin and a widow's peak hairline. His dark hair swept back from a high forehead in attractive raven wings above slender, dark brows.

Due to his business, he purposely wore clothing accessories several decades out of style, but nonetheless always managed to appear as if he were at the forefront of modern fashion. Tonight he had chosen a crimson brocade waistcoat with an ornate pocket watch tucked into it, paired with a high, stiff collar that dug into the bottom of his jaw. His cravat was tied in a manner that would have made Beau Brummell swoon. Mr. Genevan's coat and trousers, however, were cut in a modern style. Somehow, the pairing of old and new was not at all offensive to the eye.

Phyllida didn't recognize a group of five people clustered around Detection Club member Anthony Berkeley, and concluded they were amateur writers who'd paid for the fête but didn't reside in Listleigh and weren't members of the local club. Mr. Berkeley was a suave, handsome man, self-assured, well-dressed, and delighting in entertaining his small, adoring audience.

Dr. Bhatt was standing in the corner, speaking to Miss Sayers and Father Tooley. Or, more accurately, Dr. Bhatt was listening to Miss Sayers speak—and appearing to hang on her every word—whilst Father Tooley, the priest at St. Wendreda's and the honorary host of the garden party, nodded along silently as he nursed a cup of tea.

Along with a thick head of ink-colored hair, John Bhatt had a glorious set of well-groomed jet-black mustaches that had attracted Phyllida's attention the moment she saw them, during the unpleasantness several weeks ago when a dead body had been discovered in the library at Mallowan Hall. The doctor was an avid reader of Mrs. Agatha's works, and Phyllida wondered if he'd fashioned his mustaches after the famous ones of M. Poirot's.

As if reading her mind, Agatha murmured, "I venture to say, if Dr. Bhatt had more of an egg-shaped head and pale skin, he could be Poirot! Do you know, Phyllie, I've actually seen Hercule twice in my life?"

Phyllida was aware of that, for she'd been on a small steamer with Agatha the first time her friend took her arm in a sudden, tight grip and pointed out a man who did, in fact, look exactly like one pictured the brilliant detective.

"What did you think of the doctor's story?" asked Phyllida, unabashedly hoping to get a hint of who might win the prize tomorrow.

"It was quite good," Agatha replied. "There were several that were surprisingly entertaining and clever, although a number of others that didn't quite cut the mustard. But it's up to Father Tooley to tally all of the votes. It really is a good prize, you know, Phyllie. Publication not only here in England, but across the ocean as well. I would have killed for that opportunity when I first started."

Phyllida smiled. "I've always thought writers to be quite bloodthirsty, so I don't doubt that for a moment."

The two laughed, then Agatha sighed. "Oh drat. Here comes my darling and faintly disloyal Max delivering Alastair Whittlesby to me after I've managed to avoid him the past hour. But I suppose poor Max didn't have a choice, did he? Alastair Whittlesby is like a barnacle."

Mr. Max was more than ten years younger than his famous wife and was a devoted archaeologist. The couple had met when Agatha went on a trip to Mesopotamia and stayed with some mutual friends. Mr. Max gave his wife an apologetic smile as he approached with Alastair Whittlesby, who had a long, slender nose, thick gray hair, and thin lips that always seemed to be expressing distaste or displeasure. He was dressed in a fine bespoke suit that nonetheless seemed strangely ill-fitted about the middle, where it hung slightly askew. He had an air of self-importance as he approached, waving away the smoke from his cigarette with an impatient gesture.

Mr. Whittlesby's wife, Lettice, who was a pretty if faded-looking woman at least ten years younger than his fifty, clung to his arm with one hand—which could account for the strange bunching of his tailored coat—whilst gripping a champagne coupe with the other. A handbag dangled from her elbow and her hat was just the slightest bit askew. Her bright pink lip color was smudged a bit at the corner, which made Phyllida itch to apply her handkerchief to the smear.

She'd heard plenty about Alastair Whittlesby from Dr. Bhatt, and most of it was not to the man's credit. Mr. Whittlesby was the only solicitor in Listleigh, however, so one was required to do business with him if one wanted to sell bonds, write a will, or parse through a contract without traveling to London or a neighboring town. The single time she'd had to engage the man's services, Phyllida had been struck by his pompous attitude, as well as an underlying sense that he didn't appreciate a well-informed, intelligent woman. However—and unfortunately—according to John Bhatt, Mr. Whittlesby, who was also the President of the Listleigh Murder Club, was a talented writer of stories about a brilliant Scotland Yard detective named Theodore Belfast—who wasn't quite as brilliant as people thought he was. It was really his gossipy sister Millie, with whom he lived, who helped him solve the crimes.

"Aha, Mrs. Mallowan," said Mr. Whittlesby as he approached in what Phyllida could only think of as a swoop—as if he were a hawk diving for its prey. His wife, still clinging, trotted behind like an afterthought. "I've been looking for you all evening."

"How nice to see you again, Mr. Whittlesby," Agatha replied, offering her hand. Phyllida was impressed that her friend sounded quite sincere. Shy as she might be, Agatha did rise to the occasion as necessary.

"Quite. It's rather a tragedy that we should live so near, and yet we've socialized only once before. The Rollingbrokes have had us up several times, you know." Still smiling pleasantly at Agatha, he shook his arm abruptly to disengage from the grip of his wife, saying, "Do let loose, Lettice. You needn't be such a bloody limpet," without sparing his spouse a glance. "I must say, Mrs. Mallowan, that I greatly enjoyed *The Murder of Roger Ackroyd*, but it wasn't quite fair, was it? I don't think it's all that sporting when writers cheat in their stories." He gave a little chuckle before drawing on his cigarette.

"The clues were all there," Agatha replied with a smile. She'd fielded this response many times since the publication of *Roger Ackroyd*.

Lettice Whittlesby, still hovering near her husband's side, lifted her glass and drained the remainder of her champagne, then looked around as if in search of a refill.

Phyllida sympathized with the woman's desire for a new pour, knowing that if a man had rebuked her the way Alastair had just rebuked his wife, *he* would have been the recipient of the contents of her glass—over the hump of his long, arrogant nose.

Just then, Phyllida noticed that one of the Japanese lanterns needed to be relit, and as she did not see any footmen with a tray of champagne to replace Mrs. Whittlesby's empty glass, she gratefully excused herself to attend to both. She thought it best to slip away before Mr. Whittlesby expressed his opinion about a housekeeper attending a cocktail party, for there was still champagne in Phyllida's glass available to be tossed onto a snobby nose if the need arose. Still holding the drink, she headed for the unobtrusive side door that led to the small kitchen inside St. Wendreda's rectory, where the maids and footmen were waiting for instruction.

"Mrs. Bright, what are you doing with *that*?"

Phyllida managed—only barely—to keep from gasping in surprise as Dobble materialized before her. She had just pushed through the door and there he was: standing in front of her like a skeletal sentry, eyeing her glass of champagne as if it were poison.

Dobble wasn't all that slender, but he was tall with long arms, a long torso, and legs that were ill-proportioned compared to the rest of him. He did have very pale skin, a bald head with an angular jaw, and a depression above his left ear that had earned him the nickname Ol' Dent, used secretly by the staff. When dressed in dark clothing—as he always was—he did give off a sort of skeleton-like impression. He was holding a bottle of spir-its in one hand—presumably not for himself, but for the bar outside.

"Why, good evening, Mr. Dobble," she replied, neatly avoiding his question, as well as his person, as she slipped past him into the small kitchen. When had he arrived? she wondered. "How kind of you to be here to assist with the footmen and serving."

The Murder Fête was big news in Listleigh, and this cocktail gathering was the most anticipated event of the weekend aside from the announcement of the grand prize winner. Neither Phyl-lida nor Dobble wanted anything to go wrong, for the local club's sake as well as Mrs. Agatha's.

"Mrs. Bright, why are you imbibing whilst on duty, and *what* are you wearing?" he demanded.

"Why, it's a cornflower-blue crepe afternoon dress with a yoke waist, shirred bodice, and pleated capelet sleeves, Mr. Dobble," she replied with a bright smile. "I particularly like the bit of braid trim at the waist and over the shoulders," she added, brushing her fingers over the decorative detail. "How kind of you to ask about it."

She fancied she could hear Dobble grind his teeth, even over the noise of the revelry outside and the clattering of dishes in the kitchen.

"*That* attire is not appropriate for a housekeeper," he replied stiffly. "It's far too . . . too . . ."

"Well, it's not chintz, Mr. Dobble, and there's not one iota of lace to be seen, so I cannot understand your disapproval. And while I do appreciate your attention to detail, my fashion choices are not up for discussion with a butler, no matter how esteemed he might be," she replied, her sweet smile still fixed in place while her words were firm. She looked past him. "Molly, one of the lanterns needs to be relit. Check on the other ones to make cer-tain they don't need new candles as well."

"Yes, Mrs. Bright," replied the maid, moving quickly to attend to the problem, although Phyllida saw a flash of disappointment in her expression. Said disappointment could be due to the fact that she'd been talking to Elton, Mr. Max's new valet, or that she didn't want to miss whatever conversation continued to transpire between her boss and the butler. Phyllida wondered briefly who had been left in charge up at Mallowan Hall, with the butler, two footmen, the valet, and three maids all in attendance at the cocktail fête. Mrs. Puffley wouldn't do, for she never left her domain of the kitchen. The house could burn down around the cook, and she'd still be stirring her stew or pummeling her bread dough with broad, muscular hands.

"Mrs. Bright," said Dobble from between clenched teeth.

"Yes, Mr. Dobble?" she replied.

"Might I remind you that one does not imbibe whilst on duty," he said. Which was actually quite hypocritical of him, for Phyllida had caught him sipping beer in his pantry more than once—and not on his day off.

"Mr. Dobble," she said kindly, "I would find speaking with you so much more enjoyable if you would not concern yourself with my attire, my hair, or the contents of my glass—especially when there is a woman out in the garden desperately in need of more champagne and I see that neither of your footmen have made their way out there with a tray. Perhaps that should be rectified."

With that, she brought her own glass to her mouth and, still smiling, took a generous sip of the sparkling vintage. "And perhaps you should have a nip of something yourself. After all, the party is nearly over and you look as if you could use a soother. Isn't that Mr. Billdop standing out there by the bar counter?"

Dobble gave her a startled look, which was quickly masked. He straightened slightly and pursed his lips. "I was taking this to the bar," he said, gesturing with the bottle in his hand. "Stanley spelled me for the moment, but Mr. Whittlesby is quite particular about his cocktail so I should be the one to mix it. His butler explained the recipe, and it's far too complicated for a footman to remember, no matter how he might aspire to butlership. Besides the champagne toast, Mr. Genevan absolutely refuses to drink anything other than port—which I have in my hand—whilst Mrs. Rollingbroke insists only on Scotch, and so I am clearly needed."

"Indeed," Phyllida said, nodding sagely.

"As you know, Mrs. Bright, I prefer to personally supervise the inventory and usage of Mr. Max's wine cellar," the butler went on airily. "And since he and Mrs. Agatha were so generous in offering the champagne, it was the least I could do to attend this event in order to ensure it wasn't being *wasted*." His emphasis clearly indicated the words he didn't dare speak: *on the likes of you*.

"Mr. Max insisted I taste the vintage," Phyllida replied, deciding to put the matter at rest. "As it's one of his favorites. Incidentally, I trust Bess and Lizzie put the guest chambers in readiness for tonight? I checked the linens and spoke to both of them before returning here at half five."

All three visiting members of the Detection Club—Dorothy Sayers, G. K. Chesterton, and Anthony Berkeley—were staying at Mallowan Hall. Fortunately, this weekend was a much less formal affair than a normal house party, as they were spending most of their time and taking many of their meals here at the Murder Fête.

Still, Phyllida was fully aware of Dobble's exasperation over her absences . . . as well as the fact that the pink chintz sofa pillows had been removed from the large sitting room. The fact that her two cats, Stilton and Rye, were particularly moody when she was back at the house also suggested Dobble's handiwork. Clearly, the felines hadn't been allowed to do their daily mouse hunt while Phyllida was gone attending to the Murder Fête.

"Yes," replied the butler. "I checked them myself and made corrections as necessary. Now if you'll excuse me, Mrs. Bright."

Corrections as necessary, hmm? Since he was walking away and couldn't see, she allowed herself to glare at his shoulder blades. As a rule, her chambermaids did *not* need "corrections."

Phyllida watched as Dobble made his way out into the courtyard, stopping to speak sharply to Stanley, the head footman. Stanley looked out into the courtyard in Mrs. Whittlesby's direction, then back at Dobble, and gesticulated in a questioning manner. Dobble spoke again, more firmly this time, and the footman shrugged. Moments later, Stanley was filling a tray with coupes and flutes of champagne. The mismatched glasses had been a deliberate decision on Phyllida's part; she liked the way the different heights and shapes mingled on the tray.

On that note . . . assured that all was well in hand, and that the party was soon to be over, she helped herself to a second glass of the sparkling wine. Before making her way back out into the garden, she told Stanley to deliver a glass to Mrs. Whittlesby.

"But, Mrs. Bright, he told me not to bring any more to her," said Stanley.

Phyllida frowned. "Do you mean Mr. Whittlesby asked you to refrain from serving his wife any more drinks?"

"Yes, ma'am," he replied.

She smoothed out her frown lines, but warred internally. Perhaps Mr. Whittlesby was merely looking out for his wife by keeping her from embarrassing herself from overimbibing in a public setting, or perhaps he was merely being overbearing. Based on both of her encounters with Mr. Whittlesby, she suspected it was the latter.

"Very well. Don't offer her anything more, but if she approaches and takes one, I don't suppose there's anything you can do. Certainly don't refuse her," she advised, deciding on a compromise.

The party would be ending very soon, leaving everyone to make their respective ways for their evening meal. The Detection Club members were being hosted for a private dinner at Mallowan Hall, and the amateur writers would dine wherever they chose—possibly the Screaming Magpie, or their own homes.

Back out in the courtyard, Phyllida paused for a moment to survey the scene. John Bhatt caught her eye from a short distance away, and he lifted his glass in a silent toast to her, smiling warmly beneath his mustaches, then returned his attention to a conversation with Anthony Berkeley, Dorothy Sayers, Agatha, and Mr. Max.

She hoped the doctor won the prize tomorrow.

As if the thought had manifested into reality, she caught sight of Father Tooley, who would surely have calculated the contest results by now, at the bar. He was conversing with Mr. Whittlesby, who Phyllida was certain would be attempting to acquire any sort of hints about the winning story. The vicar, Mr. Billdop, and the antiques dealer, Mr. Genevan, hovered on the outskirts of the conversation, likely for the same reason.

As Phyllida watched, Mrs. Rollingbroke and her cunning yellow hat joined the little group. She appeared to have resigned her notebook for the time being, for she sipped from a champagne flute and her other hand was empty of pen and paper.

Dobble had taken his place behind the counter, mixing two dark cocktails with several different types of spirit whilst Stanley poured fresh glasses of champagne.

She noticed that Dobble suddenly frowned, pausing in his task. He looked around, then ducked behind the counter as if searching for something. When he rose, he had a small bottle in his hand, which he used to finish the drinks he was mixing.

"Oh, Mrs. Bright, how lovely to see you here tonight. Am I correct in assuming this is all your handiwork?"

Phyllida turned to see Miss Crowley in her dark, uninteresting suit. The spinsterish creator of the charming and flamboyant Filberto Fiero was holding her teacup at half-mast as if to protect herself from the evils of wine and spirits.

"I had quite a lot of assistance, but I do thank you for your kind words," Phyllida replied. "How did you find the macarons?"

"They were quite lovely indeed. Just the sort of thing my Filberto would enjoy, you know. He really does have exquisite taste when it comes to food," she replied, revealing a crooked front tooth when she smiled.

Phyllida nodded. "Quite." She was, of course, very used to writers talking about their characters as if they were real people.

"I'm just so very *anxious* about the contest announcement," Miss Crowley went on, hardly pausing for Phyllida's response. "I *so* want dear Filberto to be set free into the public eye for all to enjoy. He really is a most charming man! And a bit of a scoundrel, too, of course."

"Scoundrels can be quite intoxicating—and tiresome," Phyllida said with feeling.

But Miss Crowley hadn't taken a breath. "I'm not shy about admitting he was inspired by that Flambeau character in Mr. Chesterton's stories. But, of course, my Filberto is more of a charmer than a thief. Did I tell you that his latest adventure is about a man mauled by a tiger who's got loose from its master? It's a pet tiger, but he has a wild, feral side, of course, and the victim has been smeared with raw steak—which makes it murder, of course, and—"

Phyllida heard a clink and a crash, followed by a strange, horrible sound behind her. It made the hair on the back of her neck stand on end. As she spun, she was aware that everyone had gone silent and still and they were staring at someone.

It was Father Tooley.

He was clutching his middle with both hands and moaning as if in great pain. His face was pale, and his skin appeared clammy.

Phyllida's battlefield nurse's training was instinctive, and she pushed her way through the staring crowd as the priest collapsed onto the ground, convulsing violently.

But she was too late.

Father Tooley gave one strangled scream of pain . . . and then he went horribly, horrifically still.

CHAPTER 3

"**G**OOD *HEAVENS!*" CRIED SOMEONE, AND THIS REACTION WAS EX-
pressed in several different ways and phrases by nearly everyone
in attendance as they stood in a cluster some distance away from
the scene.

Everyone fell silent, staring . . . and then, suddenly, Mr. Genevan began to chuckle, and then to clap his hands. He looked
around at the others and offered his applause toward the collapsed priest, his eyes lit with appreciation.

Miss Crowley and Miss Sayers were the first to catch on. The
horrified spinster heaved a relieved sigh and she joined the celebrated author in smiling as they joined the antiques dealer in his
applause. Soon the tension snapped and everyone was chuckling
and doing the same.

"Absolutely *screaming!*" cried Mrs. Rollingbroke enthusiastically. "What a perfect way to end the cocktail party—with a game
of murder for all of us to solve! I cannot wait to tell Rolly! He
should be here any moment. Now, shall we begin to gather clues?
Obviously, it was poison."

"I'm not quite certain . . ." Agatha said hesitantly. "Max . . ."

Phyllida, who was crouching next to Father Tooley and smelled
the results of his violent bodily discharges, looked up and
around. She found Dr. Bhatt's gaze in the crowd, and the glim-
mer of delight in it evaporated when he saw the truth in her eyes.

Without a word, he made his way to where she'd remained

next to the priest, even as the rest of the attendees buzzed excitedly among themselves.

It wasn't until Dr. Bhatt silently closed Father Tooley's eyes that the buzzing began to subside. A second unnatural silence fell over the courtyard, but this time it lasted longer.

"Dear God . . . Is he . . . is he really . . . dead?" murmured a voice that might have been Mrs. Whittlesby.

Dr. Bhatt rose from next to Father Tooley, having covered the priest's face with his coat, and said simply, "I'm sorry."

Mr. Billdop pushed his way forward and knelt next to the dead priest. He did a final blessing during the pregnant silence, which was broken only by the distant sound of the church bell tolling seven.

Then someone whispered, "He was poisoned."

The undertones of agreement rippled through the small crowd as the reality set in—for what *else* was a group of a dozen murder writers to think after a man actually fell dead in front of them?

And before Phyllida could react, everyone was talking—mostly murmuring—in tight, excited voices.

"But who . . . ?"

"Strychnine. It *must* be strychnine. It was in his drink."

"And why?"

"Arsenic?"

"No, not strychnine. It takes longer. It had to be cyanide. Arsenic doesn't kill that quickly, either. It takes hours."

"I simply can't believe it! I thought it was playacting!"

"But he might have ingested it earlier. Perhaps it *was* strychnine."

"Digitalis! It had to be digitalis!"

"He was such a kind man! Do you think it was hemlock? Just like Socrates!"

"No, no, no. Don't you see? It had to be belladonna! Did you not notice the way he shivered and convulsed?"

"But his face wasn't red, and he wasn't hallucinating—and aren't those signs of belladonna poisoning? Cyanide kills quite quickly—a man just drops to the ground with a lethal dose."

"Then he should smell of bitter almonds."

"Well, *I'm* not about to get close enough to smell him."

Because she needed something physical to do while her mind attempted to focus, Phyllida picked up the broken pieces of the glass Father Tooley had been holding. It had shattered on one of the walkway stones. Though on its side, the bottom was mostly intact, and a bit of dark brown liquid remained collected in the vessel.

Although she was wearing gloves, Phyllida used her handkerchief when she picked up the fragment. When she brought it to her nose and sniffed its contents, she smelled rye whisky, something heavy and cloying, and the definite scent of tobacco.

Phyllida rose abruptly and sought another face in the crowd. As if reading her mind, Agatha met her gaze, then her attention dropped to the handkerchief-wrapped cup Phyllida was holding.

Hushed discussion about poisons and the employment thereof continued among the writers, and no one seemed to notice as Phyllida swiftly made her way to Agatha, where she stood with Mr. Max and Mr. Chesterton. Agatha was not taking part in the discussion; she was still watching Phyllida, and as her friend approached, Agatha eased away from the men, both of whom wore grave expressions.

Without speaking, Phyllida handed the handkerchief-wrapped glass to Agatha.

Also properly gloved, she took it, then sniffed the contents. Her eyes widened, and Phyllida nodded in agreement and acknowledgment.

"Nicotine," Agatha said. Then, projecting a little more loudly, she said again, "Nicotine. There was nicotine in his drink."

Everyone turned to look at her, and Phyllida saw Agatha reach to take her husband's arm as if to anchor herself whilst she was under the unrelenting gaze of so many people.

"What?" exclaimed Mr. Whittlesby, as his wife whimpered next to him. His face was white. "Nicotine? Are you quite certain?"

"There is the distinct smell of tobacco in Father Tooley's drink," Phyllida said in her crisp, no-nonsense tone. "Which, of course, is a strong indicator of a great amount of nicotine."

"But nicotine isn't deadly," said the vicar, fingering the cleft of his plump chin. "Is it?"

"The gardener sprays it on our flowers to keep the pests away," said Mrs. Rollingbroke. Her large hazel eyes sparkled beneath the hat Phyllida coveted as she whipped out her notebook from the depths of her large pocketbook. "I didn't realize it was deadly to humans as well."

"Is it?" said Miss Crowley. She was still holding Phyllida's champagne glass, but it was now, perhaps not surprisingly, empty. "I've never *heard* of such a thing, and I've been researching poisons for *years.*"

"Mrs. Mallowan worked in the dispensary during the war and has been certified as an apothecary's assistant," said Mr. Max firmly, his voice carrying. "She is extremely well versed in the characteristics and identification of any number of poisons, which is why she employs them quite often in her work."

His tone indicated he wasn't making a joke, and there were no chuckles, only the nodding of heads. However, only a very few people in their household knew that one of the Poirot stories his wife was currently working on utilized nicotine as the murder weapon—which was why Phyllida had been so arrested by the scent of tobacco in the dead man's drink. There had been many discussions at Mallowan Hall about the efficacy and convenience of nicotine as a poison, how it worked, where to obtain it, and what symptoms it produced. It was a speedy killer, and usually attacked the lungs and heart, paralyzing the respiratory muscles and causing heart irregularities.

Phyllida noticed that Mr. Berkeley and Mr. Genevan were suspiciously eyeing the cigarettes they'd been smoking, while Mr. Chesterton continued to puff away on his cigar, unconcerned. Perhaps he assumed that, at his relatively advanced age, it didn't matter.

As Phyllida watched, Mr. Genevan frowned, then dropped his smoke and smushed the butt into the ground with his heel. His dark skin had acquired a decidedly greenish tint.

"Nicotine in high, unadulterated quantities is an extremely effective and speedy poison," said Agatha with a ring of authority. "My assessment will, of course, be contingent upon confirmation from the authorities. But I can think of no other explanation for the strong smell of tobacco in Father Tooley's drink and his subsequent—er—demise."

Just then, the sound of new arrivals had everyone turning toward the gate leading into the courtyard. Presumably, someone had had the wherewithal to telephone the authorities. Phyllida didn't spare a moment of regret that she hadn't seen to it herself; apparently, she'd had the murder weapon to attend to.

She recognized Constable Greensticks from the unpleasantries a few months ago up at Mallowan Hall. He had a pompous air about him, and despite his name, he wasn't at all "green" in his role as constable. However, Phyllida couldn't say whether he was actually efficient at his job, for evidence from her previous interactions with him hadn't suggested a high level of competency.

At least this time, the constable didn't seem to find the situation as amusing as he had done previously, when Phyllida telephoned to report that a dead body had been found in Agatha Christie's library. Although when Constable Greensticks realized Father Tooley's poisoning had occurred at a gathering of murder writers, his eyes did widen a bit and his mustache spasmed as if he were attempting to control a guffaw.

The constable was accompanied by another figure familiar to Phyllida, and for the same reasons: Inspector Cork.

She was mildly surprised that the investigator was already here in Listleigh instead of needing to be called in, but made no comment. During their previous interactions, her initial impression of the inspector had been that he seemed too young to be an accomplished murder solver. The smattering of freckles over his face gave him a youthful look even though he was in his thirties, and his slightly protuberant eyes suggested that he was always in a state of mild shock.

As the policemen spoke to Dr. Bhatt, Phyllida realized Mr. Dobble was attempting to get her attention. With an inward sigh, she made her way over to the butler. He was back at the bar counter, automatically arranging clean glasses and bottles of liquor to be at the ready. And quite so, for Phyllida expected the partygoers to suddenly develop a desperate thirst, all things considered.

"I suppose dinner will have to be pushed back," Mr. Dobble said grimly.

"Indubitably," Phyllida replied.

"Mrs. Puffley will be in quite a state over her lamb puffed pastry," he went on. "Perhaps you should be the one to notify her, Mrs. Bright. You could telephone up to the house."

"Of course, Mr. Dobble," she said demurely. "I will be happy to relay your message."

He looked down his nose at her, clearly comprehending her delicate implication that it was he who would be the recipient of Mrs. Puffley's wrath or weeping, depending upon her mood, when she received the news that her fragile leg of lamb Wellington—an elaborate production done up with chicken mousse in puffed pastry—would have to be served hours late, if at all.

Phyllida was about to sweep off to crush Mrs. Puffley's dreams in the name of Mr. Dobble when the inspector caught her attention.

"Mrs. Bright. We meet again," he said in a tone that indicated he hadn't forgotten she'd been the one to put all the clues together to identify a murderer during the last time a killer struck in Listleigh—including clues she'd delivered to him on a proverbial silver platter.

"Good evening, Inspector Cork," she replied, eyeing his untidy mustache with disapproval. "Unfortunately, I cannot say that it is a pleasure to see you again, considering the reason for your presence. Poor Father Tooley."

He nodded, and she noticed it had been over a month and he still hadn't fixed the loose hem on his coat. Her fingers itched to attend to it, and to tighten the third coat button that sagged mournfully from its place. Certainly a bachelor could afford a seamstress to see to such things. "I understand you were a witness to the event," he went on, "and that afterward you collected the glass from which Father Tooley was drinking."

"Indeed," she replied. "I was wearing gloves, but wrapped it in a handkerchief so as to protect it from any other fingerprints. There is the distinct smell of tobacco in the remains of Father Tooley's glass, the implications of which I am certain are not lost on you." She looked at him closely in order to ascertain whether the implications were, in fact, not lost on him.

"Tobacco, hmm?" he said.

"Father Tooley did not smoke tobacco," Phyllida said, giving him a gentle prompt. "And I can think of no alcoholic spirit that has such an essence."

"You cannot?" he replied, and she noted the tiniest flicker of a grin from beneath his untrimmed mustache. Was the man *teasing* her? Younger people were astonishingly impertinent nowadays. (Although he was not *that* much younger than she.)

Phyllida gave Cork a severe look but refrained from calling him out. "Is there any other information I can give you, Inspector?"

The hint of levity evaporated from his expression. "Mrs. Mallowan knows her poisons, does she?"

"Exceedingly well. She's passed the Apothecaries' Hall test and worked in a hospital dispensary during the war."

"Mmm." He nodded, and only then did he free the notepad from the depths of his coat pocket. A pencil followed, and he flipped through the pages, presumably in search of a blank one. "We'll have the glass tested, of course, but—"

"Inspector! I say, Inspector, I *must* speak with you."

Phyllida recognized Alastair Whittlesby's self-important voice, and she managed to school her features into a blank expression as she turned, along with Cork, toward the man.

"And you are . . . ?" said Cork, taking his measure of the man, whose wife was still clinging to him like a bloody limpet. Mrs. Whittlesby appeared even more faded and wispy than she had previously, and her lipstick was completely gone. She had, however, acquired a new glass of champagne.

"Why, I'm Alastair Whittlesby," the newcomer replied, clearly taken aback that his identity hadn't preceded him. "Of Whittlesby & Konkle, Solicitors & Lawyers, and President of the Listleigh Murder Club—"

"The *what?*" Cork's watery blue eyes bulged even more than usual.

"The local writers' club, of course," replied Mr. Whittlesby. "We write detective stories. Some of us more skillfully than others."

"I see," replied the inspector.

"There's something I must tell you," said Mr. Whittlesby in a carrying voice. "Quite alarming. Quite, *quite* alarming."

"Oi, then, go on with it," said Cork, who seemed anything but alarmed.

"Do tell him, Allie," Mrs. Whittlesby said, giving the arm to which she clung a little shake. She appeared to be close to tears. *"Do."*

"Right, then," said her husband, seeming to brace himself up. "Of course I must. It's only that . . . someone's tried to murder me!"

Phyllida's brows lifted and despite the fact that Mr. Dobble was once again making agitations from across the way as if he wanted to speak to her, she wasn't going anywhere out of earshot of Alastair Whittlesby anytime soon.

"Someone tried . . . hmm. And when was this?" asked Inspector Cork.

"Why—why . . . only a short while ago," Mr. Whittlesby spluttered. "Only, they got Father Tooley *instead!*"

The inspector pursed his lips beneath a mustache that hadn't been approached by a pair of scissors in weeks. "You're saying whoever poisoned the priest meant to poison you instead?"

"That's precisely what I'm saying," replied Mr. Whittlesby. "*I* was the intended victim, not Father Tooley!"

"Tell him, Allie," pressed Mrs. Whittlesby. "*Tell* him! Tell him about *me*, too!"

"The priest collected both of our cocktails from the bar, and he took a drink from one of them as he brought them over." As the solicitor went on, his voice spiraled up in volume and pitch. "And then he died. That drink was meant for *me*—I mean to say, Inspector, someone is trying to kill me!"

"All right, all right, then." Cork held up a hand. "Let's just slow down a bit now and take this one step at a time. Constable," he said, and Greensticks produced his own notepad and a pencil. "What exactly happened, Mr. . . . . er . . . ?"

"*Whittlesby.*"

"Right, then. Go on now."

"Father Tooley went to the bar to bring back our drinks." He gave a little shudder. "Other than the occasional glass of champagne, I only drink Vieux Carrés—*everyone* knows that. They're made with rye instead of whisky, along with cognac and vermouth and—"

"Yes, yes, thank you," said Inspector Cork. "Why do you think he mixed up your drink with his? Didn't the man know his own cocktails?"

"No, no, *no*, you don't understand!" Mr. Whittlesby said. "Father Tooley is—er, was—not quite an accomplished drinker. I mean to say, he usually confines—confined—himself to a small glass of port, but it seemed that tonight he wanted to try something different."

"And so he drank yours and died."

"Yes," replied Mr. Whittlesby. "Well, no, not exactly. You see, I encouraged him to try a Vieux Carré, and so he went to collect both of them, for I was loathe to interrupt my conversation with Mr. Chesterton. It's so preposterously difficult to get to the man through all of the hangers-on you know, I didn't want to step away. But you see, it was the same drink! And obviously one of them was meant for me! And my wife"—he shrugged the arm Mrs. Whittlesby was clinging to as if to indicate her identity— "why, she was just about to taste my drink when he *died*!"

Mrs. Whittlesby whimpered and clung more tightly to her spouse. Phyllida glanced over to see Mr. Dobble giving her a stony glare and making insistent gestures that she should attend to him.

"They were the same drink, but only one of them was poisoned, and Father Tooley happened to drink the poisoned one?" Inspector Cork said, as if pushing his way through some sort of murk. "How do you know that it was meant for you?"

"Inspector, I am the only person in Listleigh who has even *heard* of a Vieux Carré, let alone who drinks them." Mr. Whittlesby's nose and tone lifted condescendingly. "If a Vieux Carré was mixed at the bar, everyone knows it was meant for me."

"Oh, *Allie,* I simply can't believe it," said Lettice Whittlesby as she looked around urgently. Phyllida noticed that her champagne glass was empty again, and that the hand holding it was very unsteady.

"Very well, then," said the inspector. "I see your point, sir. It is quite concerning."

Mr. Whittlesby tugged at the collar of his shirt, and his Adam's apple bobbed and jerked. His face was shiny with perspiration. "It's quite frightening, really, to realize someone has just tried to do away with you."

"Oh, *Allie,*" said the clinging limpet. "It's simply *horrid.*"

"Where is the other drink, then, Mr. Whittlesby?" asked Cork. "The second—erm—View-whatsits."

"Why, that's what's even *worse*—Father Tooley brought it to me and Lettice took it from him whilst I was talking to Mr. Chesterton. Thank heavens she didn't drink it!" he said, his eyes widening in sudden realization as his wife made a sound of horrified agreement.

"Where is the drink now, er, Mrs. Whittlesby?" asked Cork.

"Why, I—I must have set it down when I saw the tray of champagne," she said. "I'd been looking for a footman and I hadn't been able to find one. I prefer champagne, you know, but I don't mind a real cocktail—"

"Where would it be if you did set it down, Mrs. Whittlesby?" The detective's interruption was quite advisable in this case, Phyllida thought, for they needed to locate the other drink before someone—likely the murderer—disposed of it.

"Why . . . why, oh dear . . ." Mrs. Whittlesby looked around, but Phyllida wasn't certain whether she was looking for the abandoned drink or a new glass of bubbly.

"It's just there, Lettice—over on the table next to where we were standing. Why, I could have just picked it up and started drinking it, and that would have been it!" Mr. Whittlesby said, his eyes wide and horrified. "You didn't taste it, did you, Lettice?" he demanded. "Do you feel quite all right, then, darling?"

Constable Greensticks immediately retrieved the drink Mr. Whittlesby had indicated. As he did so, the constable put his short, stub nose and a good portion of his dark mustache inside the glass. "Smells like tobacco, sir," he said.

"Good *Lord*," breathed Mr. Whittlesby, as if his most dire fears had come to pass. "They were *both* poisoned. I might have been *killed!*"

"All three of you might have been killed," said the detective.

Phyllida could no longer ignore Mr. Dobble's agitations; she was afraid the older man would do himself severe harm if she didn't respond.

Besides, she had a few questions for the butler—including who had made the two poisoned cocktails.

CHAPTER 4

"ARE YOU SUGGESTING THAT *I* POISONED THOSE COCKTAILS?" Mr. Dobble did not like the direction of Phyllida's queries. "Are you mad?"

"Of course not, Mr. Dobble, and *certainly* not," she replied, answering both of his questions. "But clearly someone did, and the fact that both of the drinks appear to have nicotine in them is troubling, to say the least."

Stanley passed by, still doggedly making his way about the courtyard with a tray of coupes and flutes. No one had approached the bar—perhaps out of self-preservation—which left Phyllida and Mr. Dobble free to have a private conversation.

"Indeed." Mr. Dobble seemed to be following along Phyllida's train of thought now. "The implication being: someone either poisoned both drinks, being uncertain which was meant for Mr. Whittlesby—or perhaps the poisoner simply assumed *both* cocktails were for him—or perhaps him and his wife."

"That's a slight possibility, but a far more likely one is that one of the ingredients of the cocktail already had the nicotine in it. That would be much easier to accomplish than to add poison to two different glasses without being noticed," Phyllida said.

"But that would mean anyone could have drunk the poison if they had a cocktail made with the ingredient!" Mr. Dobble was incensed. "Mr. Max! Miss Sayers! Or . . . or even the vicar! Why, that's *despicable*. And who would be blamed for it anyway? The person who *made* the cocktails, of course!"

"Now, now, Mr. Dobble," Phyllida said soothingly. "I'm certain no one would even consider you a murder suspect. After all, *you* have no motive for murdering Mr. Whittlesby, do you? You don't even know the man."

To her surprise, Mr. Dobble's expression tightened. "No, of course not," he said. "But from everything I hear about him, there are any number of people who might be tempted to do so."

Phyllida pursed her lips but chose to neither agree nor disagree with his statement. Still, there was something Mr. Dobble wasn't telling her. She wondered what and why.

As her attention trailed over the partygoers, most of whom had gathered in small clusters where they seemed to be discussing matters whilst draining their glasses of the presumably safe choice of champagne, she understood that one of them was a killer.

She wondered whether *they* had yet realized one of their companions was a killer.

The Whittlesbys were still monopolizing Constable Greensticks and Inspector Cork, leaving Phyllida to contemplate whether the policemen would ever get to the actual investigation portion of the event. Lettice Whittlesby had released her husband's arm at last and now held two glasses of sparkling wine. With all of her bright lipstick gone and her mascara smudged under her eyes, she appeared even more faded and wispy than before.

Mr. Chesterton, having been liberated from the attentions of Alastair Whittlesby, was now holding forth in a small group of amateur writers, all of whom clustered around him with wide, fascinated eyes as he weighed in with his opinions about the choice of murder weapon. None of his current audience were from Listleigh, and Phyllida thought it might be acceptable to take them off the list of suspects. After all, if they weren't from Listleigh, they likely couldn't have a motive for killing Alastair Whittlesby.

But she'd been fooled by Agatha's twisty plots before, and Phyllida knew better than to summarily dismiss anyone. Everyone knew that truth was stranger than fiction.

Mathilda Crowley and Vera Rollingbroke were huddled together, making an unusual pair. Miss Crowley, in her dark, drab suit and boxlike hat, looked like a straggly wren next to the silky

yellow and blue of Mrs. Rollingbroke's slender and exuberant figure and her far better chapeau. The latter had tucked away her
notebook once more, and both women held glasses of champagne.

Digby Billdop stood a bit away from the others, appearing ill at
ease and unsure what to do with himself. The vicar was within
hearing distance of the two female members of the Listleigh writers' club, as well as Louis Genevan in his Beau Brummell cravat.
He was hovering near the Whittlesbys and the authorities, perhaps in hopes of overhearing some of the conversation.

Agatha and Mr. Max were ensconced in a corner of the garden
with Mr. Berkeley, who had lit up a cigarette once again, perhaps
having been assured by Agatha that a cigarette wasn't going to kill
him. And Miss Sayers had collected her own flock of an audience
nearby—three individuals whom Phyllida didn't recognize, and
who could also possibly be moved to the bottom of the list of suspects.

Molly, as one would expect from a member of Phyllida's staff,
was efficiently clearing used glasses and plates, piling them on a
tray to take into the rectory's kitchen. However, Rita, the maid
from St. Wendreda's, was standing there with an empty tray. Her
eyes were glassy with tears, and her squat nose was bright red on
its rounded tip. She seemed incapable of movement, and Phyllida
was just about to go to the poor girl and offer her a handkerchief
when Mr. Dobble spoke.

"Mrs. Bright!"

The terseness of his voice had her turning sharply to face him.
She smothered her acerbic response when she saw that he was offering her a small bottle.

Taking it wordlessly, she brought it carefully to her nose and
sniffed.

Tobacco. Very strong tobacco.

"So that's how he did it," she said, looking at the label on the
bottle, which was filled with a dark liquid. "'Monteleone's Special
Bitters,'" she read, then looked up at Mr. Dobble. "I've never
heard of it." She couldn't help but be mildly irritated by her ig-
norance.

"That is because this type of bitters is only used in Mr. Whittlesby's Vieux Carré cocktail," said the butler, a little pompously. "Only someone who ordered that particular drink would have this ingredient, for Mr. Whittlesby has this particular brand of bitters shipped from New Orleans, Louisiana."

"Well, that makes things quite a bit clearer," Phyllida said, wondering how Mr. Dobble knew that interesting bit of information. "We shall have to inform the inspector."

"Of course," he replied.

Phyllida examined the bottle more minutely, pleased that both she and the butler were properly wearing gloves. "There might be fingerprints by the culprit," she said. Then she looked up. "The poison might have been added at any time. Even before tonight. That greatly widens the array of suspects."

Mr. Dobble nodded grimly. He, too, had read his share of detective stories. "However, a curious thing happened. I was making the cocktails for Mr. Whittlesby and Father Tooley, and I couldn't find the Monteleone's Special Bitters. I had seen it previously, but it had gone. I assumed Stanley had been trying to be helpful and put away some of the bottles. It took me a moment to find the bottle of bitters—it had been stuck on the shelf behind me with the extra glasses."

Phyllida nodded. She had seen Mr. Dobble looking about for something. "Yes, I noticed your agitation."

He frowned. Butlers were not supposed to show agitation. "The curious thing, however, is that it wasn't the same bottle as before."

"Indeed," Phyllida said. "Now that is quite interesting." Once again, she looked out over the courtyard. The sunlight was fading, and the inadequacy of the Japanese lanterns' illumination would soon become obvious. She tsked to herself; had the cocktail party ended on time thirty minutes ago, this wouldn't have been a problem. Now she had to either bring out candles and lanterns—fortunately, she had brought a supply from Mallowan Hall—or urge the authorities to move their interrogations inside.

However, at the moment, the authorities didn't seem to be doing any serious interrogations, for they were still being subjected to the Whittlesbys' theatrics. By now, the tone of the conversation seemed to have moved from shock and horror to remonstrations about widespread crime in Listleigh, people being murdered in their beds, and the responsibility of the constable to prevent it.

"So someone removed the bottle and later replaced it with another one containing the poison," said Phyllida, returning her attention to Mr. Dobble. "Since the bitters wouldn't be used except to make Mr. Whittlesby's drink, their absence wouldn't be missed—and no one else would be poisoned by it. But how do you know it wasn't the same bottle of bitters?"

"The original bottle was more than half full, while this one, as you can see, only has some small amount left at the bottom. I suppose whoever added the nicotine might have emptied it out first so as to ensure that a high enough dosage was administered. The cocktail requires eight shakes. Mr. Whittlesby made certain I knew to count them," he added grimly.

Phyllida nodded. "So either there were two bottles—one prepared already with the poison, or someone removed one and poured out a portion of the contents and added the poison. Had you made any of that particular drink for Mr. Whittlesby previously tonight?" she asked.

"No, he'd been drinking champagne."

She was prevented from any further comment by the expected, but sudden, appearance of Bradford. He was here to assist with driving people back to the house. Mr. Max had motored down himself with his wife and Mr. Chesterton, but a second automobile was needed to bring the other guests back at the same time.

As was proper, Bradford edged his way into the courtyard from St. Wendreda's kitchen, rather than through the main gate as a guest would do. He also held a pair of chocolate macarons in his hand, which wasn't quite as proper. At least he didn't have Myrtle with him. When he saw Phyllida, he started in her direction.

She resisted the impulse to smooth the yoke front of her dress's waistline or check her hair. Instead, she lifted her nose a trifle as he approached.

"Someone died?" he said without preamble.

"Murdered," she told him. "Poisoned."

His expression flickered. "Who was it?"

"Not Mrs. Agatha or Mr. Max," she said, and was rewarded for her instinctive response by the slight lowering of his shoulders. Only then did he slip one of the cookies into his mouth. "It was Father Tooley, the priest here at St. Wendreda's," she told him.

Munching the pastry, Bradford nodded, then looked around. His dark eyes scanned the crowd in a manner that made Phyllida wonder what he'd actually done during the war.

"But it appears the poison was meant for Alastair Whittlesby," she went on.

Bradford grunted in a manner that had Phyllida mentally shaking her head at his gaucherie. At least this evening he was wearing a proper chauffeur's uniform, including gloves and cap—which, she knew, would likely disappear after he conveyed the Mallowans' guests back to the house and was required to drive only herself, Mr. Dobble, and the maids. Bradford seemed to have a selective memory when it came to wearing hats and gloves.

"Mrs. Puffley is in quite a state," he said, glancing at Mr. Dobble. The butler fumbled a glass that he was wiping, catching it just before it rolled off the counter. "Something about soft and damp pastry . . . ?"

"There's nothing to be done about it," Phyllida said crisply. "Puffley will have to realize that murder takes precedence over lamb Wellington. She does, after all, live in the home of Agatha Christie."

Because he wore no facial hair, Phyllida saw the way Bradford's mouth twitched, then quickly settled. "Right."

"Unfortunately, your arrival is likely premature, Mr. Bradford," Phyllida went on in the same tone. "I doubt Inspector Cork will allow anyone to leave in the near future."

Bradford grunted again, then, without even a proper taking of leave, he strode off toward the authorities, who seemed to just now be extricating themselves from the Whittlesbys.

That man, Phyllida thought, then realized she was staring after him and turned away. Rita, the rectory maid, needed to be seen to. The poor thing hadn't moved for the last five minutes, and her tray was beginning to tilt. Fortunately, it was empty.

As she made her way to the stricken maid, Phyllida saw that Bradford was assisting Constable Greensticks in preparing to remove Father Tooley's body. At least he was making himself useful instead of eating macarons.

"Let's take that inside now, shall we, Rita?" Phyllida said, sliding an arm around the girl and removing the empty tray from her grip.

Rita seemed startled by Phyllida's presence, but she allowed herself to be directed to the door to the inside of the rectory. The girl, who could be no more than eighteen and was built like a boxer, was trembling, and she sniffled quietly as they went inside.

"I c-can't believe it," Rita said as she sank onto a chair at the small table. "Wh-who would do such a thing?" Tears streamed freely down her rectangular, freckled cheeks. The poor thing either didn't have a handkerchief or couldn't summon the energy to find it. Phyllida offered her a napkin, for her own handkerchief was currently wrapped around a murder weapon. "F-Father was such a nice man."

"It was an accident," she told Rita, deciding it was best to get the correct information disseminated immediately. She knew that servants—well, everyone—liked to gossip, and it was always Phyllida's opinion that if people were going to buzz about a scandal, at least they should be buzzing with facts. Aside from that, she knew everyone in the vicinity of the courtyard had already heard Mr. Whittlesby's revelations. "The drink Father Tooley had was poisoned, but the poison seems to have been meant for Mr. Whittlesby."

Rita gawped at her. "How arful. How *arful*. Me mum keeps saying how this world is goin' to the devil in an oak barrel, and she's right! And now poor Father Tooley—he's *gone!*"

Phyllida soothed the grieving maid by offering a cup of tea and telling her she could remain inside and help tidy up after she'd had a moment to collect herself.

Just as she was about to send for Stanley and Molly to put out the lanterns, Dr. Bhatt came into the kitchen.

"Phyllida," he said. She'd given him permission to use her familiar name after the second time they'd met for tea at the café, but she preferred he not do so in front of her staff. "I have been looking for you."

"What a horrible thing to have happen," she said with great feeling. "I wonder if the inspector will cancel the rest of the event."

Dr. Bhatt grimaced a little. "He has not said, but I hope not. Father Tooley would want the fundraiser to go on, for the money will help the orphans." English was not his first language, but he spoke it fluently and formally, with only the faintest of accents.

"I do hope you're right," she replied.

"The inspector has given me permission to take a small sample from the cocktail to test for poison," Dr. Bhatt went on with a gleam in his dark eyes. "I can do it much faster than him sending off to London. But Scotland Yard will test it as well, in order to confirm my results. I suppose that is only right, for I suppose I am a suspect as well the attending coroner."

"I suppose we all are," murmured Phyllida. Then she gave him a curious look. "I didn't realize you had the capability to do that sort of testing."

He couldn't seem to contain a small smile beneath his glorious mustaches. "Of course I am very interested in poisons and how they cause the body to react—being both a physician and a crime writer," he said. "I have been building up my laboratory for that purpose for quite some time. I have even acquired all of the equipment for a Marsh test—that is what one uses to test for arsenic. If only I could have a sample from the *body*," he said gloomily. "This would be a fine opportunity to actually attempt the testing from a real victim. It will be excellent research for my Dr. Graceley stories, for I've decided to outfit him with his own postmortem laboratory."

"How very dedicated of you, John," Phyllida replied, having read several of Dr. Bhatt's tales about a physician turned amateur detective. "I should like to watch the testing sometime, if I may."

"Of course you may," he replied, clearly delighted with the prospect. "Erm . . . perhaps if *you* approached the inspector about it, he would permit me to have a sample—just a *sliver*, of course—from Father Tooley."

Just then, Bradford and Stanley came into the kitchen, saving Phyllida from having to reply.

"It's getting dark out there," said Bradford, whose attention went from Phyllida to Dr. Bhatt and then back again. One of his eyebrows rose. "Don't want anyone to trip and fall; some of those stones are quite uneven. If you'll permit, we'll set out the lanterns, Mrs. Bright."

Annoyed that Bradford had beaten her to the punch of directing the lanterns to be set out, Phyllida nodded. "Of course—I had just come in here with the intention of doing just that."

"So I see," Bradford replied dryly, looking at Dr. Bhatt as his brow lifted.

She refused to rise to the bait. "Thank you, Mr. Bradford."

Dr. Bhatt took his leave, and Phyllida returned her attention to the matter at hand: namely, determining whether the crime scene needed to be kept intact, or whether her staff could begin to clean up the courtyard.

Back outside, she saw with approval that Molly had cleared nearly all of the glasses and was beginning to stack up the plates from the pastries. Inspector Cork must have given her permission. Stanley was refilling more champagne glasses—he'd moved from offering them on a tray to actually filling the coupes and flutes held by each of the guests. She had advised him of this tactic, which was meant to prevent dirtying more glasses this late in the evening.

"Inspector Cork," Phyllida said, grateful to catch him making notes instead of in the midst of a conversation. "Would you like to settle inside, where there's better light and more comfortable places to sit?"

He nodded. "Yes. I'll finish speaking to the members of the, er, Murder Club"—his voice held a note of disbelief as if astonished by the name—"here, and then perhaps I could speak to Mr. and Mrs. Mallowan and their guests at Mallowan Hall later."

"Whatever you like, Inspector," she replied, mildly surprised that he would be willing to relocate himself up to the hall. And then she remembered Mrs. Puffley and her apple cinnamon scones. The inspector clearly hadn't had dinner, and he would certainly remember Mrs. Puffley's cooking talents.

Aside from that, Phyllida was quite delighted that the inspector wanted to return to Mallowan Hall, for that would give her much more of an opportunity to listen in on his interrogations.

"Why don't you come inside and sit in the rectory's parlor," she suggested. "I can bring some coffee, and you can interview everyone in there."

Phyllida would be thrilled to serve coffee and whatever leftover treats were available. That would enable her to listen in on those conversations as well, for her experience with Inspector Cork suggested he was likely to miss some important information.

Phyllida was just preparing a tray to take to the inspector in the sitting room when Molly came into the rectory kitchen.

"I found this, ma'am," she said, and offered her a small dark bottle.

"Where did you find it?" Phyllida took the bottle of Monteleone's Special Bitters, ruing the fact that her maid didn't wear gloves and hadn't thought to pick it up with a napkin. This bottle of bitters was half full and was presumably the one that had been replaced with a poisoned bottle.

Someone had come prepared.

"It was on the ground behind one of the stone benches under a bush," replied Molly, once again attesting to her efficiency and attention to detail. "I nearly didn't see it from the shadows."

"Thank you very much. You'll have to show me which bench," Phyllida said. It might not be important, but then again, if everyone's movements during the party needed to be accounted for— which of course they would—then it could be instrumental in determining who had the opportunity to replace the bitters with poison.

Outside in the courtyard, the lanterns cast a pleasant yellow glow. The summer day had cooled into early night, and Phyllida saw that clouds were gathering, beginning to obstruct the moon and stars. Nonetheless, she looked around with satisfaction. All of the table decorations had been removed, as well as most of the tablecloths. The glasses and plates were in the kitchen, where Rita was washing them in between sniffles.

Stanley and Bradford, who'd already returned from driving Miss Sayers and Mr. Berkeley—as well as Mr. Dobble—back to Mallowan Hall, had begun to remove the tables.

"Going to rain soon," said Bradford, who'd easily slung a heavy table over one shoulder and was now setting it against the wall to be loaded and taken away.

"Yes, indeed," Phyllida replied. "The paper lanterns will be soaked."

"I'll see to them before it rains, ma'am," said Molly.

"First show me where you found the bottle, if you please," Phyllida said.

As she trailed Molly over to the bench, Bradford followed. Phyllida suppressed comment, even when he came to stand next to them with his broad-shouldered shadow spilling over the bench.

"It was right there, under the rosebush," Molly told her.

"Where no one would notice it until the gardener came," Phyllida mused. As Molly went off to see to the lanterns, Phyllida stood there for a moment, trying to remember if she'd observed anyone standing or sitting in this corner. It was away from where most of the attendees had congregated, although the courtyard wasn't so large than any area was left neglected. It also wasn't far from the bar counter. There was a small, unobtrusive gate nearby through which the supplies of spirits and champagne had been delivered.

"Doing some detecting again, are we, Mrs. Bright?"

"*We* aren't doing any detecting, Mr. Bradford," she replied. "However, *I* am paying attention to small details that might come in handy for the investigation."

"What is this about a bottle?" he asked.

Phyllida commenced to explain, reasoning that articulating what she knew and didn't know would help to organize her thoughts.

When she finished describing the bitters bottle substitution, he made a thoughtful sound. "Poison in the bitters, is it," he said. "Not a bad idea, that. And you're certain it was nicotine?"

"Of course," she told him. "Mrs. Agatha knows her poisons, and we all smelt the tobacco."

"Stanley said the man had convulsions and seemed to be in pain in his belly," Bradford said thoughtfully. "And that he hadn't been feeling quite right earlier. Sounds more like arsenic."

"I didn't realize you were an expert on poisons, Mr. Bradford," Phyllida responded.

"Not really," he said. "But I do know about arsenic."

And with that ominous statement, he turned to heft up the last of the tables, leaving Phyllida to glare down at the innocent rose-bush that had obscured the bottle. Men like Bradford and Mr. Dobble, and Mr. Whittlesby for that matter—different though they were—always thought they knew everything, and that women were dunderheads.

And what precisely did he mean when he said, "I do know about arsenic"?

Phyllida realized she was grinding her teeth. She unclenched her jaw and smoothed the front of her dress. Bradford could make his little superior comments; she didn't care one whit what he thought. She had more important things on her mind—like finding out who exactly knew what was in a Vieux Carré, and how someone would get hold of Monteleone's Special Bitters.

But first, she was going to assist Inspector Cork with his inter-views.

Once back inside the rectory kitchen, Phyllida finished prepar-ing the tray of coffee and brought it into the sitting room.

Inspector Cork and Constable Greensticks made no effort to hide their pleasure at the delivery of the hot beverages, as well as the small platter of food she'd culled together from a few items in the priest's larder and the cocktail party leftovers. The two police-men were alone in the room, having just finished an interview with the last of the amateur writers who'd traveled from out of town for the fête.

"My maid found this outside," Phyllida told Inspector Cork, handing him the small bottle, which she'd wrapped in a napkin. "Unfortunately, she wasn't wearing gloves when she retrieved it." She explained what she and Mr. Dobble had concluded about the bitters being substituted with a poisoned version. "This confirms that a second bottle was procured, tainted with nicotine, and then used to replace the one at the bar."

"Mmph," said the inspector from behind a mouthful of macaron.

"Indeed," replied Phyllida, well versed in translating food-distorted comments. "Now to determine from whence it came."

"Fancy drink, that View-whatsits," said Inspector Cork once he'd washed down the cookie with some coffee. "Don't understand why the bloke can't drink a plain whisky or ale like every other man."

Phyllida privately agreed, although she also admitted she was intrigued enough to want to sample a Vieux Carré herself. She was quite partial to a good rye whisky.

"It would be reasonable to conclude that whoever poisoned the bitters must be fully aware of Mr. Whittlesby's cocktail preference—and not only that, but have some way to obtain this very specialized ingredient," said Phyllida as she poured coffee into another cup for the constable. "Someone visiting from outside of Listleigh for the Murder Fête would be far less likely to know about it. And whoever obtained it must have planned well in advance. It's hardly an item one can pick up at the local market."

"Right," said Cork. "But we'll interview every attendee, regardless. Constable, take your coffee into the next room. You can finish speaking to anyone who's not local, and I'll talk to those from around here. That will speed things up a bit."

"Quite so," she replied, pleased at the inspector's efficient suggestion. "And it's of paramount importance to determine who had the opportunity to swap the bottles at the bar counter. Determining the movement of each individual as much as possible during the evening would be very instructive. Perhaps even creating a diagram," she murmured, more for herself than as a suggestion to the inspector.

That was an excellent idea, she thought. Between her own observations—of which there were varied and excellent ones—and that of Molly, Stanley, and Mr. Dobble, Phyllida was fairly confident she could plot out the guests' movements for much of the evening.

The constable left the room with his coffee, as well as a small plate of food. Moments later, there was a knock at the door, which was ajar, and Miss Crowley's face peered hesitantly through the opening.

"Yes, yes, come in," said the inspector.

Phyllida took her time fussing with the tray, adjusting the pillows on the sofa, drawing the curtains, turning on lamps, and every other bit of tidying she could think of whilst Miss Crowley spoke to the authorities. She would even locate and use a carpet sweep if it became necessary.

Miss Crowley introduced herself but remained near the door as if hedging her bets on escape. Then, without waiting for the inspector to begin, she launched right into her own speech.

"I don't drink spirits," she said, obviously forgetting or ignoring the two glasses of champagne in which she'd indulged that evening. "When Mr. Whittlesby invited us on Wednesday, I had no intention of drinking anything but tea. And now I'm *particularly* glad that I didn't. Is it *true* that someone poisoned him with his *own* spirits? Why, he could have served any *one* of us one of those Carry-thingabobs! That's why I never touch the stuff."

"Have a seat, Miss Crowley," said the inspector.

She eyed the sofa but settled for a straight-backed chair that looked utterly uncomfortable but was closest to the door.

"Now what's this about Mr. Whittlesby inviting you on Wednesday?" asked Cork.

"Why, he had all of us from the Murder Club over for tea. He *said* it was to go over the final details for the Murder Fête, but it was really about him preparing us all for the contest judging results. He's going to win, of course." Her lips pursed sourly. "Everyone knows it. He made it quite clear he anticipated the results."

"Oh, yes, the story contest," Cork said vaguely. "What's the prize? Money, I suppose. Can't be very much, can it?"

Miss Crowley sat up even straighter. "Why, it's *publication*, Inspector. In *Cosmopolitan* over in New York, and in *The Strand* here. Both very reputable publications, as I'm certain you know. *And* an offer of representation from a literary agent."

"Right." The inspector seemed unimpressed. Phyllida would have to enlighten him about the desperation of writers to have their work published, for if Miss Crowley was correct—that Mr. Whittlesby being the winner was a foregone conclusion—then that could very well be a motive for murder, no matter how inconsequential it might seem to a non-writer.

"Who attended tea at Mr. Whittlesby's home Wednesday?" asked Cork.

"Why, all of us who were here tonight—that is to say, myself, Mrs. Rollingbroke, Mr. Genevan, Mr. Billdop, Dr. Bhatt, and Mr. Whittlesby. And even though the gathering was *supposedly* for the members of the Murder Club, Sir Rolly came along with his wife, and Mrs. Whittlesby was there as well, being the hostess. Oh, and Mr. Whittlesby's brother, Eugene, dropped in to get a drink near the end, but he didn't stay. It really *was* only for the Murder Club, you see. Despite the spouses."

"I see." The inspector scrawled the names on his notepad, then lapsed into silence as he helped himself to a thick piece of cheddar.

Phyllida took the opportunity to interject. "Miss Crowley, do you happen to know whether Mr. Whittlesby had one of his particular cocktails Wednesday at the tea?"

"I have no idea," replied Miss Crowley in a gruff voice. "Quite frankly, I pay as little attention to that man and his overbearing nastiness as possible. The only reason I deigned to attend his little soiree was because I was—" She stopped herself abruptly. Folding her hands, still appropriately gloved, she settled them in her lap and looked unblinkingly at Inspector Cork.

Just as he was about to speak, Miss Crowley launched herself down a different tangent. "If you want to know who really has it in for Mr. Whittlesby, you need to look no further than his own."

"What do you mean by that, Miss Crowley?" said the inspector.

"Well, I don't believe there's any love lost between him and his brother, you know. Filberto had a case like that once—always look at family first, you know, and he did, of course—even though the sister *had* an alibi, it turned out to be *faked* and *she* was the one who did it. It was quite clever, if I do say so myself—not even Mrs. Christie could have come up with such a twist. You see, she used blue ink." Miss Crowley nodded sagely.

"Erm . . . Mrs. Christie?" The detective blinked owlishly, pausing in his notes.

"No, no, of course not. The sister with the fake alibi," Miss Crowley said impatiently. "Filberto discovered the discrepancy and—"

"Filberto?" said Inspector Cork.

"Filberto Fiero," Miss Crowley replied. "My detective. He spends most of the time in the French Riviera and is particularly adept at finding stolen jewels—there are so many that go missing down there, you know, with all of the rich people. Filberto has gotten into solving murder cases, though, and I think he might well do more. It really does seem to be what readers want, you know. A stolen tiara simply can't compete with a good old, cold-blooded, gory *murder*."

"I see," said the inspector, although he clearly did not. "Right. You say Mr. Whittlesby's brother might have it in for him?"

Miss Crowley leaned forward as if to impart some great secret. "They don't like each other much. Eugene—the brother—has never been fond of Alastair. It has something to do with an old hound dog of theirs, I believe."

"An old hound dog?" The inspector brushed crumbs from his mustache—or perhaps he was merely attempting to hide a smile or grimace; Phyllida wasn't certain.

"Yes, although I'm not sure of the particulars. Something about how it died."

"How did it die?" Phyllida said.

"I haven't the faintest idea," Miss Crowley said, as if it was absurd she should even be asked. "All I know is that it started the rift between the brothers and it's not been any better since."

"Does Mr. Eugene Whittlesby live here in Listleigh?" asked Cork.

"Yes, of course. He lives with his brother."

"They live together but they don't get along," confirmed the detective.

"Not at all." Miss Crowley shook her head definitely. "Their mother is an invalid and never leaves her bedchamber. They all live in the same house, which has been in their family for years, of course. They do have *some* money—but they don't have as much money as that nasty, boastful Alastair would like everyone to think. Poor Lettice—to have to abide those boys *and* to have to help take care of their demanding, self-serving mother. If you want to know where Alastair learnt his behavior, it's right up there in that bedroom his mother never leaves."

The conversation went on like this for some time, with Miss Crowley offering no relevant information about the feud between the Whittlesby brothers while giving many laborious details about Filberto Fiero's fictional adventures until Phyllida intervened by knocking over a coffee cup.

Phyllida disliked having to pretend such gauche clumsiness, but desperate times called for desperate measures. The beverage splashed everywhere, including on Miss Crowley's stockings—which had not been intentional; Phyllida had been aiming for her shoes—and left many pieces of china to be picked up.

This provided an excuse for an overset Miss Crowley to gather up her handbag and take her leave, and for Phyllida to remain in the sitting room for the next interview, which turned out to be Louis Genevan, the well-dressed antiques dealer.

As if he'd learned his lesson from the previous meeting, Inspector Cork immediately took control of the conversation by asking about the gathering for tea at Mr. Whittlesby's two days earlier.

Phyllida paused in her cleanup duties to pour Mr. Genevan a cup of coffee, then did her best to melt into the background while remaining quietly busy as the interview continued.

"Oh, yes, I was there of course," said Mr. Genevan as he adjusted his Regency-era waistcoat. He seemed far more at ease than Miss Crowley had been, settling on the sofa and crossing his long legs. He paused in whatever he was about to say when he noticed the small piecrust table next to his seat. His brows rose and he brushed his fingers over the ripply edge of the table, then made a quiet, satisfied noise. He looked up and realized the detective was waiting for him to say more.

"It was Alastair's way of setting the stage, so to speak," the antiques dealer went on. "Wednesday's tea, I mean. He's so very confident he's going to win the prize on Sunday." His thin lips pursed with distaste. "I wouldn't be so certain about that if I were him. His work has moments of cleverness, but it's certainly not all that witty or entertaining." He sat up a little and his expression turned a little crafty. "Is it true that he was the intended victim?"

"Do you know anyone who'd want to kill Alastair Whittlesby?" countered the inspector.

Mr. Genevan's deep-set eyes glinted with malice. "It might be best to ask who *wouldn't* want to kill Alastair Whittlesby."

"And do you include yourself in that group, Mr. Genevan?" asked Cork, and Phyllida gave an approving nod at his pointed response.

Mr. Genevan shrugged, but the gleam remained in his eyes. "I hardly know the man, other than from the Murder Club meetings. Never been to his house before yesterday—we usually meet at Vera's—Mrs. Rollingbroke's, I mean to say. Sometimes we meet at John's—Dr. Bhatt's. He's got quite a laboratory there, you know. Studies the effects of poisons on the body, you know." His voice had dropped and he leaned forward, giving Inspector Cork a meaningful look.

Phyllida bristled a little at the implication but said nothing and was appeased when the inspector ignored Mr. Genevan's pointed comment.

"You haven't answered my question, Mr. Genevan. What was your relationship with Alastair Whittlesby?"

"As I said, I hardly know the man. I did sell him—well, his wife, really, but he paid the bill and did come to look at it—a Johnstone, Jupe and Jeanes dining table. It was stunning, in perfect condition—1870 was the year they were in their prime, you know—and it was a metamorphic flame in mahogany *and* it came with two leaves. She wanted the matching chairs—there were twelve—but he put his foot down. That was a bloody shame, because to have a table like that and not to have the chairs . . ." He tsked and shook his head sadly.

"Quite a foolish decision, in my opinion. Those chairs were a once-in-a-lifetime opportunity, and I would have made him a very good deal on the set. Now I have the set of chairs but no table to go with them." He shrugged and lifted his brows, and Phyllida noticed his attention straying to the piecrust table again. "But that's certainly not a reason to murder someone," he added pleasantly.

Inspector Cork went on. "Have you ever had one of Mr. Whittlesby's special cocktails?"

"*I?* No, of course not. And I've no interest in doing so. An excellent port, or a full-bodied Bordeaux for me, if you please. Perhaps even a glass of champagne on occasion, such as tonight," he said with a smile that displayed straight white teeth below a very thin, carefully trimmed mustache.

"But you know about Mr. Whittlesby's special cocktail?" Cork went on.

"Of course I do. Anyone who's in Alastair Whittlesby's presence for longer than ten minutes has heard about his trip to New Orleans and his stay at the Hotel Monteleone and how he was introduced to the drink. One would think they'd invented it for him, the way he goes on about it. He has to order in some of the ingredients specially from over there, did you know? I mean to say, I don't mind buying foreign—French, of course—for my wine or cognac, but something as mundane as bitters? Seems a big bother over nothing, if you ask me—but that's how Alastair is. He's not got a title—it went to a cousin or whatnot somehow—but the family has got some money, and a little more from his wife, so he's got to act like he's better than anyone else. Can't be that much money if he *works*, though."

"Did you have anything to drink tonight besides champagne?" asked Cork. "Anything that you ordered from the bar?"

"I did have a whisky, neat, of course, and, yes, it was from the bar," replied Mr. Genevan. He looked around the sitting room, his eyes traveling slowly over the furnishings. "A terrible shame, it is, about Father Tooley. Absolutely awful," he said. "I mean to say, it's one thing to *write* about such things happening—which, of course, we all do—but to experience it firsthand . . . Why I thought it was only part of the entertainment tonight. That we detective writers were to solve our own puzzle about who amongst us was a killer. But it's real," he said.

His voice dropped grimly and the last bit of malice evaporated from his expression. "Fancy that—one of the murder writers is really a killer."

CHAPTER 5

WHEN SHE HEARD A CRASH IN THE KITCHEN, PHYLLIDA WAS FORCED to leave the sitting room for a moment and thus missed the last bit of Mr. Genevan's interview. Still, she felt that she'd heard a great deal that might be relevant.

Mr. Genevan, by his own admission, had been near the bar counter and could have placed the poisoned bitters. He also seemed to have nothing but disdain toward Mr. Whittlesby.

The crash in the kitchen turned out to be a chair somehow being knocked over by Rita. No harm done, except that she was sniffling and sobbing so much that Phyllida decided to protect the other furnishings and asked her to sit down.

"Do you live in here at the rectory, Rita?" she asked kindly. "If so, you could come back to Mallowan Hall tonight so you don't have to stay here alone."

"Oh, Mrs. Bright, that would be so very kind of you," sobbed the maid. "Only I can't be in here all by meself after all of this."

"Very well. As soon as you and Molly have finished in here— and I see that you're almost done—you can gather up your things."

"Oh, thank you, Mrs. Bright," she said. "But what about Saint Aloysius?"

Phyllida merely looked at her, waiting patiently for further information.

"Father Tooley's cat," Rita explained. "Only I hate to leave him all alone tonight."

"Saint Aloysius will be fine on his own," Phyllida said firmly. Stilton and Rye had very specific opinions about feline interlopers: they should not exist. "In fact, he will likely prefer to have the place to himself after all of this activity. Tomorrow will be soon enough to decide what to do with him."

If no one wanted him, perhaps Saint Aloysius could live in the garage with Bradford and Myrtle and chase down any mice or rats that might lurk. As she filled the coffee pot and arranged another small helping of food on a tray, Phyllida meditated pleasantly on the idea of Myrtle having to contend with a condescending feline in her domain.

Thus having attended to the disruption in the kitchen, the priest's sobbing maid, the cat's overnight accommodations and potential future ones, Phyllida at last went back to the sitting room, where Inspector Cork was just finishing up with Dr. Bhatt.

"Good evening, Mrs. Bright," said the doctor, giving her a smile as he left the room. She knew he would tell her about his interview later.

"More coffee, Inspector?" she asked, refilling his cup.

"Yes, thank you, Mrs. Bright," he said, giving her a shrewd look. "Everything all right in the kitchen?"

"Everything is just fine," she replied innocently. "But I have a few more things to attend to here and in the hallway. I'll be as unobtrusive as possible."

Before Cork could object, Vera Rollingbroke swept into the room.

"Oh, Inspector, I simply cannot believe this! Poor Father Tooley!" She settled onto the sofa with her pocketbook, her silky skirt billowing gently before it came to rest over all three of the seat cushions. The feather on her lovely yellow hat bobbed delicately as she spoke. "And now to be *interrogated* over such a thing—why it would be simply *screaming* if it weren't so awful. Poor Father Tooley. He was such a nice man. He officiated at our wedding, you know. But I understand it wasn't even the priest who was supposed to be killed, and that it was really Alastair who was the target!" She shook her head sadly. "Who would do such a thing?"

"Do you know anyone who might want to kill Alastair Whittlesby?" Cork asked.

"Me? Why, no, not really," said Mrs. Rollingbroke, looking at him with big hazel eyes framed by false lashes. "No, not at all."

"He gets along with everyone, then?"

"Why . . . as far as I know," she replied. "Rolly and I have had him and Lettice up for dinner several times, and he's always been quite civil."

Civil, thought Phyllida—who was hovering in the corner near the door and hoping not to be noticed, for she'd quite run out of things to fuss over—was a word used to describe someone who was generally known for *not* being civil.

"What about his brother? I understand Mr. Eugene Whittlesby lives in the same house with Mr. Alastair Whittlesby and his wife and their mother," said Cork. He glanced in Phyllida's direction and she pretended to be adjusting a doily beneath a stack of books on the table near the door. "How do the two brothers get on?"

"Oh, I have no idea," replied Mrs. Rollingbroke, flapping her hand vaguely. "I've only met Eugene a few times, and very briefly. He doesn't say much; he's rather one of those quiet types where you wonder whether he has too many thoughts to share, or none at all. Works for a film company, I think, though what he does all about here in Devonshire isn't quite obvious—to me, anyhow. Oh, Mrs. Bright, there you are—could you bring me a cup of tea? It's getting frightfully late, and I have had quite enough champagne." She gave a tinkling laugh.

"Of course, Mrs. Rollingbroke," said Phyllida, pleased for an excuse to stay longer, even if it meant leaving for a moment.

It took her only minutes to return with the tea, which she took her time pouring. She couldn't have missed more than a sentence or two in the interview, for Mrs. Rollingbroke was talking about how the Whittlesby brothers still lived with their mother, and how kind it was that Lettice helped to care for the elder Mrs. Whittlesby.

Inspector Cork gave Phyllida an exasperated look but directed his question to Mrs. Rollingbroke.

"Did you have anything to drink from the bar tonight, Mrs. Rollingbroke?" asked the detective.

"I had several glasses of champagne, and that was quite enough," she said with another laugh. "Rolly said he would pick me up tonight so I didn't have to bother with driving—I *do* dislike trying to manage the motor anytime; I always seem to get grease somewhere on my frock or gloves! But especially when I've had spirits." She leaned forward, and Phyllida caught a waft of champagne fumes when she spoke. "It was quite upsetting to actually *see* a murder. One always imagines what one would do when it happens—"

"One does?" said Cork.

"Why, yes, of course! One does think about it, especially when one is a murder writer—oh dear, that just sounds so *horrible* to say, doesn't it? A *murder writer.*" She gave a dramatic little shiver. "It's just that . . . when one thinks about writing a murder scene, one must put oneself in the position of observing all of the clues and everything about the scene—and imagining what the poor victim is feeling, and what the *murderer* is thinking and feeling— and now that it's happened to me . . . I simply don't know if I can *continue on.*"

"Continue on?" asked Cork a trifle nervously.

"Writing, of course. Rolly will be wildly disappointed if I stop, though," she said, lifting the teacup to sip, then continuing immediately. "He simply adores my stories—especially the ones about Bunkle and Mrs. Cuddlesworthy—the cat, you know. She always seems to steal the scene. Rolly's always the first one to read them, and he simply won't look away from the papers until he's finished, not even if dinner is ready." She smiled, and Phyllida thought she saw the glint of happy tears in her eyes. "He really is such a *dear* man."

"Right, then." Cork seemed a bit lost, and so Phyllida took the opportunity to step in. "Mrs. Rollingbroke, forgive me for interrupting, but you've had Mr. Whittlesby and his wife for dinner several times. Did you serve him the particular cocktail he drinks whilst he was there?"

"Oh no," Mrs. Rollingbroke replied with a smile, seemingly unbothered by Phyllida's interference. Her lipstick had either been reapplied since her arrival that evening and subsequent imbibition of champagne, or had somehow remained in place. If it was the latter, Phyllida was determined to find out what brand of lip color had such staying power. "We don't have the ingredients for it, but Alastair was quite understanding about it all. He drank whatever it was Rolly or Whalley—our butler—poured him. I don't recall what it was. Probably whisky. Rolly has quite an extensive collection of ryes and barleys, you know."

Phyllida had more questions, but she could feel the weight of the inspector's attention on her, and the last thing she wanted was to be told to leave.

"I understand you were at Mr. Whittlesby's house for tea on Wednesday, and that your husband attended with you," Cork said, taking the reins once more.

"Oh, yes, Rolly insisted on coming along since it wasn't an official club meeting, just a social event. Of course, when it's a real meeting, only the members are allowed to attend because we talk all sorts of technical writing things like grammar and plot twists that are simply *snoozing* for a non-writer.

"Even though Alastair is the president, I usually have the meeting at our house because we don't have all those people in and out like he does, and so Rolly can pop in near the end if he likes. He says he feels like an honorary member. Lettice was there, too, of course, and Eugene Whittlesby, along with the rest of us, although Eugene stayed only long enough to get a drink and then he left. He didn't seem pleased to see us."

"Right, then. Did Mr. Whittlesby have one of his special cocktails Wednesday, do you know?" said Cork.

"Oh . . . well, I daresay he did. He offered one to Rolly, but Rolly just prefers a Manhattan—you know, we had such a marvelous time the last trip to New York. Why, we saw *H.M.S. Pinafore* on Broadway, and—"

"Right, Mrs. Rollingbroke. Thank you. I think we're finished here," said the detective, flickering a glance at Phyllida as if to obtain her agreement.

She had several other questions for Mrs. Rollingbroke and she thought it would be prudent for someone to interview Mr. Rollingbroke as well, but for the moment, Phyllida was content to move on. The only other person from the local Murder Club who hadn't been interviewed yet was the vicar, and she was quite curious about his reactions.

Phyllida slipped out of the sitting room carrying Mrs. Rollingbroke's empty tea cup. When she returned to the sitting room a few moments later with a pot of tea and a clean cup for the vicar, she found Mr. Billdop perched on the edge of the sofa, clasping his plump white hands in his lap.

"I've never been interrogated by the police before," the vicar was saying. His cheeks were ruddy with anxiousness. "How does one go about it?"

"Apparently, one begins by drinking the tea so *conveniently* and *attentively* served to him," said Inspector Cork, not even attempting to hide his exasperation with Phyllida's continued presence.

She bestowed a demure smile on him and, in a subtle reminder of how she'd seen to his own comfort, said, "Would you like some more coffee, Inspector?"

"Oi, Mrs. Bright, I do believe I'll float away if I have any more to drink," he said meaningfully. "Surely you have some matters to attend to in the kitchen?"

She ignored his comment and commenced with pouring tea for the vicar, who thanked her profusely.

With a capitulating sigh, Inspector Cork turned his attention to the more accommodating Mr. Billdop. Without beating around the bush, he began with: "Do you know any reason someone might want to kill Mr. Whittlesby?"

"Oh. *Oh.*" The vicar seemed taken aback by this abrupt question. "So it's true, then? That the—uh—poison was meant for Alastair and not Father Tooley?"

"That appears to be the case, Mr. Billdop. Now, if you would answer my question."

"Oh. *Oh.* Well, hmm . . . one does hear things, you know. Being a man of the cloth." Phyllida attributed Mr. Billdop's noisy slurp of tea as due more to nerves than ill manners. "People do tend to confide in clergy, you know."

"And what does one hear, when one is a man of the cloth?" asked Inspector Cork.

"Well . . . hmm . . . I suppose I might just as well say it. Honesty is the best policy, isn't it? Inspector, the frank truth is that Alastair Whittlesby is not a popular person in Listleigh. He puts on airs that he has no business wearing, if you will, and he's simply not very Christian. Why, do you hear the way he speaks to his wife? He's even worse to his servants, and I simply don't condone rudeness to anyone, no matter how lowly. After all, didn't Jesus care for the leper and the blind man? *And* the prostitutes?"

"He did at that," replied the inspector. "Other than rudeness—which is a rather weak motive for murder—do you know of any other reason someone might want to rid themselves of Mr. Whittlesby?"

"Well," said Mr. Billdop, "nearly everyone in the Murder Club has had an altercation with him. Except for myself, of course."

"I understand Mr. Whittlesby has a high opinion of his own writing," said Cork, impressing Phyllida with his grasp of how sensitive and possessive authors were about their work.

"Quite so," replied the vicar earnestly. "Why, he had the club over to his house on Wednesday to lord it over us that soon he would be published on both sides of the Atlantic, *and* have a literary agent because he's going to win the contest."

"What sorts of altercations have the other members of your—er—club had with Alastair Whittlesby?"

"Well, Louis Genevan was quite infuriated when Mr. Whittlesby backed out of a deal a few months ago to purchase some expensive antiques from his shop. Apparently they were pieces he'd set aside just for them—Mr. and Mrs. Whittlesby, I mean—and he lost quite a lot of money when the purchase didn't go through because he'd turned away other buyers. It all came out during a meeting when Alastair criticized the characterization of Louis Genevan's sleuth, who happens to be a spinsterish old lady with a fondness for Bordeaux and cross-stitching. Not that either of *them* know anything about being a spinsterish old lady, let alone cross-stitching, but Alastair insisted that a little old lady of sixty *must* have a cat and would *never* drink anything stronger than sherry. It turned into quite a heated exchange about it. Apparently Louis Genevan quite despises cats."

Thankfully, Inspector Cork intervened. "There was a problem with an antiques sale between Mr. Whittlesby and Mr. Genevan?"

"It was something about the set being broken up and now it was worthless. . . . They didn't actually row, but it was quite uncomfortable for the rest of us. Mr. Genevan left abruptly and did not attend the next meeting, he was so furious. Wednesday was the first meeting he attended since that one."

"And who else?" asked Cork.

"Well, Mathilda Crowley claimed that Alastair poached one of her plots and put it in his own story. It was the piece he submitted for the Murder Fête contest, you see, and she felt she couldn't submit her story because the plot was so similar and so she had to use a different one." Mr. Billdop sipped from his tea more quietly this time. "And if one were being honest, Miss Crowley's second choice submission was her second choice for a reason. I mean to say, who would care about blue ink?"

"Right, then. Anyone else?"

"Dr. Bhatt and Alastair had a serious row a while back," said Mr. Billdop. "I quite thought they were going to come to blows. It was most unsettling."

Phyllida's ears perked up. John hadn't said anything to her about a set-to with Alastair Whittlesby.

"Over what?" asked the inspector.

The vicar frowned. "It was all about Alastair's circulation problems. Apparently his feet are always cold. Dr. Bhatt suggested he come in to his surgery so he could be of help, but Alastair made it clear he wasn't going to have 'a dark, foreign quack'—those were his words—medicating him and all. Said he was just as likely to end up dead or missing a limb as not. It was exceedingly unpleasant, and Dr. Bhatt was quite overset about it. Did you know that he went to Edinburgh University?"

Phyllida had indeed known John Bhatt attended the Royal College of Medicine in Edinburgh, and she was disgusted by Alastair Whittlesby's rude intolerance. But she was also somewhat surprised that John had never mentioned the incident to her. After all, they had been meeting for tea regularly over the last several months. Perhaps the row had been too upsetting for him to recount.

"I thought they might come to blows," Mr. Billdop went on with a grimace. "Dr. Bhatt was quite livid over the insults, and added a number of his own about Mr. Whittlesby's writing and his personality and his professional skills. I . . . I had the impression something else had happened between the two men previously to cause such a quick and volatile outburst."

"I see," said the inspector. "How long ago did this altercation happen?"

The vicar thought for a moment. "Perhaps two months past? We meet every fortnight, and the latest meeting was to be at Dr. Bhatt's office—the latest meeting before Wednesday's tea at Mr. Whittlesby's, of course—and I recall there being several pointed comments being made between the two men. However, they remained civil throughout the meeting."

Phyllida could hardly imagine John Bhatt angry, for he'd always been unfailingly polite and calm in her presence. She wondered if he'd mentioned the row during his interview with Inspector Cork.

"Very well," said the inspector. "Is there anyone else you can think of who had a set-to with the chap? Yourself, perhaps?"

"Oh. *Oh.*" The vicar's face turned pink. "Well, no, of course not. I don't care for Mr. Whittlesby's incivility, but I've never had a row with him. In spite of it all, he is a good writer and does offer helpful criticisms of one's work, and that is truly the purpose of the Murder Club. One doesn't have to *like* one's writing advisors in order to benefit from it. But Vera Rollingbroke seemed a bit put out with him a while back," he went on, fingering the cleft in his chin. "I don't know what prompted it, but it seemed she made a point of not inviting him to a soiree she hosted last month. She ignored his hints for a while, until finally he said something like, 'And what *would* one do about one's friends if they suddenly cut one off' . . . and then the next thing I heard, he was attending the soiree. It was as if he were hinting at her about something."

Inspector Cork narrowed his eyes. "Your impression was that his comment induced her to change her mind and invite him to the party?"

"One doesn't know for *certain*, but that was the impression I had," replied the vicar. His teacup was empty and he placed it on the table without a clink or rattle.

"Do you have any idea what he was referring to when he said that?"

"No." Mr. Billdop sounded disappointed.

"Very well. Is there anything else you'd like to tell me?"

The vicar shook his head. "It is simply horrible," he went on, flapping a hand in front of his face. "A man of the cloth is dead, and it makes one wonder who might be next! After all, if a Catholic priest could be struck down, so also could an Anglican vicar!"

"Right," said the inspector, forbearing to point out that it appeared the Catholic priest had not actually been the target of the poison, and therefore it didn't follow that a vicar might be the next in line. "Thank you, Mr. Billdop. If I need to speak with you again, I can find you at St. Thurston's, correct?"

"Yes, indeed," replied the vicar. "Except on Sunday mornings, when I am leading the service and preaching," he added with a forced laugh. "We don't have a handy, roofless orphanage for me to visit, you know."

"Right, then," said Cork, looking at him oddly. Then he closed his eyes for a moment as if to assimilate all he'd heard.

Mr. Billdop took the opportunity to leave the sitting room, closing the door behind him.

"Is that everyone, then? Everyone from the local writing club?" Cork seemed to be asking the room at large—which included only himself and Phyllida—and so she responded.

"Yes, Inspector. Miss Crowley, Mr. Billdop, Mr. Genevan, Mrs.

Rollingbroke, and Dr. Bhatt. Other than Mr. Whittlesby, from whom I expect you heard quite a bit earlier."

"Unfortunately, yes," he said, opening his eyes.

"Did Dr. Bhatt mention the altercation with Mr. Whittlesby? His was the only interview I missed," Phyllida said.

"Yes, I am fully aware of that, Mrs. Bright," replied the inspector. "I don't believe I've ever had such excellent household service and attention during a crime investigation."

"Quite," replied Phyllida, taking the compliment as her due—and the understanding that he wasn't going to fill her in on what she'd missed. Nevertheless, she'd find out. "Now I suppose you'll want to travel up to Mallowan Hall to interview all of the witnesses up there."

"Witnesses *and* potential suspects," he said, pulling himself up from his chair. Giving a little groan, he said, "I suppose there's a loo somewhere in this place?"

"Potential suspects?" Phyllida replied. "Surely you're not speaking of Mr. and Mrs. Mallowan or their guests?"

"Perhaps," replied Cork. "But I was mostly thinking about interfering housekeepers and how easily they have access to the ingredients at the bar."

Phyllida scoffed as she collected the cups and saucers. "Indeed, Inspector, I do believe your brain is coffee soaked. It's far more likely that the butler did it than a mere housekeeper."

And with that parting comment, she picked up the tray and swept from the room, leaving the detective to find his own way to the loo.

CHAPTER 6

PHYLLIDA SAT QUIETLY IN THE DAIMLER AS BRADFORD NAVIGATED the twenty-minute drive back to Mallowan Hall. They were the only vehicle on the narrow road, which was enclosed by hedgerows and tall grasses that grew several feet taller than the roof. It was well past ten o'clock, and the headlights cut into the night shadows, illuminating a darting rabbit and little else. The rain was steady but light enough not to obscure the driver's vision.

It was the first time she'd been able to sit since she'd arrived at St. Wendreda's in the very same vehicle. Molly and Rita were in the back seat, each with their heads tipped against their respective motorcar windows, and Phyllida envied the maids the ability to take a short snooze on the return trip.

She wasn't about to give in to her weariness—both mental and physical—whilst in Bradford's presence, for he'd certainly have some sardonic comment to make about a housekeeper sleeping on the job, or point out some other perceived deficiency. She had chosen to sit in the front seat, however, because the curving, bumpy, tunnel-like roads often made her queasy.

She was grateful that Bradford hadn't brought Myrtle with him tonight, so she didn't have to contend with the slathering, animated mop in a confined space whilst in her current mood, or worry about her chewing on her shoes.

In her only real concession to the long day—which had begun before dawn, an unusual circumstance, for she usually rose by half seven—and an even longer evening, once in the shadows of the vehicle's interior she'd surreptitiously slipped off her shoes. Stifling a groan of relief at ridding herself of the high heels she wore only for social occasions and allowing her toes to wriggle inside their silk stockings, she tilted her head back against the seat and thought about everything that had happened.

There was much to consider, but one of the items that settled most prominently in her mind was the information about John Bhatt and his altercation with Alastair Whittlesby. The vicar's description of the altercation seemed so far removed from her own experience with the physician that she found it troubling.

"How is Mrs. Puffley, then?" she asked in an effort to keep from dropping off—and to distract herself. "Has she recovered from the disappointment of the lamb Wellington?"

"Dobble's got an earful from her," replied Bradford. "Felt almost sorry for the bloke. It wasn't as if *he'd* planned the murder, now did he?"

Phyllida held back a smile, remembering her parting shot to Inspector Cork. Of course, the butler really never did do it—except one time in Mrs. Rinehart's book *The Door*, which, like *Roger Ackroyd*, had stirred up all sorts of hornets' nests about detective writers "not playing fair" with their readers—quite outrageously, in Phyllida's opinion. "Mr. Dobble will survive unscathed, I've no doubt," she said, smothering a yawn.

"So someone tried to do in the lawyer bloke and got a priest instead," said Bradford. "Who do you suspect, Mrs. Bright?"

"*Whom,*" she said. "And it's far too early to have any informed opinion—even if I *were* investigating the crime, which, of course, I'm not—"

"Which, of course, you *are*," he said, talking right over her. "No need to play innocent with me, Mrs. Bright. You could no more resist the urge to investigate a murder as I could resist looking under the hood of a T77."

Since Phyllida had no idea what a T77 was—some sort of newfangled, sporty motorcar, she presumed—she merely sniffed. "I'm still developing my theories," she said finally. "What is of paramount importance is to determine who had the means and opportunity to poison that bottle of bitters."

"I expect you would be inclined to leave the visitors to Listleigh off your list of suspects, then," Bradford replied.

"*If* I had a suspect list, any visitors would be far less likely candidates, to be sure," she said, "but I wouldn't discount them completely—I mean to say, *if* I were investigating the crime."

He chuckled. "Of course, Mrs. Bright. And since I am completely mistaken about you investigating the murder, then you wouldn't be interested in knowing whom I saw outside the courtyard gate during the cocktail party."

Phyllida flattened her lips into a firm line, forcing herself into silence. She was simply not going to give his arrogant self the satisfaction of asking.

But, drat it, whom *had* he seen or noticed? Surely it couldn't be that important, when none of the suspects had left the garden courtyard during the party.

Had they?

But of course they had—the loo was inside the rectory. Likely someone had made use of it.

And if someone had, Bradford might have seen them. Which likely meant nothing.

She grimaced. He was simply trying to wind her up.

When she remained mutinously silent, Bradford chuckled again. He was *enjoying* himself at her quandary, blast the man.

"I suppose you've told whatever you saw or heard to Inspector Cork," she said primly.

"No, ma'am, I haven't had the opportunity to do so," Bradford replied breezily.

If he could have constructed any response that would have piqued Phyllida more, she couldn't think what it would be. *Drat him.*

"Since Inspector Cork is going to be coming to Mallowan Hall tomorrow morning to finish his interviews—"

"Not tonight?" Bradford asked, interrupting *again*.

"The inspector felt it was too late to bother Mrs. Agatha and Mr. Max's guests after such a difficult day. After all, it is ten o'clock and they all only arrived this morning on the early train. Since none of them know Mr. Whittlesby—except for the Mallowans, of course—it seems none of them would have a motive to kill him, and therefore speaking with them doesn't seem as urgent."

Phyllida was grateful Cork had decided not to continue his interviews tonight. She feared she was distracted enough to miss something important.

Perhaps the inspector felt the same way.

"He was too tired, was he?" Bradford commented with a snort. "Poor bloke needs his beauty rest."

"As I was saying before you interrupted me," she said in a voice perhaps a trifle louder than necessary, "since I'm certain to see the inspector tomorrow when he arrives at the house, I'd be happy to tell him whatever it is you believe you saw."

"Well done, Mrs. Bright." He glanced at her, flashing a grin, then returned his attention to the road. "That was a clever mix of apparent disinterest and an overly helpful but ultimately unnecessary suggestion. I can speak with the inspector directly once he arrives—I don't need a housekeeper to act as messenger."

Phyllida stared straight ahead, unwilling to give him even a hint of reaction.

Next time, she was definitely sitting in the back of the motorcar.

Mallowan Hall was quiet when Phyllida let herself in, a yawning Molly and the guest maid from St. Wendreda's trudging on her heels. As always, they came through by the kitchen, an entrance accessed by going down three steps from the ground level and then through the door. Despite the fact that only servants and tradespeople used that rear entrance, the stairs were swept, scrubbed, and whitewashed every day by the scullery maid.

Today was no exception, and since it was dark and Mr. Dobble had kindly left the exterior lamp lit, Phyllida could see that the steps gleamed white in the light rain. Not a speck of dirt or dust marred them, either, so they must have been recently swept.

That was Opal's work, and Phyllida smiled with satisfaction.

The girl, who was thirteen, had been an excellent addition to the staff at Mallowan Hall. Phyllida had brought her on after one of the other kitchen maids had been murdered during the last investigation she'd been forced to undertake.

Not that Phyllida was undertaking any murder investigations at the moment, despite how stridently Bradford might accuse her. There was simply no reason for her to become involved—the murder hadn't happened here at Mallowan Hall, nor were any of her staff involved, suspected, or in danger.

She simply had too many other things to which she must attend to be spending time chasing clues around St. Wendreda's.

Despite the late hour, Mrs. Puffley was in the kitchen—where she nearly always was when she wasn't in her bedroom—while Molly went on to the servants' dining room to eat a late supper (and likely to avoid being seen by the cook, who'd surely find something for the kitchen maid to do). Phyllida heard the sounds of clinking and splashing from the scullery, and peeked in to see Opal, Lizzie, and Sally, the extra maid who had been brought in for the weekend, washing dishes. That meant supper had been served and was likely finished.

Phyllida stepped into the kitchen to assess the cook's mood. She also intended to find out what had been served to the Mallowans' guests in terms of a late meal—for it was hours past the normal eight o'clock serving time. It was the responsibility of Mr. Dobble and his footmen to do the serving of meals in the dining room for both guests and family, but Phyllida needed to keep her fingers on the pulse of such goings-on.

When Mrs. Puffley saw her, she immediately launched into a tirade—although it wasn't as loud as it could be. Perhaps because she'd tired herself out with previous tirades?

"D'you know how long I worked on that leg of lamb pastry, Mrs. Bright? And to have it be set aside at the very last minute! Why, it was just perfectly crisp and flaky and golden brown, and now it's nothing but a soft, mushy lump. I couldn't serve *that* to Miss Sayers! Why, I wouldn't even feed it to Peter or Myrtle!"

As was the case with many who had her position, Mrs. Puffley was opinionated, short-tempered, volatile—and a superior cook. Phyllida had come to the conclusion that it was some sort of universal requirement for a cook to possess those characteristics, as so many of them did. Just as a housekeeper such as herself must have an even temperament, excellent organizational skills and forethought, as well as a pervading sense of order and calm, the one whose domain was the kitchen surely felt the entire weight of the household upon them.

If master and mistress, guests, and staff didn't get fed—and fed well—it was a poor reflection on the entire household. Therefore, a cook must require absolute obedience from her staff, along with hard work, coordination, and perfect timing, in order to succeed—all while working in the hot, steamy dungeon of a kitchen. It was no wonder Mrs. Puffley was like a tea kettle ready to go off at any moment.

Phyllida was not fond of the kitchen and its associated work, so she had a healthy respect for those who conducted it. After all, she did enjoy eating.

"Now, Mrs. Puffley, I'm certain your creation wasn't so bad that it must be relegated as canine food. I don't suppose you saved a bit of a taste for me?" she asked with purposeful wistfulness as a way to find out whether the lamb Wellington had actually been served to the guests or not. "I do love your puff pastry."

"Right, then, of course there's a plate for you staying warm, Mrs. Bright," replied the cook, wiping her face with a tea towel. She was a tall, solid woman of forty-five with capable shoulders and muscular arms who looked as if she could withstand a gale force wind. Due to the heat in the kitchen or her own genetic makeup—or both—her cheeks were perpetually ruddy and glistened with perspiration. Her curly dark hair was mostly tucked up inside a cap, although a stray coil had escaped at the nape of her neck.

"Mr. Dobble ate the lamb fine enough," she went on, glowering. "As if it weren't his fault it were ruined! Tried to force me to serve it anyhow, but I told him in no uncertain terms there weren't going to be no soggy lamb pastry from Harriet Puffley's kitchen coming up for the likes of Miss Sayers and Mr. Chesterton. It would be mortifying, it would!"

"Quite," replied Phyllida. "But I'm certain you found something just as delicious for our guests."

As the housekeeper, Phyllida would normally approve all meals and make any decisions about changes to the menu—with Mrs. Agatha's input as necessary. But obviously tonight, someone else would have made such decisions in her absence. Phyllida needed to know what they were, for the adjustment could affect supplies and other meals for the rest of the weekend.

"Mr. Dobble, *he* told me since it was so late all they wanted was a cold supper," said Mrs. Puffley. "A *cold supper*? After a *murder*? Why, I told him in no uncertain terms that a cold supper would *not* be served from Harriet Puffley after *my* guests were witnesses to a *murder*! Someone surely dropped that man on his head when he was a bairn, for he's still got the dent in his skull to prove it."

"Quite so," Phyllida replied, chuckling internally at the exchange that must have gone on between the butler, who'd obviously been tiptoeing around the subject and the cook: he first suggesting that she serve the lamb, and then when that idea was summarily rejected, proposing a cold supper. Either way, Mr. Dobble had had no chance of emerging from that conversation unscathed.

"Quite," she said again and let Mrs. Puffley go on, as one did.

"Everyone was tired, but all they wanted to talk about was the murder and what kind of poison was used, so Harriet Puffley made certain they went to bed with full stomachs from something hearty and hot. 'Ye can't send'em to bed on a 'nempty stomach after the likes of a murder, and so ye'd best make something up fast,' I told myself. Because a cold supper ain't gonna do for a body after a shock like that!"

"Quite right," replied Phyllida patiently. Although she craved the quiet of her cozy sitting room with her cats and a cup of tea fortified with a splash of rye, she couldn't do that until Mrs. Puffley had exhausted her soliloquy.

"So what did I do, then? Well, I dismantled a good portion of that beautiful lamb pastry"—the cook's eyes glistened with tears at the memory—"and made a stew from the meat. The chicken mousse added another layer of flavor, and of course I added onions and carrots and parsnips, and served it all up with a nice loaf of crusty bread."

"That sounds delicious. Most resourceful of you," said Phyllida, her empty stomach beginning to gurgle.

"Of course it was," snapped Mrs. Puffley. "Stanley said Mr. Chesterton even commented on it. The best lamb stew he'd ever eaten. Why, I could've served that to Jesus and the Apostles, I could, and be proud of it!"

"Quite right," said Phyllida with relief. The mention of Jesus meant that the cook had wound herself down enough to end the conversation. "I should very much like to taste it myself. Could you have Opal bring a tray to my sitting room?"

"Yes, yes, of course. Mrs. Agatha and Mr. Max and all of their guests have gone to bed already. I suppose you've brought Molly back, then?"

"She's eating her own dinner, and I told her she could go up to bed after. We've got Rita, the maid from the rectory, staying here tonight as well," Phyllida replied. "I trust the additional help I brought in for the weekend has been suitable," she added to forestall any argument from the cook. Mrs. Puffley could be rather miserly about her kitchen staff, but Phyllida had pulled rank and conscripted Molly to help her for the entire Murder Fête weekend.

Murder Fête. How horrible it was to realize that what had been an amusing title for the event had actually come to pass.

"Sally's not cut off her finger or spilt any of the batter, but she could be a trifle speedier with her work," grumbled Mrs. Puffley. "Took her nearly an hour to peel half a bushel of potatoes."

"I suppose one always wishes every maid to be speedier and more efficient," said Phyllida with a sympathetic smile.

Mrs. Puffley chuckled and mopped her face again with the towel. "It's part o' my prayers every night it is—'speed up their fingers and hands without cuttin'em off, if you will, Lord.'" Her smile faded. "So it's a murder, is it, then? Poor Father Tooley. I ain't no papist, but there ain't no reason to wish for a priest to be offed. Why would anyone do such a thing? Murder's bad enough, but when it's a man of the cloth, it's a real sin!"

"It is quite awful," Phyllida replied. "It appears a drink was poisoned and was meant for a Mr. Alastair Whittlesby, but the priest drank it instead. A terrible shame, but the inspector has agreed to allow the fête to go on tomorrow and Sunday as planned. Now, if you'll have Opal bring up that tray for me, I'll get out of your kitchen."

"She'll have it right up for you, Mrs. Bright," said Mrs. Puffley. "We'll all be glad when you're back here instead of at St. Wendreda's every day."

"Thank you, Mrs. Puffley," Phyllida told her, relieved that she could make her exit.

"You say Alastair Whittlesby was the intended victim?" said Mrs. Puffley suddenly. "Why, I know his cook, I do." Her words stopped Phyllida in her tracks and she turned back into the kitchen.

"You do?"

"We have the same day off on Tuesdays and meet up for cards every fortnight whilst chaperoning the young'uns at the dance hall," replied Mrs. Puffley. "Her name's Mrs. Dilly, and she's the one gave me that new tea biscuit recipe I've been trying out—the thin, flaky lemon wafers with the apricot compote centers."

Phyllida knew exactly what she was talking about. "Thank you for the reminder—I'll have Molly make more apricot compote," she said with a smile. "They were delicious biscuits. Does the Whittlesbys' cook talk about them at all? From what I've heard, Mr. Whittlesby and his brother don't get on."

"She's looking for a new position," Mrs. Puffley said, lowering her voice as if afraid of being overheard. "She don't like working for them. Been there two years and she says it feels like ten."

Phyllida's interest perked up even more. "Someone tried to kill Mr. Whittlesby, so the inspector will be looking for motives." She met Mrs. Puffley's eyes and saw the light of interest in her gaze.

"Now you mention it, I might be needin' to ask Dilly for some pointers about those lemon biscuits," said the cook. "Mebbe I can find time to get away for a short while tomorrow after breakfast and ask her."

Phyllida smiled. "I think that's an excellent idea. Those biscuits have become one of my favorites."

As she made her way up the stairs to her rooms at last, Phyllida suddenly froze.

"I just don't see any way around it. He's simply got to be done away with . . . cannot bear his boastful, overbearing nastiness any longer."

Good heavens. Had the exchange she'd overheard this morning from outside the church window actually been about killing Alastair Whittlesby, and not some fictional character?

She continued climbing, her hand on the railing and her eyes unfocused whilst her mind went back to this morning, trying to remember exactly what she'd overheard.

"I just don't see any way around it. He's simply got to be done away with . . . cannot bear his boastful, overbearing nastiness any longer."

"Right. The problem is . . . how to do it."

"Poison . . . Coffee. Or a drink . . . ?"

This morning she'd overheard someone plotting to poison someone's drink, and tonight someone had died from a poisoned cocktail. Surely it wasn't a coincidence.

"Poison . . . Coffee. Or a drink?"

"There is . . . that . . . new car, eh?"

New car, eh?

She nearly stumbled on the steps, gasping as the realization swept her.

"New car, eh?" she said aloud, turning the syllables over in her mind as she spoke them with different inflections. "New car-*eh . . .* Vieux Carré . . ."

Good heavens. Had she overheard the murderer—no, *murderers*; there'd been two of them!—plotting to kill Mr. Whittlesby?

Drat. *Now* what was she going to do?

CHAPTER 7

Saturday

THE NEXT MORNING, PHYLLIDA WAS IN HER SITTING ROOM REVIEWING bills and writing drafts to pay them when she heard the sounds of people descending on the main stairs. It was rather difficult to not hear the six-foot-four, twenty-one stone Mr. Chesterton making his way down the steps, a fact she had counted on to alert her to his—and the others'—arrival to breakfast.

Phyllida closed up the accounting book and pushed back from the desk, apologizing to Stilton and Rye for having to leave them again. She would find something to occupy herself in the dining room—or nearby—for a while so she could listen in on what the writers were saying. The Mallowans and their guests had already gone to bed last night by the time she returned, so she'd been unable to hear any exchanges about the events at the cocktail party.

Instead, she'd tossed and turned in her bed—which normally invited deep slumber—unable to dismiss the conversation she'd overheard that morning. Over and over she replayed it in her mind, like a record going on and on and on, but she was able to extract no further clues from her memory other than a wispy thought that she might have heard something that could identify the speakers. But though she racked her brain, nothing surfaced.

If only she'd gone to look out the window at St. Wendreda's to see who might have been plotting below the window at half past nine yesterday morning.

But she hadn't.

As she vacated her quarters, Phyllida smoothed the front of her dress and patted the comb in her hair. It wouldn't do for her to appear the least bit out of sorts in front of staff or guests, despite her lack of sleep the night before. She'd powdered the circles beneath her eyes and added a bit of mascara to distract from the drawn look on her face.

Mallowan Hall was a large, rectangular structure with five stories, including the attic, and an expansive garden and adjacent lawn that butted up to a small apple orchard. Beyond the orchard were trees that eventually became a pleasant forest.

Phyllida knew there was a small creek that ran along the far edge of the orchard and into the woods, but she hadn't seen the need to venture that far from the house. She took issue with snakes slithering across one's path. Aside from that, there were charming paths through the gardens managed by Amsi that offered plenty of opportunity for fresh air and the rich scents of flowers.

The Mallowans each had their own sitting room or office on the first floor, as well as their bedroom. On the second and third floors there were plenty of guest rooms, and the floor above accommodated the maids. There were also a number of bathrooms on the upper floors, and the house had been fully converted to electricity nearly a decade ago. That feature had been one of the deciding factors for Phyllida taking on the role of housekeeper, for she detested the work involved in filling and cleaning gas lamps, even though it would be her staff, and not her, who were required to do it.

The kitchen, servants' dining room, scullery, laundry, and distilling room were all in the cellar—along with bedrooms for the footmen and gardener. For obvious reasons, Phyllida preferred to keep the male servants as far away from the maids' beds as possible. While not foolproof, she felt that a six-floor distance was at least a buffer.

Although the kitchen was generally hot and steamy from the activity within, it did have several small windows at the top that allowed in fresh air and some light, and its subterranean location helped keep the temperature from becoming unbearable.

As neither of the Mallowans rode horses or hunted, the stable had been converted to a garage with an apartment for the driver that, in Bradford's case, also accommodated his dog.

Phyllida's apartments—which included a sunny sitting room and a cozy bedchamber—were located on the west side near the back of the building but were close enough that she could hear anyone coming or going, or descending from the bedrooms above. Mr. Dobble had his own pantry and adjoining bedroom next to Phyllida's apartments, but his faced the rear of the property. Phyllida acknowledged that he had the better view of the gardens and that his space was slightly larger, but she preferred to be nearer to the front of the residence so as to hear what was happening.

As she made her way quickly through the house, Phyllida automatically checked for dust on the tops of picture frames, that the items on the side tables along the halls were arranged properly and in an appealing manner, that the curtains had been opened in the library and front parlor—both of which she had to pass by—and that none of the fresh flowers in vases throughout were drooping or browning. Everything was in order, of course, for the maids and footmen had been up and working since dawn. Rita had been returned to the St. Wendreda's rectory earlier when Bradford took the supply of Mrs. Agatha's books to where the festival was to be set up today on the church's lawn.

When Phyllida reached the front foyer, she saw that Agatha was just making her way down the stairs in the wake of their guests.

"Oh, Mrs. Bright, there you are," said her employer and friend. Agatha never used Phyllida's familiar name when outsiders were around, a custom that Phyllida wholeheartedly approved.

"Good morning, Mrs. Agatha. I trust Peter enjoyed his biscuit on your tea tray?" she replied as Agatha edged off toward the hallway, away from the dining room. Evidently her employer wished to speak with her out of the hearing of the others.

"Oh, yes, of course," Agatha replied with a smile. Although Phyllida couldn't relate to her friend's love for canines, she did know that having Peter around for cuddles and petting was extremely important to Agatha. In fact, during her difficult divorce from Archie Christie, Agatha had relied greatly on Peter for support. "He crunched it down quite happily. It's so sweet of Mrs. Puffley to make him his own biscuits.

"Oh, good morning, Dorothy," went on Agatha, giving a little wave to her colleague as she stepped onto the foyer floor. "I do hope you slept well, after all of the excitement. I'll be right in for breakfast, but make yourself comfortable. Ask Mr. Dobble to bring you a cup of coffee—he makes it perfectly sweet but wonderfully strong at the same time."

"Thank you, dear Agatha. Do hurry and join us—I've several theories to discuss about the murder." Miss Sayers swept into the dining room, once again wearing one of the long, shapeless dresses she favored.

"What a ghastly thing to have happen," Agatha said to Phyllida, gripping her hand as she stood next to a tall, potted palm that had come back with Mr. Max from one of his expeditions. "I feel terribly for Father Tooley and St. Wendreda's, and it's simply unfathomable that someone poisoned a man at our little fête!" There was worry in her eyes, and Phyllida understood why.

Ever since Agatha had famously disappeared for eleven days during the split from her first husband, she had been extremely shy about publicity and journalists. And rightly so, for whenever the writer did any sort of interview or met with the press, the topic always came back to that infamous eleven days, as the public continued to be fixated on it.

Some journalists and reviewers even used the fact that Agatha had disappeared—and somehow "played" or "fooled" the world (for what purpose, Phyllida couldn't imagine)—as an excuse for accusations of her untrustworthiness as a writer of detective fiction. The extremely clever and surprising solution to *The Murder of Roger Ackroyd* was cited as an example of such "cheating" of Mrs. Christie's readers.

Thus, Agatha was extremely opposed to doing anything that brought—as she put it—hordes of reporters down upon her life. When a murder had happened here at Mallowan Hall only a few months ago, the estate had been surrounded by reporters and photographers for days.

That was part of the reason Phyllida had had to take charge of that investigation. She wanted not only to protect her friend and the entire household from the demands of the press but also to get rid of them as soon as possible. If she'd left matters to Inspector Cork, it might have been weeks—or never.

And now it had happened again—a murder tied closely not only to Agatha Christie but also to a group of her writing colleagues. The press would have a jolly time with that! There already would be reporters present for today's events, which were open to the public, but now with Father Tooley's death, the hunger for news would be even more savage.

"We'll keep the reporters away from Mallowan Hall, don't you worry," Phyllida said, squeezing her friend's hand. "And I'm certain Bradford will be able to navigate the motor up to St. Wendreda's and get you inside the fair without any problem— although I am concerned about the weather ruining it all. Mrs. Puffley said her hip joint is bothering her, and you know that's a sign of coming rain. At any rate, I'll post Stanley and Elton by your table to keep the journalists from crowding about and blocking your fans."

"Thank you for all of that," Agatha replied with a wan smile. "Max will be with me, too, and you know he might seem quiet and unassuming, but he knows how to stand up to things."

"Of course he does." Phyllida herself wasn't particularly keen on nosy reporters and determined photographers getting into her own business. Her shared loathing for the press was one of the reasons Agatha had been delighted she'd taken the housekeeping position.

"But more importantly, what are you doing about it all, Phyllie?" Agatha asked. "Are you employing your little gray cells? Using your method and order?" She adopted the slightest of Poirot-ish accents and smiled, then the smile faded into an uncomfortable grimace.

"I hadn't really thought about it," Phyllida prevaricated. She *had* been thinking about it, all night long when she reviewed the conversation she'd overheard, which now in hindsight seemed obviously to be two people discussing how to kill a man by poisoning his very specific and unusual drink.

"Of course, Anthony and Dorothy think we ought to all put our heads together and solve the murder. You heard what she said only just now. After all, we are detective writers, aren't we? And it would be great publicity for the Detection Club." Agatha stopped just short of rolling her eyes at the idea. "But since you're the only one of us who actually *has* solved a murder—two of them, in fact," she went on with a smile, "I am putting my trust in you, and not my fellow writers. Much as I appreciate their work and their stories, I simply don't think they're up to snuff over it. This isn't *The Poisoned Chocolates Case*, you know," she said, referring to the well-known novel by Mr. Berkeley where the members of a Crime Club tried to solve a murder that had stymied Scotland Yard. Each character had come up with their own unique, reasonable solution to the crime, but only one was the correct explanation. "Please do what you think is best, Phyllida. If you need to bring in more help here while you're busy, simply do so. Max agrees with me."

"Of course," Phyllida replied, a little stunned by her friend's confidence in her abilities. But she expected that Agatha's blithe trust was likely wishful thinking due to her fears about unwanted publicity and being in the public eye.

And neither of them had been quite convinced of Inspector Cork's capabilities during the previous events.

"Of course, G. K. already has his own ideas of what happened, and obviously Dorothy as well," Agatha went on. If her colleagues from the Detection Club took it upon themselves to try to solve the murder, Agatha would be caught in the middle of that as well—especially since Miss Sayers might use it as a publicity tactic. Miss Sayers was always looking for ways to grab the attention of the press. "I suppose that's what one can expect when a death happens in front of a slew of murder writers. Everyone thought it was a joke at first," Agatha said, shaking her head sadly. "Poor Father Tooley. And the poison wasn't even meant for him!

"I do think you ought to go round to the Whittlesbys today before all of the fair gets started," Agatha continued. "Have Puffley make up a basket of something for you to bring over as a gift from Max and me. It will give you an opportunity to talk to the servants."

There was a glint in Agatha's eyes that suggested she was becoming less overset and anxious about the events, now that she had turned the problem over to her capable housekeeper.

"I shall send Mrs. Puffley herself," Phyllida told her, "as she is friendly with their cook and would be more inclined than I to receive confidences."

"Excellent plan," replied Agatha enthusiastically. "Now I must gird myself and go on into battle. I suspect it shall be an uphill one to keep G. K., Dorothy, and Anthony from pulling out their magnifying glasses and setting deerstalker hats on their heads! They're still remembering that mock trial we did back in London." She smiled and started off, then turned back suddenly.

There was an arrested expression on her face as she came close enough to speak so quietly only Phyllida could hear. "You don't think any of the Detection Club could have had anything to do with it, do you?"

Phyllida didn't hesitate. "No. No, I'm certain of it. What would be the motive? If Whittlesby knew any of them—or had even met one of them, or corresponded with them—we would have known about it. He would have announced it to all and sundry, and rubbed the noses of his Murder Club friends in it. And besides, how would any of them know about Mr. Whittlesby's special bitters?"

Agatha's expression relaxed and she nodded. "Yes, Max and I said the same thing to each other. Only, I wanted to talk to you about it as well. Just in case you noticed something that we hadn't."

Phyllida hesitated, then plunged on. "I did overhear something yesterday that might be relevant. I haven't told Inspector Cork about it yet, but I will. He should be calling here soon."

Phyllida recounted the hushed conversation she'd been privy to the day before.

"Good heavens! Do you mean to say you overheard the murderers talking about what they were going to do—and that's precisely what happened?" Agatha said. A familiar light came into her eyes as she paused to let the thought settle. "What an interesting way to start a book," she said, tilting her head as her gaze went blank. "To have someone overhear what they think is an innocent conversation—and then have it turn out to be precisely what occurs!" Her eyes lit up.

"Quite," said Phyllida, handing Agatha the small notebook she had tucked in her pocket. "You'd best write it all down before you forget," she said with a smile. It was fortunate that Phyllida had a generous supply of notebooks and notepads, for her employer was a bit of a kleptomaniac when it came to pads of paper. She was always conscripting random notepads, notebooks, or cards to jot down her ideas—whether or not they'd already been used, regardless of where she'd found them. Phyllida had taken to carrying an extra one in her pocket and supplying random drawers throughout the house with notepads.

"Oh, thank you, Phyllie," she said, and took the pencil Phyllida gave her as well.

Phyllida waited patiently whilst Agatha scribbled her notes, murmuring, "Poirot, of course." Then said, "And it will be an odious person that everyone wants dead anyhow. And so everyone is a suspect."

"Isn't that always the case?" Phyllida said with a smile as she took the pencil Agatha offered back to her. "Everyone is a suspect." Her smile faded. That was certainly true in this case.

"Quite," replied Agatha. The glaze of creative distraction had left her eyes and she looked at Phyllida. "Now, when did you hear this conversation?"

"It was just before you arrived—about half nine. And only moments later, you and Miss Sayers, Mr. Chesterton, and Mr. Berkeley came into the hall. Presumably they were with you until that moment, so it couldn't have been any of them having that conversation."

Agatha looked relieved. "Indeed. We had just alighted from the motorcar—as you know, I drove us up—and walked over together from there. There was no opportunity for any of them to have such an exchange that you overheard. So that lets all of them off. That's a relief. Now if I can only keep them from haring off like Tuppence, looking for clues."

"Then I shall make certain to tell Inspector Cork just that when I speak to him," replied Phyllida, trying and failing to imagine the large and stodgy Mr. Chesterton, who employed a walking stick, haring off looking for anything. As if on cue, the front knocker clunked. "I suppose that will be the inspector."

"Very well. Thank you for seeing to all of this, Phyllida. I know that I rely upon you for so many things and now this, but . . . I know you are up to it." She squeezed Phyllida's hand and, notebook still in hand, went off to join her guests.

Stanley, the first footman, had appeared from somewhere in the house and was opening the door to Inspector Cork and Constable Greensticks when Phyllida returned to the foyer.

"Ah, good morning, Inspector. Constable," she said. "Would you like to sit in the sitting room or join the guests for breakfast?" Unlike when he conducted the last murder investigation, the detective wouldn't have to interview her entire staff, disrupting their schedules, as well as providing fodder for gossip—which in turn meant less efficient work.

"Erm . . . perhaps I should go down to the kitchen," said Constable Greensticks. "Interview the staff down there." And, Phyllida thought, likely acquire one of Mrs. Puffley's scones whilst he was at it.

"Indeed, Constable, some of the staff were at the fête last night, but I don't believe any of them are downstairs at the moment. Most have gone off to St. Wendreda's to set up for later."

"I'd best check to be certain, then, Inspector," said Greensticks. "One never knows."

As Phyllida always knew, she disagreed with his assessment, but declined to protest. Clearly, the constable was determined to make his way belowstairs regardless, and she didn't blame him. Mrs. Puffley's dried apple and cinnamon scones were infamous.

"Yes, yes, go on with you," said Cork, looking toward the dining room. His nose actually quivered and his protruding eyes popped a trifle more as the delicious aromas wafted from the breakfast spread. "I suppose it would be permissible for me to join the Mallowans and their guests in the dining room and have a spot of breakfast. Since the constable won't be present to . . . erm . . . notice."

"Indeed. As well, I have some information that might assist in your investigation," said Phyllida.

"Why am I not surprised?" replied Cork in a bland voice. Then his expression hardened a bit. "I do hope you aren't going to interfere with this investigation as you did the last time, Mrs. Bright."

"Interfere? Is that what you call my solving the crime and identifying the culprits single-handedly, Inspector?" she replied blithely. "How quickly one forgets."

He gritted his teeth; she could actually hear the click as his jaws came together in a snap. "Mrs. Bright, this is official business—not your . . . your housekeeping domain."

"Of course not," she replied. "For if it were my housekeeping domain, I would already have assigned the tasks to my staff and I would have excellent progress to report. Now, I do have information for you that should remove everyone in the dining room from your list of suspects. Would you like to hear it, or shall I go off to my 'housekeeping domain'?" She lifted her nose and gave him the sort of look she used when she caught one of the chambermaids standing about holding up a wall.

He made a grumbly noise, then nodded. "Of course, Mrs. Bright."

She smiled at him. "I thought so." She went on to recount the conversation she'd overheard, then explained that the Detection Club writers had all been together, just getting out of the Mallowans' motorcar, when the exchange happened. "So it couldn't have been any of them. That is, of course, assuming the individuals who were speaking are the actual perpetrators," she added as the thought struck her that *perhaps they hadn't been.*

After all, if the conversation had happened only yesterday, when would they have had time to get a second bottle of Monteleone's Special Bitters and add the poison?

Unless . . . the murderer already had the plan made out, with poisoned bitters at the ready, and was merely talking about it with one of his or her coconspirators?

Not that she thought for one moment that any of the celebrity writers would have stooped to murder. There was simply no motive and even less means and opportunity for any of them to add poison to a very rare bottle of spirits. That is . . . unless someone had brought a bottle with them from London . . .

Phyllida sighed inwardly. It was possible. Not likely, but possible. But it certainly had not been one of the Detection Club members who'd been speaking of poisoning a cocktail and Mr. Whittlesby—

She stopped her train of thought. If one was being particular, one should acknowledge that Mr. Whittlesby's name hadn't been mentioned in the exchange. It might not have been the Murder Club president who'd been the topic of the conversation.

But who else could it have been, whose "boastful, overbearing nastiness" could no longer be abided? Alastair Whittlesby certainly fit the bill.

Boastful, overbearing—

Inspector Cork grunted again, interrupting the wisp of a thought that had begun to form in her mind. "Whittlesby does seem to have acquired a number of enemies, hasn't he?" Then he flattened his mouth as if realizing he had no reason to discuss the investigation with Phyllida.

"He certainly has," she agreed, thinking of John Bhatt. She really needed to speak with him about what had happened between him and Alastair Whittlesby.

Cork smoothed his mustache, which did little to tame its wiry strands. If only he would apply a bit of wax . . . "Seems that everyone there last night had an unhealthy interest in poisons," he went on, apparently willing to talk to Phyllida about the investigation after all.

She smiled kindly at him. "They're murder writers, Inspector. That's what they spend their time doing—devising ways to kill people."

Cork nodded. "That's what is going to make this investigation even more difficult. Any of them could've had the knowledge."

By now they'd made their way to the dining room and stood just outside the door.

"Quite," Phyllida replied, hiding a smile.

After all, the inspector had no idea he was about to enter a room with a group of people who all thought they were better detectives than Scotland Yard.

She almost felt sorry for him.

Phyllida was about to follow Inspector Cork into the dining room when she heard rapid footsteps coming from the hall accompanied by a strange coughing, choking sound.

It was Ginny, the first parlourmaid, and she was carrying a duster whose feathers drooped sadly. The maid's normally pristine and starched white apron was covered with something that even from a distance Phyllida identified as great streaks of ash and soot. The dove-gray dress beneath Ginny's apron was also covered with detritus.

Phyllida hurried down the hall to meet her and, more importantly, forestall the maid from being seen by the guests and her employer. As she drew nearer, Phyllida saw that Ginny's lacy coronet cap and face were also covered with ashy streaks. Her eyes and nose were red, and she saw that the maid was sobbing and coughing.

"What on earth!" Phyllida said, already directing her back down the hall whilst offering her a handkerchief.

"I'm sorry, Mrs. Bright, I'm sorry I am, but it all came bursting out! It's everywhere in the sitting room." Ginny was beside herself, shedding ash and soot as she spoke. She wiped ineffectually at her face.

"Good heavens, get behind the door straightaway!" Phyllida said, taking the maid's arm to direct her to the green baize door that separated the back halls and stairs for the servants from the front of the house. "What were you thinking coming up this way? What if Mrs. Agatha or her guests had seen you?"

"I'm s-sorry, I'm sorry," Ginny went on, still coughing as they passed into relative safety behind the green upholstered door. "I couldn't see where I was and I got my directions mixed up, Mrs. Bright."

Phyllida sighed as she realized ash and soot were now settling on her own frock due to Ginny's agitations. "Go on now, clean yourself up. I'll send Freddie in to sweep it up. How on earth did this happen?"

"Someone closed the damper in the chimney and I was trying to open it—it was stuck—and when it came free, it clanged hard, and then everything came falling down and exploding into the room. All over me. I couldn't breathe, and—"

"Quite, quite," Phyllida said, forestalling a long explanation of obvious details. Who on earth had closed the damper in the sitting room? Everyone knew not to—

Of course. The extra maids wouldn't know, and Mr. Dobble hadn't remembered to tell them. She suppressed a groan. She could only imagine the disaster of the sitting room. Thank heavens she hadn't brought the inspector in there.

"All right, off you go," she said firmly. "Find a new uniform and wash out your eyes. And the inside of your nose and ears, too, Ginny, do you hear?"

"Yes, Mrs. Bright," she said, still sobbing a little. "I'm s-so sorry—"

"Yes, yes, that's fine," she said. "It wasn't your fault."

No, it definitely wasn't.

And so now Phyllida had to have words with Mr. Dobble instead of listening to the Detection Club tell Inspector Cork how to solve his case. Drat. She'd been rather looking forward to that.

Despite the fact that it would have punctuated the point she needed to make with Mr. Dobble, Phyllida carefully brushed off the ash and soot that had found its way onto her dress. She was not about to walk about looking like a chimney sweep.

The butler was in his pantry, but from all indications, he appeared to be doing nothing but staring into space. There was a full cup of tea on the desk in front of him, but no papers, pencils, or any other work in sight.

Since the door was ajar, Phyllida didn't feel the least bit guilty about peeking in before knocking. She also felt a mild bump of delight when the man jumped a little at the sound of her knock.

"Yes, Mrs. Bright?" he said, giving her a once-over with a disapproving expression. He'd stood, as was proper, and now loomed behind the desk in his customary dark coat and trousers.

She knew exactly what he was thinking. Instead of wearing a drab, shapeless frock, Phyllida preferred bright colors and silky fabrics for her day dresses. Today hers was a sky-blue rayon, belted neatly at her waist—which admittedly wasn't nearly as slim as it used to be, but was still defined—with a lacy white collar that lay flat over the bodice. Her sleeves were probably bothersome to the butler as well, for they were feminine, flowing cap sleeves rather than long, starched ones with buttoned cuffs. She had a watch on her left wrist and no other jewelry. Phyllida wore stockings, of course, and black shoes with heels that were just slightly less than completely practical. She never wore an apron, but always had the ring of household keys fastened to her belt, and every frock she wore was equipped with pockets into which she slipped minutiae that she came upon during her day: a shriveled leaf or petal from the flower arrangements, a scrap of paper, a random thread or button, and the like.

But it was her hair—a unique and bright strawberry gold—that irritated Mr. Dobble the most. Since Phyllida was well aware of this, she always made certain to coif herself in a modern fashion that did nothing to "subdue it," as the butler had once demanded she do; his intention being clear that she should wear a cap to cover the distraction. In fact, she'd recently had it cut off into a shorter, more fashionable style, which produced an unexpected benefit in her subtle digs at Mr. Dobble's intolerance: her hair had become even less restrained.

Now, instead of having a smooth head of hair parted slightly off-center with an intricate knot or roll resting at the back of her neck, Phyllida had a soft mass of just-below-chin-length waves erupting from all over her head. She used pretty pins and combs to keep it from falling messily into her face or obstructing her vision, and which had the added benefit of butler annoyance for the glittering of the jet beads or false pearls that decorated them. No one but herself, and the woman who'd cut her hair, ever got close enough to notice that there were plenty of silver hairs mingling among the bright curls.

"I've just come from the sitting room where the damper was stuck again," Phyllida said. "It's made a horrendous mess, and I've sent Freddie to begin sweeping it up. Which of the extra maids did you assign there yesterday?"

Mr. Dobble's eyes widened a trifle so quickly she nearly missed it. "It was . . . hmph . . . I do believe it was the dark-haired one. With the, uh, the large nose. I didn't expect anyone would be using the room with everyone gone."

"Presumably Nancy—which is the name of the dark one with the large nose—wasn't informed about the damper," Phyllida went on mercilessly. "But apparently she *was* instructed to remove three of the chintz pillows."

"They needed to be cleaned," he replied. "The pillows."

"Well, now the *entire* room needs to be cleaned because there is ash and soot *everywhere*. Including on Ginny. And Inspector Cork has just arrived—"

"I am aware of that," he said stiffly. It was a matter of his personal pride that Mr. Dobble should know everyone who came and went from the house.

"And I was going to put him in the sitting room," she added meaningfully.

Mr. Dobble heaved a sigh but gave no response or attempt to divert the blame. That was so uncharacteristic of him that Phyllida sat down in the chair in front of the desk.

With a sigh, he folded his long, slender body down into his own seat.

"It's only a matter of time until the press arrive," she said in an easier voice.

"Quite right," he replied.

"Perhaps you could station Freddie to keep an eye out and chase them away when they do."

He nodded absently. Phyllida waited, hoping her silence would induce him to speak about whatever was on his mind.

She had a suspicion she knew what it was, for she had her own similar concerns.

Her patience was rewarded after a pregnant silence, but Mr. Dobble's response was not what she'd expected.

"Who the bloody hell would have done such a thing?"

Such an outburst could only elicit one response: the simple truth. "One of the murder writers," Phyllida said. "Someone who's planned many a death on paper, and now, at last, has decided to execute one—quite literally."

"That," replied Mr. Dobble grimly, "is precisely what I'm afraid of."

She nodded. He was slowly confirming her suspicion. Feeling as though it would be permissible to allow a hint of her own worry to be revealed, she said, "Would someone from the Murder Club actually kill in order to win the writing prize?"

Mr. Dobble lifted his gray-blue eyes to meet hers. They were surprisingly clear. "I'm very much afraid they might, Mrs. Bright."

Before Phyllida could respond, they heard the distant jangling of the telephone. "Shall I answer it?" she asked in deference to his mood.

"Yes, yes, go ahead, Mrs. Bright," he replied.

She hurried from the butler's pantry to the nearest telephone, which was on a table in the hall.

"Mallowan Hall," she said into the receiver.

"Oh, oh, is it M-Mrs. B-Bright?" someone was sobbing on the other end.

"Yes, it is," Phyllida replied. The feminine voice was familiar, but she couldn't immediately place it. "What is it? Are you all right? Who is calling?"

"This is Rita, f-from St. Wendreda's," said the maid. "I-I didn't know who to r-ring, but I h-had to tell s-someone."

"What is it, then?" asked Phyllida.

"I-it's Saint Aloysius," cried Rita. "He's dead! He's just . . . *dead*!"

While a deceased feline was a tragedy in and of itself, Phyllida sensed there was something else wrong about the loss of Saint Aloysius.

"H-He was eating the cake! His paw prints are all over it . . . and now h-he's dead! He m-must have died last night . . . all a-alone." Several hiccups interrupted her wailing, but Phyllida was able to interpret her words nonetheless. "All by himself! And after Father—"

"What cake are you speaking of, Rita?" asked Phyllida. She was starting to have a very bad feeling about this.

"The . . . the cake that come for Father Tooley yesterday morning."

The bad feeling became a certainty. "Did Father Tooley eat any of the cake?" she asked, thinking about the convulsions and release of bodily fluids that had gripped the poor priest during his last moments of life.

"*Sounds more like arsenic.*" Wasn't that what Bradford had said? She gritted her teeth. Surely he was wrong. Surely there weren't *two* poisons going about willy-nilly in Listleigh. . . .

"Oh, yes, ma'am, he ate a good portion of it. F-Father Tooley loved his sweets, he did, and—"

Phyllida couldn't listen any longer. "Yes, right, I shall be there as quickly as possible. Don't touch anything—"

"B-but what about S-Saint Aloysius? I c-can't just *leave* him there—"

"Yes, you can, Rita. You need to. Do you understand me? Close up the room and I'll be there straightaway."

CHAPTER 8

"WHAT'S THE RUSH, THEN, MRS. BRIGHT?" SAID BRADFORD AS SHE climbed into the motorcar.

Against her better judgment, she'd taken a seat next to him in the front. She couldn't risk sitting in the back and feeling nauseated by the time they arrived at St. Wendreda's. She knew she would need all of her faculties once she got to the crime scene, for she was quite certain the death of Saint Aloysius was murder.

"There's a dead cat up at the rectory, and Rita is quite overset about it," she said. "Could we please drive rather quickly then, Mr. Bradford?"

He gave her a curious look but set the vehicle into motion. She settled back into the seat, her thoughts whirling.

Unfortunately, the driver's silence was far too brief, for they were just turning onto the lane that led into Listleigh when he spoke again. "I can't help but wonder why the eminently practical and persnickety Mrs. Bright would rush up to a church to see to a dead cat when she has so many other things to manage."

Persnickety?

"You may wonder all you like, Mr. Bradford—"

"I prefer just Bradford, no Mister, as you well know," he interrupted.

"You may wonder all you like, Mr. Bradford—and there's really no cause for such informality in my form of address—"

"Other than my personal preference," he muttered.

"Very well, then, *Bradford*," she said, then consciously ungritted her teeth and forced herself to speak calmly. "I shall endeavor to remember to leave your honorific aside when addressing you."

"I greatly appreciate that, Mrs. Bright," he replied. "As I know you never forget anything."

She lapsed into a stony silence, grateful to have distracted him from his questions.

"But I'm still wondering why you're in such a rush to see to a dead cat," he said. Although she wasn't looking at him, Phyllida was certain the corner of his mouth quivered, as if he were suppressing a grin. "Especially when you were already planning to be there at half eleven. What could cause such a rush that you're going an hour early?"

"A deceased feline, someone's *pet*, is reason enough," she told him frostily. "Wouldn't you be quite beside yourself should something happen to that bounding, slathering beast of yours? As a cat owner, I find myself completely sympathetic to poor Rita's grief, and I told her I would assist with its—er—disposal."

He took his eyes from the road to gape at her, then burst into laughter. "*You? You're* going to dispose of a dead cat?"

With his eyes alight and his mouth upturned with glee, Bradford looked almost handsome—a thought that Phyllida noted with complete objectivity, and then firmly dismissed. Any attractive physical characteristics of the driver—including his broad shoulders and strong, dark hands (ungloved, of course)—were utterly irrelevant.

She kept her lips primly closed, despite the number of tart responses that ran through her mind. There was no need to engage with the impossible man. He could cackle and giggle and poke at her all he liked, but she would give him no further ammunition.

And next time, she *would* sit in the back.

Still chuckling, he focused his eyes on the curving road, easily navigating around an approaching wagon, then taking a curve with a bit too much enthusiasm. Since she suspected he'd done so in order to elicit a reaction from her, Phyllida kept quiet and gripped the seat where he couldn't see her white knuckles.

"Right, then. So the great and practical Mrs. Bright has suddenly left all of her responsibilities at the hall to fly up to the village more than an hour early in order to dispose of a dead cat," he said. "Surely it could have nothing to do with the murder that she definitely isn't investigating."

When had he become so dratted talkative? When she'd first met him, he'd been surly and spare of words. Now it was as if a dam had burst and he couldn't contain himself.

Oh, how she wished she could escape . . . and then, horrified, she stopped the thought and instead gave herself a firm talking-to. Phyllida Bright did not run or escape adversity or discomfort or smug chauffeurs.

She *managed* them.

"Right, then, it's the stony silence you're giving me now, is it?" he said, still grinning.

Ignoring him, she stared out the window as the hedgerows flew by.

At last the motorcar pulled up to the rectory, which was a squat brick building adjacent to St. Wendreda's Church.

Although she would have liked to remove herself from the vehicle as quickly as possible, Phyllida forced herself to wait for him to come around to open the door. She even allowed him to help her out, grateful for the gloves *she* at least wore for the barrier they provided between his large, calloused hand and hers.

"Thank you, Mist—erm, Bradford," she said airily. "You may return to Mallowan Hall and see to bringing the rest of the supplies at half eleven as planned."

"Thank you, Mrs. Bright," he said gravely.

The rectory door nearest the parking place had swung open, and there was Rita, wringing her hands in her apron. "Oh, thank you for coming, Mrs. Bright," she said.

"Of course," replied Phyllida, starting along the graveled path. The walk was flanked on either side by clumps of red geraniums interspersed with mounds of tiny white daisies, although one of the geranium plants appeared to have been crushed by something heavy, leaving bloodred petals scattered over the walkway and the fragrance of geranium in the air. There were definite signs of portending rain as well, Phyllida noted.

Because she didn't give Bradford a backward glance and her shoes made crunching noises on the stone, Phyllida didn't realize he was following in her wake until she was well inside the rectory.

She supposed, in retrospect, she should have known he wouldn't leave without bothering her further.

"It's just arful, Mrs. Bright, just arful," Rita was saying in a variety of forms, volumes, and inflections. "Poor Saint Aloysius. He never deserved anything like this."

"Saint Aloysius?" Phyllida heard Bradford mutter in a strangled voice as they walked down the cool, shadowy hall.

"He's right in there," said Rita, at last stopping by a closed door at the end of the hall.

"And where is the cake?" Phyllida asked.

"It's in there, too. I did what you said—I closed it all up, even though there ain't no one here but me right now, although when I got back this morning, I thought someone *had* been here."

Phyllida opened the door to what turned out to be Father Tooley's office.

It was a well-appointed room for a man who'd taken a vow of poverty. The furnishings were heavy oak and walnut pieces arranged over a red and blue Persian rug: a solid desk; three straight-back chairs; a long, low, glass-topped table; and a chintz-upholstered sofa that even Dobble might have admired for its ornately carved arms and legs. The curtains were still open, likely not having been closed in the wake of the priest's death and Rita's hasty abandonment of the place. A number of icons and other religious images decorated the walls, and the room held the faint smells of incense, sugar, and death.

Phyllida saw Saint Aloysius as soon as she stepped in, and felt a pang of grief for the still, furred figure on the floor near the sofa. He'd been a large brindled tom with a handsome, sleek tail. From his appearance—bulging, open eyes; contorted paws; bowed spine; protruding tongue—she concluded he'd experienced great pain before succumbing to what Phyllida was certain was poison. Most likely arsenic, she had to admit. Her conclusion was based on the time that had elapsed between ingestion and the death throes that had followed, *not* Bradford's comments last night.

Bradford made a quiet sound behind her, then crouched next to the cat.

"Poor boy," Phyllida said, blinking back tears. At the moment, she didn't care whether Bradford or Rita saw them. The cat had died a horrific death, and she wouldn't wish such a thing on anyone—even arrogant chauffeurs. She lowered herself to the floor, balancing carefully on her slightly impractical heels. "Poor, lovely boy."

"Looks like he had a time of it," said Bradford in a surprisingly quiet voice with the cat on the floor between them. "I'll take him out if you like, Mrs. Bright."

"Yes, if you would," she replied, blinking rapidly and finding it necessary to use her handkerchief.

"I'll sh-show you where to bury h-him," said Rita, sobbing quite vocally. "I sh-should have stayed with h-him last night. I sh-shouldn't have g-gone. The p-poor thing, all b-by hisself . . ." She ended with a loud hiccup.

Phyllida looked at her, tamping back her impatience over the repetitive whimpering. "If you had stayed with him, you'd likely have eaten some of the cake, now wouldn't you? And then *you'd* be dead as well."

Her words shocked Rita into silence.

"B-but . . ." The maid stared at her. Phyllida could almost see the thoughts unrolling through her head: *Cake doesn't kill people . . . only cats if they eat too much of it . . . right? . . . So why would Mrs. Bright say so . . . ?* Here in the procession of thoughts Rita's eyes went wide. *Does that mean the cake was poisoned?*—And here the maid's jaw dropped. *What if I would have eaten it, too?*

Ignoring Bradford's proffered hand, Phyllida rose gracefully as Rita lapsed into sobs once more. This time, her wailing was accompanied by expressions of disbelief and fear over her narrowly averted demise.

Bradford stood as well, and before Phyllida could look away, he met her eyes.

"Thank you for taking care of him," she said in a voice that was a little unsteady.

"I told you it was arsenic."

She bristled. "That's not certain—"

He scoffed.

She spun away and walked over to what was left of Father Tooley's cake. It was on the credenza behind his desk, as if the priest had turned from reviewing whatever he'd been working on in order to sample the delectable pastry, then swiveled back to the workspace. The cat prints and uneven edges of the dessert left no doubt that Saint Aloysius had helped himself to a generous portion. However, that fact that more than half of the cake was gone indicated Father Tooley had previously decimated a good bit of the treat.

She could understand why. The confection had been a beautiful, delicious-looking thing, composed of three layers of white sponge approximately six inches in diameter. One filling between two of the layers was a generous slathering of strawberry jam, whilst the other two layers were divided by chocolate mousse. A frosting of white royal icing glittering with sugar finished it, with a layer of strawberry jam spread over the top like a glistening red mirror. It wasn't particularly fancy, but it did look delicious. Even Phyllida, who was sensitive to the lessening definition of her waistline, would have been hard put to resist.

"Rita," said Phyllida sharply.

"Y-yes, ma'am?" said the girl.

"Where did this cake come from?" she asked, aware that Bradford was poking around at the papers on Father Tooley's desk.

Now who was investigating?

"I-I'm not certain, Mrs. Bright. It was delivered yesterday, in the morning."

"Who delivered it? What time did it come?" Phyllida pressed. "Tell me everything you remember about it."

"I . . . I . . ."

Phyllida silently applauded when Rita drew in a shaky breath, apparently attempting to collect her thoughts. After a moment, the maid spoke carefully.

"It come in a white box, Mrs. Bright. With a note that said something like, 'Compliments of the Detection Club, with our thanks.' Father said as how it must have been a thank-you for him letting all of the festival events happen here at the church. He was all proud about it happening here instead of at St. Thurston's, you know. But St. Thurston's doesn't have an orphanage that needs a new roof—or, even, anything that does, so it was out of the question having it there. It was the bakery delivery man from Panson's what brought it. Benny is his name."

"Do you remember what time it arrived?" Phyllida pressed, watching Bradford from out of the corner of her eye. He'd moved on from perusing the papers on Father Tooley's desk to digging through the trash receptacle on the floor next to it.

"It were before half ten, Mrs. Bright."

"Here's the note and the cake box," Bradford said suddenly, withdrawing said objects from the waste can. "I suppose I'd best save them for Inspector Cork, as you're not doing any investigating, eh, Mrs. Bright?" Despite his provoking words, he placed the items on the desk within easy reach of where she stood.

Phyllida lifted her nose and looked down at him—which was difficult as he was standing and he was quite a bit taller than she. But she was certain he got the message. Without a word, she picked up the note and the cake box and began to examine them.

The enclosure was written in simple block letters on a piece of white card. It said almost exactly what Rita had recalled: *COMPLIMENTS OF THE DETECTION CLUB, WITH IT'S GRATITUDE.*

She frowned at the apostrophe, then sniffed the card. She smelled only confection, and noted that it was the sort of stock readily obtained or already on hand in most households. The ink was an unassuming black, and there were no smudges or signs of hesitancy in the writing.

Turning her attention to the box, she noted that Father Tooley seemed to have been in a hurry to reveal its contents, for the top was torn as if the opener had been impatient in unfolding its cardboard tabs. It was the same sort of box she'd seen any number of times, for she often ordered extra pastries from Panson's. It was definitely one of their boxes for it had a large P stamped on the top.

But when Phyllida examined the inside of the box, she noticed a small crumb wedged deep in the corner. Further careful investigation revealed that it was not a bit of dried icing or white sponge, but a bit of nut. Walnut, to be precise.

As there were no nuts on or in the cake, Phyllida came to the obvious conclusion: the box had previously been used, and therefore the cake had not been placed inside it by someone at Panson's.

Not that she had thought it had.

Bradford, who'd wrapped up Saint Aloysius in a tablecloth and removed the swaddled corpse, reappeared at that moment. She noticed he had to duck slightly to get through the doorway.

"This box has been previously used," Phyllida told him. "The perpetrator must have ordered something from Panson's and saved the box, then prepared the cake and put it inside. The question is, how did he or she get the box added to the delivery lorry?"

"Clever," he replied, and she wasn't certain whether he was referring to her deductions or the murderer's tactics.

"I suppose I'd best call Inspector Cork and have the rest of this cake tested for poison."

"Arsenic," he said, as if it were a foregone conclusion. "As I said."

Phyllida gritted her teeth. "We won't know for certain until the testing is completed. Dr. Bhatt has a laboratory at his surgery. Perhaps, in the interest of efficiency, he could do the test."

"Have one of the suspects test the murder weapon? Are you daft?" Bradford's reaction was quick and sharp.

Phyllida shot him a glower. She knew John Bhatt hadn't added arsenic—or any poison—to anyone's food. She *knew* it. But she supposed Bradford had a point. "Perhaps with some supervision, then," she conceded.

Bradford snorted. "And who's going to provide the supervision? His lady friend?"

Phyllida felt her face go hot, for his arch expression made it clear he was referring to her. Not only was she put out with Bradford for making such a snide comment, but she was furious with herself for reacting with a *blush*. Dear heaven, she hadn't blushed like this since . . . well, since the last time he'd made one of his snide comments.

"I'm going to telephone up to Mallowan Hall and explain to Inspector Cork what I've discovered," she said. "Perhaps *he'll* want to supervise the testing."

Bradford made another derisive noise, then turned to Rita, who'd been standing in the corner watching them with wide eyes. "I'll dig a hole for Saint Aloysius, then, if you show me where. But surely he'll need to be tested as well."

Phyllida's conversation with Inspector Cork was brief and to the point.

When she disconnected the call and replaced the receiver, Rita approached. "Ma'am, Mrs. Bright, I . . . there's something else."

"Well, what is it, then?" Phyllida prompted when the maid fell into silence.

"I . . . I think it might be important, now it seems that Father Tooley's cake was poisoned."

"Yes . . . ?" Phyllida said encouragingly after another pause.

"I . . . I think someone was here last night," Rita said. "After we left."

"Why do you think that?" Phyllida could never be a real detective; she had little patience for conversations like this.

"Some things have been moved. And . . . and there was a flower inside the door on the floor, like someone had stepped on it and it fell off their shoe. I know it was after because I had already swept yesterday. Before the party. And no one used that door last night."

"It was the door we entered today?" Phyllida asked. She had

seen the crushed geranium outside but hadn't noticed a flower on the floor. Rita must have already swept it up by the time she arrived.

"Yes, ma'am."

"Show me what things have been moved, if you please," Phyllida said. She was completely ignoring Bradford, who stood aside with his arms folded over his chest, seemingly disinterested in their exchange.

Sure enough, when she and Rita left the priest's office, Bradford followed. The maid led them into the sitting room, where Inspector Cork had done his interviews last night.

"The piecrust table is gone," Phyllida said as soon as she entered the room. "It was sitting right next to the sofa."

"Yes, ma'am," Rita said, eyes wide with surprise. "It's a different table there now, but the one that was there is gone. How did you know that?"

"I notice everything," Phyllida replied, ignoring the snort from Bradford. Really, the man was abominably rude. "Where did this table come from, then?"

"It were over there by the window," replied the maid. "I liked to keep flowers on it."

The piecrust table that Mr. Genevan had admired had not been placed in front of the window, or in any other location. It was simply gone from the room.

"Is there anything else, Rita?" Phyllida asked.

"I haven't looked through the whole rectory yet, ma'am. Only the kitchen and in here and in F-Father's office." Her eyes suddenly glistened and her lip quivered.

Phyllida forestalled another session of wailing and said, "Very well, then, you'll need to go through the entire rectory and see if anything else has been moved or is missing. The inspector will want to know and so do I. Can you do that now, very quickly but thoroughly? And write everything down."

"Yes, ma'am, yes, I can."

"Very well, then, off with you," Phyllida said when the maid hesitated.

As soon as Rita was gone, Bradford spoke. "Someone took an antique table."

"Obviously," Phyllida said. "But it wasn't the murderer."

He folded his arms across his chest again and arched one dark eyebrow so high it disappeared into the hair falling over his forehead. "Do explain, Mrs. Bright. I know you're bursting to enlighten me."

"There were any number of people in this room last night who might have noticed the piecrust table. One in particular must have realized its worth—I need not mention his name, as it is quite obvious to whom I refer—but he might not have been the only one who did. I suspect whoever it was decided the empty rectory, and the loss of its resident, would be the perfect opportunity to acquire the table. He or she assumed no one would notice it missing."

"Right, then, Mrs. Bright. That's so obvious even *I* could have deduced that." That eyebrow was still anchored behind a lock of dark hair.

"Yes, well," Phyllida went on in a clipped manner, "if it had been the murderer who came back for the table, wouldn't he—or she—have looked for the evidence—meaning, the cake—and disposed of that as well? Especially since everyone left the cocktail party believing that Father Tooley had died from nicotine poison meant for Alastair Whittlesby."

"I didn't," Bradford said.

"A fact which you will, no doubt, continue to point out. One might wonder how a motorcar mechanic is so well versed in poisons," Phyllida said.

"One might wonder the same about a persnickety housekeeper."

She didn't rise to the bait. "If it were the murderer who decided to help himself to an antique table—and I suppose we must determine whether it was, in fact, a costly piece of furniture—surely he or she would have searched for the remnants of the cake to destroy the evidence. It wouldn't have been difficult to locate. Therefore, I conclude that the murderer and the antiques thief are two different people."

"So by your account, Mrs. Bright, we have a murderer who employs arsenic, a would-be murderer who employs nicotine, and an antiques thief? And they are not the same people."

Phyllida gave him a smug smile. "We are dealing with murder writers, Bradford. Their plots are *meant* to be complicated."

CHAPTER 9

*I*NSPECTOR CORK TOOK THE NEWS ABOUT THE POISONED CAKE RATHER well, Phyllida thought. His bushy mustache rippled for only a few moments.

Once she had apprised him of her observations and deductions—and insisted that he have the cake and the cat tested for poisons as quickly as possible—Phyllida decided she had time to return to Mallowan Hall to freshen up and to ensure that everything had been packed up for delivery to the fair before the festivities began.

The side lawn at St. Wendreda's had been designated as the location for the public fair. It was a square of lush green grass bordered on one side by the church, on the next by the rectory, on the third by the small river that wended its way through Listleigh, and on the fourth by a wrought iron fence. The entire area had been cordoned off with ropes that would do little to keep out anyone determined to make their way into the festival via random locations instead of the front entrance, but at least it was an effort to keep things organized.

Each of the celebrity authors had a table piled with books and his or her own small tent. The Murder Fête attendees—both amateur writers and mere readers—could make their way to each table and have a book signed by the author, and then take all of the books to one table, where they would pay.

All proceeds from the sales would go to the orphanage, for the publishers of Agatha Christie, G. K. Chesterton, Dorothy L. Sayers, and Anthony Berkeley had donated the copies to the cause. Publishers saw the benefits of publicity just as much as authors did.

Along with the book tables, the festival included booths set up with tea, pastries, sandwiches, and other foodstuffs for sale. Another table offered pretty bookmarks to buy, made from ribbons trimmed with beads or charms. A small booth offered buttons with THE MURDER FÊTE emblazoned enthusiastically on them, and the image of a dagger dripping with blood beneath. Another enterprising soul was selling film and theatrical posters from some of the adaptations by murder writers—or any suspense or thriller story. The proprietors at each of these tables could keep their proceeds, but they'd had to make a donation to the orphanage's roof fund in order to reserve their table.

All in all, Phyllida was confident the festival would be a success . . . even with the pall of a real murder hanging over it.

In fact, she thought ruefully, news of the horrendous crime and its intended victim would probably bring *more* people to the Murder Fête. People were far too enamored with violent death.

As she made her way to the Daimler, where Bradford was waiting to drive her back, Phyllida decided to make a short detour to Panson's Bakery. It was only a brief walk from the church, and her questions shouldn't take long.

Even though she hoped the inspector would be proactive enough to question the delivery boy Benny and Mrs. Panson, Phyllida felt the urge to do so herself. Just to be sure.

"I'm going to stop into Panson's to see about some tea tarts," Phyllida told Bradford. "I won't be a minute."

"Tea tarts? Of course, Mrs. Bright," he said dryly.

She sailed past him without further comment, and moments later stepped into the bakery. The scents of pastry, sugar, and yeast assailed her.

"Ah, Mrs. Bright, good mornin' to ye," said Mrs. Panson. She was a round, shiny-faced woman with pudgy hands and a white apron. She reminded Phyllida of a polished red apple. Her husband was the baker and she managed the front counter, boxing up the confections he made and gossiping with the customers.

It was this latter activity that had prompted Phyllida to come in to speak with her.

"Good morning, Mrs. Panson. I'm in need of some of those tiny currant tarts Mr. Panson makes—with the glaze on them?"

"Oh, yes, indeed, and here I am happy to box them up for you. How many will you have, then, Mrs. Bright?" Her hand hovered over the two stacks of flattened cardboard boxes, waiting to determine which size to choose.

"Two dozen will suffice," Phyllida said. Two dozen was a generous order, and she anticipated that such a large order would likewise prompt a generous outpouring of gossip.

Mrs. Panson beamed with delight as she began to construct two of the larger pastry boxes by tucking tabs into slots. "Why, you're going to wipe us all out of currant tarts, you are, Mrs. Bright. *Milton!*" she hollered back into the kitchen. "We'll need more currant tarts now! I suppose they're for the murder writers staying up to Mallowan Hall, aren't they, Mrs. Bright?"

"Indeed, they are," Phyllida replied. "Although I confess I'm particularly fond of them myself." She smiled, for it was the truth, and the delicious smells and the sight of glistening tarts and rolls and other pastries were making her hungry. Her breakfast had consisted of a cup of tea and a single hard-boiled egg too many hours ago.

"Simply terrible about Father Tooley," said Mrs. Panson as she carefully began to slide the tarts into one of the boxes, which Phyllida noted was larger than the one that had contained Father Tooley's cake. "The poor man! I heard it was poison put in one of that Alastair Whittlesby's fancy cocktails!"

Phyllida waffled for a moment about whether to reveal her suspicions to Mrs. Panson, then said, "It was a terrible moment. Everyone was quite shocked—and, yes, it does appear that Mr. Whittlesby had been the intended victim."

"Poor Father Tooley," said Mrs. Panson, still taking her time sliding the tarts into their cardboard homes so that she would have more opportunity to question Phyllida further. "He was a nice man—liked his sweets, he did. He'd walk over here most days in the morning after mass to get a small treat for his after-noon tea. His maid isn't the best baker, you see."

"Oh, yes, that reminds me—Father Tooley was enjoying a beau-tiful cake yesterday afternoon. It came in a Panson's box, but I don't see one like it in your case—it was a three-layer white sponge with chocolate mousse layered with strawberry jam, and more jam on top. Do you have another one?" Phyllida asked. "It looked delicious."

Mrs. Panson looked at her in surprise. "No . . . we ain't had any-thing like that for weeks, Mrs. Bright. You say he was eating it yes-terday?"

"His maid said it was delivered by Benny at half ten yesterday morning," Phyllida said. "In a Panson's box."

"*Milton!*" Mrs. Panson whirled and stomped over to the open door to the kitchen. "Did you make a three-layer white-sponge this week? With chocolate mousse? And jam?"

Phyllida couldn't hear Mr. Panson's response, but when his wife turned back, she saw the confirmation on her face. "That cake did *not* come from here," she said. Her eyes blazed. "Who on earth would use *our* box and *our* delivery boy and claim a cake was ours? Why, that's—that's—*fraud!*" Her face was turning an alarm-ing shade of purple.

"Someone must have simply reused one of your boxes, then. The cake was a gift to Father Tooley for all of his work with the Murder Fête," she said. "May I speak with Benny? I wonder when that person put the cake in his delivery lorry. Perhaps he saw who it was."

"*I'll* be speaking with Benny," said Mrs. Panson flatly. "We pay for him to deliver our orders, and now we got someone *hijacking* our lorry driver! *Benny!*" she bellowed, opening the side door to reveal a narrow alley.

A moment later, a short, skinny man stumbled into the bakery from the side door. "Yes, Mrs. Panson?" he said, his eyes wide with trepidation.

"You let someone put a box on your lorry yesterday that *warn't* from here." Mrs. Panson was shaking a finger at him. "Don't you be charging us for those extra deliveries, now, and you'd best be watching more careful!"

"Wh-what? I . . . I don't know what you're talking ab-bout."

Phyllida decide to intervene, simply in the interest of keeping the little man from expiring from terror. "Mr.—er—Benny," she said kindly, "it appears that you delivered a Panson's box to the rectory for Father Tooley yesterday morning at approximately half ten. The dessert inside did not come from the bakery, and so we are trying to determine who might have—er—camouflaged a cake in one of the boxes. Do you know how the box came to be placed in your lorry?"

Benny wasn't trembling quite so much now, and he removed his cap to scratch his head—an event that made Phyllida wince at the thought of stray hairs and heaven knew what else being disseminated into the bakery and its offerings. Fortunately, he was standing away from the counter—and from Phyllida—and her tarts had already been safely packaged up.

"It were just there in the truck, ma'am," he said, darting a glance at Mrs. Panson. "I thought as how Mrs. Panson musta put it on when I were in the back talking to Mr. Panson—"

"Of course I didn't put it on," snapped the baker's wife. "Have I ever in the five years you been delivering for us put a box on your lorry?"

"N-no, ma'am, you ain't. I shoulda asked you about it when I saw it, but it was right there and the rectory was just over across the way and I thought I'd take it there first." He replaced his cap and gnawed on his lower lip.

"Did you notice anyone nearby who might have been the person to put it in your lorry?" Phyllida asked before Mrs. Panson could start up again.

"I—well, mebbe." Benny appeared as uncertain as he sounded.

"Can you think about whom you might have seen in the vicinity around that time?" she pressed. "Perhaps Miss Crowley? Mr. Genevan? What about Mrs. Rollingbroke?"

"Oh, yes, ma'am, I did see Miss Crowley as she was parking her bicycle right there." He gestured vaguely to "right there," which appeared to be across the street by the village center.

"Did her bicycle have a basket on it, where the cake might have been resting in its box?" Phyllida asked.

"Seems to me it did," he said, but the tone in his voice made her wonder if he was simply giving her the answers he believed she wanted.

"And what about Mr. Genevan?" Phyllida realized if she could identify two individuals from the Murder Club who might have been together yesterday morning, they could have been the two whose conversation to which she'd been privy. It had been just after nine when she'd overheard it, and although she wasn't certain of the sex of both of the speakers, she'd been certain one was male. "Or anyone else?"

"I saw Mr. Genevan walk by the front window yesterday morning," said Mrs. Panson. "He was walking with Mrs. Rollingbroke and Mr. Billdop. I remember because they stopped in front of the shop and I thought they were going to come inside, but none of them did." She sounded offended. "But that nice Dr. Bhatt came in only a few moments later. He likes the walnut pastries with the glaze—says it reminds him of ballycalva."

Phyllida grimaced internally. She'd hoped to place only one of the Murder Club members near the bakery at the time the box was put in the lorry, but it appeared that all of them had been in the vicinity. "Were any of them carrying anything?" she asked.

"Not that I recall," said Mrs. Panson.

"Have any of them purchased anything from you in the last week?" Phyllida asked.

"Heavens, of course they did! Everyone does. Only bakery in town," Mrs. Panson told her, then she realized Benny was still standing there. "And what're you doing now, then? Get off with you and get those deliveries made!"

Benny fled, and Phyllida decided it was time for her to make her exit as well. "Thank you, Mrs. Panson. Please add these to our account," she said, collecting the boxes of tarts.

She left the baker's wife muttering about the nerve of people using *her* deliveryman and *her* boxes—which they bought and paid for with their hard-earned money—and what if the cake inside wasn't as good as Milton's—well, of *course* it wasn't—and now if someone thought *that* had come from Panson's, why, it wasn't just the *box* they'd abused, it was Panson's reputation, it was, and it was *fraudulent*, it was!

Mrs. Panson was already picking up the telephone as Phyllida closed the door behind her. It wouldn't be long before the whole of Listleigh was being warned about fraudulent bakery items.

Bradford took the pastry boxes from Phyllida, then opened the front passenger door before she could tell him she intended to sit in the rear. Rather than make a fuss, she slid into the front seat whilst he placed the tarts in the back, then closed the door.

"Well, Mrs. Bright," he said, giving her a look as he navigated the Daimler down the road. "What did you find out?"

"Mr. Panson is going to need to make more currant tarts," she said.

He chuckled. "Very well, then, Mrs. Bright. Have it your way."

"I shall tell you what I learned from Mrs. Panson if you tell me what you saw or heard last night," she said after a bit of thought.

"I will agree to that if you will admit you *are* investigating the murder," Bradford replied.

"Mrs. Agatha insisted that I do so," Phyllida told him frostily. "She wants the matter settled as quickly as possible. The last thing we need is press camped out at Mallowan Hall again. Or any of us in the news."

He gave her a curious look but made no immediate comment. After a moment, he said, "When I arrived outside the cocktail party last night, I saw Mr. Rollingbroke there. He was standing near the courtyard."

"Mr. Rollingbroke? But he wasn't supposed to be there until the party was over—to pick up Mrs. Rollingbroke."

Bradford gave her a significant look, then returned his attention to the road.

"He didn't come inside the courtyard—at least, I didn't see him," Phyllida mused. "So he couldn't have been the one to place the poisoned bitters. I presume that's why you feel that information is relevant."

"Obviously," replied Bradford.

She mulled over that for a moment. It was important to determine who had access to the bar—or who'd at least been in proximity of it—during the evening. The bar counter had been near a small side entrance to the garden, however, where the supplies had been brought in. She hadn't yet had a chance to question Dobble and Stanley about who had approached the bar during the evening and had been close enough to put the poisoned bitters on the shelf behind.

"I suppose Sir Rolly might have been able to slip inside and then back out again without being noticed," she mused.

"When I saw him, he was walking around from the front of the rectory," Bradford said.

"Was that where his motorcar was parked?" Phyllida asked.

"No."

She frowned. Why would Sir Rolly want to do away with Mr. Whittlesby? According to his wife, they interacted socially, and if not close friends, they were at least friendly. Neither of the Rollingbrokes seemed to have a reason to murder the man. Unless Vera Rollingbroke was desperate to eliminate Mr. Whittlesby as competition for publication.

And according to his wife, Sir Rolly knew about Alastair Whittlesby's cocktail preference. Perhaps he'd taken to heart Mr. Whittlesby's disappointment over not having a Vieux Carré when they had dinner at the Rollingbroke home, and ordered a bottle of Monteleone's Special Bitters to have on hand.

And perhaps he wanted his wife to succeed in getting her stories published.

Or perhaps there was another reason, related to whatever Mr. Whittlesby had said—which had sounded almost like a threat, hadn't it?—that prompted Mrs. Rollingbroke to decide to invite him to her soiree at the last minute.

"Thank you for that information," Phyllida said. "As for what I learned from Mrs. Panson—the cake was definitely not from the bakery, and the perpetrator used one of the smaller boxes. All of the suspects have ordered pastries from Panson's in the last week, and since it was the smaller box, it could have been any of them."

"What does the smaller box have to do with it?" Bradford asked in a tone that was, for once, simply curious.

"A smaller box means a smaller order, and many of our—er, my—suspects live alone: the vicar, Miss Crowley, Mr. Genevan . . ."

"Dr. Bhatt."

"Yes," Phyllida replied a little shortly. "If it had been the larger box, it might have been easier to determine who did it because a larger household might have had a larger order."

"Right."

"What must be determined is whether the same perpetrator who attempted to kill Mr. Whittlesby is also the person who murdered Father Tooley. One cannot assume it is the same individual," she said, giving him a sidewise look.

"No, one cannot," he replied.

"But if it isn't the same individual—I suppose even if it *is*—there must be some motive for putting arsenic in his cake. By all accounts, Father Tooley was a great consumer of sweets, and so one would expect he'd eat the cake as soon as possible. It was delivered at about half ten yesterday morning, and its appearance would have negated his usual trip to the bakery for a treat after mass, as he usually did. Whoever poisoned the cake knew his habits well and made certain it was delivered before he visited the bakery so that he would eat it right away."

Bradford made a sound of agreement.

"The timing is suspect as well," Phyllida went on, marshaling her little gray cells into Poirot-like order. The cake was delivered yesterday, and the obvious intention was that he should eat it yesterday. Presumably, there was enough arsenic in it to ensure it was a fatal dose, rather than a slow poisoning. The size of the confection was indicative of that—it was large enough to harbor a good amount of arsenic, but small enough that someone like Father Tooley wouldn't hesitate to eat a good portion of it."

"So someone wanted him to die yesterday," Bradford said.

"Precisely."

"Whoever poisoned that cake would have known it would take some time before he died," Bradford went on.

"An hour or perhaps more for someone like Father Tooley, who was rather large due to his love of sugary sweets."

"Did they want him dead *before* the cocktail party?" Bradford mused.

"That is an excellent question," Phyllida replied, forgetting for the moment that she didn't need any assistance from the driver for her investigation. Still, it *was* nice to be able to discuss such matters with a relatively quick-minded individual. "One can't help but wonder if that was precisely the point—to get rid of Father Tooley before the Murder Club gathered. Perhaps," she said as a little idea began to solidify in her mind, "the poisoner didn't want Father Tooley to give any indication as to who had won the publishing prize. He'd finished calculating the results earlier this week."

Suddenly she straightened. "I didn't see anything on his desk that was indicative of the results of the short story contest, or his calculations."

"He might have already given them to Mr. Chesterton or Mrs. Agatha," Bradford said.

"I don't believe he could have done," Phyllida said, frowning. "He joined the cocktail party a bit late—perhaps he was already feeling the effects of the arsenic—and the Detection Club members were absolutely swarmed all evening. Surely if he'd presented one of them with the results, it would have been noticed or remarked upon." She shook her head. "No, I don't believe he delivered the results. And I didn't see anything like that on his desk."

"They could be in his pocket," Bradford said. "He may have intended to give them up but died first."

"Yes," Phyllida said, turning over the thought in her mind. "Yes, that's quite possible. Someone will have to go through his pockets to determine whether he has them."

Bradford looked at her. "I suppose you'll insist on doing so."

"It would be preferable," she replied agreeably. "I, at least, wouldn't overlook anything. If the contest information is missing, and the one who calculated the scores is dead . . . anyone could change the winner."

"Do you truly think one of those writers offed a priest and attempted to poison someone else just to win a publishing contract?" Bradford scoffed.

"I certainly do," Phyllida replied. "Writers by nature are competitive and desperate to be published, and murder writers are the worst of the lot. They're appallingly bloodthirsty—and they spend all their time thinking about ways to kill people."

"I don't believe it," Bradford said. "Killing two people in order to have a bloody story printed in a magazine? Best find another motive, Mrs. Bright, because I think that one is a load of rubbish."

She gave him a dark look. "Believe what you want, Bradford, but you'll see. When the scores for the short story contest are discovered to be missing—and mark my words, they've gone—*or*," she added with a rush to forestall any argument he might make, "when the results are discovered and can be proven to have been falsified with someone other than Alastair Whittlesby as the winner, you'll see just how desperate an unpublished writer can be."

He gave a sardonic chuckle and shook his head. "Whatever you say, Mrs. Bright. You're the detective. But remember who was right about the arsenic."

She sat up straight, folding her hands over her lap, and declined to speak with him for the remainder of the journey.

CHAPTER 10

Saturday afternoon

ONCE THE FESTIVAL WAS UNDER WAY, PHYLLIDA DIDN'T HAVE MUCH to do. A good number of her staff had been brought up to St. Wendreda's for the day, for she preferred to have maids she knew and trusted helping out for such a public event. They all had their assignments, and she knew them well enough not to have to watch over them.

Nonetheless, she did observe with satisfaction the maids and footmen scurrying about, refreshing tea, coffee, or water for the authors at their respective tables; bringing new supplies of books as needed; and doing their best to keep the press out of the way. Even Mr. Dobble had come up for the festival, although Phyllida wasn't certain whether his presence was more to criticize her organizational skills, determine whether she really *needed* most of the staff at the festival (of course she did), or purchase a signed book from Miss Sayers.

She was hoping for the opportunity to speak with each of the Murder Club members in an effort to try to identify the clandestine speakers from yesterday morning.

Phyllida noted that Mr. Billdop was standing off to the side, as if uncertain which author's queue he should join—or perhaps he was merely watching to see which wait was shorter. Miss Crowley had been standing at Miss Sayers's table for quite some time—

much longer than it would take to purchase a signed book—and the queue behind her had begun to snake around into the center of the festival. The people on line did not look pleased.

Mrs. Rollingbroke and her husband were strolling about, arm in arm. She was speaking with great animation, and Sir Rolly, who was carrying several hardback books, seemed to be hanging on her every word.

Phyllida didn't see Mr. Genevan or Mr. and Mrs. Whittlesby, but Dr. Bhatt was standing near one of the food booths, speaking with Mrs. Tattersall, who lived in the village and was always complaining about her corns and bunions.

Agatha's line was the longest—even longer than Miss Sayers's—but she moved through the people quickly and efficiently, likely due to her shyness. Mr. Max was in the tent with her, and he assisted by handing her books. Being an archaeologist, he was not unused to manual labor, and so he moved the heavy boxes around as necessary.

"You're doing an excellent job keeping the reporters from Mrs. Agatha's table, Elton," Phyllida said, speaking to Mr. Max's valet, who'd been conscripted for that particular purpose.

Elton was a relatively new addition to the Mallowan Hall staff, having joined just after the last murder investigation Phyllida had conducted. An unusually handsome young man in his early twenties, Elton had usurped Stanley, the first footman, as the favorite of the maids—although to the chagrin of Ginny, Molly, and Lizzie, the valet seemed uninterested in any sort of flirtation with them. He was, however, unfailingly polite and exceedingly helpful when not assisting Mr. Max—who'd originally claimed he didn't need a valet and now found him quite invaluable. He was even considering taking Elton on his next archaeological dig, which would be quite a tragedy insofar as the housemaids were concerned.

"Thank you, Mrs. Bright," Elton said. He straightened his broad shoulders, and Phyllida noticed that his cheeks were a bit flushed.

"It's rather warm out here today, isn't it, Elton?" she said.

"Oh, no, ma'am, not for me—but I can find you a fan or a glass of cool water if you like," he said. "If you're uncomfortable, that is."

She smiled, for she'd been about to offer to get him a drink so that he didn't need to leave his post. "No, no, I'm quite comfortable." Her pale-blue day dress was light and airy and she hadn't worn a sweater.

Just then, John Bhatt gave her a little wave from across the green. "But I do think I'll have a meat pasty, as I've missed luncheon. Carry on, Elton," she said. "Don't let any of the reporters talk to Mrs. Agatha, mind. Today she is speaking only to readers. Stanley will be here to give you a break in short order," she added, knowing both young men had been up and moving heavy boxes of books and setting up tents since dawn. "He's just finishing his break."

"Yes, ma'am, Mrs. Bright," he said, his cheeks still flushed. "Thank you."

Phyllida made her way to Dr. Bhatt and found him carefully eating a flaky Cornish pasty. There wasn't even a hint of crumb in his mustache—a feat that she found quite impressive. He smiled at her as she approached.

"Good afternoon, Phyllida," he said, using her familiar name since no one was near enough to hear. He looked particularly dapper in a gray linen suit and snowy shirt with a striped gray and blue tie and matching pocket scarf. His ink-black hair was covered by a white fedora ornamented with a bright red feather.

"How are you today?" she asked, touching his arm briefly in greeting as well as support. Although she and John had been meeting occasionally for luncheon or tea, their relationship hadn't progressed to anything more intimate than that. She knew John was more than receptive to such a development, but whilst she very much enjoyed him and his company, she simply had no interest in pursuing such a relationship with any man.

But that didn't mean she didn't care about him, or for him. And now, she couldn't help but be worried.

Not for a moment did she believe that John Bhatt, who'd taken the Hippocratic Oath to "first, do no harm," could have poisoned anyone. But the fact remained that he looked like a "foreigner," and she well knew the prejudices that abounded in small village and large city alike. A man with dark skin and a slight accent would often be considered an outsider—and an easy scapegoat.

When he responded, "I'm worried," Phyllida's concern heightened.

She gave him a sympathetic look. "As am I . . . especially as it appears Father Tooley was actually poisoned by a cake and not a cocktail." She watched his reaction closely in spite of herself and was relieved to see unabashed shock and confusion in his eyes.

"What are you saying?" he replied.

Phyllida explained, watching his eyes grow wider as she did so.

"Are you saying the man was poisoned *twice?*"

"That appears to be the case. I suggested to the inspector that, in the interest of time, he allow you to test the cake and the cat—"

"I would certainly do that," he replied, the light of enthusiasm in his eyes. "I'll finally be able to use my Marsh test equipment." Then his delight faded. "I was able to test the small sample of bitters last night and found copious amounts of nicotine—as expected. But the inspector has already brought in someone from London to do the official testing. He arrived this morning. They're using my lab to do the work, because of course *I* am considered a suspect—and so I cannot be trusted to do it—even with witnesses. They will not even allow me to watch them do the testing," he added morosely.

"Yes, you are a suspect. And a strong one, I must say—with your laboratory all set up to test poisons clearly indicating your deep interest in them," Phyllida said. When he looked at her as if surprised she would agree, his mustache drooped.

"I vow to you, I *never* would do such—"

"I know," she interrupted, patting his arm again. She certainly would have recognized John's voice if he had been one of the speakers. She hesitated, but decided not to tell him about the conversation just yet. "I *know*," she said again. "It's all in the name of research, of course. Nonetheless, the cake and poor Saint Aloysius should be tested immediately."

"Surely the work has already begun at my own laboratory, unfortunately." He sounded exceedingly disappointed. "I do wish they would allow me to observe!"

"John, whom do *you* suspect? You know all the members of the

Murder Club better than I do—and definitely better than Inspector Cork."

He heaved a sigh. "None of them. I do not suspect any of them . . . and yet it must be someone who was there last night."

"It's certainly not Mr. Chesterton or any of the other members of the Detection Club," Phyllida said. "And it certainly wasn't me or any of my staff. There was no one else there—aside from Rita, the maid at the rectory—and where would she get a bottle of Monteleone's Special Bitters? For that matter, where would anyone get one?"

"Indeed," he replied.

Noticing the queue for the food table had shortened, she excused herself from Dr. Bhatt to procure a pasty for herself—his smelled and looked far too delicious to ignore. She also intended for her absence to give him time to think. By the time she returned her attention to him with her own paper-wrapped pasty stuffed with beef, potatoes, and rutabaga, he'd finished his own.

"John," she said carefully, "you should know Mr. Billdop told Inspector Cork about the—er—altercation between you and Mr. Whittlesby."

Dr. Bhatt's mustache flattened and his dark cheeks turned darker. "I dislike speaking ill of anyone, but I admit, I have very little good to say about Alastair Whittlesby—other than that he is a good writer. He has won the contest, I am quite certain of it. He very nearly told us he did on Wednesday. I wish it were not so, but one cannot argue with talent." He sighed. "His work is good, and that is the only merit on which this contest has been judged."

"Did your altercation become physical at all?" Phyllida asked. "Or threatening? On the part of either of you? You must tell me all of it, for Inspector Cork will find out regardless."

His mustache, which she'd previously observed was a barometer for his mood and reactions, bristled and shivered. "He did put his hand on me—it was rough, but there was no injury; he shoved at me a bit. I did not respond in kind. I am ashamed to say, however, that I allowed my temper to get the best of me, and I . . . I did make statements that could have been construed as threats."

Phyllida nodded. "All right, then. We have established your motive—revenge, I suppose, for . . . for harsh words and a shove."

John made an uncharacteristically rude noise. "If harsh words were a sufficient motive for murder, far more killings would occur."

Phyllida gave him a sympathetic look. Dr. Bhatt was a proud, calm man, and she sensed this conversation was intensely uncomfortable for him—particularly with her, a woman whom she knew he admired. "I cannot disagree, but I am looking at this situation through the eyes of the inspector. You were physically accosted, embarrassed, and slandered in the presence of friends and colleagues," she went on.

His thick, luxurious mustache thinned as he flattened his mouth. His dark eyes turned empty. "I *was* angry. I did not contain my temper well enough. I said things I should not have done. But I did not attempt to poison Alastair Whittlesby."

She nodded again. "Does your housekeeper bake?"

His eyes revealed confusion, and then comprehension. "Yes, on occasion. But I most often acquire my desserts from Panson's. I particularly enjoy the sticky-glazed tarts. I do not eat sponge cake, and my housekeeper has never made one for me. It is too English for my taste."

"Very well." She hesitated, then plunged on. "Since it wasn't you, *who was it?*"

He was silent for a moment, then spoke carefully. "I have been racking my brain—that is the correct phrase, is it?" When Phyllida nodded, he continued. "I have been racking by brain since last night. No one likes Alastair Whittlesby, but he is a useful member of the Murder Club. He does offer constructive suggestions and criticism. There are times when his suggestions are not well received—particularly when he is pointing out very particular grammatical or spelling errors in a rough draft—but I cannot imagine Miss Crowley or Mrs. Rollingbroke being so upset as to try and kill him. None of us would."

"And why Father Tooley?" Phyllida said.

"That is even more of a mystery to me. Who would wish ill on a man of religion?" He shook his head.

"When you were in the village yesterday morning, did you see any of the Murder Club members carrying anything that might have been the cake?" she asked.

"I did not, but Digby Billdop seemed rather startled when he came round the corner and saw me. I did not think anything about it at the time, but it was near the bakery."

"So it was possible he had just put the box in the lorry," Phyllida mused, "and he was afraid someone had seen him." She frowned, nibbling on the crust of her pasty. She couldn't imagine the quiet, unassuming vicar as a murderer, but she would not discount it as impossible. "And on Wednesday, when the Murder Club met at Mr. Whittlesby's house . . . did anyone seem interested in the Vieux Carré cocktail?"

John's expression turned sour. "The meeting on Wednesday was nothing more than an opportunity for Alastair Whittlesby to lord it over the rest of us that he was going to win the competition. Louis Genevan was livid. I thought he was going to dash the man's drink in his own face."

"Mr. Whittlesby had one of his cocktails then," Phyllida confirmed. "Did anyone else?"

John sighed. "No, I don't believe anyone did, but he did talk about how he'd come upon the cocktail in New Orleans and how he had to buy special ingredients that no one could get here in England. But I don't believe he offered that particular drink to anyone—although he did pour a whisky for Sir Rolly, and I had a small glass of brandy. I don't usually imbibe so early in the day, but . . . well, Mr. Whittlesby was being quite trying."

"I understand his brother came in for a drink as well," Phyllida said.

"Yes, but I don't know what he had. Everyone was drinking some sort of cocktail except for Miss Crowley," he told her. "Mrs. Whittlesby had several drinks, and she seemed rather loose for it being tea." His mustache flattened.

Phyllida's suspicion grew that Mrs. Whittlesby enjoyed her spirits a bit too much. Before she could continue her discussion, how-ever, a sudden gust of wind caught her attention. It was followed by a definite spray of *wet*.

"Drat!" she exclaimed as the rain began in earnest.

Phyllida had been so busy she hadn't noticed how quickly the clouds had rolled in. She sprang into action, thrusting what was left of her pasty into Dr. Bhatt's hand and hurrying off to limit the damage of the rain.

In moments, the lawn at St. Wendreda's turned into a melee in the rain: servants were running everywhere, shoving boxes of books beneath the tables under the tents and securing the table-cloths over them, the authors being hustled toward the dry safety of St. Wendreda's rectory, festival-goers scrambling into the church itself, vendors stowing their wares, and Phyllida stalking about, safely covered by the umbrella she'd had the forethought to bring—for Mrs. Puffley's aching hip was never wrong—super-vising the efforts.

By the time she got inside, she was out of breath and her shoes were soaked, but that was the worst of it. Thanks to her planning, there'd been ample canvas coverings for the boxes of delicate books, and the tents were sturdy enough to withstand even gusty winds.

Phyllida shook out her umbrella and turned to find Elton standing there in the foyer of the rectory. He was soaked from head to toe, his dark hair falling over his face.

"Shall I get you a cup of hot tea, Mrs. Bright?" he asked, push-ing the dripping hair from his face.

"Why, thank you, Elton, that would be very nice," she replied. "I don't suppose there's been some brewed already."

"Mr. Dobble told Molly to see to it, for Mrs. Agatha and Miss Sayers were wanting something," said the valet.

Phyllida nodded. Mr. Dobble was no doubt attempting to re-deem himself for forgetting to tell Nancy about the faulty damper. As well he should.

"Shall I find you a blanket, too, Mrs. Bright?" asked Elton, still standing there dripping—much more generously than she was. "You've gotten wet."

"You're in far more need of a blanket than I," she replied, to which he responded with a bashful smile.

"Yes, ma'am, I beg your pardon. I didn't mean to drip on you. I'll just go get your tea. Two lumps and splash of milk, is that right, ma'am?"

Phyllida paused, surprised that he should be aware of her preference. "Why, yes, thank you, Elton. Do you know where Mrs. Agatha and her guests have gone?"

More important than drying her shoes and sipping a warm brew was ensuring the Detection Club was comfortable and their needs were seen to.

At least she wouldn't need to worry about the press invading the rectory; Elton, Stanley, and the other servants had been given strict orders that no one but the Mallowans and their guests should be allowed in the rectory should it rain. That included the Murder Club members.

"I'll show you, ma'am," he said. "But should I get your tea first?"

"Yes, that would be appreciated." Phyllida changed her shoes into the second pair she'd brought along for such a circumstance, and by the time she finished, Elton had returned with her tea. Along with it was a biscuit on a small plate.

"I noticed you didn't get to finish your pasty, ma'am," he said with a definite blush, "so I brought that as well."

Slightly amused, but touched by his thoughtfulness, Phyllida walked with him down the hall.

She could hear voices and realized the Detection Club was in the same room where Inspector Cork had interviewed the Murder Club members last night. She approved, for it was the most comfortable room she'd seen in the building.

After quickly downing her tea, Phyllida broke off a piece of the biscuit to sample, then gave the rest of it and her cup to Elton with the instructions to return it to the kitchen and to send Molly back with more tea service. Then she went into the sitting room to evaluate the situation.

"Oh, there you are, Mrs. Bright," said Agatha when she caught sight of Phyllida.

Phyllida smiled at her but didn't reply. Someone had stoked up a fire in the room, and the damp writers had pulled up their chairs around the welcome blaze.

They were, of course, talking about murder.

"The question is always motive," Mr. Chesterton was saying in a manner that suggested he'd been holding forth for some time. He was waving his pince-nez for emphasis. "When my little Father Brown solves a case, he puts himself inside the head of every suspect and imagines how he or she would create evil, and why. As a priest and confessor, he hears the most vile, base, and evil stories, and thus he is not as sheltered as one might think. Nothing could be too surprising or too unbelievable for him—"

"Yes, yes, G. K., we know all about Father Brown. He's truly delightful. But he's fictional," said Mr. Berkeley, somehow still appearing suave and smooth despite the rush to come in from out of the rain. He held a cigarette between two long fingers. "And we have a very *un*fictional situation here. We ought to have our own Crime Club and attempt to solve this mystery."

"As in your *Poisoned Chocolates* book?" said Agatha. "Which I did enjoy quite a lot, Anthony—it was very clever—but I don't really think—"

"But I do, Agatha! After all, we were in the unique position of being *witnesses* to the murder," Mr. Berkeley went on. "When would such an opportunity present itself again? Hopefully never," he added quickly.

Phyllida listened to the ensuing discussion—which included Agatha demurring such a notion, whilst her colleagues seized on it. She exchanged glances with her employer as she made the rounds silently refilling teacups and offering the plate of biscuits Molly had delivered.

"What that inspector needs to do is take the fingerprints of everyone who was here last night," said Miss Sayers firmly. "And *I* didn't see him with a magnifying glass—what about you, Agatha?"

"He certainly doesn't seem quite interested in crawling about on the ground looking for clues," murmured Agatha, giving Phyllida a glance.

"I told the inspector not to waste his time interviewing us," said Mr. Berkeley on an exhale from his cigarette. "Obviously, none of *us* would have done such a thing."

"Certainly *not*," said Mr. Chesterton, who'd settled his pince-nez back into place.

"But I suppose one of us might have noticed something important," Agatha said quietly.

"But I wasn't paying any attention to much of anything, Agatha," said Miss Sayers. "I certainly didn't expect an actual *murder*, and I was discussing the difficulty of realistic characterization most of the evening, and then we went on to talking about plot twists. I don't believe I would be quite a good witness after all. Still . . . if I *had* seen anything, of course I would tell the inspector. The first thing he must do is interview all of the suspects—which I should hope he has already done. Then one must determine who is lying, because someone is. Someone *always* lies."

"Mrs. Bright has solved a murder," said Agatha, startling Phyllida so that she nearly splashed a bit of the tea she was pouring for Mr. Max. "Two of them in fact."

All four of the writers looked at her, and Phyllida saw the flash of a grin on Mr. Max's face.

"Indeed?" said Miss Sayers, her eyes lighting up. "I did attempt to help solve a murder once—you know, the Edith Thompson case—and I simply couldn't make any sense of things. It's far different looking for clues off the page than on it, you know." She gave Mr. Berkeley a pointed look.

"That's why I've asked her to investigate," said Agatha. "I'm simply hopeless at divining clues for real murders. I prefer to create the ones I need."

"Don't we all," replied Miss Sayers with a laugh.

"Phyllida's very clever," Agatha went on. "And I've asked her to solve this one. Do tell us what you've learned so far, will you, Phyllida?" In her enthusiasm, Agatha had used her familiar name, but Phyllida didn't mind. "And do sit down. I can see that your dress is wet from the rain—but how on earth did you keep your shoes dry?"

After taking a seat, Phyllida explained about her extra pair, and although she at first demurred about sitting, Mr. Max took the decision from her when he placed a chair next to the fire and said, "Sit, please, Mrs. Bright. We are all friends here, and of course we want to hear what you've learned."

Phyllida explained about the second bottle of bitters, which was, of course, a prime clue. "But the most startling development happened this morning," she went on. "When a dead cat was discovered and a table went missing."

Her audience listened with rapt attention as she told them about poor Saint Aloysius, the presumably poisoned cake, and the missing piecrust table.

"All of this has led me to the conclusion that someone wanted Father Tooley dead before the cocktail party last night," Phyllida concluded.

"In order to steal a piecrust table during—or after—the party?" said Miss Sayers doubtfully.

"And when he didn't die, the murderer decided to poison him *again*, but with a faster-working poison," said Mr. Berkeley, gesturing with his cigarette. "That's quite, quite clever. An excellent plot twist, I must admit."

"I think not," Phyllida said, not the least bit concerned about correcting the man in front of his peers. "Whoever poisoned the cocktail had to have planned it in advance in order to have procured the bitters."

"And why would someone want to kill a priest?" asked Mr. Chesterton. He had removed his pince-nez once again and fixed on her with his steady dark eyes. He was an intimidating figure, but Phyllida was not intimidated. "One would have to be very evil to want to off a man of the cloth."

"I don't have the answer to that yet," she said. "Father Tooley was calculating the results of the Murder Fête Short Story Contest, was he not? Unless he presented them to one of you before he died, whatever the results were we shan't know. For they are missing, and so are the score sheets." She looked around at them, but each shook his or her head. "As I suspected. The only other place remaining to look is on Father Tooley's person, to see whether he had them in his possession last night at the party."

"I suppose we'd best discuss and pool our scoring of the stories, then," said Mr. Chesterton. "So that we can determine who the winner is to be."

"But that's quite impossible, for Hugh and Freeman mailed their choices to me at Mallowan Hall," Agatha said. "I didn't open their envelopes, of course, but I gave them to Father Tooley."

"You should telephone to them and find out what they wrote," said Mr. Max, settling a gentle hand on her arm.

"Yes, of course. I can do that," replied Agatha in a relieved tone. "That would be simple to do."

Phyllida was about to speak when she noticed a flurry of agitated movement just outside the door. "If you'll excuse me for a moment," she said, rising from her chair. "It appears I'm needed."

She walked briskly out of the room and found Molly, Elton, Stanley, and Rita clustered in the corridor, clearly upset about something and arguing with one another as to whether or not they should interrupt her.

"Oh, Mrs. Bright!" cried Molly at a volume that required Phyllida to shush her whilst prodding her out of sight and hearing from those inside the sitting room.

"What is it?" Phyllida said when they were at a distance.

"It's Mr. Dobble—he's, well, he's quite . . . not himself. I—I think you ought to talk to him," Molly said in a slightly less agitated voice.

"Has something happened?" Phyllida asked.

"Yes, ma'am, although I don't understand why Mr. Dobble is— well, he's—well, you'll see," Stanley said. "Would you come with us, Mrs. Bright?"

Of course she would come with them, she replied, and rather grateful to no longer have to sit and talk over yet again the details of her fledgling investigation, Phyllida hurried along with her staff.

She found Mr. Dobble in the rectory kitchen, sitting in much the same way he'd been this morning when she found him in his pantry: looking into the distance at nothing. A cup of coffee—not tea—sat next to him, which also indicated something greatly amiss.

"All right, off with you," Phyllida said to the others. "I'm certain there's work to be done—see to the stragglers in the church. Perhaps the rain will stop in short order and we can resume the festival."

Having thus cleared the others out of the kitchen, Phyllida took a seat across from Mr. Dobble.

"What's happened?" she asked, although she had a niggling suspicion she already knew.

He started and looked up at her, his expression shifting from surprise to irritation to glumness. "The inspector has arrested Mr. Billdop for the murder of Father Tooley and the attempted murder of Alastair Whittlesby."

CHAPTER 11

*P*HYLLIDA WAS FULLY AWARE OF THE CLOSE FRIENDSHIP BETWEEN Mr. Dobble and Mr. Billdop. She'd suspected for some time that it might be something more than mere chess-playing on a weekly basis, and Mr. Dobble's reaction certainly supported such a possibility.

Having been on the front lines with the troops—terrified and lonely men who'd done whatever they had to do to survive, remain sane, and find love and affection during the horrors of war—Phyllida had seen and experienced many things that would have appalled or scandalized her prim and proper Victorian ancestors. However, she herself had always lived by the tenet that what happened privately between two individuals was their business, as long as no one was hurt or injured.

With this knowledge and experience weighing upon her, along with her collaboration and association with Mr. Dobble, she chose her approach carefully. "Inspector Cork is wrong, of course. The vicar is not the least bit capable of doing such a thing. Surely you agree."

Mr. Dobble shrugged, and that concerned Phyllida even more than his morose, vacant expression. A shrug coming from such a staid, stiff, *unbending* person seemed like a dismissal, a surrender.

"*Harvey,*" she said, doing the impermissible and using his given name in an effort to yank him from his stupor, "surely you don't believe it."

As she had intended, the butler's attention snapped to her. "That is quite impertinent of you, Mrs. Bright."

She merely smiled at him, albeit a little sadly. "Mr. Dobble, put yourself at ease. Mrs. Agatha has asked me to investigate the situation, and I have everything well in hand."

There was a flash of Dobble's characteristic superciliousness in his eyes, and then it faded. He frowned. "There was a cake—a white sponge—at Digby's house yesterday. It's gone now. And they found strawberry jam there at the vicarage, also mostly gone from the jar. And there was a nearly empty box of arsenic . . ."

Phyllida took in this information calmly. "Every household in Listleigh—likely in England—has strawberry jam. As well as arsenic for the rats! And might I remind you that vanilla sponge is a baked-goods mainstay."

"He didn't offer me a piece of cake," Dobble went on steadily, still looking down at the table. "When I saw him yesterday morning. We *always* have a sweet with our tea, and he *always* offers me anything his housekeeper has baked."

"I see," Phyllida replied, remaining unconvinced. "And because of that, you believe Digby Billdop is guilty?"

Dobble shook his head and lifted his eyes. His gaze fastened on Phyllida with an intent, desperate look she'd never previously witnessed on the reserved butler. "He loathes Alastair Whittlesby. He told me yesterday he wished something would happen to the man. I . . . I don't know what to think."

"Why would he kill Father Tooley?" Phyllida asked. "Surely the competition between the Catholic parish and the Anglican one isn't *that* lethal." Her comment was meant mainly as a jest, although it was, in fact, true that the competition *was* rather heated.

"Digby was quite upset that St. Thurston's wasn't chosen as the charity for the Murder Fête. He said the only reason St. Wendreda's was chosen was because it has its own orphanage."

"That was precisely the point of the charitable event," Phyllida pointed out. "To raise money for the orphanage's new roof."

"Quite so," said Dobble, who looked even more miserable. "I

don't believe it of him. I truly don't . . . but he's in jail, and he has such a delicate composition. His nerves will be simply *frayed*, and what will his *flock* think? The bishop will surely remove him even if he's released. . . ."

Ah. Now Phyllida fully understood Mr. Dobble's fears. It wasn't so much fear that Mr. Billdop had murdered someone—he clearly didn't truly believe that—it was the fear that the vicar's life would be destroyed and, even worse, he would be removed from Listleigh.

"Then we will just have to ensure that doesn't happen. Come now, Mr. Dobble, you must admit that the situation is in the most capable of hands. *Mine.*" Phyllida stood. "I shall have to have a conversation with Inspector Cork about this and insist he release Mr. Billdop. In the meanwhile, I believe it would be prudent to discover who else had cakes in their possession, and from where or how the second bottle of Monteleone's Special Bitters was obtained. I believe once we determine that, we will have identified our murderer."

"Digby was certain Mr. Whittlesby was going to win the contest," Mr. Dobble went on, likely unaware that he was referring to the vicar by his familiar name. "Everyone was."

"I've been unable to find any evidence of the scoring sheets or calculations by Father Tooley," she told him. "It seems to be missing."

"What could that mean?"

"It means that someone didn't want the winner to be made public, of course," Phyllida told him. "Everyone is so very certain it is Alastair Whittlesby. Perhaps it isn't. Or perhaps it is. But that's another thing I'm determined to find out. But first, I must speak with Inspector Cork."

It didn't take long for Phyllida to learn that the inspector had left St. Wendreda's to take Mr. Billdop to the small jail in the village, and so she decided to confront him there at the constable's office.

It was still raining, however, and her umbrella was not going to keep her dry shoes dry. She loathed having cold, wet feet. She stood at the entrance to the rectory, frowning at the streams of water ruining her plans.

"Going somewhere, Mrs. Bright?" said a deep voice behind her.

"I should very much appreciate a ride to the constable's office," she told Bradford, for once grateful to see him. "It's a bit wet out there."

"Of course," he replied with only a hint of the ironic tone she'd become used to—and without demanding why she wanted to go to the police station. "I'll bring the Daimler up to the entrance. Wait here."

As she waited, Phyllida caught sight of Molly, who was talking to a young woman Phyllida didn't recognize but suspected was another servant. Generally, servants knew servants and limited their interactions to others of their working class. Phyllida, of course, considered herself an exception to this generality.

She walked over to Molly and the other young woman. Servants were incredible gossips, and, of course, they knew everything that went on in their houses.

Pursuant to that, Phyllida knew it was no secret among the servants of Listleigh how "that Mrs. Bright up to Mallowan Hall" had not only uncovered the killer who'd murdered one of their own and cleared a servant from suspicion at the same time but had also managed to concurrently run her household *without* being a tyrant to her staff. Since those events, she'd become something of a legend in the local downstairs community—a fact that she would now use to her advantage.

Sherlock Holmes had his cadre of informants in the form of street urchins, and Phyllida Bright had hers, garbed in aprons, caps, and livery.

Pulling Molly aside, Phyllida explained what she wanted her to do. She concluded, "Do you understand? I want to know about several different things in particular: cake, strawberry jam, walnuts, geraniums, and the bottle of bitters." She didn't bother to ask about the piecrust table; it was obvious who had taken it—but traces of geranium would confirm that as well. "And any other relevant bits of information—anything that seemed odd or interesting or off—in their households over the last few days."

"Yes, ma'am," replied the maid, a light of excitement in her dark eyes. "I'll find out *everything* for you, Mrs. Bright."

"Thank you," Phyllida replied, just as she saw the Mallowans' Daimler pull up in front of the rectory.

"Ever since you helped Elton, you know, all of us in service— why, we would do anything to help you," Molly went on earnestly. "Not only at Mallowan Hall, Mrs. Bright," she said. "All of us in the village. Every one of us remembers poor Rebecca, too, and how you found out the man who did her in." Her eyes grew a little fierce here. "Lots of people wouldn't care because she was just a kitchen maid."

"Yes, yes, that's very kind," replied Phyllida, feeling a bit of a stinging in her eyes. Impatient with such emotion, she blinked it away and took her leave before Molly could say any more.

Moments later, she was climbing into the Daimler with the help of Bradford, who held the umbrella over her from rectory door to motorcar door. She was relieved that he remained silent as they wheeled down the street, rain rattling on the metal hood and roof of the vehicle.

However, when they arrived at the police station, Bradford not only covered her with the umbrella from door to door but also accompanied her all the way inside.

Phyllida resisted the urge to comment; instead, she merely ignored him.

"Mrs. Bright," said the inspector wearily. "What can I do for you?"

"I'm here about Mr. Billdop," she said without preamble. "You've made a mistake, and a man's life and livelihood are at stake. I suggest you release him posthaste before word gets out about it."

"Of course I'm not going to release him," replied Cork testily.

"What evidence do you have to hold him?" Phyllida fired back. "A cake? A pot of jam?" She scoffed and speared the inspector with her most severe expression. "I'd be quite surprised if you didn't have a pot of strawberry jam in *your* kitchen. And no one would believe that Mr. Billdop *baked himself a cake* so he could add poison to it. The very idea is absurd. That man hasn't the first idea about turning on a stove, let alone *baking* anything. And everyone has arsenic for rats."

The detective seemed a bit taken aback by her ferocity, but he did stand his ground. "Oi now, Mrs. Bright, I realize you fancy yourself a crime-solver, but you ain't got all of the information. Turns out the arsenic was in the strawberry jam on top of the cake, and in the frosting on the sides—looked like sugar crystals—so *anyone* could have spread it on there. They didn't have to bake the cake themselves."

This bit of fascinating information silenced Phyllida for the mere breath of a second before she regrouped and went on. "That is correct. *Anyone* could have done so. Have you determined from whence the cake at Father Tooley's had come?"

"Not yet," he admitted. "But—"

Before he could go on, she parried and thrust once more. "Inspector Cork, Mr. Billdop is a man of the cloth. He is meant to save souls, not to release them. If word of his arrest—which I must add has the flimsiest of evidence behind it—gets to his flock, it will ruin him as their vicar. Not to mention that the bishop will likely remove him, and then what will happen to the people at St. Thurston's without their good shepherd?" She knew she was laying it on a bit thick—and the soft jeering sound from Bradford supported this belief—but the hesitancy was growing in Inspector Cork's eyes, and she wasn't about to stand down. "Perhaps you acted a bit hastily and only needed to question Mr. Billdop about what he might have seen and heard relative to the events of yesterday, hmm?"

She kept her eyes pinned on him until, like every little boy of her acquaintance (and a significant number of grown ones), he squirmed under her unrelenting stare. She continued to advance. "If you release him now, there will be no harm done, Inspector. His reputation will be protected—and if it does unfold that Mr. Billdop is a murderous thug," she said, "I shan't stand in your way."

"Right, right, all right then, Mrs. Bright," Inspector Cork said.

"I suppose you've got a point there—but he was acting suspiciously, and everyone wanted the culprit to be caught so the bloody—er—ahem—so the, erm, Murder Fête could go on. Now we still got a murderer going on about, and everyone's gonna be all nervous about it."

"I'm quite convinced that even with Mr. Billdop in custody there is still a murderer walking about freely," she said firmly. "And rest assured, I shall be the first to admit my error should it become clear that he is the perpetrator." Once again, she ignored the mocking sound from behind her, for something the detective had said made her pause and look at him shrewdly. "Inspector, you seem particularly pleased that the Murder Fête is able to go on now that a suspect—however erroneously—might be in custody." And then she remembered how easy it had been for Inspector Cork to be convinced that the fête should not be canceled despite a murder . . . and how quickly the Scotland Yard investigator had appeared on the scene last night. "I'm certain you're wanting to return to the festival's activities as soon as possible, aren't you, Inspector?"

She ignored the quiet, surprised cough from Bradford and merely smiled at Cork when his eyes widened. An actual tinge of pink swarmed over his cheeks beneath the freckles that had so put her off.

"It was a shame the rain had to interrupt it," Phyllida went on.

"Oh, er, yes," said Cork. "Now, I suppose you've finished what you've come here for?"

Phyllida repressed the urge to correct his grammar and instead elected to answer his question. "There is only one thing remaining—I wish to see Father Tooley."

Bradford wasn't quite as circumspect with his reaction this time; she heard a definitely loud and scornful snort. As always, however, she readily ignored him.

"Erm . . . um . . . ma'am," stammered Cork, clearly still feeling the effects of her previous staredown. "I don't think that's quite . . ."

"More specifically," she went on, "I wish to see his personal effects. There is a document that has gone missing, and I mean to ensure that it wasn't tucked into his coat."

"I see," replied Cork. "Well, that might be more permissible . . . *if* it were appropriate for us to release his belongings into your custody."

"Of course it's appropriate," Phyllida told him. "I've taken the rectory's maid, Rita, under my wing, and as she is in my care, and Father Tooley's possessions would likely be sent back to the rectory, it's quite obvious that no one will quibble if you allow *me* to be the one to conduct those effects back to his most recent residence."

Even Phyllida wasn't quite convinced of the merits of her convoluted argument, but she didn't reveal even a chink in her armor. Instead, she waited for Inspector Cork to capitulate.

After all, the rain had nearly stopped, which meant the festival could start up again at any moment. He must be chafing at the delay. She wondered if he had been waiting in line for a book from Agatha or for someone else.

"I suppose that would be all right," said the detective. "Weren't naught of importance anyway."

"I shall be the judge of that," she informed him, and this time when Bradford snorted behind her, she accidentally-on-purpose stepped backward and trod heavily on his boot. The resulting "oof" indicated she'd won that battle, at least. "Now, perhaps you could attend to releasing Mr. Billdop whilst I look over Father Tooley's effects. We've contacted the bishop to find out his next of kin."

The priest's clothing was in a small office in the back of the constable's building. It took only a few moments for Phyllida to search through Father Tooley's pockets. They were empty of everything but a rosary and a small stole, which she suspected the priest would wear if he was required to unexpectedly perform any sort of last rites, just as Mr. Billdop had done for him.

"No sign of the story contest results," she said to Bradford, who'd hovered in the doorway as she ducked her hands in and out of the priest's pockets. "Perhaps we should check the waste can in his office again—unless you noticed something in there."

"I wasn't looking for score sheets or notes about the contest," he replied, "but the only items in the waste can were remnants of the cake box and a few crumpled papers."

"I shall uncrumple those papers," Phyllida said decisively, "and look through every other waste can in the rectory." Then a thought occurred to her and she pushed past Bradford, hurrying to accost Inspector Cork before he left the constable's office.

"What is it now, Mrs. Bright? Did you find what you were looking for?" The inspector's hand was on the door's latch and he definitely rolled his eyes.

"I did not. But I would like to know whether the testing on the bitters is complete, and whether there are any results from Father Tooley's body. Did he die from arsenic poisoning or nicotine poisoning? And what about the cat? And might I compliment you on your efficiency—it was an excellent notion to use Dr. Bhatt's laboratory." Phyllida was always of the mind that positive reinforcement and compliments should be given whenever appropriate.

"Why thank you, Mrs. Bright," replied the inspector in a tone that did not sound the least bit complimented. "I'm relieved you approve. However, I have no intention of giving you that information. Confidential police business, not for civilians."

She pursed her lips. "Inspector, you know that I will find some way to acquire it. In the interest of efficiency and simplicity, you might just go ahead and tell me."

"I might, but I won't, Mrs. Bright," he said, and then, to her dismay, he opened the door and slipped out onto the street, leaving her frowning after him.

Bradford obviously found it all quite amusing, for his lips were twitching when she turned to him. "Well," she said, "don't *you* want to know as well?"

"I'm not investigating the case," he replied. "I'm just the driver."

She pursed her lips and made no immediate reply. How *would* she get that information? "It's not necessary, I suppose," she replied. "We already know there was nicotine in the bitters—

there's no other explanation for such a strong tobacco smell—
and Cork did let slip that there was arsenic in the cake. In the jam
and in the frosting. Quite ingenious, really, and yet it broadens
the realm of suspects—as I indicated to the inspector, the vicar
wasn't about to bake his own cake and add poison to it—nor was
Mrs. Rollingbroke or Mr. Genevan."

"Or Dr. Bhatt," said Bradford. "Unless their housekeepers or
cooks made it for them."

"Correct," she said. "But I *would* like to know whether Father
Tooley expired from arsenic or nicotine."

"It was arsenic," Bradford replied as he opened the door for
her to precede him out onto the street.

She stepped outside. The rain had stopped, and the fresh,
damp air also held a tinge of floral. "How do you know so much
about arsenic? You seem positively obsessed with it."

He shook his head, smirking a little. "I wondered when you'd
get around to demanding that information. You're so bloody
nosy, Mrs. Bright. I think I'll let you stew over that for a while."

But the smile playing about his mouth didn't reach his eyes.

As Harriet Puffley approached the hill at Tangled Vines Cottage, she considered whether to attempt to force her bicycle to as-
cend by pumping the pedals whilst astride, or whether she ought
to simply climb off and wheel it up. The road was wet from the
short but heavy rain that had swept through the village and its environs, and she already had a good splatter of mud up the back-
side of her coat.

It was a rather steep hill, but she was a strong, muscular woman
who was used to cycling about the village on her day off, not to
mention what she did in the kitchen. Kneading dough and playing butcher weren't for the weak and slight. Still, she didn't want
to arrive at the Whittlesbys' kitchen to visit with Mrs. Dilly dripping with perspiration—although any cook worth her salt grinder
was quite familiar with sweat trickling down one's cheeks and
back. And it was more likely the tires would slip in the muddy
ground, possibly causing a spill.

Thus, she elected to climb off and push the bicycle, reasoning also that it was more likely the basket she'd filled with fresh and fragrant rosemary popovers would remain intact.

It was too bad Bradford and his darling puppy hadn't been available to drive her; such a proposition would have taken much less time than cycling and would have been far more agreeable.

She always enjoyed her conversations with Bradford, filled as they were with discussions about her latest recipe, how he most recently repaired a tricky engine problem, and stories of her previous life in Cornwall, raising her daughter and managing Mr. Puffley. She could have snuggled little Myrtle in her lap whilst he drove, for Mrs. Bright was severe in her rule that the puppy was not allowed into the house—despite Peter's freedom to go where he chose—and as Mrs. Puffley rarely left the kitchen, she had far less opportunity than she liked to cuddle the soft and fluffy canine, who was utterly the sweetest dog she'd ever met.

Mrs. Puffley sensed that Mrs. Bright's banishment of Myrtle was more due to her dislike of Bradford than the actual dog herself, although, she allowed, it was likely a close thing. Mrs. Puffley had no idea why the housekeeper was so put off by the chauffeur. The man was polite and interesting, and he always complimented her on whatever she served him at the table. Even if it were just the heel of a loaf of bread and a hunk of cheddar, he was grateful and unassuming.

Not that Mrs. Bright didn't properly compliment her work in the kitchen. She certainly did—for if she didn't, Mrs. Puffley would have been looking for a new position, as Harriet Puffley was fully aware of her worth.

Had there ever been a delayed meal—except on the occasion of murder, which, of course, she had no control over—or a disastrous course? Had there ever been an accident created by one of her maids that she hadn't been able to put right—most of the time without Mrs. Bright even knowing? Had there ever been waste in the kitchen or supplies gone missing or a menu not be perfectly suitable for event or guests?

Of course not.

Still, the way Mrs. Bright lifted her chin and spoke in a lofty manner whenever she encountered Bradford puzzled Mrs. Puffley. She simply couldn't understand why Mrs. Bright didn't set her cap for the man. He was civil and intelligent and, if not precisely handsome, he was, at least, deliciously broad-shouldered and muscular, though a bit dark for Mrs. Puffley's personal taste. Though he would be a bit much to manage, she allowed, in the way of husbanding. Certainly not as easy as her dear Mr. Puffley had been.

Still, if she *were* in the market for another husband—albeit a challenging one—and was as nicely turned-out as Mrs. Bright always was (perspiration and flushed cheeks weren't permitted for the likes of Phyllida Bright), Harriet Puffley might be doing a good amount of extra cooking in order to capture Bradford's attention—just as she had done for Mr. Puffley, long before he realized he would be marrying her. He'd been the type to tinker around about engines and motors, too. Perhaps that was why she liked Joshua Bradford so much; in some ways he did remind her of Mr. Puffley.

Come to think of it, Mrs. Bright never did talk about her own husband. If there even had been one.

All housekeepers took on the honorific Mrs. whether or not they had been a bride, so it was impossible to know for certain. Perhaps that was why Mrs. Bright didn't seem interested in Bradford—it was possible Mr. Bright was still a factor in her life. Although, Mrs. Bright *had* been dining at the café with that nice Dr. Bhatt several times over the last few months, so it would seem she was open to at least some male attentions. Mrs. Puffley did not think for one moment that Dr. Bhatt was merely looking for a dining companion.

As efficient and capable as she was, and as pleasant and reasonable as she acted, Mrs. Bright was still rather a mystery to Mrs. Puffley. Even though they'd been working together at Mallowan Hall for three years, they were cordial colleagues, but not what one would call friends. Of course, Mrs. Bright was one of the upper servants, and they normally didn't fraternize much with the lower servants. But she'd never given the impression to Mrs. Puffley that she thought herself above her—certainly not. The woman simply kept her own counsel regarding her past—although Mrs. Bright certainly did not keep her opinions to herself about anything *other* than her past, Mrs. Puffley thought with a short laugh. She was fairly certain Mrs. Bright was younger than her own forty-five years, and had somehow landed the coveted position as housekeeper at a relatively young age.

Propelled by these ruminations, Mrs. Puffley had by now reached the top of the hill. She pushed her bicycle past the BMW sedan parked in the drive, eyeing it with appreciation, for Mr. Puffley's love of automobiles had rubbed off on her.

Moments later she was knocking at the back door.

"Why, Harriet! What a nice surprise!" cried Mrs. Dilly, wiping off her flour-dusted hands with her apron. "I daresay I have a suspicion why you've come by this afternoon," she added in a lower voice, looking about conspiratorially.

"Not at all, Betty," said Mrs. Puffley, giving her a sly wink as she offered the basket. "It's only that I've been forever promising to bring over some of my rosemary popovers, and with Mrs. Bright and Mr. Dobble and half the staff away at the Murder Fête, I was able to slip away for a bit this afternoon. Good fortune I waited until after the rain shower." She'd also had to sit in the kitchen and visit with Constable Greensticks for a time this morning—*he* certainly had enjoyed the rosemary popovers—but that hadn't been as much of a hardship as one might expect. The man clearly needed a wife, or at least a decent day maid who could cook, for he acted as if he'd not been properly fed in weeks. Still, he'd been polite and very complimentary over her cooking.

"Oh, yes, you have been teasing me with those popovers for months now," said Mrs. Dilly—fully aware that until this very moment the subject of rosemary popovers had never crossed either set of the cooks' lips. "My! They do smell delicious," she said, pausing a moment to lift the napkin and stick her nose into the basket. "Even after a long cycle ride!" They took another few moments for professional discussion—how long the pastries had been baked, whether the butter was chilled or soft when used, how finely chopped the rosemary had been.

"I add a bit of rosemary oil to the batter along with the fresh herb needles," Mrs. Puffley said, confiding one of her most treasured secrets. She decided it was worth it, considering the information she hoped to extract today. "It's what makes the scent just strong enough without being too bold and brassy."

"Why, that's so very clever," said Mrs. Dilly. "I suppose Mrs. Bright infuses the oil?"

"Land's! She doesn't actually *do* it herself, of course, but she supervises Molly and Opal to do it. First house I've been at that has its own distilling room, and I must say, you couldn't get me to a house without one now't I've had it. It's a pleasure to have all that sort of stuff made right there next to my kitchen."

Mrs. Dilly's expression sank. "At least someone is happy at their post." She sighed. "Have a seat, Harriet. I should be happy for an excuse to get off me feet for a bit. Mr. Drewson won't mind. He's probably hiding in his pantry wishing he could have a drink."

Mrs. Puffley chuckled, unsure how serious her friend was about the Whittlesbys' butler. "It's been quite upsetting here, I'm certain," she said. "Having your master nearly poisoned."

"And mistress! Why, Mrs. Alastair had her husband's drink in her hand last night. She could have—probably would have—had a taste if Father Tooley hadn't bought it at that moment." Mrs. Dilly tsked and shook her head.

"So that's three people who might have died instead of just the one," Mrs. Puffley said. "Good heavens."

"Makes a body wonder about whether I should check me own food before I eat it," said Mrs. Dilly. "Or before I send it upstairs," she added glumly, speaking figuratively since the kitchen was on the same floor as the dining room in this particular house. "They—the poisoner—tries again, next thing you know, I'll be blamed for it."

"It's a right horror it is," said Mrs. Puffley, nodding companionably. "Being the cook. Anyone gets a bit of a tummy ache and who gets blamed? The cook. Don't matter if we eat all the same food, it's all 'our cook's tainted things,' and there's hardly a way around it if they start to give you the dirty eye. Not that I've had any of *that* sort of experience."

"Oh, here she comes now," said Mrs. Dilly, tilting as if to listen to the sound of feet coming down the stairs from somewhere in the house. "That's Mrs. Alastair. She's already had two vodkas, and no breakfast." She shook her head.

"Dear me," said Mrs. Puffley, her brows lifting. "Has she always been such a sot?"

"Not at all. It's only recent—at least that it's become obvious."

"Well, why do you think she started drinking so?"

Mrs. Dilly shook her head. "I don't know. It's not as if things seem that bad between her and Mr. Alastair. They don't row or anything like that. I mean to say, he talks to her the same way he talks to everyone—short and sharp and like he always knows best about everything."

"I knew a man like that once," Mrs. Puffley said grimly, but, taking a page from Mrs. Bright's book, chose not to give any further details about his outcome. "Who do you think could be trying to do away with Mr. Alastair, then? Could it be his brother?"

Mrs. Dilly shook her head again. "Do you think I know anything? Oh, that's him now coming down, too. Mr. Eugene. Mr. Alastair has already gone into the village."

She paused and Mrs. Puffley could hear the sounds of male and female voices. She couldn't make out what they were saying, but it sounded cordial, if brief and to the point.

Moments later, Drewson came into the kitchen. "Mrs. Alastair wants her tea right away in the breakfast room, and then she is leaving to join Mr. Alastair at the Murder Fête. She's none too pleased he left her the sedan, might I add. And the old dragon"—his eyes rolled up to indicate the invalid upstairs—"is complaining that her hard-boiled egg was too hard-boiled."

Mrs. Dilly muttered under her breath but rose from her seat. "Give her this one," she said, placing an egg in its cup. "I boilt it twenty seconds less than the other," she said, looking at Mrs. Puffley. "I make several each morning, as it depends what *mood* Herself is in as to how hard she wants her egg boilt."

"It's always a good policy to have other options," replied Mrs. Puffley, thinking of Mr. Dobble and his ridiculous requirement that boiled eggs be turned often whilst cooking so the yolks ended up in the middle instead of at one end. "But it seems as if old Mrs. Whittlesby would have more important things on her mind than her boiled eggs. After all, her son was nearly poisoned."

"I don't suppose old Mrs. Whittlesby has much cared about anyone else but herself in the last five years, since she became an invalid. And probably before," said Drewson.

"I suppose she wants new toast, too," said Mrs. Dilly.

"Of course she does," replied Drewson.

"Where's Louella?" asked Mrs. Dilly.

"Lacquering the old dragon's nails," replied Drewson.

"Then how the bloody hell is she going to eat a boilt egg?" muttered Mrs. Dilly.

"How should I know? I'm only the bloody butler," replied Drewson. "God, I wish I had a drink."

"Better get it whilst you can before Mrs. Alastair dries up the bar," said Mrs. Dilly dryly.

"Speaking of the bar," Mrs. Puffley interjected. "Do you have any idea who might have tried to poison Mr. Whittlesby last night, Mr. Drewson?"

"Oh, I have many ideas," he said. "Many of them. If only whoever it was had succeeded."

"Good heavens, Mr. Drewson, someone might hear you!" said Mrs. Puffley.

"Then perhaps they'd fire me. One can only hope. Do you have any idea how miserable it is working in this house?" he said. "The entire family is uncivil and arrogant. Thinks they're better than they are. Especially the old dragon. The only reason I stay is because they pay well. But even that might not be enough. I suppose Mr. Dobble is quite settled at Mallowan Hall?"

Mrs. Puffley shook her head. She really did have it quite good at Mallowan Hall—not that she'd ever tell Mrs. Bright about that. It would never do to have one's boss get too comfortable that you were there for the long haul, now, did it?

"Oh, Mr. Dobble isn't about to leave Mrs. Agatha," said Mrs.

Puffley, before turning the conversation back to where it should be. "Surely it had to be one of the murder writers who tried to do away with your master."

"He and Mrs. Rollingbroke did have a bit of a testy exchange on the telephone a while back," said Mr. Drewson. "I only heard one side of the conversation, but he was quite annoyed and it sounded as if he were threatening her."

"Threatening her?" Mrs. Puffley leaned forward. "Do you mean he was threatening to kill her?"

"No, no, not like that—though the man is always talking about how to kill people, isn't he?" Mr. Drewson looked at Mrs. Dilly for affirmation, and she nodded earnestly. "Takes his writing awfully seriously. Don't let anyone look at his notes or pages till they're done, though, and he keeps 'em in a locked drawer. A *locked* drawer! It's not as if it's some sort of treasure map or stock certificate or even that it's worth anything but the paper it's typed on!"

"What did you hear in the conversation with Mr. Alastair and Mrs. Rollingbroke?"

"The only thing that struck me was when Mr. Alastair said, 'I'm sure Sir Rolly would want to know all about *that*,' or something of that nature. It was the look on his face when he said it—sent a shiver up my spine it did. Shortly after that, Mr. and Mrs. Alastair received an invitation to a soiree at the Rollingbrokes'."

"Good heavens," said Mrs. Puffley. "That certainly sounds like a threat to me! I wonder what he was talking about."

"I haven't any idea. Of course, Mr. Alastair, being a solicitor, must know a lot of secrets about a lot of people," said Drewson, nodding knowingly.

"Quite so," replied Mrs. Puffley, turning that over in her mind. She was suddenly grateful she'd never had occasion to speak to a solicitor here in Listleigh.

She was just about to ask another question when they heard the roar of the motorcar starting up outside. She glanced out and noticed that Mr. Eugene and Mrs. Alastair were in the sedan.

"Mrs. Alastair is driving her husband's estranged brother?" Mrs. Puffley said as the vehicle started down the hill.

"Mr. Alastair refuses to allow Mr. Eugene to drive either of their motorcars, so he has to get a ride when he can," said Drewson.

Mrs. Puffley's eyes narrowed. "Does Mrs. Alastair drive him very often?"

"Most often Mr. Eugene takes his bicycle, but if she is going to the village, she will drive him on occasion. She spends most of her days at home in her sitting room, and when he's not in London, Mr. Eugene is usually out and about around here. He works for a film company, finding locations for them to film and also antiques and furniture to be used on the—what's it called? Oh, yes, the *set*. The stage where they film. He's a . . . what is it? Oh, yes, a set dresser. Sounds rather raunchy to me," Drewson said with a chuckle.

Mrs. Puffley's interest waned. It certainly didn't *sound* as if Mrs. Alastair and Mr. Eugene were having an affair. But it was worth passing that bit of information on to Mrs. Bright.

Just then, off in the distance, there was a sudden, ugly sound . . . like a crash or a great thud.

"What on earth . . . ?"

They hesitated, then the three of them hurried outside, shortly joined by a young woman who Mrs. Puffley identified as the maid Louella.

Drewson stood in the drive, looking down the hill and its winding road. "Sounded like it came from that way," he said, hands on his hips.

"Maybe she hit a tree," said Louella grimly. "Wouldn't surprise me, after the way she downed those vodkas this morning."

"Should we take a look?"

"I don't see any smoke, and I don't hear anything else," said Drewson, scratching the side of his nose. "It's prolly nothing."

But only a few moments later, there was a loud, urgent pounding on the back door.

CHAPTER 12

"MRS. BRIGHT! MRS. BRIGHT!"

Phyllida had just stepped out of the Daimler at St. Wendreda's when Molly ran up to her. The maid was out of breath, and her eyes were wide.

"Did you hear?"

"Did I hear what?" Phyllida replied. She hoped Molly wasn't gossiping about Mr. Billdop's arrest.

"It's Mrs. Whittlesby! She's crashed her motorcar!"

"Good heavens!" Phyllida replied, looking around. The festival, which had started up again now that the rain had stopped, consisted of clumps of people standing about, probably discussing murder and motorcar crashes along with detective novels. "Is she all right?"

"I don't know," Molly said, shaking her head. "She was with Mr. Eugene Whittlesby and he ain't—I mean, he didn't make it."

"How *awful*," said Phyllida. "How badly is Mrs. Whittlesby injured?"

"She's hurt real bad. They called in Dr. Bhatt."

"Is Alastair Whittlesby still here at the festival?" Phyllida asked. How terrible for the family to have to face such a tragedy after Mr. Whittlesby nearly being murdered the day before.

"No, ma'am. He rushed right off as soon as he heard."

"Thank you, Molly," Phyllida said. "Oh, and have you been able to discern anything about those particular items I brought to your attention?"

"Only everyone's been so busy with the rain, and in and out, and now the motor crash. But I put the questions to them and asked them to spread it round, and now I'm waiting for them all to report back," Molly replied, standing up straight. Phyllida almost expected her to salute.

"Very good. Thank you. Do you know where Mr. Dobble is?"

Molly pointed—Phyllida would speak to her later about the gaucheness of such a gesture—across the green. Mr. Dobble was standing alone near Agatha's table, but far enough away that he wasn't engaged in any conversation. Phyllida would have liked to believe he was overseeing the work of the maids and footmen, but the expression on his face and his downcast eyes said otherwise.

"Very well. Thank you, Molly." Her thoughts were spinning as the maid hurried off—likely to share the news about the tragedy.

Phyllida was already wondering how to find a reason to visit the Whittlesbys to learn more about what happened. For, being a murder mystery reader and, now, an amateur detective, Phyllida was inclined to connect the crash to the previous poisoning incidents. Although she would obtain more information before drawing a definite conclusion, her instinct was to wonder whether the motorcar accident was yet another attempted murder . . . and if so, who was the intended victim? Mr. Whittlesby or his wife? Or both of them?

And what was Lettice Whittlesby doing in the motor with her brother-in-law, Eugene?

"I suppose you'll be wanting to go up to the Whittlesby home, now, won't you, Mrs. Bright," said Bradford.

"That would be lovely," Phyllida replied. She'd forgotten he had climbed out of the Daimler as well. "However, I need to speak to Mr. Dobble first." She decided she had time to put the butler out of his misery.

She hurried over, aware that the wet grass was, in fact, dampening her second set of shoes, but there was nothing for it.

"Mr. Dobble," she said crisply on approach. "I've attended to the—er—matter we discussed, and it has been rectified to my satisfaction. I would appreciate it if you could manage things here whilst I make a brief visit to the Whittlesbys' on behalf of Mrs. Agatha and Mr. Max."

"Very well, Mrs. Bright," Dobble replied. His expression gave nothing away, as usual, but the promptness and agreeability of his response expressed his relief.

"And if you please, would you advise Mrs. Agatha of the reason for my absence?"

"Indeed."

Moments later, Phyllida was back in the Daimler, now with wet shoes but without having to wait for Bradford to cover her with an umbrella.

"The Whittlesbys live at Tangled Vines Cottage in Marlake Hill," Phyllida told Bradford as he navigated the motorcar down the street, which was filled with festival-goers returning to the Murder Fête. She had a moment of satisfaction that the event was sure to be a success, despite—or perhaps even because of—the unpleasantries around it. "There's quite a steep, curving road coming down from the house."

"I see," Bradford replied.

And she suspected that he did, in fact, see why she had mentioned that detail. Not that she'd needed to do; it would be obvious even to him when they approached the house.

Other than that brief response, Bradford remained silent as he drove out of town and toward Marlake Hill, which gave her time to think.

As they approached, they came upon the wreck of the motorcar. It had crashed into a large elm tree, and the left corner of the hood was crumpled as if the driver had attempted to avoid the tree but didn't quite succeed. The windshield was shattered, and as she drew near, Phyllida saw blood on the interior of the motorcar. The roof was dented where one of the elm's branches had splintered during the force of the impact.

"Good heavens," she murmured.

Bradford had stepped out of the Mallowans' Daimler and was eyeing the crashed-up vehicle. "Bloody good bang-up," he said soberly, then turned to look in the direction from which Mrs.

Whittlesby had come down the hill from the cottage. He'd removed his coat and began to roll up his shirt sleeves. "Mr. Eugene Whittlesby died, and Mrs. Whittlesby is injured? She must have been driving, then, as most of the blood and damage is on the passenger side."

"She got banged up pretty well," Phyllida said. "I don't know how badly she's injured."

As she'd pointed out, the road from Marlake Hill was steep and there was a turn at the bottom of it. It was obvious what had happened: the motorcar had been trundling down the hill, picking up speed, and when Mrs. Whittlesby approached the curve at the bottom, she somehow couldn't make the turn and perhaps had overcorrected, tried to miss the tree, but the motorcar smashed into it anyway.

"Check the—" Phyllida stopped; Bradford was crawling under the vehicle, which was slightly elevated on one side due to how it had landed against the tree during a swerve. Presumably he meant to check the brake lines—or for any other sabotage. She wasn't certain he'd see anything with the front of the motorcar as crushed as it was, but it was certainly worth a try. For the first time, she was grateful for his stubborn presence and his expertise with motors.

She watched for a moment, concerned that the tilted vehicle might somehow fall onto him, but it seemed stable and she didn't want to make a fuss. The last thing she needed was Bradford teasing her about concern for his safety—which, of course, she would feel for anyone in a similar situation. Still, she didn't breathe easily until he worked himself out from beneath the tilted vehicle, his dark hair mussed and grass clinging to his trousers.

Whilst Bradford continued his examination, Phyllida took it upon herself to explore the area around the motorcar. Of course, whoever had removed Mr. Eugene's body and Mrs. Whittlesby had trampled the area quite handily. Shattered glass glittered on the ground, and there was a horrible amount of blood splatters on the inside of the motor, as well as on the flattened grass and a dead tree branch next to it. A man's hat lay crumpled on the ground amidst the glass, and she saw what must have been Mrs. Whittlesby's hat on the ground next to the driver's side—both testaments to the severity of the motor's impact.

Two tire tracks flattened the grass and told the tale of where the BMW sedan had left the road. Phyllida observed the way the gravel and dirt had been thrown up by the swerving tires, and was caught up for a moment imagining Mrs. Whittlesby's and Mr. Eugene's last seconds of horror before crashing into the huge elm. She offered up a swift prayer for the victim, as well as for Mrs. Whittlesby.

Just as she was about to conclude her examination, Phyllida noticed a woman's handbag on the ground. It had obviously been thrown from the vehicle, but, surprisingly, its clasp had held and the bag was still closed.

She swiftly retrieved it and lost no time in opening the pocketbook. She didn't expect to find anything relevant inside, but of course one must be thorough in a murder investigation.

"Brake lines were cut," Bradford said when he joined her. He was wiping his hands with a rag that had appeared from somewhere. She noticed a dark smudge on his clean-shaven cheek that somehow reminded her of a dangerous pirate or highwayman.

She saw that he was holding a toolbox. "Found this in the boot. No cutters inside."

Phyllida frowned. "Is that important?"

He shrugged. "You tell me, Mrs. Bright. You're the investigator. I will tell you that one would expect to find wire or metal cutters inside a toolbox for a motorcar. What's that you have there?"

"Her handbag," she replied, returning to rummaging inside.

The contents were precisely what she expected: lipstick, a compact, and a comb. However, there was also a small metal flask and a crumpled paper. Phyllida shook the flask and then opened it, confirming that it was empty. Then she smoothed out the crumpled paper and was able to read it. "A receipt from a milliner in Wenville Heath. She bought a hat from them; it was picked up on Thursday."

"What's on the back of it?" asked Bradford.

Phyllida turned it over and saw that someone had scrawled a note on the reverse. WILL PUT PETROL IN THE MG. TAKE SEDAN; PLENTY IN ITS TANK TO GET TO AND FROM. She frowned at the lettering. It was simple, blocky, and all capitals. After a moment's thought, she tucked the note into her own handbag. "Shall we proceed?"

Bradford opened the door of the Daimler for her and she climbed in. She still hadn't settled on a suitable excuse for making a visit to the family during such a difficult time, but Phyllida was confident that something would present itself.

It always did.

As she alighted from the Daimler, the back door at Tangled Vines Cottage—which was not, as far as she could ascertain, suitably named, for there wasn't any sign of vines, tangled or otherwise—opened to reveal Mrs. Puffley.

"Oh, Mrs. Bright! There you are! I told you she would be here in short order," she added to someone inside. "Now, come on in, will you," she said to Phyllida. "And you, too, Bradford," she added, beaming up at the driver. "You can set at the table and have a cuppa, and Mrs. Dilly will put a nice bowl of pea soup in front of you."

Slightly irritated that Bradford would be joining them—and clearly, he, at least, was to be fed, for the suggestion of soup had been directed at him—Phyllida nonetheless did as suggested and went inside.

She found herself in a kitchen far smaller and less well appointed than the one at Mallowan Hall, but it had larger windows since it wasn't partially underground. Unlike at Mallowan Hall, there was a large, scarred trestle table in the kitchen that would accommodate the servants as well as any work that needed to be done. Mrs. Dilly had obviously been in the midst of rolling out some sort of pastry dough at some point in the morning. From the looks of the cracks and dryness, however, Phyllida thought it had been some time since the cook had given the dough any attention.

While the lapse was quite understandable, all things considered, Phyllida would not have stood for such inattention at Mallowan Hall. Surely a cook worth her salt (as Mrs. Puffley was) could roll out pastry whilst gossiping.

"Thank you, Mrs. Puffley," Bradford said. "And who might I have the pleasure of meeting? The soup smells delicious."

Phyllida's jaw dropped, but she realized it immediately and closed it. She had never heard Bradford speak in such a cordial, almost cajoling manner. Nor had she seen such a warm, boyish smile on his countenance. She noticed with a bit of malice that there was another grease streak on his chin.

She took control of the conversation as soon as introductions had been made, which included a chambermaid named Louella who came into the kitchen just as they were sitting down at the table. The soup did smell delicious.

"Tell me, if you please, what happened with your mistress and Mr. Eugene, and what the doctor is saying," Phyllida said, looking at both of the Whittlesbys' servants.

Mrs. Dilly, whose appearance was quite the opposite of what one expected from someone whose life required her to constantly sample food, looked at Louella. The cook was skinny as a stick and had butter-yellow hair fashioned in a braid pinned around the crown of her head, but her hands appeared strong and capable. "Poor Mr. Eugene. God rest his soul," she said, shaking her head. "You tell'em, Lou—you've got more information than me, bein' all stuck over here in the kitchen and scullery."

"Mrs. Alastair probably ain't gonna die," Louella said in a blunt manner that Phyllida appreciated. "But she's bunged up good, and Dr. Bhatt wants to send her to hospital, but Mr. Alastair don't want her to go and she don't want to go neither."

"Mr. Whittlesby is allowing Dr. Bhatt to treat his wife?" Phyllida asked, remembering that the man had called Dr. Bhatt a foreign quack. Of course, desperate times called for desperate measures, and Dr. Bhatt was the only physician in the village.

"I don't see as how he had any choice, but he ain't happy about it. Ask me, he should send her to hospital," said Louella.

"But he won't do that?" Phyllida was appalled.

"He don't wanna listen to Dr. Bhatt's advice, such as it is. Don't know why. Dr. Bhatt's such a nice man," Louella said. Her cheeks had turned pink.

"Do you know why Mr. Eugene was in the motor with Mrs. Alastair?" Phyllida asked. "And why she was driving?" As much as Phyllida knew, members of her sex were quite capable of driving a motorcar—or in fact doing nearly everything a man could do—but the fact remained that when a man and woman were in a vehicle together, the man usually presumed to be the driver.

"Oh, yes, Mr. Alastair *refuses* to allow Mr. Eugene to drive any of the motorcars. And so Mrs. Alastair drove him into town when she left for the festival," said Mrs. Dilly. "Mr. Eugene wasn't going to the festival, mind, but he said as how he had business in Listleigh. It's awful bad blood between those brothers," she added, shaking her head sadly. "And now what does Mr. Alastair think? Mrs. Alastair was driving, and now his brother is dead and she is in a bad way. If only Mr. Eugene had been driving, this never would have happened!"

Before Phyllida could respond, a tidy blond man in formal wear strode into the kitchen. She immediately realized he was the butler—although he was the shortest, slightest butler she'd ever seen.

"Mrs. Bright! Is that you?" he said, confirming the fact that either her reputation or the color of her hair had preceded her. She preferred to believe it was the former.

"That's Drewson," said Mrs. Dilly. The fact that neither she nor Louella seemed alarmed to be caught sitting around in the middle of the day indicated plenty to Phyllida. Clearly the Whittlesby servants disliked their employers and working at Tangled Vine Cottage. "Is there news?"

"Mr. Alastair has finally agreed to take Mrs. Alastair to Dr. Bhatt's surgery, but he insists on driving her himself," said Drewson. "She does not see the need to go, and so they are rowing a bit."

"Might want to check the brake lines on his motor," Bradford said dryly. Everyone turned to look at him. He shrugged. "Brake lines were cut on the vehicle Mrs. Whittlesby was driving."

Drewson's eyes widened. "I thought—why, I thought the accident was because she'd been"—his voice dropped a notch—"imbibing."

Mrs. Dilly nodded sagely. "You'd'a thought it, wouldn't ya? She's quite a drinker, she is," she added, looking significantly at Mrs. Puffley. "I was telling you. She specially hates it here with *her*, you know." The cook's gaze lifted, and Phyllida understood Mrs. Dilly was indicating the senior Mrs. Whittlesby, the mother of Alastair and Eugene.

"I had noticed," was all Phyllida said. Then, thinking of the note she'd found in Mrs. Whittlesby's handbag, she said, "Was it unusual for Mrs. Alastair Whittlesby to drive the sedan?"

"Yes, Mr. Alastair usually drives that one. She don't like it because she says it's too big to handle. She usually drives the MG."

"Do you know why she didn't drive her usual motorcar today?" Phyllida asked.

"Mr. Alastair said as how he was going to drive the MG today because it needed petrol, and Mrs. Alastair doesn't like to fill the petrol because it's so messy," said Louella. "She always gets it on her gloves. We ain't got a chauffeur here, you see, to do it." She glanced at Bradford.

"But why didn't they come to the festival together?" asked Phyllida.

The servants exchanged looks. "Because Mrs. Alastair sleeps late. Every day. Too much . . ." Drewson mimicked tossing back a drink.

Phyllida nodded. Presumably, Mr. Whittlesby wanted to arrive at the festival as early as possible in order to hobnob with the writers. "Do you know the last time anyone drove the BMW?"

Once again the servants exchanged looks, but this time it seemed they were calculating information rather than deciding whether to share it. At last Drewson said, "It would've been to the cocktail party at the rectory last night. Mr. Whittlesby drove both of them in that motor."

So someone had sabotaged the brake lines on the sedan some-time overnight. And didn't put the wire cutters back in their place? Or perhaps they brought their own wire cutters and the toolbox never had them to begin with.

"Is the vehicle kept in a locked garage?" asked Bradford.

"Yes, most of the time. But last night Mr. Alastair—he was so distraught about what happened—about him almost getting poi-soned—that he just left it out there. Right in the yard," Louella said.

Phyllida sighed. That meant anyone could have tampered with it.

"Mrs. Bright, Mr. Drewson's got something to tell you," said Mrs. Puffley. "Go on, now, tell her what you told me. About them bitters."

Drewson did as directed. "There were three bottles of Mon-teleone's Special Bitters in the bar. Mr. Alastair orders them spe-cial from New Orleans"—he pronounced it "New Orlanes"—"and he doesn't like to chance not having any, as it takes so long for it to arrive. So he orders extra before he runs out."

"Do you know when the bottle went missing?" Phyllida said.

The butler's eyes widened and then he smiled. "That's what I was going to tell you—you're right, there, Mrs. Puffley, she's a good detective, Mrs. Bright is. Er—I mean, you are, Mrs. Bright. A jolly good detective."

Phyllida took this statement as her due. "When did you notice the bitters were missing?" she asked.

"It was when I was packing up supplies for the cocktail party. Mr. Alastair wouldn't abide it not having his particular Vieux Carré at the event. I think he liked to show off for the authors, you know. Make it sound as if he were more important than he is."

"He's like that, Mr. Alastair is," put in Louella. "And Mrs. Alas-tair always just tucked away in her sitting room, typing out her let-ters and reading and such, clickety-clack, and hardly wanting much of anything. Only when old Mrs. Whittlesby calls on her to read to her or sit with her, which she don't really much like doing." She rolled her eyes at Mrs. Whittlesby's room above them.

Drewson went on. "I knew for certain there had been three bottles—two new ones, unopened, and one only half full, but when I went to pack up the supplies—it was Friday morning, of course—I noticed one of the unopened bottles was missing."

"When was the last time you had actually seen three bottles?" Phyllida asked.

"Well, the two extra ones were on the lower shelf, and the one that was open, the one we were using, was on the top shelf, where everything else was for easy access. But I am certain I saw the other two bottles on Wednesday before the Murder Club meeting. I was seeing to the supplies for that as well, even though it was tea. I knew Mrs. Alastair would want her cocktail, and Mr. Alastair would want to show off his to the rest of his writer friends."

"Did Mrs. Alastair drink Vieux Carré cocktails as well?" Phyllida asked.

The staff exchanged looks. "She drank whatever was at hand, Mrs. Bright, and that's the honest truth," said Mrs. Dilly. "Over the last two months, we began to notice how much she came to like her spirits."

"She'd sit in that pretty blue chair by the Tiffany lamp and work her crossword puzzles and drink her whisky or port or whatever her fancy was that day," said Louella. "I'm surprised there ain't a path in the rug how many times Mr. Drewson or Mr. Alastair walked over to bring her a drink."

"How did she get on with Mr. Eugene?" asked Phyllida. She didn't find it necessary to ask what Mr. Alastair Whittlesby thought about his wife's excessive drinking; she'd been witness to his discomfort last evening. "Did he ever bring her drinks?"

Drewson shrugged. "Mr. Eugene—God rest his soul—didn't spend much time in the sitting room because he and Mr. Alastair didn't get along. I don't think Mrs. Alastair got on with him much, either, but I hardly ever saw them together except during dinner. If there was any conversation, it was polite and brief."

The sounds of footsteps coming down from the upstairs drew the attention of all of them. It wasn't difficult to discern that the noises belonged to Mr. Whittlesby and Dr. Bhatt assisting Mrs. Whittlesby—who was protesting weakly—down the stairs.

Drewson and Louella left the kitchen to assist, and moments later, Phyllida looked out the window and saw them carefully helping Lettice Whittlesby into a little MG. Dr. Bhatt's motor was parked nearby as well, and she hoped to get the opportunity to speak to him before he left.

She also hoped to have the chance to poke around the Whittlesbys' home now that they were leaving. One never knew what one might find.

She looked up to see Bradford eyeing her speculatively, as if he were reading her mind. She looked away. He could finish his soup. She would investigate.

CHAPTER 13

"*L*ETTICE WHITTLESBY WILL SURVIVE," SAID DR. BHATT. HE'D JOINED them in the kitchen to tell the staff what he knew, but indicated that he had to leave very quickly in order to meet the Whittlesbys at his surgery. "She is bunged up, and a bit out of her head from the shock as one might expect, but the worst of it is a sprained wrist and some bruises. She was very fortunate."

After having made that pronouncement, he accepted a muffin from Mrs. Dilly, then made his excuses to be on his way.

Phyllida walked out with him for a private conversation. "Mr. Eugene wasn't so fortunate."

"Not at all," said Dr. Bhatt grimly. "He was already dead when I arrived. He had been flung from the motor. Head and face smashed up pretty badly. Poor bloke was hardly recognizable."

"Mr. Bradford says the brake lines on the motorcar were cut," she told him.

His eyes widened. "When I arrived and found her—she was still in the driver seat, barely conscious—I could smell the alcohol. I assumed she had simply been driving recklessly and had caused the crash. I said as much to Alastair, and, surprisingly, he agreed. He is quite traumatized about it—especially over Eugene's death, despite their differences. He blames himself for leaving Lettice to drive the larger motor this morning. He knew she didn't like to handle it as well as she did the MG, but he didn't permit his brother to drive any of the motors. But now to learn that the brake lines were cut . . ." His expression turned even more grim. "Someone tried to kill Alastair Whittlesby again."

Phyllida nodded. "So it appears. John, when you were here on Wednesday, did you notice anything?"

He shook his head. "Not particularly. What do you mean?"

"Someone took the bottle of bitters between Wednesday morning and Friday morning—which means someone from the Murder Club could very well have done so. In fact, I should say most definitely that was when the bitters went missing, which puts all of the members of the Murder Club as having opportunity. Do you remember anyone who was standing near the bar counter and who might have had the opportunity to look behind it and take one of the bottles?"

Dr. Bhatt thought for a moment. "Well, Sir Rolly and I were standing there for a bit whilst Alastair saw to our drinks. I believe I sat down first, so Sir Rolly would have been up there longer, but I didn't see him look behind it. Miss Crowley walked over that way to admire a photograph on the wall above it—it was of the Riviera—and she stood there for a time muttering on about Filberto."

"What about Mr. Genevan and Mrs. Rollingbroke?"

"Oh, everyone was over there at one time or another, I suppose," said Dr. Bhatt, frustration in his voice. "Yes, they were over there getting their drinks."

"Did Mr. Whittlesby make a big production of it when he mixed his cocktail?" Phyllida asked, realizing that probably had to have happened in order for the murderer to know about the specific bitters.

"Of course he did. He declined to offer one to anyone else, might I add." He looked at Phyllida. "I really must get on now—Lettice was quite vehement about not going to hospital, and I am afraid she might convince Alastair to bring her back if I'm not at the surgery when they arrive."

"Very well, of course you must go," Phyllida said, patting him on the arm. "By the by, we still have not located the scores for the short story contest."

He paused in the action of opening his motorcar door. "Where on earth could they be?"

"I don't know, but I'm going to find them," she replied, then gave a little wave as he slid into the driver's seat.

Back inside Tangled Vines Cottage, Phyllida wasted no time. "Could you show me the sitting room where everyone was during the Murder Club meeting on Wednesday?" she asked Drewson as the kitchen bell buzzed loudly.

"Of course, Mrs. Bright. Louella, you'd best go up and see what the old dragon is ringing for this time," he said. "Someone ought to put poison in *her* drink."

The sitting room was quite what Phyllida expected: several comfortable chairs and two sofas arranged in a few different clusters to promote conversation—or to segregate brother from brother. She spotted the blue chair where Mrs. Whittlesby sat to do her crossword puzzles and frowned at the potted ficus in the corner with a haze of tiny fruit flies about it. She saw no reason to keep an unattractive, dying plant in the sitting room, and someone needed to clean up the scattering of dead leaves on the rug. But it seemed that Louella wasn't motivated to do any such tidying, for there was a fine layer of dust on the bookshelves as well. It was also obvious a carpet sweeper had not been employed in the recent past. Even the pillows on the sofas were off-kilter and hadn't been plumped.

Murder attempts were no excuse for not doing one's job, Phyllida thought grimly. Especially when the attempt was not on the worker.

The bar counter was at one end of the rectangular room, and the photograph of the Riviera that had been so admired by Miss Crowley was located in such a position that it would have been very simple for her to edge behind the bar and reach under the counter. And, being a woman, she would have had a handbag—a convenient place to stow the small bottle.

Mrs. Rollingbroke would have had a handbag as well.

That thought brought another to Phyllida's mind: whoever planted the poisoned bottle of bitters at the cocktail party last night would have had to unobtrusively transport the item to the party. The bottle was small enough to fit easily into nearly any handbag—except the tiniest, flattest, envelope style, which neither Miss Crowley nor Mrs. Rollingbroke had carried last night at the courtyard event. Both had had their handbags dangling from their respective arms.

The bottle would also fit into the outside pocket of a man's coat. It would fit into an inside pocket as well, but its shape would mar the fit and lines of the coat and would be more noticeable.

These realizations left Phyllida no closer to determining who might have brought the poison, as any of the men could have had it in their pocket, or any of the women could have had it in their bag.

Phyllida was beginning to wonder if this murderer was going to be able to outsmart her.

She set her jaw grimly. No. She wouldn't allow that to happen.

"Is there anything else you'd like to see, Mrs. Bright?" said Drewson.

"Is it possible to see Mr. and Mrs. Whittlesby's bedchambers and sitting rooms?" she asked. She didn't know what she was looking for, but she'd know when she found it.

If someone had tried to kill Mr. Whittlesby twice, perhaps there was some clue among his personal effects—or his wife's—as to why.

What she really wanted was to get access to his solicitor's office. There could be an entire *mine* of information there. But that would be far more difficult to arrange.

Still . . . surely Molly or Ginny or Mrs. Puffley knew someone who worked there.

"Oh, certainly," replied Drewson, gesturing to the stairs. "Just keep your voice down so the old dragon doesn't hear you."

Phyllida hurried up the steps in Drewson's wake and was shown into the adjoining bedrooms used by Alastair Whittlesby and his wife. The beds in both rooms were rumpled and unmade, a testament to Louella's lack of efficiency and motivation, and there was clothing strewn about Mrs. Whittlesby's dressing area. Two merchant's hat boxes sat on a side table, and Phyllida ascertained that they were from the milliner on whose receipt Mr. Alastair had written his note, and there was also a shopping bag from a clothing shop in Wenville Heath.

"Does Louella attend to Mrs. Whittlesby as her lady's maid?" she asked Drewson, mildly appalled at the mess in the bedroom.

"Oh, yes, when she's able," replied Drewson. His eyebrows lifted as if noticing the disarray for the first time. "Mrs. Whittlesby doesn't like anyone in her room whilst she's sleeping—which is quite often," he added in a disapproving tone. "Or when she's in her sitting room, typing her letters. She says Louella makes too much noise for her head. Not a surprise."

A vase of roses sat on Mrs. Whittlesby's bedside table, and there was another on the desk in her connecting sitting room, which seemed to serve as a sort of office. One wall in the office contained bookshelves, and Phyllida noted an extensive collection of murder novels, as well as other books on gardening, fashion, cooking, and sewing.

A typewriter sat on the desk, and there was a sheaf of stationery in a tray next to it. An ink pen, pencils, scissors, and an eraser were organized in another small tray.

Phyllida automatically tried to open the main desk drawer, but to her surprise it was locked.

"What does she keep in here?" she asked Drewson, opening another drawer to find plain typing paper. In another, there was an extra pair of gloves, a nail cutter, and a tube of lip color.

"Her correspondence," he replied, seemingly unconcerned by the locked drawer.

Phyllida frowned. What sort of correspondence needed to be kept under lock and key? If she were alone, she would open the drawer to find out. But of course she couldn't with the butler hovering. There was no need to advertise her lock-picking skills.

After finishing in Mrs. Whittlesby's rooms, Phyllida went into Mr. Alastair Whittlesby's bedroom. She discovered it was only marginally less disorganized than his wife's. Presumably, in the absence of a valet, Drewson attended to his master's clothing, shoes, and toilette, and therefore was responsible for keeping the room tidy.

Phyllida made a firm mental note to never consider employing any member of the staff currently at Tangled Vines Cottage.

Mr. Whittlesby's office, which was a mirror image of his wife's, turned out to be where he wrote his detective stories. A typewriter sat in the middle of a large, imposing desk. There were crumpled papers in the waste can, which Phyllida pulled out. They were, as she expected, pages from an Inspector Belfast story, and some apostrophe and grammar corrections, as well as plot notations, were marked with a pencil.

Next to the typewriter was a stack of plain paper, and on its other side was a stack of typewritten pages, turned upside down with the first page on the bottom. Phyllida picked up the stack despite Drewson's sharp intake of breath.

"The staff don't touch his papers," said the butler.

"I'm not staff," Phyllida replied smoothly. She was reading the first page of the story. She frowned, then went on to the second and third pages. By the time she'd finished the fifth, she could force herself to read no further, and replaced the stack of papers. She couldn't help but wonder why those pages hadn't found their way into the waste can, for the contents of the crumpled one she'd fished out had been far more compelling than the pristine pages on the desk.

Perhaps Mr. Whittlesby was a ten-draft writer, and these were his first attempts at a new story.

Or perhaps he was more liberal in borrowing ideas from the likes of Miss Crowley—and presumably others in the Murder Club—than anyone realized. That would be an excellent motive for murder, especially if the odious man won the short story contest with *someone else's* idea.

Drewson, who'd been watching her in dismay, relaxed when she straightened the stacks of papers and walked away from the desk to survey the books that stuffed Mr. Whittlesby's bookshelf: murder novels; history books; tomes on chemistry, anatomy, medicine, and mechanics; and an extensive collection of volumes on the law. Precisely what she would expect from a murder writer who did his research.

She did extract Taylor's *Medical Jurisprudence* from its place on the shelf and flipped through the heavy volume about medical forensics, toxicology, and how to use such analyses within the English court system. Notations in the margin indicated that Mr. Whittlesby was a particular fan of strychnine poisoning, as well as arsenic.

She replaced the book. Every other murder writer likely had a copy of the same or a similar title; she knew Mrs. Agatha did, despite her personal and extensive knowledge of poisons. It would be interesting to look at the copies belonging to all of the suspects and determine whether any of them had nicotine as a preferred poison.

"Is there anything else, Mrs. Bright?" asked Drewson. He sounded a bit nervous and kept looking through the front window. "Mr. Eugene's bedroom, perhaps?"

She nodded thoughtfully. Might just as well be thorough. She didn't *think* Mr. Eugene and Mrs. Alastair had been having an affair, but it would be worth her time to survey his personal effects in an effort to make certain.

To her surprise, Mr. Eugene Whittlesby kept a bedroom that was quite neat and orderly. Since his brother didn't allow him the ability to drive either of his motorcars, it was logical to expect he hardly allowed him access to the butler as a valet. Thus, the younger Whittlesby brother likely took care of his own things. Phyllida approved.

There was only one shirt hanging over a chair in the corner, and a single pair of shoes lined up next to the wardrobe, although there were several other pairs inside. Phyllida found receipts from antique dealers with items Mr. Eugene had acquired for Rengate Pictures, his employer: a silver tea set, a beveled mirror, a table gas lamp from 1900, a coat rack, and more.

One of the receipts caught her attention, for it was from a small shop in Belgravia. The proprietor's name was printed across the top: LOUIS GENEVAN.

She pursed her lips. So Mr. Genevan had done business with both Whittlesby brothers: one had purchased an expensive table—but not its chairs—and the other had purchased an American spittoon dating from the middle of last century. Hardly comparable in cost and size, but very interesting nonetheless.

"What about Mr. Genevan?" asked Phyllida. "When he was here on Wednesday, did he speak to Mr. Eugene?"

"I don't recall," replied Drewson. "Possibly. I was busy bringing in tea for Miss Crowley, for she doesn't touch spirits. I had to bring in an entire service just for her! She even complained that the cinnamon buns had nuts on them, and why didn't I cut the lemon bars into smaller sizes. Everyone else was happy with the sherry and cocktails."

"And on Thursday, it appears Mrs. Whittlesby drove to Wenville Heath to pick up her hat," Phyllida said. "Did Mr. Eugene go with her?"

"Thursday . . . let me think about Thursday," replied Drewson distractedly. He was looking pointedly from the entrance to the bedroom to the windows overlooking the front drive. Clearly, he was ready for Phyllida to leave the bedroom. "Ah, yes, when Mr. and Mrs. Alastair returned from their trip into town that morning, she took the MG and went over to Wenville Heath to get her hats, and I believe she did some shopping. Mr. Eugene was not at home at the time; I don't know where he was. He took his bicycle and went off, as he does."

Phyllida mulled over this information as she started down the stairs. "What were Mr. and Mrs. Alastair doing in Listleigh? Did Mrs. Alastair get up unusually early?" she asked.

"She was up unusually early that day, but it was because she was bringing flowers to St. Wendreda's. She does that once every month—makes us run about all morning getting them together—and decorates the altar or something. It's part of her donation and service to the church—that and the money Mr. Alastair gives. When she goes, it has to be after morning mass but before the midday prayer service, so she has to rise early."

"And Mr. Whittlesby went with her into town?" Phyllida found that interesting. Had Mr. Whittlesby spoken to Father Tooley and somehow learned about the results of the story contest? But he had been gloating about it during the Murder Club meeting on

Wednesday, which was the day before, so he must have known before he accompanied his wife on Thursday.

But what if Mr. Alastair had spoken to Father Tooley on Thursday and learned that perhaps he *wasn't* going to be the winner of the contest . . . ?

"Oh, yes. Mr. Alastair likes to meet with Father Tooley; or perhaps it's the other way around, with Father Tooley wanting to talk to Mr. Alastair to get more money from him. But I suppose he won't be doing that anymore, now will he?—now, wait a moment. *Wait* a moment. That wasn't Thursday, now, was it? No, no, no, it was Wednesday morning, Mrs. Bright. It was *Wednesday* that Mr. Alastair and Mrs. Alastair brought the flowers in to St. Wendreda's. I remember now, because on Thursday, it was the morning *after* the Murder Club meeting and, unsurprisingly, Mrs. Alastair did *not* get up early that day."

"But she went into Wenville Heath later that afternoon. On Thursday. And you're certain Mr. Eugene wasn't with her."

"I'm quite certain he wasn't."

"What about Mr. Alastair? Did he go with her to Wenville Heath?"

"No, he was closed away in his office, typing. We aren't to bother him whilst he's writing, you know."

Just then, they heard the sound of a motor approaching. A quick glance out the window indicated that it was not Mr. Whittlesby returning early.

"Ah. Someone must have telephoned to the constable. And it appears the inspector is with him," Phyllida said, then hurried lightly down the stairs. It wouldn't do for her to be caught snooping around in the private areas of the Whittlesbys' house.

She was sitting innocently in the kitchen when Constable Greensticks and Inspector Cork were shown in.

The inspector did not appear pleased. "Why am I not surprised to find you here, Mrs. Bright." As there was clearly no question mark at the end of his statement, Phyllida took it as rhetorical and declined to respond—at least on that topic.

"The car crash that took Mr. Eugene Whittlesby's life and injured Mrs. Alastair Whittlesby was murder," Phyllida told him instead.

"And why do you think that?" he replied dismissively. "It's obvious she's a bit of a sot, and from what I've heard, there was the smell of spirits all over her when they pulled her out of the car. Appears she lost control and hit a tree. Oi, unless you're suggesting she was attempting to off her own brother-in-law by driving whilst intoxicated," said Cork with a rude guffaw. "And nearly offing herself in the process."

"The brake hoses on the motorcar were cut," said Bradford evenly.

The inspector turned to him with such overt appreciation and relief that Phyllida could hardly keep from being offended. "What's that you say?" asked Cork, adopting a completely different tone than the snide one he used with Phyllida. "You've examined the motorcar?"

"I have," said Bradford firmly. "And you see how steep and curving that hill is. It would be a miracle for a motorcar to make it down safely without the ability to brake. I expect it would crash at any speed."

"Mr. Bradford is a fine mechanic, and if he says so, I believe him," said Phyllida, wresting the detective's attention back to herself. She was aware that the other servants were watching with great fascination. "Obviously, whoever cut those brake hoses anticipated that the driver would lose control coming down Marlake Hill—which is precisely what happened. This is a second attempt at murdering Mr. Whittlesby. And Mrs. Whittlesby was once again nearly the victim." She lifted an eyebrow. "She is either a very lucky woman . . . or a very unlucky one. I haven't quite decided which."

"Right, then, Mrs. Bright, thank you," said Cork. His body was still angled more in Bradford's direction than hers.

"Now, Inspector," Phyllida said. "I hope that since I've given you some extremely relevant information you will reciprocate and share the results of the testing on Father Tooley. I understand your man from London has been using Dr. Bhatt's laboratory, and that the work is being done here in Listleigh. I must compliment you on such forethought and competence."

Cork looked at her as if attempting to determine what to make of this compliment. "That's confidential information," he said finally.

"Oh, pish, Inspector. It's perfectly within your realm of legality to share the cause of death—it will be at the inquest, you know," she said.

Cork sighed, then capitulated. "Father Tooley had high levels of both nicotine and arsenic in his system. It's anyone's guess as to which actually killed him—it could have been either or both of them."

"As I suspected," Phyllida replied, ignoring Bradford, who simply could not keep his sardonic noises to himself. "And Saint Aloysius—presumably the cat had high levels of arsenic as well."

"Yes," said Cork.

Phyllida nodded, then looked at him in speculation. "One must assume since you weren't aware of the foul play of the Whittlesbys' motorcar, and you weren't here to disclose the cause of death of Father Tooley—such secrecy, as I've indicated, is quite unnecessary—that you've come here to the cottage for a different reason. Presumably to help determine where and how the poisoner obtained the Monteleone's Special Bitters. And possibly to interview the servants about who might want to kill their employer."

"Yes, among other things," replied Cork in a more subdued manner. At least he seemed to be taking *that* element of the investigation seriously.

"Mr. Drewson will confirm the information I am about to relate to you in a far more succinct and efficient manner than you would be able to discover yourself." She glanced at the butler, who nodded. She continued.

"A bottle of bitters went missing sometime between Wednesday morning, when Mr. Drewson was preparing for the Murder Club meeting that afternoon, and yesterday morning, when Mr. Drewson was packing up the supplies to be taken to St. Wendreda's for the cocktail party. As all of the members of the Murder Club were here—along with Mr. Rollingbroke and Mr. Eugene Whittlesby— it appears that was when the bitters was taken from the Whittles- bys' bar. Any one of them could have taken it; they were all, at various times, standing near the bar, which is where the bitters are kept."

Cork's mustache quivered and his eyes popped a little more than usual, but he didn't speak. Constable Greensticks, who sat at the other end of the table, seemed quite taken by the rosemary popover that had been placed on a plate in front of him. Even from where she sat, Phyllida could see the rivulets of melted but- ter over its crispy golden top, and she silently mourned the fact that she hadn't finished her Cornish pasty.

"Mr. Whittlesby did not park his sedan in the garage last night, which is unusual and also means that anyone could have had ac- cess to it overnight to cut the brake hoses," she went on. "Under normal circumstances, I would suggest you skillfully interview the suspects to determine who has a mechanical ability or such perti- nent knowledge, but in this case that would be a moot point. All of them are murder plotters, and so likely all of them would be well aware of where and how to cut a set of brake hoses in order to cause a lethal accident. It's a rather common occurrence in de- tective stories," she explained. "An easy way to get rid of a charac- ter, and often an excellent plot twist. And good writers do extensive research for their murder plots, so surely all of our sus- pects would know where to locate the brake hoses."

"Yes, thank you, Mrs. Bright," Cork replied with heavy irony. After a moment of silence, he said, "Is there anything else I should know, Mrs. Bright?"

She thought for a moment, then replied in the negative. After all, she hadn't gotten the reports back from her network of down- stairs folk via Molly.

"Are you quite certain?" Inspector Cork pressed. "You've noth- ing else to add, to suggest, to direct, or to command?"

Phyllida lifted her chin, ignoring the soft snicker from some- one behind her—Bradford; for who else would dare?—and replied regally, "Not at all, Inspector. I have the utmost confidence in your ability to continue the investigation now that I've set you on the right path. There is clearly someone determined to do away with Mr. Whittlesby. And that someone doesn't care whether anyone else might be hurt or killed in the process."

With that, she rose from the table. "Good day, Inspector. Constable." She paused to look at the three Whittlesby servants, fixing each of them with a severe gaze in turn. "I suggest the lot of you see about doing your jobs—and properly. The state of this household leaves much to be desired, and there is simply no excuse for it."

With that, she swept from the room.

"A fine mechanic am I?" said Bradford, the *moment* he settled into his seat. "Why, Mrs. Bright, I can't remember when I have been so lauded. I thought you hadn't noticed."

She studiously kept her attention on the road as the odious man navigated the Daimler down the steep, curving hill that had taken Mr. Eugene Whittlesby's life, and wished quite vehemently that Bradford would find a new employer and be on his merry way.

Obviously having made his point—for what reason, Phyllida couldn't imagine—Bradford drove in silence for a few moments, glancing out the window as they passed by the motorcar crash. The BMW was still there and would likely remain so for another day or so until a towing lorry could remove it.

"Thought you might like to know that I looked around outside at the cottage for any footprints or other clues that might have given an indication as to who or when the brake hoses were cut," said Bradford once they were past the crash site.

"Did you find anything instructive?" Phyllida asked, irritated that she hadn't thought to do so herself.

"Too many people and motorcars have tracked over the area since this morning," he said. "Hard to say when the hoses were cut; I didn't see any sign of brake fluid, but there was quite a bit of activity—tires, footsteps—over the area and it rained earlier, so much of the evidence would have been obliterated anyway."

She frowned in disappointment. "So you found nothing of importance?"

"Not that I could tell," he replied cheerfully. "Of course, I'm not the intrepid Phyllida Bright, hunting down clues and diving into danger like Tuppence Beresford." He paused as if to see whether she'd respond positively to what he must have considered a compliment, then, when she remained silent, went on. "But I did happen to look in the boot of the MG, and that toolbox has a pair of cutters in it."

"Was there any sign of recent use?" Phyllida asked. "Traces of brake fluid? I suppose you didn't bother to look," she added.

"No sign of recent use," he said firmly. "I did look."

"Right, then, Bradford. You might make a competent detective someday after all."

He looked at her, his eyes wide and mocking. "Is it possible I've received two compliments from Mrs. Bright in one day? No, in one *hour*? How can that be?"

She scoffed and rolled her own eyes, then instantly regretted the display of emotion. It was her policy not to allow Bradford—or anyone, for that matter—to know when they'd gotten her goat or irritated or annoyed her.

"Mrs. Puffley appears to have an admirer," he said a few minutes later, causing Phyllida to once again wonder what had happened to the surly and sulky chauffeur who previously couldn't be bothered to carry on a conversation.

"Indeed?" she replied, curious nonetheless.

"Did you not notice the way Constable Greensticks was acting in her presence?" he went on. "How he blushed when he sat down next to her? He nearly overset her teacup."

"The constable? And Mrs. Puffley?" Phyllida couldn't hold back her surprise.

"You didn't notice? The great Inspector Bright didn't notice the constable fumbling around and making cow eyes at her cook?"

"I was engaged in my conversation with Inspector Cork," she told him in a lofty tone. But she did remember how eager the constable had been to visit the kitchen at Mallowan Hall this morning. "Bringing a murderer to justice is far more important than gossiping about a possible romance."

But . . . Mrs. Puffley and Constable Greensticks? Why on earth would Mrs. Puffley be interested in that short, pompous, mustachioed policeman? Nonsense. She'd believe it when she saw it.

However . . .

Phyllida's mood changed swiftly. If Mrs. Puffley and the constable developed a mutual tendre, then surely the cook could extract all sorts of valuable information from the policeman, should Phyllida need it.

She settled back into the seat and plotted about how to assist the constable in making his case with Mrs. Puffley. It would be an uphill battle, she was certain, but Phyllida Bright was undaunted.

If anyone could make such a strange match happen, it was she.

CHAPTER 14

I MMEDIATELY UPON THEIR ARRIVAL IN LISTLEIGH, PHYLLIDA DIRECTED
Bradford to drop her off near the Screaming Magpie.

"Fancy a pint, do you, Mrs. Bright? At least it's well after noon,"
he said.

"Of course not," she replied primly, but declined to correct his
assumption that her destination was the local pub.

In fact, she intended to visit Dr. Bhatt's surgery, and saw no reason to advertise this fact to Bradford—for he'd surely attach himself to her once again and insist on poking his nose into her
investigation.

"I shall walk back to St. Wendreda's, so there's no need for you
to wait," she told him.

"Very well, Mrs. Bright," he said, giving her an enigmatic look.
"Do give the good doctor my regards."

Not even bothering to grit her teeth this time, Phyllida simply
nodded and walked off.

Her brisk stride took her to Dr. Bhatt's surgery in a matter of
minutes, and Tracy, his maid-of-all-work, was there to greet her as
she came in.

"I'm here to see Mrs. Whittlesby," said Phyllida, deciding to
take the bull by the horns. "If she's feeling up to a visitor."

"Oh, hello, Mrs. Bright. Mrs. Whittlesby is resting in the back
room. Mr. Whittlesby is with her. Dr. Bhatt got her settled, then
stepped out for a few moments. I believe he intended to nip down

to the Murder Fête and get a copy of *Strong Poison* before the festival closes down for the day," she added in a conspiratorial tone. "He does enjoy the Peter Wimsey stories, and Miss Sayers's queue was so very long earlier. But he only left once he was confident Mrs. Whittlesby was improving."

Phyllida nodded, declining to comment on the irony of the title of the book John was seeking. "Thank you. I'll just duck to the back and express my sympathy. I promise not to tire her out."

Having both of the Whittlesbys together wasn't optimal for her purposes, but Phyllida had no choice. She didn't know whether John would mind if she questioned his patient, so she had best do so before he returned. It was better to ask for forgiveness than for permission when one wasn't certain.

Alastair Whittlesby sat in a chair next to his wife's bed. He was hatless but still wore his coat. His foot, which was tapping impatiently on the floor when Phyllida approached, ceased its movements.

Lettice Whittlesby was propped up by several pillows. Her wrist was bound up and rested uselessly across her lap, but other than a small bandage at her temple, she showed no other outward signs of injury. But her eyes seemed vacant and slightly glazed, and they barely fluttered open when Phyllida greeted her.

"Mrs. . . . er, Bright, is it?" said Mr. Whittlesby.

Since he'd previously met with her in his office and had seen her again last night, Phyllida was not fooled. Nevertheless, she gave him a warm smile as if pleased and surprised he'd remembered her lowly self. "Yes. Mr. and Mrs. Mallowan suggested I stop up and offer their condolences—and to see if there is anything we can do to help," she said. "I cannot imagine how terrifying and trying these last days have been!"

"And all in the midst of the Murder Fête," he said, sounding more petulant than alarmed. "It's quite ruined it all."

"I'm very sorry about your brother," Phyllida said, taking the only tack available in the face of childish male complaints: ignoring them. "But I'm pleased to see that Mrs. Whittlesby's prognosis appears positive."

"Yes, at least according to that foreign quack," he said, taking not the least bit of care to keep his voice down. "Lettice, you really ought to let me take you to the hospital. I don't trust him."

"No, no, Allie . . . I'm fine," she said wearily. "I just need to rest. My head is absolutely *thudding*." She reached out with her uninjured hand as if to pat her husband's arm, but he was sitting too far away. Then her eyes lit on Phyllida. "Mrs. Bright? What are you doing here?"

Phyllida smiled. "I am bringing condolences and best wishes from Mr. and Mrs. Mallowan. I'm very sorry that they won't be able to visit with you until the festival is over."

"Oh, yes . . . the festival. Oh, dear, Allie . . . do you think they'll give up the contest?" Her voice sounded a little stronger. "Cancel the rest of the festival?"

"Surely not," he replied flatly. "I should hope not! Why, they have to announce the winner! It's a publishing contract!"

"It would be quite a tragedy for all of those poor orphans," Phyllida said, "if they canceled the rest of the festival and weren't able to raise enough money for the new roof."

"Quite right," replied Mr. Whittlesby absently.

"How do you feel, Mrs. Whittlesby?" Phyllida asked.

"I've certainly felt better," she replied with a weak smile. "But it could have been so much worse. I cannot believe Eugene is *gone*." Her voice caught on a sob. "I'm so sorry, Allie. I'm just *so* sorry. I tried to avoid the tree, but the car wouldn't stop and—"

"Perhaps it was the vodka you'd had this morning," said Mr. Whittlesby flatly. "Drewson told me."

"Perhaps it was the cut brake lines," Phyllida said firmly, and perhaps a trifle too loudly. She simply could not stand by and let Alastair Whittlesby berate his injured wife.

"What?" He goggled at her.

It was no surprise to Phyllida that he was unaware of the sabotage; after all, she had only just informed Inspector Cork of it, and he was presumably still at Tangled Vines Cottage.

"What are you saying?" said Mrs. Whittlesby. She shifted awkwardly, as if trying to sit up higher. Her husband ignored her, for he was still gaping at Phyllida.

"Someone cut the brake lines on the sedan," Phyllida told them. "So you wouldn't have been able to stop or even slow down, Mrs. Whittlesby, no matter how you tried. It was another case of attempted murder—and since it ultimately resulted in the death of Mr. Eugene, the killer did succeed . . . though not perhaps how he or she intended."

"Good God!" Mr. Whittlesby's face had gone white. "Why, that might have been *me* driving the BMW—it *should* have been me! I always drive—if you hadn't been out of petrol, I would have driven it into town!" This last was directed at his wife, who lay there, still and wide-eyed.

"Someone tried to kill you again," Mrs. Whittlesby wailed. "Oh, *Allie*, what is happening?"

"Someone tried to kill your husband," said Phyllida firmly, "but very nearly killed *you* in the process, Mrs. Whittlesby. *Again*. While Mr. Eugene was the real victim. . . ."

"Good heavens," said Mr. Whittlesby, grasping his wife's pale hand as it occurred to him that his life wasn't the only one that had been in danger. Phyllida wondered when—if ever—it would sink in that his brother had actually been killed. "It might have been you, Lettice! And then what would I have done?"

She shook her head slowly, as if in pain. "You would have carried on, darling, as you always do. Belfast and Millie would have been just fine in your—"

"But how could someone have done it?" he said, his voice spiraling higher and tighter than before. "Sneaking around our house? Cutting brake lines?" Horror filled his voice. "*Someone is trying to kill me, Lettice!* What will they do next? Shoot at me through a window?"

"Don't be ridiculous," Phyllida said, cutting into his hysterics. "Thus far, the murderer has limited himself or herself to secretive, anonymous tactics. There's simply no reason to think someone would march up to your home and point a gun at you. It doesn't match the psychology of the killer. Still," she went on, "you ought to take extra care, Mr. Whittlesby. And you as well, Mrs. Whittlesby. But at least you'll be here tonight, won't you?"

"Yes," replied Mrs. Whittlesby. "Yes, I agreed to stay overnight here instead of going to hospital. It was simply too far away. And I *will*," she said in a surprisingly firm tone when her husband began to object. "I'm in no danger. It's you who's the target, Allie. Not me. Besides, Dr. Bhatt will be here."

"*Doctor* Bhatt." Mr. Whittlesby's mouth twisted, and Phyllida heard him mutter an appalling phrase under his breath. It was all she could do not to lash out at him.

Instead, she swallowed her outrage and said, "Indeed." She rose. "I suppose I should be going now. There's much to attend to at the fête."

"I should return to the festival myself," said Mr. Whittlesby, standing. "Surely they're missing me. Mr. Chesterton and I were having quite an animated conversation about characterization through backstory." He reached for his hat. "Not that he's done much of that at all with Father Brown, you know. You will be all right, now, won't you, Lettice?"

"Of course, darling. Tracy will be here if I need anything," she replied. "You must get back to the festival and find out whether they will be announcing the winner after all." She gave him a weak smile.

"Ah, yes . . . I suppose I should mention that the calculations for the short story contest have gone missing," Phyllida told them.

"They've *what?*" cried Mr. Whittlesby. "You must be *mad*—of course they haven't gone missing! Why I *saw* them—" He stopped short. "I mean to say, I saw Father Tooley with them on—what day was it we were visiting him, Lettice?"

"I can't remember," she said vaguely. Lifting her uninjured hand, she pressed it to her forehead. "Perhaps yesterday? No, no, that was—"

"It was Wednesday," her husband interrupted. "Don't you recall? Before the Murder Club meeting."

"Oh, quite," she said. "And you say they've gone missing? The calculations? The winner?"

"No one has been able to find them. You say you saw them when you visited with Father Tooley?" Phyllida asked. "Where were they?"

"Why, they were in his study! Right there on the desk."

Right where Father Tooley had been eating the cake on Friday afternoon, two days later.

"Well, that's very helpful. But they aren't there any longer," Phyllida said.

"Well, someone *must* find those contest results!" cried Mr. Whittlesby. "It's . . . it's . . . it's simply pre*pos*terous that someone has taken them! *That's* why they want to kill me, Lettice! It's because they all know I'm going to win! And someone wants to do away with me so *they* can claim the prize!" By now he was stalking about the room, waving his hat. "I'll bet it's that damned foreign quack," he said bitterly, and Mrs. Whittlesby gasped. "Always ranting on about his Dr. Graceley—and he does all sorts of experiments with poisons, doesn't he? Wouldn't put it past him, being a bloody infidel—"

"John Bhatt would *never* do such a thing," Phyllida snapped, unable to keep her emotions in check any longer. "And you ought to think very carefully about making such boundless accusations, Mr. Whittlesby. As a solicitor, you must be very well versed in the principles of defamation law." She wanted to say more, but held back. An intolerant, overbearing, *nasty* man he was *indeed*!

Mr. Whittlesby gave her a withering look but kept his mouth closed. Perhaps he saw the fury in her eyes. "Well, I certainly hope someone finds those contest results very soon," he said after a moment. "Because I want my bloody publishing contract."

Phyllida had a number of other things she wanted to say to him—and in a loud, biting voice—but she controlled the urge. "You must have seen the results of the contest then, Mr. Whittlesby—to be so confident of your win."

He fixed her with a malevolent look. "Not at all, Mrs. Bright. I did not happen to see the results. But there's simply no one else who has a chance of winning. My story is the best of the lot."

"I understand Miss Crowley had to change the story she wanted to submit because it was too similar to your plot—even though she had written hers first," Phyllida said evenly. "Word is that you took her idea."

Mr. Whittlesby's expression grew darker, even threatening. "You might take your own advice about defamation, Mrs. Bright," he said. "In fact, Miss Crowley is wrong—as she often is. The old pussy can't place a comma properly, let alone plot a cohesive story. If she's mucking about accusing me of stealing her story ideas, then I shall have to have words with her. Now," he said, jamming the hat on his head, "I shall go off to the festival. Someone has to see to getting the story contest results." He took two steps toward the door before turning abruptly. He bent to kiss his wife on the cheek, then strode out of the room.

When Phyllida marched out of Dr. Bhatt's surgery, she was surprised to find Bradford approaching.

"What are you doing here?" she said ungraciously. She was still quite irate over Mr. Whittlesby's intolerant accusations. Her hands were even shaking a bit.

"I came to fetch you," replied Bradford. Then he paused. "Is everything all right?"

"Yes, of course. It's only that I have come to see quite plainly why everyone seems to want to do away with Alastair Whittlesby," she said. The heat in her cheeks grew hotter as she remembered what the horrible man had said. "He really is an odious, boastful arse."

Bradford nodded. "I see."

Phyllida collected herself and automatically reached up to check that her hat was still in position. "You came to fetch me?"

"Yes, Molly needs to speak with you," he replied. "It sounded important, so I offered to track you down—although I was certain I knew where you had gone."

"Obviously," she replied as he fell into step with her.

"You spoke with Mr. Whittlesby?" said Bradford.

"As well as with his wife. They were unaware that the motorcar crash was another murder attempt," she said.

"And how did they take the news?"

"As one would expect." She walked a bit in silence, thinking about the exchange. Then suddenly she burst out, "I'm finding it difficult to believe it a mere coincidence that both attempts on Mr. Whittlesby's life nearly took his wife's as well—or instead."

"Right," said Bradford. "It does seem a bit much to swallow."

"With that in mind, one must begin to wonder whether *Mrs. Whittlesby* is actually the target," she said, mulling aloud. "And not her husband."

Bradford hesitated only a moment, then said thoughtfully, "I don't see how. Wasn't it quite accidental that she nearly took a drink from Whittlesby's cocktail? A murderer couldn't have planned that."

"I suppose," Phyllida replied, stopping short from actually saying that he was correct. The man already had the arsenic deduction in his tally; he didn't need another checkmark. Especially since he wasn't actually doing the investigation.

"We have to find the story contest calculations," Phyllida said after another few steps. She noticed he had shortened his lengthy stride to remain even with hers.

"We?"

She ignored the sardonic comment. "It seems certain they figure into this mess somehow. I haven't had the opportunity to search the rectory thoroughly. I suppose I shall have to attend to it myself."

"Didn't Rita already do that?" he asked.

Phyllida gave him an exasperated look. "Supposedly. But that doesn't mean she did a thorough job of it. That reminds me, I haven't heard from her whether she noticed anything else missing."

"Such as an antique piecrust table."

"Indeed."

They were just approaching St. Wendreda's. To Phyllida's satisfaction, the festival seemed to be going on in full swing. If anything, the crowd seemed bigger now that the rain-interrupted fair had started up again. She nodded grimly. Sadly, tragedy had its way of bringing out the curious. Based on the number of people and the length of the queues, she felt confident the orphanage would have money left over after paying for the new roof.

"Oh, Mrs. Bright, there you are!" Molly hurried up to her. She was flanked by several people—three women and two men, all of different ages and appearances. Based on their attire, Phyllida deduced they were some of the servants working in the homes of Murder Club members. Presumably, they'd been given the day or part of the day off to attend the festival.

"Indeed, here I am," Phyllida replied.

"We've got information for you, the things you asked about, Mrs. Bright," said Molly. "They wanted to tell you themselves. If that's all right."

Phyllida looked at the small cluster of people, noting that two of the maids held back a bit and one of the footmen (or perhaps he was a valet or driver) seemed a little bashful.

Taking these expressions of awed intimidation as her due, Phyllida nonetheless strove to put them at ease. "Of course. Where shall we sit?"

Moments later, they were gathered around a garden bench under a tree near the church. Phyllida wasn't about to sit on the ground in her pretty blue day frock—or ever—but the footmen and some of the maids didn't mind at all. She was a trifle concerned about grass stains from the still-damp lawn, but any housemaid worth her salt knew how to care for such occurrences, so she declined to advise them. It was no surprise when Bradford decided to lean against the tree and listen in.

"All right, now, what have you to tell me? Presumably each of you have relevant information. Shall we begin with you?" Phyllida nodded to the young woman who appeared to be the least shy of the housemaids.

The girl jolted and her face turned bright red when everyone looked at her. Phyllida saw her swallow hard, but nevertheless, the maid spoke without hesitation, albeit a little softly. It was fortunate Phyllida had excellent hearing. "Yes, Mrs. Bright. I'm Miss Crowley's maid-of-all work, and I just wanted to say thank you for asking me here."

At this point, Phyllida braced herself for the lumbering process that would likely take place as she attempted to extricate whatever each of them had to tell her. After all, it wasn't as if she'd invited the servants to a fête. This was a murder investigation. She nodded encouragingly but didn't speak for fear of terrifying the maid into silence.

"Right. And you wanted to know about a-a cake, strawberry jam, walnuts . . . um . . . geraniums, and bitters?" The girl listed off the items as if she'd memorized a verse for school, then, looking up at the sky as if retrieving the data from the depths of her brain, continued her recitation without pausing even to take a breath. "Miss Crowley had a small cake this week, but it wasn't white sponge but lemon sponge. I made it and she ate it herself. She did have some tarts from Panson's, but she hates nuts—she just about sacked me one day when I baked a walnut-twist teacake with cinnamon—and she would never have them in the house. Makes her throat go tight, she says. She always has got strawberry jam, and there is a jar with some of it missing, but that's not quite unusual, for she prefers it to orange marmalade or lemon curd. There were no geranium leaves on her shoes . . . and . . . um . . . oh, right—I never saw any bottles of a bitter anything anywhere—I don't even know what they look like, but I never saw any." She finished in a rush and with a renewed flush in her cheeks. "Mum."

"Thank you very much—what is your name, then?" Phyllida said, making an effort to soften her normally blunt tone.

"Amy, mum. I'm Amy."

"Very well. Thank you, Amy. Did Miss Crowley ever talk about Alastair Whittlesby or the Murder Club?"

"Oh, yes, mum, all the time. She *hates* the man. Says he's overbearing and nasty and . . . and something else." She frowned.

"Boastful?" Phyllida suggested, all at once realizing what her wispy fragments of memory had been trying to tell her.

"Oh, yes, that's it, mum! That's what she says. Overbearing and boastful, an utterly nasty man. Those are her exact words. And she says she wishes how Filberto Fiero were a real person so she could run off with him, she says." Amy nodded, her cheeks pink with pleasure, now that she had finished her speech. "And that the Dr. Bhatt is a very nice man, for him being a foreigner."

"Is there anything else you noticed about Miss Crowley over the last few days that was unusual?"

"Well . . . it was very strange that when I come in this morning, she wasn't up and about yet. It was just about half nine, and she was still in bed! Said she had a bit of a headache and was awful dour about it all." Amy shrugged. "I ain't never seen her in bed past half seven before, in all the years I've done for her."

Phyllida hid her amusement. Presumably Miss Crowley's lying-in had been due to her unaccustomed imbibition of champagne. Several glasses would give anyone a headache and keep them in bed late, but it would be especially potent for a teetotaler.

Still, there could be another excuse for her sleeping late: if she had been out in the middle of the night to cut brake hoses. It would have been a thirty-minute walk at the very least to get from the village where Miss Crowley lived out to Tangled Vine Cottage; less, of course, if she bicycled. Surely she wouldn't risk the noise of driving a motorcar.

"Excellent. Is there anything else you can think of that might be interesting?" Phyllida asked.

"I'm sorry, mum, but no," said Amy. She sounded disappointed.

"Very well, then. If you do think of anything else, please find a way to get the information to me. Now, what about you?" Phyllida said, turning her attention to one of the men. He seemed to have the most intelligent expression of the bunch.

"Yes, ma'am, Mrs. Bright. I'm Mr. Genevan's valet, and when Molly told me about how you were wanting information about Mr. Whittlesby and all, I remembered some things."

"And your name?" she asked. The valet was older than the other servants, possibly in his early thirties.

"Oh, right. It's Preston, ma'am." When Phyllida nodded encouragingly, he went on. "Mr. Louis, he doesn't like Mr. Whittlesby at all and he was very angry when Mr. Whittlesby didn't buy the chairs that went with the metamorphic table. He had a lot to say about that matter," Preston said, shaking his head. "I heard about it for weeks. Once he was so mad he crumpled his neckcloth. Another time he tore his cufflinks off before I could help, and ripped up his shirt.

"Talked about what a bloody arse—begging your pardon, Mrs. Bright," he said with a grimace. "But that was how he talks about him. About a cake . . . there was a cake in Mr. Louis's kitchen. I saw it. It might have been white sponge; I don't rightly know, but it had white icing on it. The housekeeper went off on Thursday to Brighton for her goddaughter's new baby, and I don't know if she baked it or whether Mr. Louis got it from Panson's. He did have some pastries from there last week and some of them did have nuts, although I can't be certain what type." He paused, then went on. "I didn't see any geraniums anywhere—not sure I'd know what they were—"

"But I showed you," Molly interjected impatiently. "The crinkly, smelly leaves? They're a little soft on the top."

"Right." Preston shrugged. "I didn't see any leaves on Mr. Louis's shoes or anywhere. And nothing like a small brown bottle of bitters."

"Last night, was Mr. Louis wearing a coat that had a pocket large enough to hide a bottle about this big?" Phyllida asked, showing him the basic dimensions of the bitters bottle. "Without it upsetting the cut of his coat, I mean to say."

"I would say, yes, it might have done. He didn't have anything in his pocket when I dressed him, though, Mrs. Bright. I can say that for certain—I would have noticed."

She nodded. "Very good. Now, is there anything else that happened over the last few days that was unusual?"

"Not that I can say . . . although now I think about it, he might have gone out again last night. He came home from the cocktail party and was quite upset. He didn't want any assistance from me before bed, and I last saw him sitting in his office where he writes the Miss McClatchery stories—which are rather entertaining, I must say. It was nearly midnight. He was drinking whisky, but he wasn't writing. I went to bed, but I thought I heard a sound later—someone moving around in the front room, then perhaps the sound of a motor. My quarters are in the back, of course, and I'm not certain what I heard. But I wouldn't be surprised if he went out."

"Did you notice any grease on any of his shoes or clothing?" she asked.

"No, ma'am."

"Amy, I should have asked you the same question: was there any sign of oil or grease on any of Miss Crowley's shoes or clothing?"

The maid jolted a little at the attention abruptly being focused on her once more, but she shook her head. "No, mum."

"How many new items of furniture have appeared at Mr. Genevan's house since yesterday?" Phyllida asked Preston.

His eyes widened. "How did you know?" Phyllida merely smiled and waited for him to continue, which he did. "I nearly tripped over it, I did; right in the back hallway, a small round table with crinkled edges. And there was a cushioned wooden footstool I never saw before, and three porcelain statues."

Apparently Louis Genevan had been quite busy in the wee hours of the night. But whether he was a murderer remained to be seen.

"Thank you," said Phyllida. "Is there anything else?"

"No, ma'am, not that I can think of, Mrs. Bright."

"No telephone conversations, or—"

"Oh! That's right," said Preston, his eyes lighting with pleasure that he had more information to give. "I did hear him speaking this morning on the telephone. Someone rang, and he answered it. I could only hear his side of the conversation, but it sounded as if he were arguing about whether to tell about something. He said something like 'no one could have' and 'that would be quite stupid!' And then he became very angry and said, 'Of course I didn't, and you had best not!' He finally slammed down the telephone; I thought he might have broken the receiver, but it still seems to be working."

"Do you have any idea to whom he might have been speaking?" Phyllida asked, although she was certain she already knew the identity of the other person.

"Not at all, Mrs. Bright."

"Think now . . . did he curse or swear at all during the conversation? Even though he was very angry?"

"No, ma'am, I don't believe he did so."

Phyllida nodded. "Very well. That is quite excellent information. Now, who is next?"

One of the maids raised her hand shyly. "Mrs. Bright," she said, then managed a tremulous smile that revealed a large gap between her bottom teeth. "It's only one thing I have to tell you, it is, but I wanted to sit for all of it, even though it's only the one thing."

"And what is your name, and who is your employer?" Phyllida asked.

"Oh, yes, ma'am. I'm Lucinda and I'm an upstairs chambermaid at Wilding, ma'am. Three years going now."

Phyllida knew that Wilding House was the name of the estate where Sir Rolly and Vera Rollingbroke lived. "And what have you to report?"

"Only, ma'am, I didn't see no cakes or walnuts or bitter bottles, didn't I? But there was some of them geranium leaves I swept up on the floor, I did. Me mum used to make geranium water for her mistress, ma'am, and it always reminds me of her when I smells me some geranium leaves. It were definitely geraniums, ma'am, from last night, and we ain't got no geraniums right now at Wilding, only Michaelmas daisies and roses and some carnations, we do."

Phyllida found that information quite interesting. "Thank you, Lucinda. That's very helpful. Now, have you heard Mrs. Rollingbroke talk about Mr. Alastair Whittlesby at all?"

"Not very much, only I don't think she likes him too well. She don't say much, but Sir Rolly always rolls his eyes whenever Mrs. Rollingbroke mentions the Murder Club—not because he don't like it, not at all—he's famously addicted to her stories."

"The ones with the talking cat?" Phyllida asked, imagining the reaction of Stilton and Rye if she told them someone had written stories about a cat that could speak. Surely they would be mortified by the idea of a feline stooping to such undignified communication skills—let alone one named Mrs. Cuddlesworthy.

"Yes, ma'am. Sir Rolly asks her every day what pages Mrs. Vera has written, and he insists on looking at them when they meet in the sitting room for cocktails—unless they're having guests, of course."

"The Murder Club meets at Wilding quite often," Phyllida said. "Have you ever heard any arguments between the members, or any indication that someone might want to kill Mr. Whittlesby?"

Lucinda glanced at the young man who hadn't spoken. "I usually work upstairs in the bedchambers, but Noel could tell you more."

"I'm a footman at Wilding," said Noel. He was young, and his voice cracked a little. "I've helped Mr. Whalley, our butler, serve some of the Murder Club meetings. Pardon me for saying so, Mrs. Bright, but I don't think anyone likes Mr. Whittlesby very much. There were lots of murmurings, you know, whenever he would speak, and the dark-haired man with the thin mustache . . . I can't remember his name, but he dresses like a nob all the time."

"Mr. Genevan," Phyllida supplied the name.

"Him . . . he *really* didn't like Mr. Whittlesby. I heard him say some words under his breath more'n once—words I dare not repeat, ma'am—when Mr. Whittlesby was talking or carrying on."

"Did you notice anything else?" Phyllida asked. "Anything over the last day or two that might seem strange?"

"No, ma'am. Not that I can think of."

"Do either of you, Lucinda and Noel, have any idea what Mr. Whittlesby might have said to Mrs. Rollingbroke to make her invite him to their soiree? I understand she didn't intend to ask him, but changed her mind near the last minute."

Both of the Wilding House servants shook their heads in tandem.

"Is there any chance Mrs. Rollingbroke had some sort of secret that she was keeping from Sir Rolly?" Phyllida asked. "That Mr. Whittlesby might know about?"

"Do you mean like a-a *lover*?" whispered Lucinda.

"Or gambling debts?" said Noel a bit lasciviously, as if the very idea delighted him.

"Anything like that," Phyllida replied.

"No, ma'am, I don't think so," replied Lucinda. "Only, I know Mrs. Vera's maid well enough she'd tell me if there was, she would." She nodded firmly, and Noel shook his head with definite regret.

"Very well, thank you," Phyllida said. "All of this has been very helpful. And now, for whom do you work?" she asked the third woman, who hadn't yet spoken.

"Mr. Billdop, ma'am. I'm his housekeeper, but I don't live in. But I come in for him every day, I do, and he's a very nice, kind man when he's not wound up about St. Wendreda's."

Phyllida was fully aware of the underlying tension between the Anglicans and the papists in Listleigh, so she made no comment. Instead, she nodded encouragingly.

"Mr. Billdop, he did have a small white cake yesterday, ma'am. I don't know where it come from; I didn't make it for him and he didn't eat it and then it was gone. The policemen, they asked me about it, and I had to tell them, you know. About that and the strawberry jam. The vicar said the jar broke and he threw it away, but I didn't see no evidence of that, either, so I told the constable all about it. And maybe I shouldn'ta." Her small, dark eyes filled with worry. "But Mr. Billdop wouldn't do anything to hurt someone—even a priest! He's too nervous and fluttery, ma'am. You know a murderer has to have a very strong mind, he does, and . . . what's it—determination, right?—and a body who's gonna plan a murder can't be all soggy and twisted up like a tub of wet laundry."

"Quite so," replied Phyllida. "How does Mr. Billdop feel about Mr. Whittlesby?"

"He surely don't like him, ma'am. Not at all. That isn't no secret. He's said some un-Christian things in my hearing, he has, but it's only words, ma'am. And he just wanted bad things to happen to his stories, not Mr. Whittlesby himself, you know. Once he said as how he wouldn't mind seeing all his Inspector Belfast papers get blown into the stove or fireplace."

"Mr. and Mrs. Whittlesby attend St. Wendreda's, not St. Thurston's," said Phyllida. "Is that part of the reason Mr. Billdop didn't like him?"

"Only because they give a lot of money to St. Wendreda's," said the housekeeper. "They and the Rollingbrokes, you know. I hear about *that* all the time. Why none of the rich people in Listleigh come to St. Thurston's, and that's why St. Wendreda's has an orphanage."

Phyllida wasn't certain how Mr. Billdop felt about the Mallowans—neither of whom attended church regularly as Mr. Max was Catholic and Agatha was Anglican. "Did anything strange happen over the last few days with Mr. Billdop? Did you notice anything unusual?"

"Only the cake, ma'am. And I wouldn'ta thought anything of it if poor Father Tooley hadn't died from a poisoned one." The vicarage housekeeper shrugged. "For all I know, Mr. Billdop ate it all hisself and didn't want no one to know about it. Wouldn'ta put it past him; he was very anxious about meeting all of the writers yesterday. Wouldn'ta been the first time someone stuffed themselves up with sweets."

"Any grease or oil spots on his clothing or shoes? Or geranium leaves?"

"No, ma'am, not that I've noticed."

"Very well, then." Phyllida looked around the small cluster of servants, satisfied that she'd asked everything she meant to, and content with what she'd learned.

Things were starting to fall into place, and her little gray cells were working deftly to fill in the holes.

Now, if she could only find the short story scoring sheets.

CHAPTER 15

Saturday evening

AFTER SHE FINISHED SPEAKING WITH MOLLY'S GROUP OF FRIENDS, Phyllida turned her attention from murder investigations to the Murder Fête, or, more specifically, the closing down of the festival for the evening.

By all accounts, the second day of the fête had been a great success, despite its temporary suspension due to rain and the tragedy of two deaths related to the festival. But when it was time for the attendees to return to their houses, that meant Phyllida's work was only beginning.

There were tents to dismantle, booths to close up, unused books (fortunately there weren't many of them) to box away, chairs and tables to fold and store, and a myriad of other tasks.

Tomorrow's final event would be a small, informal tea served on the green, with a public speech about the mystery genre by Mr. Berkeley—which was one more opportunity for people to make donations to the orphanage. At that time, as the local celebrity, Agatha Christie would award the funds to the orphanage director (a brief yet simple task that she had agreed to conduct). Mr. Berkeley was meant to announce the short story prize winner at the same time.

Since the official scores from Father Tooley were nowhere to be found, Agatha had promised to telephone Hugh Walpole and Freeman Wills Crofts to obtain their scores for the story contest, and then she and her guests would write up their own notations once again. All would be provided to Phyllida, who had offered to do the calculations when she returned to Mallowan Hall later tonight.

Phyllida sighed, surveying the takedown efforts happening around her. At the rate things were going, she wouldn't be back to the hall until after eleven o'clock.

It wasn't as if her staff wasn't doing their jobs efficiently; it was just that there was a great deal to do, and Mr. Dobble had left with half of them in order to ensure dinner was waiting for the Detection Club members. Both he and Phyllida had agreed that it was of paramount importance not only for the guests, but for Mrs. Puffley, that a superb dinner was served this evening in light of last night's debacle.

Phyllida was just about to go into the rectory to do her own search for the contest scores when she caught sight of Miss Crowley. Phyllida spun on her heel and started off toward the older woman.

"Miss Crowley," she said as she approached.

The woman turned. "Mrs. Bright. What can I do for you? Have the score sheets for the story contest been found yet?"

Apparently, word had gotten around.

"I'm afraid they haven't, but the Detection Club will announce a winner tomorrow nonetheless. They will simply resubmit their scores to me and I will do the calculations."

Miss Crowley seemed relieved, then annoyed. "Not that it matters. That boastful Alastair Whittlesby is bound to win."

Boastful. There was that word again.

Phyllida decided to plunge in. "Miss Crowley, I do believe you ought to tell Inspector Cork about your conversation with Mr. Genevan."

The other woman stumbled a bit. Her eyes were wide when she looked at Phyllida. "What on earth are you talking about?" she said angrily. But Phyllida recognized fear beneath the anger.

"Your conversation with Mr. Genevan yesterday morning. About doing away with Alastair Whittlesby by poisoning his Vieux Carré."

"But—" Miss Crowley's face went white. "How did you know?" she whispered. "Did *he* tell you?"

"I overheard the two of you talking," Phyllida told her. "At the time, I didn't recognize the voices, and I didn't know about whom you were speaking. But then Father Tooley died, and I realized later it was you and Louis Genevan who'd been speaking."

Miss Crowley didn't respond immediately. Phyllida could almost see her reviewing all the options in her mind, so she decided to prod her in the proper direction. "I've already reported the details of the conversation to Inspector Cork. I have not told him who was speaking, but now that I've identified who they were—and you've confirmed it—I have no choice but to tell him. I do believe it would shine a more positive light on yourself and the possibility of your innocence should you confess to the inspector first."

"The *possibility* of my innocence?" Miss Crowley said. "Of course I'm innocent! I would never do such a thing. It was just . . . just talking, you know. It didn't mean anything. It was a *joke* more than anything!"

"And yet Father Tooley died from a poisoned Vieux Carré that was meant for Alastair Whittlesby—which was precisely what you and Mr. Genevan had plotted to do."

"We didn't *plot* anything," Miss Crowley replied, her voice cracking with stress. "I tell you, it was just talk. Neither of us can abide that man and his boastful nastiness, and it was just a bit of letting off steam."

"That is why you should tell the inspector voluntarily," Phyllida told her.

"Perhaps."

"After all, you claim it was only talk—but what if it wasn't only talk for Louis Genevan?" Phyllida asked.

"Good *heavens.*" Miss Crowley's words were shocked, but Phyllida saw more fear than surprise in her eyes. As if the older woman worried about that very thing. "Surely not."

"You might feel that, by telling Inspector Cork of the conversation, you'll incriminate yourself, but I believe he should know, and I believe that if you confess, as I previously said, it would go a long way toward suggesting your innocence."

"Hmm. Yes, yes, perhaps you have a point," said Miss Crowley.

"Of course I do."

"But . . . Louis would kill me if I told the inspector," said Miss Crowley. "I don't mean literally . . . well . . ." Her eyes went wide and her face turned from pale to a sickly gray. "Oh dear, Mrs. Bright! I don't know what to do! He was very angry this morning when I suggested we ought to tell. I telephoned him."

"I suspect he was," Phyllida said. "Do *you* think he poisoned Mr. Whittlesby's cocktail bitters?"

"I . . . I don't know. I truly don't know. I've been worrying *horribly* about it ever since it happened . . . ever since our conversation. I truly have," she said, reaching for Phyllida's hand. Her fingers were strong as they closed around Phyllida's wrist. "You can have no idea how awful it's been for me."

"Probably not as awful as for Father Tooley," Phyllida replied dryly.

"And now I hear that the Whittlesby's motorcar was sabotaged? It's simply awful. Just awful."

"Indeed."

Miss Crowley gripped her wrist even tighter as she leaned closer. "I understand you're investigating the murder, aren't you, Mrs. Bright?"

Phyllida firmly removed her limb from the other woman's claws. "Inspector Cork is investigating. I'm merely offering suggestions and direction as necessary." There was no need to explain how vitally necessary her intervention was.

"Aren't you worried that—well, that you'll be next?" Miss Crowley said in a voice barely above a whisper. Her eyes glittered with something dark. "Someone like that wouldn't take kindly to a housekeeper sticking her nose in other peoples' business."

And with that, she turned and walked away—leaving Phyllida to wonder whether her words had been meant as a threat or a concern.

* * *

Phyllida couldn't find Rita anywhere. Molly, Stanley, or Elton hadn't seen the rectory's maid for at least an hour, and they'd expected her to be helping with the closedown of the festival.

It was nearly ten o'clock, and the only illumination on the church lawn was from a half-moon and a few weak streetlamps. The festival-goers, writers, and amateur writers had all ebbed away hours ago. The white of the last tent gleamed in the darkness, and Phyllida saw the Mallowans' Daimler waiting patiently to bring the rest of the staff back to the hall.

Bradford was helping Elton to stack the last of the tent cloths and poles, and Stanley and Molly were loading boxes into the boot and back seat of the motorcar.

But Phyllida couldn't go back to Mallowan Hall without Rita. She'd promised the woman she could stay there for a few days because of poor Saint Aloysius—and the fact that a murderer was loose in the area. She didn't blame the housemaid for not wanting to stay in the rectory alone.

But where was she? The last time anyone had seen Rita, she'd been carrying a basket of tablecloths into the rectory kitchen. That had been some time ago, and the rectory windows were completely dark, so surely she wasn't still inside.

"Go ahead and take them back home," she told Bradford, indicating Elton, Molly, and Stanley. The servants were drooping with fatigue. "There's not enough room in the motor for all of us and those boxes anyway."

"You'll be all right here by yourself?" Bradford said hesitantly. "There is a murderer loose, you know."

Phyllida hadn't previously given Miss Crowley's warning any serious consideration, and she certainly didn't now. "I shall be fine. I have quite a healthy set of lungs, and aside from that, there's no reason anyone should want to harm *me*."

Bradford made a strangled sound but didn't argue further. "I won't be long."

"Of course not. I will spend my time looking for Rita. I cannot imagine where she's gotten to. Perhaps in the church, praying. She did say something about lighting a candle for Father Tooley. Or perhaps she rode back with someone else. I'll call back to the house from inside the rectory and ask Mr. Dobble."

Bradford hesitated one last time, then, to her surprise, he fished something out of the motorcar and handed it to her.

"What on earth—" She stared at the pocketknife. It appeared heavy, and as large as her hand when folded.

"Just in case," he said enigmatically, pressing it into her hand. "And take this as well." He pulled a torch from his pocket.

"Very well," she replied, closing her fingers around the knife and the light. They could come in handy, she supposed—especially since she was finally going to have the chance to do a thorough search inside the rectory for the contest information. A knife tip could be quite useful in opening a lock; perhaps Father Tooley had secreted the information in a strongbox.

"Stay here in the light," Bradford said.

"I shall be quite fine," she said firmly. "Now the sooner you go off, the sooner you can be back."

He nodded, then climbed into the motor. Phyllida could see that Molly was already asleep, leaning against the window in the front. Stanley and Elton were crammed in the back with several boxes.

"You're not coming, Mrs. Bright?" said Elton, poking his head out the window.

"There's no room in the motor, and I want to find out where Rita has gone off to."

"I can stay with you," said Elton, opening the motorcar door. One of his feet appeared on the ground. "You shouldn't stay here alone."

"That's not necessary," Phyllida said firmly, wondering what was wrong with all of these people who thought she couldn't take care of herself.

Even if there *was* a chance that the murderer might be lurking about, thus far all he or she had done was poison food and cut brake lines—as she had pointed out to Mr. Whittlesby. And as

Phyllida had no intention of eating or driving, she felt no worry over her safety.

"Now go off with you," she said. "I should like to return before midnight tonight."

Elton hesitated, but Bradford murmured something to him that sounded suspiciously like "addled" and "goat," then started the motor.

No sooner had the Daimler cruised off than Phyllida left the pool of light from the streetlamp and went into the church.

The nave was shadowy and dark, and its high ceiling rose in a series of gothic arches above Phyllida's head. Faint red, blue, and gold light spilled over the altar from the moonlight shining through stained glass behind it. Six very small lamps were lit along the sides of the rows of pews in the nave—three lanterns on each side—and did little more than to provide long shadows and dark patches. Seven offering candles winked and danced in their red holders in one of the small alcoves off to the side.

"Oh, there you are!" Phyllida said when she saw the figure kneeling in one of the pews next to the offering candles. "Rita?"

She hadn't expected to need Bradford's torch so soon, but here she was. The light beamed bright and strong and she shone it toward the maid, who still hadn't moved.

That was not good.

Phyllida's heart surged into her throat as she approached. Her fingers had suddenly gone stiff and icy.

"Rita?"

But she already knew it was no good. The flashlight shone over the maid's inert body, which was slumped over the pew in front of her—not in prayer, but in death.

CHAPTER 16

*P*HYLLIDA TOOK A MOMENT TO OFFER A PRAYER OF GODSPEED FOR the poor maid's soul. Then, using the torch, she began a cursory examination of Rita's body . . . which was still slightly warm to the touch.

This realization had Phyllida straightening sharply to look around, beaming her light slowly and carefully into the shadowy corners of the church. Whoever had killed Rita was not long gone.

She hesitated, then, much as she wanted to finish her examination of the body, Phyllida hurried toward the closest door, reasoning that whoever had murdered the maid would have made for the nearest exit in order to melt into the night. She certainly hadn't seen or passed anyone near the main entrance of the church, so they hadn't come that way.

The side door was only a few feet from the stand of red offering candles, and Phyllida pushed it open slowly, peering into the churchyard, which was cloaked in shadows from the trees that grew in a stately line next to the church. Surely this was the direction the killer had gone; it was dark and unobtrusive. She kept her torch turned off in an effort to not give away her presence, listening and straining to look into the shadows, but the night was still and silent. The only sound was the scream of a fox in the distance.

After a moment, Phyllida eased back inside the church, closing the door behind her and, after brief consideration, bolting it from the inside.

Now she returned her attention to the body of the unfortunate maid, shining her torch over the scene.

Blood darkened the back of Rita's uniform, and Phyllida could see where a blade had been shoved in, right into the heart from behind, and then withdrawn. A single, silent wound had done the deed—and the weapon was nowhere to be found.

It seemed the murderer had graduated from subtle, less precise methods to something more accurate—and desperate—in less than a day.

Phyllida suspected that had something to do with the perpetrator becoming concerned about being identified. Which meant *she* had been doing her job. She found herself looking out into the shadows of the church once more. Normally a peace-inducing place with its flickering candles, tall, graceful arches, and softly lit stained glass, now the church was eerily silent and forbidding—a somber witness not to life eternal, but to brutal death.

Once more assuring herself that she was alone, Phyllida turned again to the dead girl. Though she wanted to ease Rita down into a more respectful position or to at least cover her, she knew better than that. The inspector would want to see the scene of the crime just as she'd found it.

She did, however, cast the torch's beam along the floor, looking for footprints or anything that might be helpful in identifying the culprit.

But other than the pool of blood that had run and dripped onto the stone floor and kneeler in front of Rita, she found nothing of interest. No footprints, no bloody fingerprints, no conveniently dropped button or item from one's pocket . . .

The murderer was not only very clever but also slick and silent as a wraith.

The thought had Phyllida going still once more. She'd been here for at least fifteen minutes and hadn't sensed the presence of anyone else in the church . . . and even now she didn't feel as though she were being watched.

Still, she shined the torch around the church again and listened very carefully.

Nothing.

Phyllida had examined the floor and pews around Rita, but not the maid's body itself. The single stab wound indicated a near-instant cause of death, but there could be more information to be had.

Carefully, so as not to move the body out of place, Phyllida continued her examination. Rita's fingers had a rosary tangled within them, and those digits had remained curled tightly around the beads. Her weight had sagged forward as she died, the pew in front and the kneeler propping her upright.

Phyllida beamed the torch over Rita's body on one side, then went around and did the same on the other, looking for anything of interest . . . and her diligence was rewarded when she saw the corner of a paper peeking from Rita's apron pocket.

It wasn't a single paper, but a sheaf of papers, folded and haphazardly shoved into the pocket. Phyllida extricated them, and when she played the light beam over the collection of papers, she gave a quiet sound of satisfaction.

The missing story contest results.

There would be plenty of time to wonder how and why they were in Rita's possession—and how long they'd been there. Now she needed to alert Constable Greensticks and Inspector Cork about yet another dead person. There was a telephone in the rectory that would be more efficient than walking several blocks to the constabulary.

Phyllida stuffed the papers into her own pocket and rose from the pew. She had just slipped into the aisle to walk down and out when she heard the quiet sound of a door shift and thunk in its frame.

Someone was trying to get in through the side door she'd locked.

Phyllida turned off her torch and ran silently down the aisle to the main entrance, planning to hurry around to the side door and head off whoever was there. She didn't want to open the door to a murderer; she'd rather take him or her—although she'd fairly well decided upon the culprit's sex by now—by surprise.

Slipping out into the night through the main door, Phyllida

dashed on light feet toward the side of the church, then stopped when she got to the edge of the building.

Peering carefully around the corner, she squinted into the dark, seeking any sort of movement, listening for any sound of humanity. The oak trees cast long, bushy shadows in the half moon, and their leafy branches skittered and scattered against one another in the soft breeze.

Everything was silent. There was no sign of human movement. Only the sound of her heightened breathing filled her ears.

Then, suddenly, she felt something—*someone*—behind her.

With a strangled cry, she spun—just in time to dodge something dark and heavy. It whooshed down, skimming past her ear and banging hard onto her shoulder. Her defensive movement and the blow knocked her off balance, and she stumbled, dropping her torch as she caught herself against a tree trunk.

"Stop!" cried Phyllida, but her attacker had darted off into the shadows.

She didn't wait, but took off after the figure who accosted her. The weight of Bradford's pocketknife bounced comfortingly—if a bit awkwardly—in her dress pocket, and Phyllida put her hand over the opening to keep it from falling out as she ran.

She could see only hints of the figure as it darted away from the church, away from the village green, and into the center of town, all the while staying in the shadows. Whoever it was wore a hat and a long, flowing coat, which, along with the darkness, obstructed any details of the culprit.

Phyllida followed the figure down the main throughway, then down a curving, narrow road that made its way between buildings with doorsteps right off the passage. The uneven street was dangerous, and she was beginning to get a stitch in her side, but at least the dry shoes she'd changed into earlier were ones with more practical heels than her original footwear.

Down the curving road, she ran; then across a small garden, onto another narrow street, dodging parked motorcars, flowerpots, garden gates, and one irritated feline who hissed when she nearly knocked over the waste can it was surveying.

Then all at once, Phyllida realized she no longer heard running footsteps ahead of her. There was suddenly no sign of her attacker.

She'd lost him. Or her.

She paused, breathing heavily, standing in the middle of a curving cobblestone road she recognized as being on the near east side of the village. Brick houses and retaining walls created a narrow throughway that had been constructed for horse and carriage and was barely wide enough for a motorcar to pass through.

Drat. Whoever it was—and she was beginning to believe she knew the cunning, brilliant murderer's identity—had gotten away.

Phyllida rubbed her sore shoulder and started to trace her steps back to the church. Perhaps the attacker had dropped something during the pell-mell dash.

She heard the sound of a motorcar engine just as she approached the opening of the narrow street, and all at once, the glare of two bright headlights was in her eyes.

Phyllida was blinded, her eyes watering from the sudden sharp light that was much, much too close, and she held up her hand in an effort to ward off the brightness.

The engine revved and suddenly the headlights leaped toward her. Fast.

Phyllida gasped—there was nowhere for her to go! She turned, darting back up the narrow street with the headlights spilling their beams around her.

The motorcar growled and spurted closer, and Phyllida didn't dare look behind her. She knew it was close, and gaining . . . and she was trapped in this narrow, winding road between brick walls.

She couldn't draw in a breath to scream—not that it would do much good anyway. By the time anyone realized what was happening, she'd be pinned beneath the tires of the motor. All she could do was focus on pumping her legs as fast as possible and keeping herself as far away from the deadly vehicle as she could.

But it was a losing battle. Even hampered by the narrow, winding passage, the motorcar was nearly upon her, and Phyllida couldn't outrun it.

She had to find another option.

And then she saw it.

The crenelation on the retaining wall just ahead, where the road took a right turn. Brickwork jutted out in regular decorative channels, like the merlons on a castle wall, leaving narrow indentations between them.

Phyllida headed for the nearest of these indentations. She could feel the heat of the motorcar as it roared up behind her as she practically dove into the alcove.

She plastered herself tightly against the wall as the blaring headlights and vicious machine leaped toward her in a loud, angry growl.

She closed her eyes, held her breath, and prayed.

CHAPTER 17

BRADFORD SIMPLY COULDN'T SAY NO TO HER. WITH THOSE BIG, SAD brown eyes and that unruly mop of soft-as-silk dark hair, and the absolute *joy* with which she greeted him every time he returned from anywhere—even just going into the house to eat—she was utterly irresistible.

"Mrs. Bright isn't going to like it," he told Myrtle as he opened the door to the Daimler.

The dog—she was just barely past being a puppy—leaped in and wriggled about in such delight, bouncing from seat to seat, that he couldn't help but laugh.

"I know—she'll just have to live with it, won't she?" he said, imagining the prune-like fashion into which the housekeeper's pretty lips would shrink when she saw the extra passenger. She'd lift her chin in that way she did when she was irritated—which was nearly all the time when he was around; a fact that Bradford not only enjoyed but deliberately provoked. A man who'd been to war had to have some levity in his life.

Bradford had wasted no time in bringing back the servants to Mallowan Hall after the festival and enlisting them to help unload the supplies from the motorcar. Mrs. Bright claimed she wasn't worried about being left alone at night when a murderer was about, but Bradford did have a bit of a conscience when it came to leaving females—even annoying ones—alone in potentially dangerous situations.

God knew, he'd learned not to waste his breath arguing with Mrs. Bright. The blasted woman was as immovable as Stonehenge. Instead, he was determined to return to Listleigh and retrieve her—as well as the ominously missing Rita—as quickly as possible. And since he hadn't seen much of Myrtle all day, he decided she deserved to ride along, particularly since she'd asked so sweetly.

"Make certain you sniff at her as much as possible," he told the mop of dog hair, who sat in the front seat, panting, drooling, and, doubtlessly, shedding hair on which Mrs. Bright would likely place a remarkably fine posterior for a woman her age. "You know how much she hates it when you lick at her through her stockings, too, Myrtle, so have at it. It's always a pleasure to hear her shriek a little." He chuckled.

It was quite a sight, watching the uptight and proper Mrs. Bright attempt to keep herself calm and collected when the wet-nosed dog unexpectedly nudged her palm or slurped at her shin.

Uncharacteristically, she'd left a handkerchief in the Daimler once. Instead of returning the lacy confection to her, Bradford had kept it. He'd been teaching Myrtle to search out and find the source of the handkerchief's scent—just for the pleasure of watching Mrs. Bright try and fend off the dog.

The housekeeper couldn't understand why the dog was so attracted to her whenever she happened to walk across the yard or go to the garage, and Bradford wasn't about to divulge the reason. Instead, he watched with concealed mirth as she attempted to ignore Myrtle and her affections. She had no idea that Myrtle was handsomely rewarded by her master every time she sniffed out the owner of the handkerchief.

Bradford's grin faded as he approached St. Wendreda's and did *not* see Mrs. Bright standing where he'd left her, beneath the gas lamp in front of the church.

Was he surprised? Not at all, blast it.

But where had the addle-brained, stubborn woman got off to?

"Come on, Myrts," he said, opening the door for the mop. The dog bounded out and eagerly began to gambol about, sniffing and pausing to squat all over the place.

Bradford looked around. There was no sign of movement or life. No lights on in the rectory. Only the faintest glow emitted through the stained glass on the church. Every other building in the vicinity was dark and silent. The area was deserted.

He muttered something unflattering about prissy redheaded housekeepers under his breath and strode toward the rectory and church. If she wasn't there, she was likely at that Dr. Bhatt's office.

Or . . . surely she hadn't gotten it into her head to break into Alastair Whittlesby's office here in the village and snoop around.

He groaned. That would be precisely something Phyllida Bright would do.

A short, sharp bark from Myrtle—who'd dashed off ahead of him—had him loping a little faster. She was dancing around the entrance to the church, scrabbling at the wooden door with her nails.

When he got closer, he saw a faint glow just beyond the walkway. With a start, he recognized it as the torch he'd given Mrs. Bright. It was still on, shining from beneath a thick boxwood hedge.

Bradford picked up the torch, an unpleasant feeling coming over him. If she'd dropped it whilst it was still on, that meant—

He didn't spend time thinking about any of the possibilities.

"What is it?" he said to Myrtle, who was yapping and bouncing even more desperately in front of the church door.

Bradford pushed the door open and Myrtle bolted inside the nave.

He immediately saw the dark figure slumped over one of the rows, and he smelled the heavy rust of blood before he got halfway down the aisle. His steps faltered, and for a moment his vision wavered and memories threatened to crash into him . . . then he pushed through.

Blessedly, the moment passed.

When he realized it wasn't Mrs. Bright hanging over the back of a pew, Bradford had a moment of numb relief, followed by fury over yet another wasted life, and then the renewed frustration over the housekeeper's disappearance.

Knowing her, she'd interrupted the killer and then tried to

chase him or her down. He wasn't certain whether to hope she'd succeeded or not.

Myrtle had ceased barking and now simply sat, staring with silent concern at the inert body of Rita.

There was nothing else Bradford could do for the maid, and the absence of any of the authorities indicated that they hadn't been notified. The girl's body was cold but had not begun to stiffen, so she couldn't have been here for long. Hardly more than an hour, he guessed.

Which meant that Mrs. Bright couldn't have been gone for very long, either.

"Let's go," he said to Myrtle. "Let's find Mrs. Bright."

The dog gave a short yip of comprehension and having first done her duty of alerting him to the unfortunate maid, she now bolted toward the door for a different task.

Outside the church, Bradford looked around for any sign of where Mrs. Bright might have gone. Although he'd been playing about with Myrtle and her ability to sniff out the housekeeper, it was mostly a game in a limited area. The dog was still young and easily distracted, so he wasn't about to rely solely on the mop and her immature abilities. Aside from that, Myrtle couldn't sniff her out if she'd been bundled into a motorcar and driven off.

His jaw set grimly, Bradford started toward where he'd found the abandoned torch and looked around for footprints or any sign of struggle. There was a tree branch on the ground where it shouldn't have been, and the crushed bush next to where it had fallen indicated some sort of altercation.

Mrs. Bright definitely hadn't been alone. But had she been attacked, or was she the pursuer?

Myrtle was barking and bouncing with excitement, so—since it couldn't hurt—he said, "All right, go find the addled woman, Myrt! Find Mrs. Bright!"

Myrtle dashed off into the night, leaving Bradford to follow at a brisk run.

The dog threaded her way down the street, pausing occasionally to stop and sniff the air and the ground—and, presumably, for her master to catch up—and then bounded off again. He followed her down winding streets, through gardens and over flowerpots (the dog went over; Bradford went around) until finally Myrtle tore down a narrow street bounded on one side by a retaining wall for the small river.

The only illumination was the occasional gas lamp, but there was enough light for Bradford to see that a motorcar had crashed into the wall ahead. Its single working headlight shined on the shiny redhead of a person pinned, sagging, in front of it.

CHAPTER 18

*P*HYLLIDA LOOKED UP SHARPLY WHEN SHE HEARD THE FEROCIOUS barking and snarling.

All at once, a broad-shouldered figure emerged from the shadows from behind the crashed motor and she tensed even more. Whoever it was, he was coming toward her.

Bradford's pocketknife was in her hand—for she'd been contorted in a downward position, trying to cut her skirt away from where it had gotten pinned between motorcar and the wall—but it wouldn't be much assistance against a ferocious dog or an attacker. Still, knife in hand, she prepared to meet whatever threat approached.

"Mrs. Bright!" cried a familiar voice, and Phyllida couldn't control the surge of relief that washed through her.

"Bradford, is that you?" she called back, although by now she'd recognized the mop of dark fur. Its incessant barking didn't sound quite as ferocious anymore, either, but it was still irritating. The dratted beast would wake the entire neighborhood—although, since no one had seemed to notice the loud motorcar chase and ensuing crash, perhaps that wasn't a concern after all. Apparently, the villagers slept like the dead.

"Of course it's me," he replied. "What in the bloody—what on earth did you do?"

He paused, standing next to the crashed-up motorcar—which had hit the two jutting crenelations on either side of her, leaving

Phyllida unharmed in the narrow little indentation—and folded his arms over his middle.

"What did *I* do?" Phyllida lost every word in her vocabulary for a moment and resorted only to impotent sounds of fury.

"I can see—and hear—that you're uninjured. Were you planning to remain back there all night?" he asked, coming closer. He was holding a torch—quite possibly the one she'd dropped by St. Wendreda's.

"My skirt is caught," she managed to say, and brandished the pocketknife furiously at him—which, by the by, had taken quite a bit of maneuvering to remove from her pocket, for that was the side that had been pinned by the motor.

Bradford came closer and gave a low whistle. Myrtle continued to bark, drat the annoying beast.

"Good thing you're not any thicker," he said, looking at the shallow indentation into which she'd flattened herself in a wild bid for self-preservation. "Whose motor is this?"

"I have no idea," she replied, then, in the absence of the indication of any forthcoming assistance, she returned to sawing away at the corner of her frock in an effort to free herself.

"That was a very close call," Bradford said, shining the torchlight onto the part of her dress that had somehow been caught between vehicle and the jutting crenelation that had acted as a barrier to keep her from being crushed. "*Very* close. Another inch closer and it would have been *you* pinned there."

"I'm well aware of that," she responded.

"Lucky for you it was a Morris, with a flat front end, instead of something like a Rover or an Austin, with an angled one, otherwise . . ." He made a quiet sound of dismay.

She'd thought of that, of course, but only after the fact. There hadn't been time to consider the design of the front of the motorcar during the chase and her ensuing efforts for escape.

Bradford was still standing there, arms folded, surveying the situation. "Do you want that I should move the motor so you don't have to cut your dress?"

"That would be an excellent plan," she replied from between clenched jaws. "Mr. Bradford."

She thought she heard a little chuckle, but he moved immediately to dig around inside the motorcar. She heard a soft thunk and a click, but the motor didn't start—which wasn't surprising, as the vehicle had been coming at her so wildly, it had crashed its front end quite thoroughly.

Bradford emerged from inside the motor and after picking up the barking beast and shoving it into the driver seat—for what purpose Phyllida couldn't imagine—he gripped the open door and steering wheel and began to pull the vehicle away. To her surprise, the motorcar actually moved, rolling back silently. The corner of Phyllida's skirt fell free and then all at once her knees buckled.

She barely caught herself from falling, having been unaware of how much support the motor had been providing her.

"You all right?" Bradford asked. Apparently, he'd seen her near collapse.

"Yes," she said, but her voice came out as shaky as her knees felt. Fortunately, it was only one syllable, so perhaps he didn't notice.

"Let me help you." Bradford's tone was softer than it had been, and she allowed him to lift her clear over the hood.

Unfortunately, when he set her down, her knees gave way again, and she had to cling to his arms to keep from collapsing.

"All right, then, Mrs. Bright?" he said, taking his time steadying her.

"Yes, yes, I'm fine," she said briskly, releasing her grip on his solid forearms.

By now, the wild beast had erupted from the interior of the motorcar and seemed to think there was some sort of game happening. It bounced and bounded, barking and darting about them with what Phyllida interpreted as delight.

"You can thank Myrtle for saving your dress," Bradford said, bending to pick up the writhing, squirming mop.

"Whyever for?" Phyllida replied, unobtrusively resting her hand against the brick wall for support. Now that she was free, and safe, it seemed as if her entire body only wanted to fold into itself and heave and tremble.

It had been a very near thing.

Those last few moments as the bright, blaring headlights roared toward her, where she was tucked into a brick prison that she was by no means certain would protect her . . . the close heat of the engine of her would-be murderer . . . and then the jostle of metal against her middle—so close!—all were sensations burned into her mind.

"It was Myrt here who found you," said Bradford in an unusually light voice. "Didn't you, you little beastie?" He cooed—actually *cooed*—at the bundle of fur, who panted happily in Phyllida's direction.

Phyllida glanced at those dark, glinting eyes and the lolling pink tongue and suppressed a shudder at the thought of it swiping over her hand. And surely that was a light of smug satisfaction in the creature's eyes. "I see," she replied.

"You would have been able to free yourself," Bradford went on in the same blithe tone.

"Obviously."

"Eventually. But if Myrtle hadn't found you in time, you would have ruined your dress. Imagine if we'd come on the scene only moments after you'd sawed through the hem and released yourself—why, that would have been quite a tragedy, wouldn't it, Mrs. Bright?"

Phyllida had the notion he was teasing her somehow, but she was far too exhausted—physically as well as emotionally—to parley with him. Instead, she merely nodded and said, "Quite. Please inform Myrtle that I am very appreciative of her intervention on behalf of my frock." She was of the mind that one must give credit where credit was due.

"You can tell her yourself, Mrs. Bright," he said, his eyes dancing with unconcealed glee. "All she wants is a pat on the head."

Phyllida ground her teeth, but, again—credit where credit was due. The little beast had saved one of her favorite frocks, hadn't it? She reached out and lightly patted the creature on the top of its warm head. "There you are," she said, retracting her hand before that wild pink tongue could swipe at her. She was surprised at how soft and silky the thing's hair was, but that was neither here nor there.

"Now, shall we determine whose motorcar this is?" she said. She'd given herself sufficient recovery time and now felt safe enough to step away from the support of the brick wall.

"You don't know?"

"Of course I don't know," she retorted. "Had I known, I would have told you immediately."

"Would you care to tell me exactly what happened?" Bradford replied, setting Myrtle down within licking and jumping distance.

Phyllida automatically edged away from the threat, then she clapped a hand to her mouth. "Good heavens! Rita!" Thoughts of the poor maid had simply flown from her mind during the last hour or however long it had been since she'd chased the murderer from the church.

Bradford nodded soberly. "We saw her. I suppose you caught the murderer in action and decided to pursue him—"

"Or her," she said. "Yes, that's precisely what happened."

"Do you mean to say Inspector Bright hasn't decided on the identity of the killer yet? Why, it's been over twenty-four hours!"

Phyllida didn't give him the satisfaction of responding to his gibes. Instead, she gave a succinct explanation of what had occurred.

"For all I know, he or she could have jumped into anyone's motorcar to run me down," she concluded. "But as soon as it crashed, whoever it was got out and ran away. I was . . . understandably . . . a bit confused and out of sorts at the moment and didn't see who it was."

"Understandably," he said. He'd turned back to the motorcar and was digging around inside once again with the help of the torch. "Does the name Winnie Pankhurst mean anything to you?" he said, emerging a few moments later.

"Oh, yes—that's the woman who owns the general store," Phyllida replied.

"Well, it appears she is going to need a good mechanic to get her motorcar running again," Bradford said. He was holding a small stack of letters or papers in his hand; presumably, that was how he'd determined the name of the owner. "She's obviously not one of your suspects."

"No," Phyllida replied. She sighed. "I suppose I'd best get over to the constabulary to notify them of Rita's—death." She pushed past the sudden lump in her throat and lifted her chin. There would be time for grieving the maid later tonight, when she was alone with Stilton and Rye—neither of whom would *ever* consider going about randomly licking people who didn't like them with their sandpaper tongues.

"Perhaps I could go and report it, and you could sit in the Daimler, and, er, review your clues, Mrs. Bright," Bradford suggested.

Later, Phyllida might be mortified by how eagerly she accepted his suggestion, but for now, she wasn't going to think about that. "Yes, I do think that would be a good use of my time," she said, suddenly very weary when she thought about how far it would be to walk back to St. Wendreda's, where the Daimler was surely parked.

"If you'd like to wait here, I can run over and drive the motor back here. It won't take five minutes," he said.

"Oh, that would be—yes, I do think it would be a good idea to just sit and think for a moment," she said, ignoring the fact that she'd had some significant amount of time to think whilst pinned to a brick wall by Miss Pankhurst's motorcar.

"Myrtle will stay with you," Bradford said, and then dashed off into the darkness before she could argue—quite deliberately, she was certain.

Phyllida looked down balefully at the beast, whose dark eyes gleamed up at her. "I suppose it's all right, as long as you keep your distance and *don't even think about licking my stocking,*" she added quickly and fiercely as the mop sniffed at her leg.

To her surprise, Myrtle didn't attack. Instead, the beast plopped down onto its bottom so close to her that it sat half on top of her shoe, giving her foot the appearance of wearing a very large, dark wig.

Phyllida sighed, but for some reason, she couldn't quite bring herself to remove her foot from beneath the creature. The beast wasn't all that heavy, and it was warm and—she loathed to admit it—almost comforting to have a living, breathing creature right next to her after the horrors of her evening.

"Only this once," she informed the pile of curls. "And *only* because of my frock. It is one of my favorites."

But when she heard the sound of the Daimler approaching, Phyllida slipped her foot from beneath the mop's rump and moved away. Myrtle didn't seem to mind, for she must have recognized that the sound heralded the return of her master.

Phyllida climbed silently into the front seat of the motorcar and for the first time in her recent memory, she sat.

And closed her eyes.

It wasn't until she entered the sanctuary of her apartments that Phyllida remembered the papers she'd stuffed into her pocket.

The short story results, at last!

She had just pulled them out and was spreading them over the desk in her sitting room when there was a knock on her door.

Stifling a groan, she said, "Yes?"

To her shock, it was Agatha—and she was carrying a tea tray!

"Good heavens, what are you doing?" Phyllida said, shooting to her feet. "It's nearly midnight and you're—"

"Never mind the time—are you all right?" Agatha ignored her friend's reaction; instead, she walked right in and set the tea tray—which was laden with something that smelled delicious and comforting—on the small table next to Phyllida's favorite chair by the fire. "Oh, close your mouth, dear. I'm perfectly capable of delivering a tray of food—which you clearly could use. Why, you're white as a *ghost*. Now sit and tell me that you're *truly* all right."

"Yes, yes, I'm fine," Phyllida said, sinking into her favorite chair. She gathered Stilton into her lap and reveled in her soft, warm comfort. Rye, a tawny-gold cat named for the whisky, was annoyed that his mistress smelled like Myrtle, but Stilton—who was white with grayish blue streaks, like the cheese—was far more charitable. "Not even a minor bruise."

"Please forgive me, Phyllie," said Agatha, her eyes wide and anxious. She was half a foot taller than Phyllida, so she loomed quite a bit over her friend—especially when Phyllida was sitting. "I should never have asked you to do such a thing . . . never should have put you in such a position—"

"Not at all, Agatha. Not at *all*!" Phyllida was exhausted, but she had the energy to vigorously decry Agatha's misplaced guilt. "You know me better than that."

But Agatha shook her head sadly. "No, Phyllie. You could have *died* tonight. I should never have asked you to get involved!"

"Agatha." Phyllida adopted her stern, forbidding voice—the one that caused maids and footmen alike to go pale and trembly when she used it. Stilton looked up at her worriedly. "It's not your fault in the least. The truth is, I was already involved before you suggested I do so. I simply cannot sit back in the face of ineptitude—you must know that about me."

Agatha gave a weak laugh. "I do know that about you, but still—"

"I'll not have another word about it. I'm unhurt and—how did you even know about it all?"

"Oh. Well, Joshua telephoned ahead and told Dobble to have a tray prepared for you, and that you'd had an awful experience," Agatha said.

"Joshua?" For some reason, Phyllida's brain felt like the mush she'd eaten every morning when she'd been at the front.

"Joshua Bradford, of course. He rang from the rectory to let us know about . . . about everything. Poor Rita and . . . and what happened to you. I cannot imagine how horrific it must have been!"

Phyllida was simply too exhausted to do anything more than sigh. "How very kind of him."

"Now, Phyllida, I want you to listen to me—"

"Look what I have," Phyllida said, speaking over her friend. "The short story contest results at last!"

"Oh! And I had just put together all of the scoring sheets again for you earlier tonight. But you don't need them any longer, then, do you?" said Agatha.

Pleased at how easily she'd distracted her friend from ordering her off the case, Phyllida said, "No, no, I think it would be best if I saw them as well. Do you have the papers with you?"

Agatha did have them—tucked into her pocket—and she handed the small sheaf of papers over to Phyllida. "I didn't do the calculations yet; I didn't quite have the time—Dorothy and Anthony have been very insistent that we discuss the clues and the case. And G. K. just keeps soliloquizing about who would murder a *priest*! Just wait until I tell them about poor, poor Rita!" Suddenly, Agatha's expression turned blank. "You didn't speak to the inspector, did you, Phyllida? About Rita?"

"No," she replied. "Bradford was kind enough to notify the authorities whilst I waited in the motor. I didn't speak to them at all."

Agatha nodded, and there was something about the look on her face that had Phyllida tensing.

"What is it?" she asked.

"It's just that . . . they found the knife," Agatha told her slowly and carefully. "The knife used to kill Rita. In the grass near the side door."

Phyllida's insides tightened. "And?"

"Its hilt was engraved with the initials *J.B.*," Agatha told her, reaching over to cover Phyllida's fingers with hers.

Phyllida's breath caught.

J.B.

John Bhatt.

CHAPTER 19

Sunday morning

P HYLLIDA SLEPT BADLY THAT NIGHT.

She knew John Bhatt wasn't a murderer, but she was certain she would awaken to the news that he'd been taken into custody. The authorities in Listleigh had already demonstrated their ineptitude by arresting Mr. Billdop.

When she woke—if one could call it waking, when all she'd done was toss and turn all night in between nightmares about racing, blaring headlights bearing down on her—at half five, Phyllida surrendered to the day. She flung back the bedclothes on her bed and rose, dressing in a subdued forest-green frock and patting cold cucumber water over her face. The bags beneath her eyes were not an attractive look, so she added a bit of mascara to distract from them.

Fortunately, Opal would already be up and working in the scullery, so she rang for the young maid.

"Yes, ma'am," she said, arriving promptly at the door to Phyllida's sitting room. "You're up early, Mrs. Bright."

"I am," replied Phyllida, noticing with satisfaction that Opal was neat as a pin and seemed to be wide awake and energetic, even at six o'clock. She'd even brought a tea tray with her, anticipating Phyllida's request.

"We heard about all of what happened to you last night, we

did," said the maid as she set the small tray with tea, toast, and a hard-boiled egg on Phyllida's desk. She was conscientious enough not to muss or crinkle the papers that were spread out there. "I'm so very glad you came out of it all right, Mrs. Bright." She was earnest, and her eyes—gray and clear like her name— were filled with emotion. "I don't know what we would have done if . . . if . . ."

"Thank you, Opal. I am very glad as well."

"And how Mr. Bradford and Myrtle came to your rescue! Why, that was such good luck they were there!" Opal beamed, showing the two front teeth she had yet to grow into.

Phyllida knew her smile had gone flat. Rescue, *indeed*. But if that was how Bradford was putting it about, she saw no reason to exert any energy to minimize his viewpoint—it would only give it more credibility. Aside from that, she had far more important things on which to focus.

"Is there anything else you need, ma'am?"

"No, thank you. I just have some papers to review," Phyllida said, looking at the two piles of short story contest scores. "Please make certain if there is *any* news at all, if anyone should telephone, that I am notified immediately."

"Yes, ma'am," replied Opal. She gave a little curtsy, then slipped quietly from the room.

Phyllida poured a cup of tea and added four lumps plus a generous splash of milk. She knew she would need the extra boost.

And then she set to looking at the short story scores. They were important somehow, and she was determined to figure out how.

The first thing she did was look at the paper she'd found in Rita's pocket.

It was only the final score sheet, with the listing of each of the ten stories and the total scores for each on topics such as plot, character, tone, and overall. The pencil writing was in a fancy, old-fashioned male hand that Phyllida recognized from seeing other papers in Father Tooley's office. They were definitely his calculations.

As expected, Alastair Whittlesby's story had scored the highest overall and he would be the winner.

But. Her heart skipped a beat when she noticed that some of the numbers had been erased—the small smudges on the paper were an obvious clue. Some of the numbers had been erased and then new numbers had been written in. It was a subtle difference, but Phyllida could tell by the width of the pencil markings and also the pressure with which they'd been written that altered numbers had been changed by someone other than Father Tooley.

Now she was getting somewhere.

Next to determine who had been the *actual* winner, based on the scores submitted.

Phyllida turned to the papers Agatha had given her last night. The judging members of the Detection Club, including those who hadn't attended the Murder Fête, had been written out. Each member had one sheet with all of the story submissions listed on it, and they'd gone through and written their scores for each story by category of plot, characterization, tone, and overall.

Phyllida quickly went through and retabulated all of the results. . . .

And then she stared at the final score on Father Tooley's sheet.

They were identical.

Which didn't make any sense. Why would someone erase the scores and then put the same—the correct!—numbers back in?

Phyllida sat back with a gusty sigh and took a very large drink of oversweetened tea. Rye was still ignoring her from his perch atop her bookshelf, his delicate pink nose held aloft, but Stilton had leaped onto the desk and allowed Phyllida to stroke her along her arching spine.

Think. Think! she told herself. She'd been so close to understanding everything . . . and then *this.*

The jarring ring of the telephone in the hallway outside her sitting room had her rising swiftly to her feet before she could formulate the answer.

She hurried from the room, certain the news would be bad—news of Dr. Bhatt in custody for the murders of Rita, Father Tooley, and Eugene Whittlesby.

"Mallowan Hall," she said in a calm voice that belied her anxiety.

"Is that Mrs. Bright?" came a female voice that she recognized as Mrs. Dilly from Tangled Vines Cottage.

"It is," Phyllida replied.

"Only, I told Drewson we should ring up and tell you," said the Whittlesbys' cook. "And he said I shouldn't bother, but you said if there was anything unusual, we should be letting you know."

"Yes?" Phyllida said, hoping the cook would get to the point rather quickly and not tie up the telephone line.

"Well, the Whittlesbys were coming back home today, and seeing as how they were, Mrs. Alastair telephoned and said as how their bedchambers should be all cleaned up and ready—you know Drewson and Louella ain't allowed in there much"—Phyllida also knew that she had advised the servants to do just that yesterday, hadn't she?—"but they went about doing it all, and Drewson found something."

"Yes?" Phyllida said far more patiently than she felt.

"There was a shirt under Mr. Alastair's bed, there was, and it had *strawberry* jam on it. Right on the cuff. Or it might've been raspberry jam, he—Drewson, you know—ain't sure, and I sure ain't gonna taste it, Mrs. Bright."

"I see," Phyllida replied, her mind turning again. "When was the last time Mr. Whittlesby had strawberry—or raspberry—jam, do you think? Or, perhaps I should ask, how long do you think that shirt has been there?" Based on the state of the bedchambers, she could only guess.

"Oh, that's why I thought to ring you, Mrs. Bright. You said anything unusual, you did. It's only, Mr. Alastair—he *never* has red jam, ma'am. He only takes orange or lemon marmalade ever."

Phyllida's eyes grew wide. "Now that is quite interesting," she said. "Quite interesting indeed. Thank you very much, Mrs. Dilly. That is, I think, quite helpful."

She replaced the telephone receiver and just as it settled into place, so did all of the little pieces that had been churning about in her mind—just like the tumblers of a safe when the correct combination had been spun: *click, clank, clunk.*

CHAPTER 20

Sunday afternoon

PHYLLIDA WALKED INTO THE SITTING ROOM AT ST. WENDREDA'S JUST in time to hear Alastair Whittlesby.

He was complaining.

"What is the meaning of this?" demanded the man with a tone of self-importance. "What are *they* doing here?"

They, presumably, referred not only to Inspector Cork and Constable Greensticks but also Phyllida herself—as well as Mr. Dobble, Bradford, Molly, and nearly all of the household staff at Mallowan Hall.

There had been no keeping them away—the staff—and so Phyllida and Mr. Dobble had reluctantly agreed to allow them to attend what was *supposed* to be the announcement of the winning short story, as long as they served tea and whatever drinks the attendees preferred. The fact that seven staff members weren't necessary to serve drinks to thirteen people was beside the point.

But obviously Mr. Whittlesby had realized there was something else occurring other than an unexpectedly large crowd to witness his triumph.

"Now, Allie, don't make a fuss," said Mrs. Whittlesby. She sat in a chair, one wrist still bound, face tight and drawn in an expression of what she'd been through in the last two days. "I'm certain it's all fine. Surely they're only here to serve everyone. I do hope they'll bring another round of drinks rather quickly."

Mr. Whittlesby grumbled a bit, but his wife's explanation seemed to appease him, so he took the chair next to hers and waved over one of the footmen, who had a tray of sherry.

Phyllida glanced at Inspector Cork, who also did not appear pleased with the turn of events. Still, if he'd been the least bit competent at his work, she wouldn't have to be giving the speech she was about to make. At that thought, she sought out Elton and Bradford with her gaze, lifting a brow in question. She was already certain her theory was correct, but it had been up to them to find the missing wire cutters so she could prove it.

Bradford nodded and lifted a small paper bag that presumably contained the wire cutters. Phyllida exhaled with satisfaction. If the cutters had been where she anticipated they were, then she most certainly was correct in her deductions.

When Mr. Chesterton and Miss Sayers learned that Phyllida had identified the murderer, they insisted she give the explanation in a public setting, filled with the suspense of how she'd come to her conclusions and pinpointing the culprit at the end of it all—just as any of their fictional detectives would have done.

"It's only right," said Miss Sayers in her grandiose fashion, hands fluttering, robe-like frock shivering. "This was a murder— no, a *series* of murders—taking place at a festival of *murder writers.* What else would be more fitting than to have an actual denouement speech?"

Mr. Chesterton, tickled by the irony of it all, had heartily agreed, although Mr. Berkeley gave Phyllida a look as if he wasn't certain a housekeeper—that is, a female—would have been able to figure it out if he and his colleagues hadn't done so.

But it was Mr. Max who'd informed Cork and Greensticks that they should be present whilst Phyllida explained what they should have figured out for themselves. And it was Mr. Max who now watched the room carefully, as if prepared to jump to her defense at any given moment. Phyllida had a moment to reflect on how grateful she was for Agatha and Mr. Max as not only her employers but also her friends. As if reading her mind, Agatha sent her a broad smile and fluttered a little wave from her lap.

"What *are* we doing here?" said Miss Crowley. "Surely . . . surely the contest isn't about to go on, after . . ." She gave Phyllida a careful glance, then dragged her eyes away. If Phyllida didn't know better, she'd think the other woman was feeling guilty about her threat yesterday.

"We are gathered here—the members of the Detection Club and those of the Listleigh Murder Club—for the announcement of the contest winner . . . and to hear a story," said Mr. Chesterton in his booming voice. He'd come to stand at the front of the room as was fitting—being the president of the Detection Club— prepared to announce the winner. "This is a tale that promises to be just as twisty and diabolically clever as any of the stories written by any of the folks in this room—or anywhere. Even Mr. Conan Doyle, God rest his soul."

Mrs. Rollingbroke, who was sitting on a sofa with her husband, leaned over to whisper to him. He nodded and patted her hand, looking about the room. Phyllida was certain she detected a bit of discomfort in his normally jovial gaze, and stifled a smile. She knew precisely why he appeared slightly discombobulated.

Mr. Genevan had taken a seat slightly behind Miss Crowley, and the vicar had pulled up a chair in such a position that he had a good view of the front of the room, but also of Mr. Dobble, who stood across from him. John Bhatt sat next to Constable Green- sticks, and the doctor wore a tense expression. It was only due to Mr. Max's influence that John hadn't already been taken into cus- tody. Phyllida caught John's gaze and gave him an abbreviated nod meant to indicate that his freedom was safely in her hands.

"Well, shall we get on with it, then, Mrs. Bright?" Mr. Chester- ton gave a theatrical bow and stepped aside. "The stage is set."

"Wait a minute! I thought you were going to announce the con- test winner," said Mr. Whittlesby, half rising. "What is *she* doing there?"

"Mrs. Bright has a tale to tell," said Mr. Chesterton. His figure was so large and imposing, and his words were so firm and powerful that even the strident Mr. Whittlesby was cowed. "And then the winner of the story contest will be announced. So sit down and listen, if you please, Mr. Whittlesby."

Mr. Whittlesby sat.

And Phyllida stepped forward. Oddly enough, she wasn't nervous.

"This story begins several months ago when the idea of having a Murder Fête charity event supported by the Detection Club was first proposed," she started off. "It was the short story contest— and the highly desirable prize of international publication—that gave the murderer the idea. Through the ensuing weeks, the plan was developed. Every detail was thought out, every plot twist accounted for, and the stage was set.

"And then the Murder Fête arrived, the story contest results were submitted and calculated, and everyone knew who the winner was going to be."

Phyllida looked around the room at the faces of the Murder Club members, then added, "Or so they thought."

A little surprised shuffling rippled through her audience—as she'd intended—and now, having fully secured the attention of everyone in the room, she went on.

"On Friday, the day of the cocktail party, whilst I was overseeing the luncheon setup, I overheard a conversation. Two people were standing outside the window, discussing someone in quite unflattering terms, and one of them said, 'He's simply *got* to be done away with,' and the other person agreed, and suggested that poisoning a drink or something about a 'new car, eh?' would do the trick.

"As we all know, later that evening, Father Tooley drank a cocktail called a Vieux Carré"—she emphasized the syllables so that they sounded less French and more like the phrase "new car, eh?" and was rewarded by gasps and more shuffling and murmuring throughout the audience—"and Father Tooley, God rest him, died.

"It became obvious quickly on that Alastair Whittlesby was the intended victim, for reasons of which you are all likely aware—

mainly that a bottle of bitters used specifically for his cocktail had been poisoned." Phyllida looked around the room, took a sip of the tea someone had thoughtfully placed on the table next to her, then went on. "And so the authorities spent much time interviewing the attendees—for it became obvious that whoever had poisoned Mr. Whittlesby's cocktail bitters had been at the party. Everyone's movements were accounted for but did little to assist in determining who had placed the poisoned bitters on the bar counter. Anyone could have had the bottle in his pocket or her pocketbook, and everyone, at one time or another, was near the bar.

"The next morning, I was called here to St. Wendreda's due to the death of Father Tooley's cat, Saint Aloysius. Upon my arrival, I noticed that a geranium plant had been crushed near the front entrance of the rectory—the entrance that had *not* been used by anyone attending the cocktail party. Rita, Father Tooley's maid, also indicated that there were geranium leaves and petals inside the front rectory door when she returned that morning and that they could only have been deposited Friday night, *during or after the cocktail party*. Someone had gained access to the rectory.

"That brought to mind the question of *why* someone would want to have access to the rectory after Father Tooley's death—accidental or otherwise." Phyllida looked around the room and settled her gaze pointedly on one countenance in particular. A countenance who was doing a poor job of appearing innocent and unbothered by her conjecturing. "It was someone who took advantage of the fact that the rectory would be empty overnight Friday . . . someone who'd been in this very room earlier and noticed a particularly nice table that had, at the time, been placed right *there*."

Phyllida gestured to the spot next to the sofa where Sir Rolly and Mrs. Rollingbroke sat. "The table was missing on Saturday morning, replaced by the uninteresting—and inexpensive—round table that Sir Rolly is currently using for his ashtray."

"Someone stole a table from the church?" Mrs. Rollingbroke

said, sitting up sharply. "Why, that's *despicable*. Who would *do* such a thing?"

Phyllida said nothing. She merely turned pointedly and looked at Mr. Genevan.

When he didn't speak, she prodded him. "Not only was the *antique* piecrust table missing but also a footstool of some value, and three pieces of porcelain statuary. I suspect the individual might have intended to return last night for another sweep through the house and were foiled when they found the place quite lit up and overrun by the authorities due to the murder of the rectory's maid, Rita, whom many of you saw on Friday evening."

"Louis, did you take the table?" Mrs. Rollingbroke said shrilly. "And the other items?"

Everyone looked at the antiques dealer, who shriveled a bit into his seat. "Fine. Yes. I . . . I didn't think anyone would miss it, now that Father Tooley is gone, and it was a lovely piece," said Mr. Genevan. "Who would care?"

"*I* care," cried Mrs. Rollingbroke. "Why, stealing from a church is just . . . just *ghastly*!"

"Fine. I'll return the—er—items. But I didn't *kill* anyone," said Mr. Genevan. He looked at Phyllida, who nodded in agreement.

"No, you aren't a murderer. A thief, yes." She looked significantly at Constable Greensticks, who nodded. Charges would be filed against Louis Genevan. "But not a killer.

"But you weren't the only visitor to the rectory Friday evening with thievery on their mind, Mr. Genevan," Phyllida went on. "Someone else used the front door to enter this building whilst we were all at the cocktail party in the courtyard. Someone who wasn't attending the party, but who was seen just outside the building during that time. That individual deposited geranium flower petals and leaves from their shoes at their home that evening, proving they'd been inside the rectory." She leveled her gaze at the culprit and was rewarded when he gulped and turned pink. "You were looking for the contest scoring results, weren't you, Sir Rolly?"

"Didn't mean any harm," he said as his wife turned to stare at him. His cheeks went even pinker under her shocked regard. "Only—well, everyone was so certain that *Alastair* was going to win that I thought it would just serve him right if he *didn't*. And . . . and I wanted to see how Vera's story had scored, and, all right, dash it all—I meant to change the score sheets to list her as the winner." He gave his wife an abashed look.

"Oh, Rolly!" cried Mrs. Rollingbroke. Her cheeks were flushed, too—but with pleasure not guilt, and she gave him an affectionate slap on the arm as she fought to hold back a smile. "What a silly, *sweet* sort of thing to do! You silly, *silly*, sweet, *foolish*, loving man!"

Phyllida cleared her throat and lifted her brows at Sir Rolly. "What happened when you broke in?"

"Well, dash it all, I didn't really *break in*—make me sound like some sort of vagrant, you know. I mean to say, we—Vera and I—were bloody good friends with Father Tooley, and I knew he wouldn't mind if I just let myself in—give enough money to the church, you know, that it really shouldn't have been even a concern," Sir Rolly went on. His pudgy face was still pink, but the color was fading. "The parish *owns* the building after all, now, don't it? But it didn't matter because I didn't find the score sheets or anything about the contest." He gave Phyllida a belligerent look. "So I didn't do anything wrong."

Her look indicated how little she agreed with *that* sentiment. However, she let that go for the moment, as there was so much more to reveal. "Sir Rolly didn't find the score sheets for the short story contest, and when Rita and I looked about for them on Saturday morning, we didn't find them, either. Quite mysterious, I thought . . . and that had me meditating about who would *want* the score sheets—that is, information about the winner—to go missing. With Father Tooley out of the way, the thief could change the scores and the winner to anyone he or she wanted it to be, and no one would be the wiser."

"Are you saying that someone killed Father Tooley in order to change the contest results?" said Mr. Chesterton, his eyes popping from behind his pince-nez.

"That was precisely what I wondered," Phyllida said. "Particularly when, on Saturday morning, it was discovered that Saint Aloysius—the rectory cat—had died after eating part of a cake that had been left in Father Tooley's office. A cake that Father Tooley had already consumed a large portion thereof."

Heads nodded—apparently, this wasn't news to anyone in the room. But Phyllida felt it necessary to lay it out anyhow. "Thus, it seemed that someone wanted Father Tooley *and* Alastair Whittlesby dead. And that someone also was, presumably, in possession of the story contest scores. It was beginning to look more and more as if someone wanted the presumed winner of the publishing contest out of the way—actually *dead*—and they wanted the ability to change the contest winner."

Phyllida paused to take another sip of tea, for now things were about to become more complicated. Then she went on with her tale.

"Obviously Alastair Whittlesby expected to win the short story contest. In fact, he not only assumed he had done, he put it about publicly at the Murder Club meeting on Wednesday that he was to be announced as the winner.

"But when he discovered that he *wasn't* going to be named the winner, he had to take matters into his own hands—including poisoning Father Tooley, who was the only person who knew the actual results of the contest.

"Mr. Whittlesby somehow managed to have Father Tooley divulge the winner to him—or, perhaps, the priest merely indicated that Mr. Whittlesby *wasn't* the winner; most likely on Thursday, the morning after his triumphant Murder Club tea party—and so he had to act quickly. If Father Tooley died before the results were announced, Mr. Whittlesby could change them to favor himself—and save face among the other members of the Murder Club."

"Why that's preposterous!" shouted Mr. Whittlesby. "*I've* been the intended victim all along—how *dare* you accuse *me!*"

"Don't listen to her, Allie! Just don't!" cried Mrs. Whittlesby, from her usual position of clinging limpet.

"Quite, Mr. Whittlesby. There was the poisoned cocktail bitters, obviously meant for you. And then there was the cut brake lines on the motorcar you drive every day. Clearly, you have been the intended victim all along." Phyllida was aware that everyone in the room had settled into a rapt silence as the tone of her voice changed. "Or have you?"

"What on *earth*—"

Phyllida spoke over Mr. Whittlesby, gaining steam with her narrative. "It was clearly the intention to poison Father Tooley with the cake—a cake that was spread with strawberry jam liberally laced with arsenic. But we will get to that in a moment. First, shall we discuss the cocktail party?"

Phyllida wasn't asking a question meant to be answered, so she went on without pause. "At the cocktail party, two drinks were made with your special bitters, Mr. Whittlesby. One for you and one for Father Tooley. He was the only one who drank his, and he died—but whether it was from arsenic or nicotine poisoning, we don't know. Either or both of them would have killed him.

"But *was* he the intended victim of the nicotine-laced bitters? Perhaps. But since Father Tooley was not known to imbibe spirits, no one could have *expected* he would have one of your special drinks, could they, Mr. Whittlesby? And so someone else had to have been the original, actual target for the poisoned Vieux Carré cocktail."

"Of course there was—*me!*" cried Mr. Whittlesby, banging his fist on the table next to him. "No one else drinks anything with those bitters in it except for me." His eyes bulged with fury, and it seemed that only the grip of his wife's hand kept him from surging out of his chair. "Someone tried to kill me! And they killed Father Tooley, too, so they could change the contest results!"

"But Mrs. Whittlesby had *your* drink in her hand that night," Phyllida said in a carrying voice. "She would have tasted it if Father Tooley's death hadn't distracted all of us. After all, it was clear to everyone present that Mrs. Whittlesby—er—enjoyed her spirits. It would have been an accident, correct?"

"It would have been *ghastly!*" cried Mrs. Rollingbroke. "Imagine if it had been me, Rolly!"

"But what if it *hadn't* been an accident?" Phyllida went on smoothly. "When you told the footman *not* to serve your wife any more drinks, you had two motives for doing so, didn't you, Mr. Whittlesby? One, to keep her from becoming even more intoxicated and embarrassing you in front of your colleagues . . . and two . . . so that she, desperate for another drink, *would taste your cocktail.* The cocktail that you *knew* was poisoned."

Gasps rippled around the room and Mrs. Whittlesby yanked her hand from where it had curled around her husband's arm. She stared at him in shock. "Is this true, Allie?"

"No, no, no," Mr. Whittlesby said, his voice rising in volume and pitch. His forehead glistened with perspiration. "Yes, yes, it was true that I told the footman not to bring her any more drinks, but it was just as you said—I didn't want her to . . . to have anything else. But of *course* it wasn't so that she would drink my cocktail. Someone tried to poison *me*, and they nearly got my wife instead! How *dare* you try and turn this around and accuse me!" His eyes blazed with fury and indignation.

Phyllida fixed him with a steady gaze. "And then," she went on without acknowledging his outrage, "on Saturday there was the motorcar crash. Another very convenient, nearly successful murder attempt—purportedly on Alastair Whittlesby. It was the vehicle that you use nearly every day, Mr. Whittlesby, and it was sabotaged on the *one day* that your wife was left to drive it.

"*Two* attempts on your life in two days . . . two attempts *seemingly* on your life in two days, but both of them very nearly killed Mrs. Whittlesby instead. I find that far too coincidental to be believable, Mr. Whittlesby."

"What are you trying to say?" Alastair Whittlesby hissed, his eyes bulging.

"I'm suggesting that perhaps you weren't the target after all, Mr. Whittlesby, but that instead it was your wife. It was a clever arrangement—making those events appear like attempts on *your* life, but really Lettice Whittlesby was the one who was intended to be the victim all along."

"But who . . . who would do such a thing?" Mr. Whittlesby's anger turned to confusion. "Who would want Lettice dead?" He reached for his wife's arm, but she pulled it away. *"Lettice!"* he exclaimed in shock as her feelings became obvious. "You don't think . . . "

"Who *would* want Mrs. Whittlesby dead? That is an excellent question. It certainly wasn't Mr. Eugene Whittlesby, for if so, he wouldn't have ridden in the sabotaged motorcar with her and he couldn't have engineered the poisoned cocktail at the party. In fact, it had to be someone at the cocktail party on Friday night. Your embarrassment by her clinging and her heavy drinking became quite clear at the cocktail party, Mr. Whittlesby."

"Are you implying—"

Phyllida cut him off. "And perhaps you realized that, since you were about to become published on two continents and your writing career was about to take off, you no longer wanted a—what did you call her?—oh, yes, a bloody, clinging limpet, or something of that nature. You no longer wanted a clinging, whiny, boring wife in your exciting new life. And so you created this very elaborate plan to make it appear as if *you* were the intended victim while you were actually trying to kill your wife instead."

Alastair Whittlesby lunged to his feet. "Why, you impertinent little bi—"

Mr. Max half rose from his seat and Inspector Cork clapped a hand to the revolver at his waist, but it was Mr. Max who spoke. "Sit down, Alastair. You'll do yourself no favors by making a scene."

As Mr. Whittlesby sank back into his chair, Bradford took a step back to where he'd been leaning against the wall. His expression glittered dangerously as his eyes settled on Mr. Whittlesby.

"You have no proof of any of this," Mr. Whittlesby said from between clenched jaws. "I'll sue you for slander, you lying—you interfering madwoman."

"On the contrary," said Phyllida. "There was a note for your wife that you would be driving the MG on that morning—a note that you left before she rose so she didn't have an opportunity to argue. And you left the sedan outside Friday night so that it would seem that *anyone* could have access to the motor and cut the brake lines. But," she said, cutting him off when he started to speak, "you weren't taking any chances of anyone figuring it out.

"It is, after all, a classic murder plot for a presumably accidental victim to actually be the target, whilst the murderer camouflages themselves with several attempts on his or her own life." Phyllida glanced at Agatha, whose Poirot had nearly missed solving such a twisted case. In that case, as in this one, it was a printed note that helped Phyllida and Poirot solve the killings. Agatha nodded, her eyes twinkling with understanding.

"And since you weren't taking any chances of anyone figuring out that Mrs. Whittlesby was the actual target and you were the perpetrator, you staged a clever scene last night, here at St. Wendreda's," Phyllida went on. "You used John Bhatt's knife to murder Rita, and you left the evidence where it would easily be found—and then you attempted to run me down."

"That's a *lie*! She's *lying*! She's making this all up!" Mr. Whittlesby was so agitated that a fleck of spittle flew out and lodged on the corner of his mouth. "If that man's knife was found at the scene of the crime, then it's *obvious* who—"

But Phyllida went on, clearly and inexorably stating her case. "You stayed at Dr. Bhatt's surgery last night with your injured wife, didn't you, Mr. Whittlesby? I didn't know about that until I received a telephone call from Tangled Vines Cottage this morning mentioning that you had stayed with her. It would have been very simple for you—in a physician's surgery—to slip a sedative into Dr. Bhatt's drink and your wife's as well, steal a knife, and slip out to do the deed. No one would have been the wiser, and Dr. Bhatt wouldn't have had an alibi, as *you* would have claimed you were drugged. It was a very clumsy attempt to frame Dr. Bhatt, but it might have been effective had I not been on the scene."

"It's not true," Mr. Whittlesby said in a quieter voice. "It's not true *at all.* I would never . . ."

"And poor Father Tooley, twice poisoned. Fortunately, he could only perish once. The main clue in the murders of the priest and

Saint Aloysius was the poisoned cake. I admit, I spent more time than I should have done trying to determine from *where* the cake had come.

"But everything became much clearer when one of your shirts was found, stuffed under your bed, with strawberry jam on the cuff. Everyone at Tangled Vines Cottage knows you *loathe* strawberry jam and only eat orange marmalade, Mr. Whittlesby. That, along with your strong and almost obsessive preference for Vieux Carrés was what helped me to make sense of it all. You see, it was these very, very specific and unyielding tendencies of yours, Mr. Whittlesby, that made you such an easy target."

"An easy target?" Mr. Whittlesby exploded, leaping to his feet again. "I'll say I was an easy target! Someone has been trying to kill me, and now you're accusing *me* of . . . of . . ." He was so furious he couldn't seem to find the words. But, apparently mindful of the watching Max Mallowan and the glowering Bradford, he didn't lunge toward Phyllida—although his expression clearly indicated his desire to do so.

Phyllida's palms were going a little damp, for she knew what was coming . . . what she had to do next. She *knew* she was correct. The two hat boxes, the fruit flies, the dead branch . . . the misplaced apostrophe . . .

It was the only explanation.

"You were a target . . . but of a very diabolical and twisted plot, Mr. Whittlesby." Phyllida drew in a steadying breath and looked directly at Lettice Whittlesby. "Why did you kill Mr. Eugene Whittlesby?"

CHAPTER 21

THERE WAS A SHOCKED SILENCE, THEN MRS. WHITTLESBY FROWNED, confusion in her expression. "Are you speaking to me?" Her tone was perfectly calm, but Phyllida saw her forefinger tremble a bit as her unwrapped hand pressed to her chest.

"Yes, Mrs. Whittlesby. I'd like to know why you killed your brother-in-law."

Gasps and low murmurs filled the room, and Mr. Whittlesby appeared just as shocked as his wife did.

But Phyllida knew better.

"I think she's out of her mind," said Mrs. Whittlesby to her husband. "First, she accuses you of trying to kill me, and now she accuses me of killing Eugene!"

"It was incredibly risky for you," Phyllida went on, looking steadily at Mrs. Whittlesby. She saw the flicker of fear that was quickly banked in the other woman's eyes. "To stage the motorcar accident in such a way for it to be believable—and to facilitate Mr. Eugene's death—but not enough to actually injure yourself. It was very, very clever. I nearly believed it."

"But . . . ?" said Mrs. Whittlesby in a challenging voice. "Something somehow made you believe I faked nearly dying in a motor crash? How appallingly ludicrous. She *is* mad," she added in a stage whisper to her husband.

Phyllida looked around the room. The faces of her audience were still shocked, and the silence was so taut that she felt the air vibrate. "Mrs. Whittlesby purposely drove the motorcar into the tree, taking care, one must assume, that Mr. Eugene's side of the vehicle sustained the greater damage. The crash wasn't enough to kill him, but she took care of that herself. Whilst he was recovering from the shock—or perhaps, you were fortunate enough that he'd been knocked unconscious; but it hardly matters, does it, Mrs. Whittlesby?—you used a tree branch to smash him on the head and make certain he was dead.

"That was one of the mistakes, you know. Bringing your own weapon. You see, that particular branch obviously didn't belong there. And you were the only one who could have put it there because it had blood on it."

At first Mrs. Whittlesby didn't speak or react. Then, after a moment of sharp, jerky breathing, she pulled away from her husband, for the first time putting significant distance between them.

"I had no choice," said Mrs. Whittlesby at last. "I had to make certain there was something handy to use. I knew I only had a few minutes before someone would come to investigate the sound of the crash." Her voice was a little unsteady, as if she couldn't believe she was making the admission.

"And so you put a small but hefty tree branch in the back of the motor to use after the accident, thinking it would simply blend into the environs after you were finished with it. However, it was obviously an old, dead branch, and the motor had driven into a living tree. Any branches that had been knocked loose—as you clearly expected us to believe—would have been green wood. Any old, dead branches that might have already been on the ground wouldn't have blood on them.

"Aside from that, I asked Amsi, the gardener at Mallowan Hall, to identify the variety of tree from which the branch came. There was no maple in the vicinity of the car crash. Only that single, bloodstained branch."

Mrs. Whittlesby pursed her lips, then nodded grudgingly.

"The other mistake you made was not returning the cutters to the toolbox in the back of the motorcar after you cut the brake lines. Yes," Phyllida said, once more needing to clarify for her audience, "she cut the brake lines *after* the accident in order to make it appear as if the crash had been an attempt on her life. Or her husband's. Either suited her purpose, although she was certainly doing her best to incriminate Mr. Alastair in any way possible, weren't you, Mrs. Whittlesby?"

"What?" cried Alastair Whittlesby.

More murmurs of surprise rippled through the room.

"We'll get to that as well in a moment, but first I'd like to finish with poor Mr. Eugene. Since you haven't answered my question, shall I conjecture as to why you decided to rid yourself of Mr. Eugene Whittlesby as well as your husband." Phyllida purposely made her words a statement rather than a query. "Presumably, he'd seen something—most likely, you with the bottle of bitters, or perhaps the strawberry jam. He wouldn't have thought anything of it at the time, but later, of course, he might remember and it would make sense to him. And so he had to be gotten rid of."

"It wasn't only that," Lettice Whittlesby burst out. "He was always grabbing me, trying to back me into a corner. I think he thought he was getting something over on Alastair. It became even worse when I started drinking more heavily over the last few months. He must have assumed that, drunk, I would be an easier target." Her mouth twisted with distaste.

"You mean to say, when you *pretended* to start drinking more heavily," Phyllida said, skewering her with a pointed look. She saw the flare of surprise in Lettice Whittlesby's face and knew the woman hadn't expected her to have deduced so much.

"H-how did you know that?" said Mrs. Whittlesby.

"The ficus in your sitting room is dying and its soil is swarming with fruit flies due to being overwatered with whisky, port, sherry— whatever you had on hand. You were pouring your drinks into the soil instead of drinking them. And you dumped your morning vodka into the vase of roses next to your bed or on your desk because it was clear like the water and no one would notice.

"You planned it all very well, and were very patient, Mrs. Whittlesby. The idea surely came to you when the Murder Fête was first announced. You had some time to set the stage, so to speak.

Or, to be more relevant, to plot the story. And that's what you did, isn't it? You plotted your own murder story, complete with red herrings, clues, and a very clever killer."

Mrs. Whittlesby's expression now held a hint of admiration. "But how did you figure out it was me?"

"There were three things that gave you away. First, the two hat boxes in your bedchamber from your Thursday visit to Wenville Heath. The receipt in your pocketbook—which you had specifically placed therein to prove that Mr. Whittlesby had decided to drive the MG into town; that was very clever—indicated that only one hat had been purchased. So why were there two hat boxes but only one hat?"

Phyllida smiled, noticing by their expressions that some people—Agatha, of course, and Miss Sayers—had already caught on. "A hat box is very similar to a bakery box, isn't it? That's how you brought the cake into the house unnoticed—the cake that you poisoned for Father Tooley and purchased from a bakery in Wenville Heath. Then you framed your husband for the priest's murder by stuffing a shirt under his bed with strawberry jam on it.

"The second item that caught my interest I've already mentioned—the fruit flies about the ficus. Once I realized you were dumping your drinks, I began to look at everything quite differently.

"Then there was the motorcar crash. Not only was there a branch that didn't belong, but there were no wire cutters in the toolbox in the sedan's boot. I'm told," Phyllida said, glancing at Bradford, "that wire cutters are a basic tool that would nearly always be in a vehicle's toolbox. You bashed Mr. Eugene on the head and killed him, then used the wire cutters to snip the brake hoses. But you were afraid of leaving fingerprints on the wire cutters, so you threw them into the woods as far from the scene as possible. You couldn't wear your gloves whilst cutting the brake lines because you couldn't chance getting grease or oil or anything on them—there would be no good explanation for that.

"I wasn't certain about the wire cutters until I had Bradford and Elton look around the motorcar crash—and they found them. There is no other reason for such a tool to be in the woods nearby, and I'm quite certain we will find your fingerprints on them."

Phyllida heard Inspector Cork's muttered, *"We?"*

"Last night, you arranged to meet Rita in the church, where you knew she'd be lighting an offering candle for Father Tooley and Saint Aloysius," Phyllida said, still speaking to Mrs. Whittlesby. "You took the story contest results—which you had previously stolen from the rectory, probably either Thursday or Friday, when you slipped the cake onto the Panson's delivery truck—and gave them to her to make certain we would find them on her body. Then you killed her with Dr. Bhatt's knife—something you'd easily found and taken from his surgery."

"That's ridiculous," said Mr. Whittlesby. "Why, Lettice has a sprained wrist, and she was in a terrible accident and . . ." His voice trailed off when he noticed the disdainful expression on his wife's face.

"Presumably the sprained wrist is either faked or exaggerated," Phyllida said. "Just as were all of her injuries. She needed to be hurt enough to stay the night at Dr. Bhatt's surgery—with proximity to the church and village—but not so hurt that she had to go to hospital. It was a stroke of genius to get your husband to stay with you at the surgery last night, Mrs. Whittlesby," she went on. "I can only guess that you used his distrust of Dr. Bhatt's medical abilities to convince him to do so."

The expression on Mrs. Whittlesby's face told Phyllida she had guessed correctly.

"I . . . I can't believe this," said Alastair Whittlesby. "And I don't quite understand . . . you . . . you tried to kill me? But you also tried to frame Dr. Bhatt for the murder?"

"It is quite complicated, but it makes great sense when one considers with *whom* we are dealing in this situation. A collection of murder writers," Phyllida said. "People who read and write and are familiar with the most twisty and devious plots ever created . . . and so Mrs. Whittlesby had to outsmart them all.

"And so she cleverly made it appear that she was meant to be the victim of the killings even though her husband seemed the obvious target, and then she clumsily—purposely clumsily— attempted to frame Dr. Bhatt, so that it would seem that you, Mr. Whittlesby, were in fact the killer and were framing Dr. Bhatt as the culprit in an effort to turn suspicion away from yourself. But it was such a clumsy tactic that she knew it wouldn't hold up for very long." Phyllida cast a sidelong look at Inspector Cork, hoping he was paying close attention to this part. He'd been just about to put handcuffs on John Bhatt when Mr. Max convinced him to stand down. "And so once the false framing was exposed, and the jam-stained shirt was discovered—that was also quite clever of you, Mrs. Whittlesby, to call and tell the servants to clean up the bedchambers for your return home. You needed the shirt to be found at the perfect time, and that was it. Once the framing of Dr. Bhatt was exposed, it would become clear and obvious that Alastair Whittlesby was not the victim, but the murderer—and that he'd been trying to rid himself of his own wife."

The room was silent for a moment as Phyllida's words were di-gested, and everyone's brains caught up with her explanation. She saw the light of understanding come into pairs of eyes around the room; saw nods and heard murmurs and even noticed a few admiring grins—from Miss Sayers and Mr. Berkeley in particular.

"So Mrs. Whittlesby has been trying to get rid of her husband while framing him for trying to kill her—or possibly even killing him outright at some point," said Dr. Bhatt after a moment. "What I don't understand is . . . why?"

Phyllida smiled. "Because Lettice Whittlesby is the real author of the Inspector Theodore Belfast stories."

CHAPTER 22

*T*HE ROOM ERUPTED WITH EXCLAMATIONS; THE LOUDEST BEING Mr. Whittlesby himself.

"Why, that's . . . that's . . ."

"It's true, Alastair," said Mrs. Whittlesby flatly. "You know it's true. You can't hide behind me any longer. *I* wanted the recognition and the prize, and he simply wouldn't agree to it. Said no one would believe it of me, little plain, wispy Lettice Whittlesby writing the smart Millie and Belfast stories. If I were rid of him—either through death, or in prison for murder—then no one could hold me back. Besides," she went on, a furious, unholy light coming into her eyes, "I was tired of being called a clinging limpet and being spoken to like I'm a child. I'm *through* with you, Alastair."

Having finished that impassioned speech, Mrs. Whittlesby turned her attention to Phyllida. "You're the first person to figure it out. How did you know?"

"There were several clues. The first is the nature of the stories themselves. The entire premise is that Theodore Belfast is a brilliant detective, but it's really his sister Millie who's the brilliant one. No one would believe that about her—she's rather Miss Marple-ish in a way, though much younger and more energetic than Mrs. Christie's Jane—and so she guides her brother, who takes all of the credit for solving the cases. It's so very obvious, I'm surprised no one figured it out before now," Phyllida said, looking at the other members of the Murder Club, all of whom appeared stunned. She gave Mr. Whittlesby a pitying look. "Often the person who crows the loudest about his or her accomplishments is the one who actually has the fewest of them all."

Phyllida paused for another sip of tea; she had been talking for a long while. "I didn't even think of it myself at first, but there were two things that made it clear to me. First, the note that was enclosed with Father Tooley's cake included an incorrect apostrophe with the possessive form of the word *its*. Everything I had heard about Mr. Whittlesby was that, despite his smugness and boorishness, he was very particular and knowledgeable about grammar, and that was one of his most relevant contributions to the club.

"Still, I didn't think much of it—so many people make that error—until I saw the note your husband left for you yesterday morning about driving the motorcar. In that note was the possessive form of the word *its*, correctly *without* the apostrophe. Again, I didn't draw any firm conclusions until I . . . er . . . had a look at the papers in Mr. Whittlesby's sitting room."

"You *what?*" cried Mr. Whittlesby, bolting from his chair. "You were snooping about my sitting room?"

Phyllida gave him her best quelling look. "If I hadn't done so, you'd either be dead or going to prison for attempted murder."

He gave her a malevolent look—which in Phyllida's opinion should have been directed at the woman who'd tried to kill him instead of the one who'd saved him—but closed his mouth and sat down.

"There was a stack of papers next to Mr. Whittlesby's typewriter—presumably his current work in progress. So of course I took a look at them. And they were . . . well, they weren't very good at all."

"Do you mean to say that you were writing your *own* Inspector Belfast stories, Alastair?" cried Mrs. Whittlesby. "Without me? Why you—" She clamped her mouth shut, but her fingers were opening and closing furiously as if they'd like nothing better than to slip around his throat.

Phyllida suspected that at that moment Mrs. Whittlesby had the strength and ability to succeed if she attempted to strangle her husband. As one with her vast experience well knew, hell hath no fury like a scorned woman.

"You have nothing to worry about—in that regard at least, Mrs. Whittlesby. I am a connoisseur of detective stories and I can attest that your husband's work might be grammatically correct with proper sentence structure and spelling, but there's little else to recommend it. On the other hand, I discovered several crumpled papers in Mr. Whittlesby's waste can. The writing on those papers—typed, one must presume, by yourself in your own sitting room and locked in the drawer so that no one would discover them—was far better and much more compelling. In truth, I wanted to read more of the story."

"Oh, was that the one with the green bus ticket?" asked Mrs. Whittlesby, preening a little. "I thought it was a rather clever premise myself."

"Yes," replied Phyllida. "There was, in fact, a green bus ticket that seemed to play a significant role—although I only saw two pages. It seemed that your husband had decided to toss your work and strike out on his own, now that he expected to win the short story contest . . . which was quite a foolish decision since it was one of your stories that had been submitted and would be announced as the winner.

"And perhaps that was your final twist of the knife, so to speak, Mrs. Whittlesby. That when your husband was announced as the winner—and it became clear from your diabolical machinations, framing him up to be your own would-be murderer—that you would divulge the fact that you were the actual author of the stories, and that that was part of the reason he wanted to get rid of you: so he could write his own stories and not have to share the credit.

"And that brings me to the final point I wish to make, and then I will turn the floor over to Mr. Chesterton and Inspector Cork." And, she hoped, have Mr. Dobble or someone pour her *several* fingers of whisky.

It had been a long, *very* long Murder Fête.

The inspector muttered something that might have been "finally," but Phyllida ignored him and went on to elucidate her last plot point.

"The short story results I found on Rita's person were quite interesting. It appeared that some numbers had been erased and new numbers put in. The winner on that sheet was, as everyone expected, the Inspector Belfast story. *But* the scores seemed to have been altered—and that was the final nail in the coffin that you had created for your husband, wasn't it, Mrs. Whittlesby?

"Because the scores had obviously been altered—but not *too* obviously; the erasures were very subtle—and the winner was Mr. Whittlesby. That would make it appear that *he* had stolen the score sheets and altered them to make himself the winner. That would thus seal his fate as the presumed murderer of Father Tooley—who would have known the real winner of the contest—and also, logically, the attempted murderer of his own wife.

"But what the murderer couldn't have anticipated was that, in the absence of Father Tooley's tally sheets, the Detection Club provided their raw scores again, and I was able to recalculate the *correct* winner of the contest. And the correct winner was . . . Alastair Whittlesby."

Anticipation was replaced by confusion on the expression of everyone in the room, except Bradford, who merely nodded as if he understood. Which surely he didn't; how could he when Phyllida hadn't figured it out until only hours ago?

"So someone erased some of the numbers but put the same scores back in?" said Miss Crowley. "I don't understand . . ."

"I didn't at first, either," said Phyllida. "But when I realized that this entire plot was a frame-up of Mr. Whittlesby, then it made sense: Mrs. Whittlesby knew the score sheets had to look as if someone had altered them to make certain her husband was the winner so that he had the motive to kill Father Tooley. It was that simple."

"Simple, and yet so very, very complicated," said Mr. Chesterton, rising as if on cue to take the stage. "And since Mrs. Bright has taken the wind out of my sails by announcing the contest winner—no, no, not at all," he said, waving off Phyllida's apology, "I now call this meeting to an end, and close the festival. And my last task as grandmaster of the Listleigh Murder Fête is to invite Inspector Cork and Constable Greensticks to conduct this clever and diabolical woman into custody. And the rest of us—especially Mrs. Bright—should have a very stiff cocktail."

"Indeed," Phyllida replied. "I should be most grateful to imbibe . . . just so long as it isn't a Vieux Carré!"

CHAPTER 23

Monday afternoon

W RITERS REALLY ARE CURIOUS PEOPLE," SAID AGATHA, WAVING AS the motorcar took Mr. Chesterton, Miss Sayers, and Mr. Berkeley down the drive, heading back to London. The driver gave a gay toot of the horn as the vehicle disappeared around the bend.

"Curious and bloodthirsty," Phyllida said dryly, causing her friend to laugh. "Did you hear the way everyone was arguing about poisons when poor Father Tooley died?"

They were standing on the front porch of Mallowan Hall, the day after Lettice Whittlesby was arrested for murder and Mr. Genevan for theft. The authorities had declined to press charges against Sir Rolly for unlawful entry, for obvious reasons.

"Indeed I did. That made me think—I ought to bring back Mrs. Oliver in a full book sometime," Agatha replied. "Perhaps I'll even do a story with a murder that happens at a Detection Club meeting. She would be a member, you know, being an international bestselling writer of sensational novels. And so they'd all be suspects, of course. The Detection Club members."

"I should certainly like to know more about her, other than her penchant for apples," Phyllida said, wondering how much of herself Agatha would put into the writer character of Ariadne Oliver.

"She has a detective named Sven or something like that—he's

Norwegian," Agatha said, her eyes going cloudy with thought. "And everyone loves him, but she's come to loathe him. No—perhaps he'll be Finnish. Or Swedish. I'll have to think on that. Either way, Mrs. Oliver is finished with him, but the public simply won't let her kill him off."

"I should hope not," Phyllida said vehemently, thinking of her beloved Poirot. "It's really not quite done for a writer to murder her own detectives. Look how it turned out for Mr. Conan Doyle—he had to bring back Holmes."

"He'll be simply impossible," Agatha went on, trundling along on her train of thought. With a chuckle, Phyllida handed her a notebook and pencil. "This Sven or Gunnar or whoever he is. And perhaps even a bit ridiculous—like Hercule. But people will like him, so Mrs. Oliver simply can't get away from him." She sighed.

The sound of wild barking drew Phyllida's attention. Sure enough, Myrtle came hurtling around from the back of the house, ears streaming out behind her, tail flying.

She automatically dodged the animated mop—which, as always, seemed to make a beeline for her—but Agatha bent to greet the slathering beast, thus encouraging its depravity. "You're such a sweet thing, aren't you? Saving our Phyllida like you did. You quite definitely deserve to be inducted into the Order of Faithful Dogs."

Phyllida's lips flattened into a straight line. "The beast didn't actually *save* me, you know. I was perfectly fine and quite capable of freeing myself from the situation. It only hurried things on a bit."

Agatha stood, laughing. "Yes, of course, dear Phyllida. You are the most competent, brilliant, efficient of women, and I am quite delighted to have you on *my* side, at least. I shudder to think what it would be like if you weren't."

Phyllida shook her head, giving her friend a wry smile even as she expertly dodged Myrtle's attentions. "You're only relieved everyone has gone off and you can return to your work."

"And that I don't have to do any *speeches*," replied Agatha with a laugh. Then she sobered. "I do thank you for stepping in and sorting it all out. If you had not done, I fear G. K. and Dorothy would have insisted on staying another week—or more—in order to investigate!" She looked down at the scrawls she'd just made on the notepad. "Perhaps he'll be a vegetarian," she said.

"Who?"

"Why, Ivar or Sven or whatever his name is going to be. Mrs. Oliver's detective, of course." Murmuring to herself, Agatha turned and went back inside, leaving Phyllida alone with Myrtle, who was still attempting to acquire her attention.

"You've simply got to stop going about and telling people that you *rescued* me," Phyllida told the mop severely. "It's not at all accurate."

To her surprise, instead of leaping up and nipping at the hem of her frock, or scrabbling at her shins, Myrtle plopped down in front of her. The creature looked up at her with its beady eyes, pink tongue unfurling from its mouth like a ribbon. The thing panted so hard Phyllida could feel the heat through her hose.

"Precisely," she told the bundle of dark curls. Really, canines were so much more *disorderly* than felines. "I'm relieved we've come to an understanding. Now, if you'd only—"

"Are you lecturing my dog?"

Phyllida's attention snapped up from one unruly dark mop to the matching dark head of Bradford, who'd just come from around the back of the house. He was, as per usual, without a hat, gloves, or coat.

The beast, catching sight of its master, bolted up and dashed over to him as if it hadn't seen him for days. Unfortunately, despite Phyllida's most fervent wishes, Bradford had not been the least bit absent since arriving at Mallowan Hall.

"We were merely discussing accuracy in one's reporting of events," she told him coolly.

"I see." He didn't appear to "see," but Phyllida declined to comment. Instead, he directed his next comment to the dancing mop in front of him. "You needn't listen to her, Myrts. *We* know what really happened, don't we?"

Phyllida sniffed and turned away, prepared to go back inside and ensure that Mr. Dobble hadn't removed any more chintz pillows, and that the maids weren't standing about flirting with Elton. But, credit where credit was due . . . and so she paused and turned back. "Thank you again for your assistance, Mr.—er, I mean Bradford. You were quite helpful in a number of ways."

Myrtle, who'd been pawing at its master, plopped down again in a restrained sitting position. Those beady eyes looked back and forth between the two humans.

Bradford gave Phyllida a wry look. "That must have been painful."

"What on earth do you mean?"

"Thanking me for pointing out the arsenic bit."

"I wasn't actually referring to that particular aspect," Phyllida said frostily. "I was referring to all of the times you conveyed me in the motorcar to where I needed to go, and also for finding the wire cutters in the wood. And the snipped brake hoses."

"I see," he replied—but once again, his expression did not seem to support his words.

"Well, then," she said, wondering why *he* hadn't complimented her on her excellent detective work—then realized of course he would never offer any sort of adulation toward her. "I suppose I shall retreat to my domestic domain and leave the two of you to . . . whatever it is you do in the garage all day."

"Very well. And, Mrs. Bright, I must say, it was bloody clever of you to figure out the wife was behind it all. One does always say *cherchez la femme* in those murder stories you're always reading, so it was rather obvious from the beginning that one of the spouses was attempting to off the other." Bradford's French pronunciation was shockingly accurate. "Although I do recall your certainty that it was one of the writers desperate for a publishing contract."

"And, of course, I *was* correct," replied Phyllida sharply. "It *was* a writer desperate for *her* publishing contract, under her own name and reputation."

"I suppose if one wants to split hairs, you might be correct. But, really, when one comes down to it, it was more of a domestic murder situation. She wanted rid of her husband, either through murder or prison. And she got rid of a lecherous brother-in-law *and* a dragon-like mother-in-law at the same time."

Phyllida was forced to acknowledge his point and nodded stiffly. "Very well—although she's the one ending up in prison."

"Indeed. But I do have one unanswered question," Bradford said.

"And what is that?"

"If Father Tooley hadn't had a Vieux Carré and died at the party—which your murderess could not have planned for, since the priest didn't normally imbibe—but Alastair Whittlesby had drunk the poison, how would Lettice Whittlesby have handled that? She was trying to make it look like her husband was trying to murder her."

"Of course," Phyllida replied. "If nothing else, we've seen that Mrs. Whittlesby is cunning and creative. One could assume one of two possible explanations: first, that it was her initial intention that her husband would drink the poison and die while at the cocktail party, and his death would have been on the tail of that of Father Tooley, who she had hoped would be dead prior to. She'd be rid of her husband and there'd be two deaths to investigate—and she would probably have taken a sip of the cocktail in order to throw suspicion off herself.

"The second option, and the more likely one, is that very simply, Lettice Whittlesby would have done the same thing she did with the car accident: drink from the cocktail and then drop it whilst pretending to be poisoned. She would make sure everyone knew that her husband suggested she drink from it first. Whether it was a lie or not, it wouldn't matter at that point when she was nearly a victim and someone else had already been poisoned."

Bradford blinked, frowned, then nodded. "I suppose that could be the case. It seems awfully like she would leave a lot of things to chance."

"Quite. And that is precisely what happens with most murders: the killer often leaves many things to chance. That is why they get caught."

Having decided there was nothing more to say on the matter, Phyllida once more turned to go back inside. But Bradford stopped her again.

"One more thing, Mrs. Bright. You left this in the Daimler some time ago," he said.

She took the handkerchief he offered. It was wrinkled and had clearly not been laundered recently. But it was hers. "Thank you for returning it," she said.

"Of course," he replied. "Myrtle has quite finished with it."

And with that—and a broad grin Phyllida didn't quite understand—he turned and walked away, the dark bundle of curls bounding after him.

She glowered at his broad shoulders and the overexcited dog and was, quite frankly, more than pleased to return to her far more orderly, sedate, and efficient world of cats, chintz, and housemaids.

Mrs. Bright's Cocktail Recipe

Due to the harrowing events at the Murder Fête, Mrs. Bright was curious about Mr. Whittlesby's Vieux Carré cocktail, particularly because of her fondness for rye whisky. She took it upon herself to take up a second investigation, this time into the ingredients of the cocktail that originated in New Orleans, and decided to make her own version of the drink.

She finds this a delightful libation to be sipped near a roaring fire on a winter's night, or on a cool, summer evening. Even when, as is wont to happen, there is a rainy day in Devon. A Vieux Carré, she finds, is a delightful way to take off the damp and chill. As always, the mixture of cocktail could easily be added to a cup of hot tea for a unique hot toddy.

Mrs. Bright suggests the following recipe for any interested parties who might wish to make their own version of the cocktail favored by Alastair Whittlesby.

1 oz rye whisky
1 oz cognac
1 oz sweet vermouth (although Mrs. Bright prefers a *trifle* less vermouth, and suggests the bartender might not wish to fill the measurer to the full one ounce)
.3 oz Benedictine
3-4 shakes of bitters of the mixer's preference (see note below)

Shake with ice, drain, and serve in a martini glass, coupe, or lowball, with or without ice. Garnish with orange peel and/or cocktail cherry.

Regarding the bitters:

In Mrs. Bright's research, she discovered that the original Vieux Carré recipe called for two shakes of Peychaud's bitters, and two shakes of Angostura bitters. Mr. Whittlesby, of course, preferred his Monteleone's Bitters—which are no longer available, likely due to the negative publicity surrounding the poisoning of said bitters. A suitable substitute for the Monteleone's Bitters would be the more widely available Dale DeGroff's Pimento Bitters.

However, Mrs. Bright's personal preference is three to four shakes of cardamom bitters (quite possibly due to her friendship with Dr. Bhatt, and his penchant for chai tea), as she finds it adds a unique, spicy, and warm element to the cocktail.

Don't miss the next Phyllida Bright mystery . . .

MURDER BY INVITATION ONLY by Colleen Cambridge

In this engaging historical mystery, Agatha Christie's ever-capable housekeeper, Phyllida Bright, not only keeps the celebrated author's English country home in tip-top shape, she excels as an amateur sleuth. But when a murder-themed game goes awry, can she outfox the guilty party?

"*A murder will occur tonight at Beecham House . . .*" Who could resist such a compelling invitation? Of course, the murder in question purports to be a party game, and Phyllida looks forward to using some of the deductive skills she has acquired thanks to her employer, Mrs. Agatha, who is unable to attend in person.

The hosts, Mr. and Mrs. Wokesley, are new to the area, and Phyllida gladly offers their own overwhelmed housekeeper some guidance while events get underway. Family friends have been enlisted to play the suspects, and Mr. Wokesley excels in his role of dead body. Unfortunately, when the game's solution is about to be unveiled, the participants discover that life has imitated art. Mr. Wokesley really *is* dead!

In the absence of Inspector Cork, Phyllida takes temporary charge of the investigation, guiding the local constable through interviews with the Murder Game actors. At first, there seems no motive to want Mr. Wokesley dead . . . but then Phyllida begins to connect each of the suspects with the roles they played and the motives assigned to them. It soon becomes clear that *everyone* had a reason to murder their host—both in the game and in real life. Before long, Phyllida is embroiled in a fiendishly puzzling case, with a killer who refuses to play by the rules . . .